Braving Fiery Waters
By Sarah Hanks

Praise for
Braving Fiery Waters

If you have an affinity for time travel tales, like me, you will thoroughly enjoy the second volume in the Time Sailor series. I eagerly anticipated this book and was not disappointed. Hanks again weaves together complex family dynamics with history and faith in Jesus Christ. This author knows her steamboats, understands complex families, and is well-versed in 19th-century American history. You'll enjoy this unique blend of dual timeline storytelling with fantasy and become a fan of Time Sailors

Jenny Powell, author of *But For These Chains* and *Take The Sea*

Prepare to sail away into a tale of loss, faith, motherhood, and discovering God's purpose for our lives. Braving Fiery Waters is a fresh and creative time travel story featuring a modern-day widowed mother of teens and the 1849 Great Fire of St. Louis. You'll find yourself challenged to replace voices in your life speaking lies with the truth and learn with Marina and Claire that loving the people God places in front of you is the greatest mission of all. Relatable and twist-filled, Braving Fiery Waters is Christian fiction with solid faith and comes with a resounding recommendation from me.

Heather Wood, author of the Finding Home and Gathering of Mercy series

Sarah Hanks weaves a heartfelt novel exposing a young widow's desire to strengthen her connection with her teenage children before they leave for college. The time travel aspect and road to reuniting makes for a memorable read.

Erma M. Ullrey, Author of *Journaled With Love* and *Sadie's Gift: The Christmas Cabin*

Sarah Hanks' novel, *Braving Fiery Waters*, is a standout work for fans of time-travel stories. Humor and emotional weight between key characters is well-developed with their captivating interactions, transporting the reader seamlessly between the past and present. The backdrop of the middle 1800s provides plenty of historical and speculative intrigue for readers. Marina and her two teenagers, Aiden and Brinley, navigate their separation through suspenseful plot twists, unhinged relationships, and ultimately reunite on a solid foundation of family values and love.

Becky Van Vleet, award winning author of *Her Strength Within*

Edited by Janice Boekhoff
Cover by Kelsey Gietl
ISBN   979-8-9854789-8-3

Chapter One

The traffic light ahead shone yellow, and Marina slammed her foot on the accelerator. She would not be late. Not this time.

From the back seat, Brinley poured the sass on thick. "Watch out, Mom. Speeding is dangerous."

Aiden snickered beside her.

Marina blew a strand of hair out of her eyes as she careened left. Stupid haircut. She should have left it long. "Not sure *you* should be the one warning *me* of danger." She spoke through clenched teeth. "Besides, if you would have gotten up on time, we wouldn't be late."

"I don't want to go on this stupid lake cruise." Judging by Brinley's tone, she was probably rolling her eyes.

"I don't want to be here at all." Aiden's words sliced with a hard edge.

Ungrateful. How could these be the two sweet children she'd raised? So much for a beautiful bonding experience. Fun family vacations had been the highlight of her summers growing up. Road trips and camping. Fishing with Dad. Craft fairs with Mom. Now that she was alienated from them both, she hung on to those memories like a lifeline. They reminded her that her parents had loved her, once upon a time. But her family vacation to South Haven, Michigan, was off to a horrendous start.

Why weren't there any open parking spaces? It was five thirty in the morning, for crying out loud.

"I can't believe you made me board Frankie. Poor baby." Brinley's whine grated on Marina's last nerve.

She dug deep for a chipper tone. "Oh, come on. It's a luxury dog spa boarding center. That little basset hound's never had it so good."

Aiden reached back and patted his sister's knee. "He'll be fine. He'll probably come home with blue toenail polish."

Marina's forced smile fell. Weren't siblings supposed to fight? Not these two. Apparently, they only fought her. At least Aiden's tone with his sister proved her sweet boy was in there somewhere.

A glance in the mirror reflected Brinley's scowl. "Kimmy's throwing an epic party tonight, and I won't be there."

"Did Kimmy jump off the cliff too?"

"I told you, Mom. Everyone did."

"Except Fiona." Aiden flipped down the visor mirror to ensure his blond waves were appropriately brushing his forehead. "She's too chicken."

"Sounds like Fiona is the only one in the group who has any sense."

"Did you just call us stupid?" This was from Aiden.

"You acted like it that day." Cliff diving at Johnson's Shut-Ins State Park. Of all the reckless, harebrained things to do. They could have died or ended up paralyzed. What had they been thinking?

"Whatever." Aiden crossed his arms. "Dad would have been proud of our courage. He had guts."

Brinley's scowl loomed in the rearview mirror. "He probably would have jumped too."

"Well, Dad is dead. I'm here to make sure you don't join him."

Silence.

Okay, that was harsh. Uncalled for. Remorse thickened her throat. She swallowed it down and made a sharp left into what appeared to be the last available parking space. The charter boat *Duncan's Delight* remained at the pier near the mouth of the Black River, mere yards away from where the river spilled into Lake Michigan. Her stellar speeding skills had left them six minutes before their sunrise cruise.

"You suck all the fun out of life," Brinley mumbled.

A glance in the rearview mirror showed her adjusting the spaghetti strap of her purple sundress, then flicking a strand of dirty-blonde hair over her shoulder.

Marina flung her arm in the direction of the iconic South Haven lighthouse. "Um, hello? Family vacation." Why did they think she went through all this trouble and expense? She'd envisioned a week of laughter and memories. A time of knitting their family together with each activity. Instead, all they'd done so far was fight. Add another failure to her tally.

"How long is this thing?" Disdain dripped from Aiden's voice.

"Can I go back to the hotel and sleep?" Brinley's grumbling clawed Marina's ears.

"For real. We don't want to go on some lake cruise."

Tension knotted her shoulders. Lava bubbled in her gut. "Right now, I don't want to go on a cruise with you two either."

She got out and slammed her door, clamping her lips together to avoid saying more words she would regret. She needed to calm down. A public restroom stood across the street at the pier. Barreling toward it, she left the teens and their ungratefulness in the car.

She followed a trail of sand into the foul-smelling bathroom and braced her hands on either side of the sink. Deep breaths. In through the nose. Out through the mouth. She'd let them get to her again. Why? They always played the dad card when they wanted to dig the knife in deep. What had she done wrong? She'd poured herself out for them, giving every last ounce of her energy to attempt to fill the role of two parents. And still, it wasn't enough.

Aiden had only one year at home before he graduated and left for college. Brinley, only two years. Then what? An achingly empty home. What if she'd pushed them away like her mom had done to her? At the thought of them never visiting, of her not remaining a part of their lives, bile rose in her throat. She had to do better. Win them back. Otherwise, her future looked bleak.

She splashed cool water on her face, then rushed back out the door. Good. Aiden and Brinley had peeled themselves from the car and boarded the charter after all. She wouldn't need to drag them. She returned to the car, grabbed her massive rolling cooler, and headed for the dock.

~

Arms laden with boxes of pastries, Claire swallowed back a wave of nausea. No way could she get sick here and now. Bearett was counting on her. Using her hip to open the boat's back door, she tumbled inside and nearly dumped the bakery selections onto the bar.

What a day for the caterer to cancel. Bearett had used the same company for his sunrise cruises since he'd opened his charter business. They'd always proved reliable, but a stomach bug had left them short-staffed.

Her muscles burned as she lugged the serving platters from underneath the bar. She washed her hands, then set to work arranging the pastries on the platters. Next, she placed bananas and oranges beside them. So, it wasn't Pinterest-worthy. Hopefully, their guests would take more interest in the stunning views of South Haven and Lake Michigan than an artful arrangement of breakfast options.

She carried the trays down the four steps into the lower deck and set them on the buffet table, then went back to fetch milk and orange juice from the fridge. The minute she placed them on the table, her stomach lurched. She winced as she held down its contents. From across the deck, Bearett's piercing green eyes caught her gaze. She forced a smile. Did it look genuine? Best that he not guess something was amiss. Not yet. He started to mouth something to her—maybe *Thank you*—but a passenger came up to talk to him. Good. Attention off her, at least for the moment.

Bearett's white T-shirt rustled with a breeze. He took the handheld intercom and, in his soothing tour guide voice, relayed the customary announcements, including the guests' right to partake of the breakfast spread. While a few people made a beeline for the food, most stood at the railings, far too taken with the sun awakening on the horizon than anything she had picked up from the local bakery.

A sigh fell from her lips. It *was* a stunning view. Bearett couldn't have chosen a better place to build his business. And she couldn't have chosen a better man to do life with. So why did she have this pinch in her chest?

Two teenagers—one boy and one girl, both with blond hair and blue eyes—approached the table. While the girl grabbed a muffin, the boy filled a plate with nearly every option offered.

The girl's brow lifted. "Hungry much?"

"Lay off. Who are you? Mom?" He popped a mini donut into his mouth.

The girl rolled her eyes. "Where is Mom, anyway? She better not have ditched us here."

"Hardly. She'd never miss the opportunity to torture us with family bonding."

They must be siblings. Claire angled away so it wouldn't appear she was eavesdropping. Which, of course, she was.

The girl frowned. "Yeah, but it's not like her to leave us alone. Isn't she afraid we'll get into trouble or do something dangerous?" She made air quotes with her free hand on that last word.

"What trouble could we cause on this lame boat?"

Lame? The nerve. Though she probably wouldn't have found a leisurely lake cruise at the crack of dawn exciting at that age. Had their mom truly dumped them onto the boat and left? Bearett didn't allow unaccompanied minors on his cruises. She'd better watch them and ensure their safety. Last thing their pocketbook needed was a lawsuit. That might take them under completely.

A guy dressed in khakis and a half-buttoned dress shirt swaggered to the table and placed a slice of sponge cake onto his plate. "Beautiful morning, isn't it?"

She nodded. "Gorgeous."

"So true." He wasn't looking at the sunrise. Instead, his gaze roamed her face and then her body.

Ugh. The creep. It was as though she were a magnet for these guys. She made a show of rubbing her arms, ensuring her wedding ring was in full view.

He took a step closer, apparently undeterred. "You should have some cake. It's delicious."

"I'd better not."

"Worried about keeping that amazing figure?" He leered at her.

There was a time when her waist size would have been a top concern, but not now. Fit TV was no longer breathing down her neck. She could indulge in dessert now and then if she wanted. If she deserved it. But sweets were a reward for a big accomplishment. As far back as she could remember, her parents had showered her sister with cake or ice cream for every academic achievement, each award. What had Claire done to indulge in such a treat? Nothing. She'd barely made it through her first semester of homeopathic med school before she quit. Mostly because of the financial burden, but also because it was a lot.

No cake for her.

But this slime ball didn't need an explanation. "Excuse me. I need to speak with my husband." She sidestepped the man and hurried to Bearett at the helm. Fresh morning air mingled with a fishy lake smell, undercut by her handsome husband's woodsy cologne. She leaned in closer until the notes of bergamot and cedar wood overpowered the fish.

He glanced at her, and his brow furrowed. "Everything okay? You look a little green."

"I'm fine. Just tired and some creep tried to hit on me."

He clenched the wheel. "Where is he? Want me to have a word with him?"

She placed a hand on his arm. "No need."

He huffed out a breath. "Thanks for scrambling to put breakfast together. I hate that you had to do that."

"Hey, we're a team." She bumped his shoulder. "We've got to work together if we want this venture to succeed."

A muscle twitched in his cheek. Shoot. Not the right thing to say. Why'd she remind him of their precarious finances?

She tried again. "I'm happy to help you do what you love." A little better.

He kissed the top of her head. "I'm happy to be your husband."

But with all the financial pressure they were under, would he be happy to learn he was going to be a father?

~

Aiden stuffed the last of his breakfast muffin into his mouth as he scrolled Instagram. What he wouldn't give to be just about anywhere else than lounging on the lower deck of *Duncan's Delight*. What kind of name was that, anyway? Sounded more like an old person's coffee drink than a cruise boat.

He scanned the deck. Where was his sister? Brinley'd left a while ago to get another muffin. She should have returned by now. Hopefully, she wasn't seasick. Mom had the Dramamine.

He turned his attention back to his phone. A reel. An ad. A picture of his best friend Patrick diving off that same cliff that led to this torturous "vacation." If only Mom didn't have eyes everywhere. They could have gotten away with it, and he could be spending this week with his friends rather than his psychopath of a mom. A twinge nagged his chest. Okay, so she wasn't exactly a psychopath. More like a helicopter mom with control issues. He loved her, but man, she drove him crazy.

Another reel. A picture of … Stacy. His breath caught. With Brad Bonville's arm around her. Was she with the football player now? Is that why she'd dumped him? Maybe all her honey-sweet words about growing apart were just a cover-up for her desire to date the high school quarterback.

Had she been cheating on him with Brad? No. She wouldn't do that. Not after a year together. It'd been the best year of his life with Stacy in his arms. Guilt coated him. How could he think such a thing? It couldn't have been the best year of his life without Dad. Nothing was the same without him. Mom sure wasn't.

He studied the picture for a hint of a ruse. Maybe Stacy and Brad were only hanging out as friends. But Brad sure held her tight, and their faces were far too close together. He resisted the urge to throw his phone across the deck.

A musical voice stole his attention. Good, there was Brinley, face tanned instead of green. He'd been about to wonder if she'd gone overboard. She was talking with a black-haired beauty. As the mystery girl threw her head back and laughed, a beam of sunlight spotlighted her face, making her look otherworldly. Like an angel. Then her gaze tangled with his.

Great. She'd caught him gawking at her.

With a lift of her chin, she called out to him. "Beautiful morning for a cruise, huh?"

His lips edged up. "I guess."

"You guess?" One of her eyebrows lifted.

He straightened in his chair. How should he play this? Did she like this cruise? Maybe he should pretend to. Or he could tell her his mom dragged him here. No, he couldn't mention his mom ten seconds after meeting her.

She raised her eyebrows.

Great. He was staring at her like an idiot again. His face flushed.

Brinley shot him one of her *Really, Aiden?* looks. "That's my brother, Aiden." They crossed the deck and sat in lounge chairs across from him. "Aiden, this is Nevaeh. Her family vacations here every summer."

Poor girl. "I'm sorry."

Another laugh. "Don't be. I love it here. It's the perfect place to spend the summer."

If she said so. Maybe she had a boring life back home.

The three chatted. Nevaeh was from some small town in Nebraska. No wonder she enjoyed it in South Haven. She was on her high school volleyball team, had two younger sisters, and loved to jet-ski. As she spoke, an idea formed. Maybe Stacy posted that picture to make him jealous. Two could play that game. If she thought he'd moved on, maybe she'd regret ditching him. All he'd need would be one strategic picture.

"Hey, what about a selfie?"

Nevaeh smiled. "Sure. How about right over there?" She pointed to the railing. "The lighting is perfect."

Brinley wedged herself on one side of Nevaeh, and Aiden stood on the other side. Man, she smelled good. Like coconuts. "We need to get closer." He held the phone out and brought his cheek close to Nevaeh's. Did that look intimate enough? He leaned in a little more. There. He snapped the picture. *Take that, Stacy.*

They stepped apart but remained at the railing.

"You feeling okay, Brin?"

She stuck out her tongue. "Yes, Mom. Not sure why, but I don't feel sick at all." She turned to Nevaeh. "I usually get motion sickness pretty bad."

"Aw. That stinks. Glad you're okay today." Nevaeh turned her attention to Aiden. "You didn't talk much about yourself. You're a senior, right? What are your plans after high school?"

Brinley snorted, and Nevaeh turned toward her.

"What? Doesn't he have plans?"

"He has plans all right."

Nevaeh angled toward him, frowning.

He ran a hand through his hair. "I want to be a cop … It's complicated." Far too complicated. "Anyway, how about you? What are your plans?"

Her expression smoothed. "I want to go to the University of Illinois Chicago. They have a great nursing program."

"No way." He tilted his head toward her. "I've considered Loyola University Chicago for criminal justice. Different schools, but same city."

"Hey." Nevaeh spun around to face them. "Do you want to hang out on the beach when we get back?"

Aiden spoke without hesitation. "Sure." A few more pictures would seal the deal.

Brinley frowned. "What about Mom?"

Shoot. Mom probably had the entire day planned for them. "She owes us for—" He couldn't say for making them come on this ridiculous cruise. Not when Nevaeh enjoyed it. "For stuff." Good one. He could smack himself.

But maybe he could sweet talk his way into having the afternoon free. An apology would go a long way, even if he didn't truly do anything wrong. Or maybe she'd still be ticked and not want to spend time as a family anyway.

Nevaeh smiled at him. A pretty smile, which he returned. Only, he couldn't get distracted. Stacy was his girl, and he'd win her back. One picture at a time.

Chapter Two

From where she stood at the open upper deck's railing, Marina filled her lungs with fresh morning air. Everything would be okay. Her teens were somewhere in this swarming mass of humanity, likely on the lower deck, though why they'd choose to be enclosed in walls and windows was a mystery. She'd give them another few minutes to calm down before she went to find them. She'd apologize. They'd apologize. She wasn't naive enough to expect a hug from either of them, but surely a ceasefire. Once they saw the jaw-dropping beauty of sunrise over the lake, they'd forget their protests. A sweet family-bonding vacation remained in their future.

As long as she didn't bring up their idiotic cliff-diving stunt.

And as long as they didn't bring up their father.

Her action-packed itinerary would take their minds off friends at home. A tour of the maritime museum, a close-up view of the lighthouse, biking the Kal-Haven trail, exploring the dunes at Van Buren State Park, kayaking on the lake … They'd finally connect like they used to. Yes, she could salvage this trip. She *would*. After all, Aiden and Brinley were everything to her.

Which reminded her … Brinley had forgotten to take her motion sickness pills. She dug through her monstrosity of a purse. Aloe. Sunscreen. Band-Aids. Gum. Tylenol. Tic Tacs. Lip balm. Hand sanitizer. Wet wipes. There. Dramamine. She clutched the bottle in her hand, lest it disappear into no-man's-land again.

She turned to the woman lounging in a deck chair to her right. "Crazy, isn't it? My purse is as big as a suitcase."

The woman gestured to her own handbag. "Tell me about it, sister. It takes me forever to find anything in there." Her southern accent wrapped around Marina like a hug.

Marina offered a commiserating smile. "Well, better go find my kids."

The woman's eyebrows lifted.

"Oh." Marina waved a hand in front of her as if brushing away the woman's concern. "They're not kids anymore. Teens. Both of them."

The woman's bright pink nails flew to her collarbone. "Two teens? You poor dear."

"They're good kids. Smart. They stay out of trouble." For the most part. No smoking, drinking, or sleeping around, at least not that she could tell. Just a burning desire to put themselves in harm's way. Were they trying to prove they were as fearless as their father had been? If only keeping them safe were still as simple as cutting their grapes and installing outlet covers.

The woman nodded. "That's good."

Yes. She was good. They were good. All good. With a parting smile, she straightened the purse strap on her shoulder, heaved her cooler, and wove her way toward the stairs that would take her to the lower deck. Okay, maybe the cooler was overkill. The cruise included breakfast and beverages. But what if they got dehydrated and needed a Gatorade? Or what if junk food comprised the only selections? It never hurt to bring fruit and electrolytes.

As she neared the stairwell, a glimmer of gold caught her eye. Was that … a mailbox? On a boat? Odd. Though she'd read *Duncan's Delight* had been a mailboat, so perhaps it fit. With its worn, rusty hinges, could the mailbox be an antique? She trailed her fingers over the engraved lion and yanked her hand back when she got a shock. *Yikes.* Tentatively, she opened the lid and peeked inside. Nothing. She nearly guffawed. Of course, there was nothing. It wasn't like the postman delivered letters on the lake. A couple wedged past her, followed by a burly, bare-chested man. She stepped back to give him a wide berth.

A glance down the stairwell showed a clear view of a small landing dominated by an empty bar. Four steps to the alcove, then four more steps leading in the opposite direction of the lower deck. She pulled her phone from her back pocket to check her texts. Nothing from Aiden or Brinley. Time to hunt. Phone in one hand and cooler in the other, she barreled forward. Her purse strap fell down her shoulder, and she attempted to shrug it back in place. In doing so, her sandal slipped on a step. She plummeted hard onto her backside and bounced down a step before veering forward. Her head crashed into the wall. Her phone fell from her grasp. Everything went black.

~

With only ten minutes left until docking, Claire gathered the breakfast leftovers to box up and drop off with her elderly next-door neighbors.

She donned food-service gloves, then moved the leftover bagels and pastries to one tray. Most guests stood on the outer deck near the railing, soaking up the last minutes of their cruise. Claire didn't have to duck and dodge her way back to the bar area where the empty boxes waited.

As she slid the tray onto the counter, something red caught her eye. There on the floor, tucked close to the bar, was a phone. Interesting. People were always leaving things behind. Jackets, umbrellas, water bottles, hats. But a phone? Most people had those permanently glued to their hands. Someone had to be looking for it.

The food would have to wait. With quick steps, she bounded back down the stairs and made her way to Bearett at the front of the ship. His navy ball cap read *Lake Life* and matched his cargo shorts. He looked every bit the relaxed sailor, created for the water.

"Hello, darlin'." He kissed the top of her head.

"Hi." She'd gotten into a habit over the past two days of averting his too-perceptive gaze. She evaded it now and focused on the phone. "Someone must have dropped this. Make an announcement?"

"Sure. I'll tell them to meet you at the bar if it's theirs."

"Thanks. Gotta get back to boxing up the leftovers." She turned and rushed back before he could ask annoying questions like how she was feeling and if anything was wrong. He'd know soon enough.

By the time she'd safely tucked away the leftovers and cleaned, dried, and deposited the empty trays on the shelf behind the bar, unease filled her. No one had come to claim the phone. How could that be? It had to belong to someone on this boat. Maybe the owner was hard of hearing and hadn't caught Bearett's announcement. Plausible? Maybe. Probable? No. But who would not care if their lifeline to the outside world disappeared?

Stella's face flashed in her mind. Okay, so Claire's best friend's phone had catapulted into the ocean on her bachelorette cruise, and it hadn't bothered her. Surely, Stella was an exception. Even after all the progress Claire had made detoxing from social media, she could never survive without her phone. Maybe she hadn't progressed as much as she'd like to think. A depressing thought. If someone would just claim the phone, she'd feel a lot better about herself. But as passengers filed past to exit *Duncan's Delight*, no one approached her about it. Odd.

Oh, well. She had bigger things to think about. Or smaller things. Her hand instinctively went to her tummy. The size of a pinto bean. How long before she'd start to show? Her lack of experience with these things overwhelmed her.

"There's my queen."

At the sound of Bearett's voice, she flung her hand away from her stomach as though it might burn. *Smooth, Claire.* To cover her awkwardness, she tucked a strand of hair behind her ear. "Hi." A tight smile was the best she could offer. "No one claimed the phone."

"Hmm." Bearett tilted his head to the side. "Put it with the rest of the lost and found, I guess."

"Yeah, okay." It seemed strange to tuck a phone on a shelf in between a parka and a novel, but what else could they do? Wait. She swiped at the screen. A picture of a handsome man in firefighter gear smiled back at her, as did a prompt to enter the phone's pin. So much for discovering the owner's identity by looking through the contacts. She swung the phone in Bearett's direction. "Recognize him?"

"No. You?"

"No." Not that it meant much. There were over a hundred people aboard today's cruise—weekends during the summer always brought high numbers—and she couldn't have memorized all their faces. He very well could have been on their boat.

"Don't worry." Bearett pulled off his ball cap and wiped his glistening brow with the back of his hand. "Someone is bound to come looking for it."

Yes, of course. Why had she allowed such a little thing to get under her skin? It was ridiculous, but she couldn't seem to shake the feeling of unease.

Hormones, probably. It came with the territory, and she'd have to learn how to navigate these ups and downs. Because, like it or not, the baby growing inside of her wasn't going anywhere. It would be her responsibility for the next eighteen plus years.

A wave of nausea struck her. She bent over and retched on the cabin floor.

~

Aiden squinted against the sun's glare. "I don't see Mom anywhere."

Brinley scoffed. "Guess she really did ditch us."

He pulled out his phone to call her. "She must be back at the hotel. Think she'll come get us or make us walk?"

"Not so fast." Brinley snatched his phone.

"Hey, give it back."

"Don't call her yet. Let's at least enjoy ourselves first."

Nevaeh stood a few yards away talking with a group of teenagers. When she turned and caught his eye, he couldn't help but smile. "Yeah, sure."

Brinley placed the phone in his hand. "Wait. You like her." She smirked.

"Don't be ridiculous." He pocketed the phone. "Stacy—"

"Yeah, yeah. Stacy's your girl. The two of you are meant to be. Whatever." She tilted her head in Nevaeh's direction. "But Stacy's not here, and Nevaeh is. Besides, Stacy dumped you. Time to move on."

If only it were that easy. He wouldn't waste his breath explaining how perfect Stacy was for him. How perfect her family was. How he needed her dad to vouch for him so he could get on the force despite his asthma. He said nothing as they meandered to the circle of teens.

"We're about to head to South Beach and play volleyball. You in? You could be on my team." Nevaeh's gaze included both Brinley and Aiden.

Volleyball? No way. He wasn't about to make a fool of himself in front of this beauty. Brinley must have picked up on his hesitation because she hedged. "I don't know. It's not really our thing."

What a great sister. It totally *was* her thing. She must have turned down the opportunity to help him save face. He owed her one.

A rumbling motor stole their attention. A teenager pulled up on an electric-blue moped, creating his own parking spot mere inches away from a sports car. "Hey, guys."

"Hi, Jack." Nevaeh motioned to Aiden and Brinley and made introductions. "I just met Jack yesterday. He's a local."

"You about to start a game?" Jack ran a hand through his curly black hair, though not even a strand seemed to be out of place.

When Jack got off the moped, Aiden admired it. "Sweet ride." Mom would never let him drive one of those things, even if they were far safer than a motorcycle.

"Want to take it for a spin?" Jack asked.

"Seriously?"

"Have at it. I'm going to play." He gestured to the volleyball in a blonde girl's hands.

"If you're sure." Who knew when he'd get another chance. Never, if Mom had her way.

"I'll come with you." Brinley hopped on the bike like she was born to ride. Okay. They were doing this.

"Thanks, man." Aiden grabbed helmets from the back, handed one to Brinley, and strapped one on himself. He straddled the bike in front of Brinley and started the motor.

"No problem. Have fun."

Nevaeh waved at them before the group headed down the sidewalk to the beach.

"Thanks." He didn't need to say more. They'd always understood each other.

"No problem. Now, let's go before Mom shows up and has a heart attack."

He revved the motor and pressed the gas. He'd never ridden a moped before. It took a couple of minutes before they moved smoothly, but once he found his stride, they flew.

Behind him, Brinley hooted. *This* was the life. A fresh breeze whipping around them, coasting up and down South Haven's streets. What could be more freeing?

"I think Dad used to have a motorcycle!" Brinley shouted.

That's right. Aiden had seen a picture of him standing by a motorcycle back in his high school days, hair long like a hippie. Maybe he was looking down from heaven right now smiling. Or maybe he'd be ticked since they were doing something Mom would never approve of. Yet, this was a moped, not a motorcycle. Did Brinley know the difference? Mom hadn't specifically told them *not* to ride a moped. It wasn't like they were defying her orders.

Aiden crested a hill, and his stomach dropped with the motion. Adrenaline coursed through him. He nearly hooted to himself.

Sirens blared. A glance in the mirror showed a cop trailing them. Aiden slowed and pulled to the side to let him pass, but the officer pulled over too. "Shoot." Had he been speeding? Didn't mopeds only go like thirty miles per hour? Brinley's fingernails dug into his back. He shrugged her off as the cop approached. Now Aiden's nerves buzzed for a different reason.

"Hello, officer." Aiden tossed the man his winning smile. "Is there a problem?"

The cop frowned. "Is this your moped?"

"Well, no—"

"I'm going to need you to stand to the side."

Brinley shot Aiden a wide-eyed, fear-filled glance as they got off and stepped onto the sidewalk.

"Is there a problem?" he asked again.

The officer circled the moped, scratching something on his notepad. "Driver's licenses."

Aiden fished his from his wallet, and Brinley dug hers from her cross-body purse. Why did the cop need Brinley's? If this was about speeding, Aiden was the only one at fault.

The officer's gaze flicked from their licenses to their faces. "I'm going to need you to come with me. This moped has been reported stolen."

Chapter Three

Marina blinked and slowly opened her eyes. Bursts of light flooded her vision. She cringed at the overpowering ammonia scent assaulting her nostrils. Pain radiated from the back of her head. Ouch. What had happened? Her hand trailed the throbbing spot. A bump. Had she fallen? From where? Fog clouded her brain. Hushed voices surrounded her, none familiar.

Slowly, her vision cleared. She was lying on some kind of couch. Red velvet.

"Look! She's coming to. I told you smelling salts would do the trick."

She scanned the room, searching for the source of the voice, and found a man with a handlebar mustache wearing an oversized, flat bow tie. She squeezed her eyes shut and counted to ten before opening them again. But when she did, he was still there, lingering like an actor from a Dickens's play. Cigar smoke emanated from him. What was happening?

"Miss? Are you all right?"

Was she? A dull pounding pulsed through her head.

"The poor dear." A woman's face loomed above her, hair parted down the middle and looped around her ears in the ugliest hairstyle Marina had ever seen. "She must be mortified to be caught in such a state of undress. Bertha, fetch a blanket for her, would you?"

A state of undress? Squinting against the pain, Marina lifted her head to view her surroundings. The woman who had just spoken wore a checkered dress with a voluminous skirt and a shawl draped around her shoulders.

What in the world? Three other similarly dressed women stood whispering amongst themselves a few feet from the couch. Each wore a … bonnet? No one waltzed around half naked. Unless … A glance at herself showed she wore white capris and a ribbed, sleeveless shirt. Thank goodness *she* wasn't the one lacking clothing.

"W-where am I?"

She'd no sooner asked the question when another woman rushed forward and draped a quilt over her. "There you go, miss. No need to be ashamed, though you are in the saloon. When you're feeling up to it, we'll find your berth and ensure you're properly outfitted."

Saloon? Her berth? Why couldn't she think clearly? Perhaps she had a concussion. That must be it. A concussion from her fall. But where did she fall from?

Like the sun dawning on the horizon, memories surfaced. A sunrise cruise. Standing on the top deck. Running her hand over a strange mailbox. Tripping down the stairs as she went to find Aiden and Brinley.

She sat up with a start. "Where are my children?"

Her gaze swept the old-fashioned room. No sign of them.

"You have children?" Bertha asked.

"Aiden. Brinley. Where are they?" They needed her. Or did she need them?

Nothing looked familiar. Fancy chandeliers hung from the ceiling. Oil paintings graced the walls. A dining table and straight-backed chairs filled nearly half of the space, with a bar on one side of her and a barber chair on the other. Ornate couches with engravings of fruit and vines on the legs dotted the large common room. On the far side of the space, thick velvety curtains blocked off an area.

Shouldn't she be on the lower deck of the *Duncan's Delight*? She'd only caught a glance of it before ascending the stairs to watch the sunrise from above, but this couldn't be it. The charter boat had windows on all sides for a spectacular view of the lake. Here, walls enclosed them. She seemed to be in some sort of lounge. Had someone moved her from the boat?

"How old are your children, miss? There aren't many aboard."

Aboard? So, she *was* still on the boat?

"Sixteen and seventeen. A girl and a boy."

The women exchanged glances. "We'll let you know if we locate them." The lady with the strange hair clasped her hands in front of her waist.

If? Marina swung her legs off the couch and attempted to stand. The quilt fell from her shoulders, and a collective gasp filled the space. Why? She looked down to find nothing amiss. Her head swam. Maybe she should sit back down. Only, she had to find Aiden and Brinley. She'd been about to bring her girl Dramamine. How was Brin holding up?

She took a step and swayed.

Ugly Hair Lady grasped her arm. "Miss, you really should sit down. Dr. Duncan is on his way to examine you. He was with another patient but will come straightaway." She led Marina back to the couch and sat beside her, tucking the quilt around her again.

Dr. Duncan? As in *Duncan's Delight*? If he was the ship's owner, he could possibly shed some light on what was happening and why everyone looked like they'd just stepped off a Broadway production.

She swallowed, then repeated her original question. "Where am I?" Was this some kind of secret compartment of the boat she hadn't seen before?

The woman patted her arm. "You're on the *White Cloud*, my dear, headed for Peoria. We found you collapsed on the floor over there." She pointed to the gaudily patterned carpet a few feet from them. "Only, no one knows where you were coming from or why you fell."

A lady in a bonnet stepped forward. "We hadn't seen you yet on this trip. Believe me, we would have remembered someone with such an … unconventional hairstyle. Perhaps you've taken meals in your room?"

The *White Cloud*? Her room? She must have hit her head harder than she realized. Perhaps she was dreaming. That had to be it. And what was wrong with her hair? Her fingers gravitated to the shoulder-length ends. Nothing seemed amiss, but she couldn't be sure without a mirror. Was there one on this dream ship?

"*Duncan's Delight.*" That *was* the name of the boat she'd boarded that morning, right?

"Oh yes. Dr. Duncan is delightful. A splendid chap. He'll be of great assistance." Mustache Man nodded. "Here he comes now."

A middle-aged man strode toward her. The gray hair surrounding his bald patch stuck up as if he'd inserted his finger in an electric socket. He carried a large physician's bag and wore a maroon scarf-like thing tied around his neck. He approached and put out his hand. "Dr. Duncan, at your service."

As she shook his hand, she couldn't keep herself from staring into his eyes. A deep shade of gray, they seemed to bubble with secrets.

"Marina Stone," she replied.

"Good day, Miss Stone. Reginald said you collapsed?"

"Apparently. I think I hit my head." She felt the bump and winced at the pain.

He studied her with those perceptive eyes. She shivered under his gaze. "Step aside, everyone. Step aside." He set his bag near her feet and bent to rummage through it. A moment later, he victoriously held up a strange stethoscope with only one earpiece.

Those watching stepped back a foot or so but still encircled her, gawking. Dr. Duncan's gaze swept the crowd as he cleared his throat. They took another step back. Except more oddly dressed men and women came to watch, filling in the gaps until Marina could no longer see her surroundings.

As the doctor listened to her lungs and heart behind the quilt, she studied the bystanders. The women wore dresses with big skirts, some muted solids, others modestly patterned.

Some wore bonnets, while curls framed others' faces. A few sported the same hideous hairstyle as the first lady with looped hair, mimicking a dog's ears. The men looked no less formal, most with bow ties and sport coats. In this crowd, she certainly was the one who stuck out as abnormal.

Could this truly be a dream? She bit her lip and tasted blood. No, this certainly seemed real. Had the stress of the last couple of years driven her insane?

As Dr. Duncan moved the stethoscope to her back again, he leaned close and whispered, "I can explain everything, but not presently."

"Huh?"

"You likely question where you are and how you got here. I can explain." He cast a meaningful look to the hovering crowd. "Just not now."

He must mean he couldn't disclose his top-secret intel with an audience nearby. Her breaths grew shallow. "Aiden and Brinley, where are they?"

"Your family? Friends?"

"Children. Teenagers. Are they safe?"

A reassuring smile accompanied his nod. "Yes, I'm sure they are safe. Right where you left them."

She forced herself to breathe deeply. They were on the bottom deck of *Duncan's Delight*. "And where am I?" Her squeaky voice failed to match the doctor's whisper.

Ugly Hair Lady stepped forward. "She asked this before, Doctor, and we told her she's on the *White Cloud*. Clearly, she's confused. Does she have amnesia?"

He turned to address the onlookers. "This woman has what's known as the traveling sickness. She might remain befuddled for a time, but I assure you, it's not contagious, and no one is in danger." He dropped his stethoscope into his bag. "I encourage you to help Miss Stone to reacclimate to reality. The confusion will lift in time." He adjusted his scarf, then picked up his bag. "I'll come check on you in your stateroom in a few hours."

"My stateroom?" Her mind swirled. "What stateroom?"

"What room number did they give you when you boarded the ship?" He seemed to be trying to communicate something with his eyes, but what?

"None. There were no rooms." That she knew of, at least. The *Duncan's Delight* had seemed straightforward. Two decks, the bottom surrounded by windows, the top open-air. A bar in back. The pilothouse up front.

"Ah. Room 11, then. I believe your belongings should be in the room."

What belongings? What room? He had one thing right. She certainly was *befuddled*. Maybe he was also correct in that her confusion would dissipate with time, and she'd remember what happened and make sense of everything. What choice did she have but to wait it out? Whether she had a concussion, amnesia, or lunacy, she could hardly think straight enough to formulate a complete sentence. Her head felt stuffed with cotton and tacks. A muddled, painful mess.

"Come now, dear." Ugly Hair Lady took her hand. "I'll walk you to your room."

Marina's legs shook as she stood.

"Your dizziness will dissipate momentarily." Dr. Duncan peered at her in an unnerving way. "Headache too."

Had she mentioned her headache? She pleaded with her eyes, but a small, compassionate smile was his only reply. He'd explain everything soon. Aiden and Brinley were safe. It would all be okay once this traveling sickness wore off.

"I'll carry your bag." Ugly Hair Lady scooped up Marina's purse from the foot of the couch. At last, something familiar. She allowed the woman to lead her past a dining table and an area partitioned off by curtains to a door with the number eleven on it. "Now, where is your key?"

Marina opened her mouth to tell the lady she didn't have a key, but before she could form the words, Ugly Hair Lady reached into Marina's purse and pulled out a large brass key. "Here it is."

Of all the odd things. While the woman unlocked and opened the door, she studied her surroundings, searching for something—anything—familiar. Her breath caught as her gaze zeroed in on something directly across from her room. An antique-looking mailbox identical to the one she'd admired on the *Duncan's Delight.*

~

Back at home, Claire lay on the couch while Bearett brought her saltines and 7UP. "Really, honey, I'm fine."

He raised an eyebrow. "Not buying it." He covered her with a blue-and-white-striped blanket.

"I felt a bit queasy on the boat. Motion sickness, maybe." She bit into a cracker.

Bearett sat on the coffee table and leveled her with a hard stare. She resisted the urge to squirm.

"You're telling me that after spending nearly two years going out on that boat with me without any problems, you've suddenly developed motion sickness?"

She shrugged as he placed a hand on her forehead.

"No fever. That's good."

She should just tell him. Blurt it out and let him process. He was a good man. The best. Surely, he'd understand. Her lips twitched with the weight of unsaid truth. Her heartbeat thudded in her ears as her mouth went dry.

No. She couldn't tell him yet. She needed to come to terms with it herself. Time to change the subject.

"How'd we make out today?"

He stood and raked a hand through his hair. "We might end up breaking even."

Ouch. "We were filled to capacity this morning." Unlike in the cooler months or on weekdays.

He harrumphed. "I need my own boat. Leasing is killing me."

"You'll get there." She gave his pants leg a tug, and he reclaimed his spot on the coffee table. She took his hand and squeezed. "It takes time."

"Yeah. I know. Thanks for always supporting me." His smile looked forced. "No matter what I choose to do, you always have my back."

Was he thinking about the mission trips he used to go on each summer? They'd been the highlight of each year, but now he couldn't take time off to go. Couldn't rely on her measly income to tide them over. Some support she was.

"Of course." She inched upward until she was propped against her pillow instead of lying flat. "I feel bad that I'm not doing more to help financially. If I was a homeopathic doctor, if I'd finished my schooling …"

He waved her off. "You do plenty. We'll get there in time. Once we save up enough money for you to continue your training without taking on a boatload of debt, you can go back to school."

She wouldn't argue, but her chest burned with the thought of trying again. What if she couldn't do it? Better to stick with what she was obviously good at. "What if I took on a couple more classes? I could teach step aerobics, or maybe one of the water classes." Even as the words tumbled out, the impossibility of their situation flooded her. What were a few more classes at the YMCA compared to a thirty-five-thousand-dollar-a-week lease, plus fuel and fees? Besides, it would only be a temporary solution. It wasn't like she could bring a baby to work.

He laced his fingers in between his knees and licked his lips. Uh oh. She wouldn't like whatever he had to say.

"What if you dipped your toe back into your old fitness channel? I'm sure you could get some of your previous sponsors back."

She shook her head. "No. I can't. I mean, I could, but I … You know how hard I've fought to get out of the social media cycle."

He frowned. "I know."

"It would be backtracking on all my progress." But what if she did videos on exercising while pregnant? Or doing Pilates with a baby in tow? It could work. But no. She'd gotten out of that lifestyle for a reason. The pressure had nearly incapacitated her. There would always be the push to do more, be more. It wasn't healthy. "I can't do it, Bearett."

"Okay. Sorry." He handed her the bottle of 7UP. "I get it. Rest for now, and we'll pray about the boat later."

She took a swig of soda and closed her eyes. She could go for a nap. If only her racing thoughts would quiet and let her sleep. Captaining *Duncan's Delight* was Bearett's dream. He was a Duncan, after all, and Duncans were drawn to the water. He honored his heritage by leasing a mailboat and installing an antique mailbox on board, similar to the one Claire and Wendy had used to communicate with Stella when she'd time-sailed to 1856. It was the perfect boat for him, and she couldn't allow him to lose it. But how could she generate significant income without selling her soul to the social media devil?

Oh, Lord. What should I do?

~

Light crept through the small, barred window in Aiden's cell. Spending the night in jail had so not been on his bucket list. Had Mom been looking for them? She hadn't answered her cell when he'd used his one phone call, and the police hadn't stopped trying to contact her since they'd arrived. No luck. She couldn't still be ticked at them, could she? At least, not enough to let them rot in jail.

"Brinley, you awake?" He kept his voice to a whisper. Were there some kind of quiet hours? Surely, he could talk to his sister on the cot across from his.

"Yep." She sounded defeated.

"I can't believe Mom hasn't bailed us out by now."

"She probably doesn't know we're here."

"I left a message." And that was something like nine hours ago. "Besides, if she couldn't find us anywhere, don't you think she'd go straight to the police?"

A beat of silence. "She'll come."

She'd better. The cops had taken down their side of the story, but their pleas of innocence had availed them nothing.

The bike had been stolen. Aiden and Brinley had been riding the bike. End of story. Were the cops even looking for Jack? Doubtful. They were far more concerned with badgering Aiden about where he was from and where his legal guardians were.

"Guardian," Aiden had said. "My dad died a couple of years ago."

"Ah." The officer had nodded like that explained everything. He mumbled something about how it was always the fatherless getting into trouble, stealing and such.

Whatever. When he became a cop, he wouldn't badger the innocent.

The police had threatened to hand Brinley over to child services when Mom didn't answer, but she and Aiden had begged to stay together. Apparently, the law considered a seventeen-year-old to be an adult and a sixteen-year-old to be a child. The officer kept saying, "We'll hold off another hour or so. See if we can get ahold of your mother." But as the hours marched on, they ended up letting them stay together "just for one night." Where was Mom, anyway? If she'd just show up, they could straighten out this mess.

"I'm scared." Brinley's voice shook.

"Aw, Brin." He should tell her everything would be fine, but he couldn't lie to her. How this would play out was anyone's guess.

Heavy footsteps approached, and Aiden straightened on his cot. "Aiden and Brinley Stone, come with me." The guard, with more frown lines than hair, unlocked his cell. Aiden jumped up and nearly bolted out the door.

Brinley offered a smile. "Guess Mom showed up after all."

Ahead of them, the guard grunted. He led them into a small room with a conference table in the center. At the table, in a black plastic chair, sat Jack.

"That little …" Aiden mumbled under his breath.

Brinley put a hand on his arm.

A cop with a clipboard sat next to the black-haired traitor. "Are these the ones you lent the moped to?"

"Yes!" Aiden blurted.

The officer cast him a warning glance, and he clamped his mouth shut.

"That's them." Jack had the audacity to look sheepish with hunched shoulders and red cheeks. "I met them near South Beach and asked if they wanted to take the moped out for a spin. They had nothing to do with the … theft."

The officer gave a single nod, then angled toward Aiden and Brinley, still standing near the doorway. "Since Mr. Barr's testimony corroborated your innocence, you are free to go as soon as a family member can pick you up."

"For real?" Aiden attempted to hold back a smile.

"Yes. Stop at the front desk for your things."

"Cool. Thanks."

The guard opened the door, and Aiden followed Brinley through it. At the front desk, he retrieved his wallet, phone, and hotel keycard, and Brinley got her purse. They sat in the waiting room under the watchful eye of the front desk attendant.

Aiden wasted no time calling Mom again. Straight to voicemail. So strange.

"Did you get ahold of someone?" the attendant asked.

"Yeah," he said. "She'll be here in a few minutes."

"Really?" Brinley whispered through the side of her mouth.

He gave a slight shake of his head. They had to get out of there somehow. If only there were someone else he could call.

Two officers burst through the door, belligerent man in tow. The handcuffed, bearded man pitched and writhed, mouthing off curses.

"Assistance, please!" one of the cops shouted.

The attendant ran for backup.

"Go. Now," Aiden whispered.

Brinley jumped up and headed for the front door. "Here's Mom now. Thanks!" she shouted behind her.

They rushed out the front door before anyone could question them.

At the corner, they stopped to catch their breath.

Brinley beamed. "I knew Jack wasn't a bad guy."

"Are you serious right now? He stole a moped." What was with his sister's flushed cheeks? Was it from their prison escape, or was she actually developing feelings for that creep?

"He could have pinned it on us, but he didn't." She twirled a strand of hair around her finger. "Besides, there's probably more to the story."

Whatever. He had bigger worries than his sister falling for a thief she'd never see again anyway. Where was Mom? Why hadn't she answered her phone or bailed them out of jail? To say it wasn't like her would be the understatement of the century. Something was wrong. He had to find out what.

Chapter Four

Out of breath from the thirty-minute walk, Aiden swung open the hotel room door and barged into the room, only to skid to a stop. "Brinley?"

"Yeah?" Her voice lapped at his back, shaky and small.

"Where's Mom's suitcase?"

"What?" She came around to his side. "How am I supposed to know?"

Both beds were meticulously made—no surprise there—but while one side of the room contained their suitcases, snacks, and clothes, Mom's side was bare. As if she'd never been there at all.

Brinley rushed to the closet. The sliding door banged open to reveal nothing but empty hangers. Aiden yanked open dresser drawers. Not even a sock on Mom's side.

Brinley wrapped her arms around herself and spun in a slow circle. "What's going on?"

If only he had a clue. Mouth dry and hands sweaty, he plopped onto Mom's bed to think. Where could she have gone? He pulled out his cell and dialed her number. Voicemail.

His sister sat next to him. "Do you think she drove home?"

Ridiculous. "She would never leave us here alone."

"Maybe she had some kind of breakdown?"

Possible. But to ditch them in another city? She'd have to be literally insane. "Maybe she wanted to teach us a lesson." She'd been ticked enough the last time they saw her, her face red as a tomato and that vein bulging at her temple. "She could have moved her stuff to a different room."

Brinley looked at him as though he were the insane one. "You think she'd pay for two hotel rooms just to teach us a lesson?"

It wasn't like her to waste money, but … "She did waste her cruise ticket." Not the same thing. He rubbed his temples. *Think!*

"We could ask at the front desk." Brinley worried her lip, eyes wide. "But what if that's not it, and they kick us out?"

They wouldn't, would they? But what if they did?

Brinley's breath hitched. "Should we call the police?"

"No way." With their luck, they'd be accused of killing their mother. He projected confidence into his voice. He couldn't give in to the fear that rose in his gut. His sister needed him to remain calm. "Why don't we try going back to the last place we saw her?"

"That boat?"

"Yeah. Couldn't hurt." If she wasn't there … well, he'd figure out what to do then.

As they walked for another forty-something minutes to the Southside Marina, they talked through everything they could think of about Mom. Nothing added up. How could she disappear? If she'd been attacked, she always carried Mace. If she'd changed plans, she would for sure call.

Neither of them spoke as they neared the pier, both of their gazes sweeping the area. The beach was just out of sight. People of all ages swarmed the sidewalk, many dressed in bathing suits. The scent of sunscreen lingered in the air. Seagulls swept the sky. The noise of spraying water and children's laughter from a nearby splash pad competed with the lapping of the river. Boats—large and small—bobbed in their slips. No sign of Mom.

"Might as well check the boat." He tried to keep from sounding as discouraged as he felt. No need to scare his sister any more than she already was.

Duncan's Delight bobbed at its place on the pier, quiet and empty. Aiden led the way onto the gangplank. "Hello?" He ducked under a chain and boarded the boat. "Anybody here?"

A blonde emerged from inside, rag in hand, hair tied up with a red bandana. "Can I help you?"

Now what? He pressed his lips together, scrambling for how to explain.

Brinley held out her phone. "We're looking for our mother. Have you seen her?"

The woman stepped closer and studied Mom's picture on Brinley's screen. "I don't remember her, but that doesn't mean much. Did she take a cruise with us, or are you asking everyone in the area?" A strand of hair fell in front of her face, and she tucked it back under the bandana. "Wait. I *do* remember you two. You did the sunrise cruise yesterday, right?"

"Right." Aiden stepped closer. "Mom was supposed to be on that cruise with us, only we don't think she made it. Do you know what happened?"

The woman brought a hand up to her chin, as if thinking. "Tell me more."

How much should he confess to this stranger?

"We had a fight right before we were supposed to board. We didn't see her get on, but assumed …" Brinley squeezed her eyes shut, a sure sign she was fighting back tears.

"It's not like her to leave us on our own," he said.

"And when we got to the hotel room, all her things were gone," Brinley said.

That might have been TMI. He pinned Brinley with a glare, but she only shrugged.

The woman's jaw dropped. She put out her hand. "Wait. What?"

Now Brinley's eyes brimmed with tears. "Her suitcase, clothes, the book she kept on the nightstand, all gone."

The woman gave a slow nod. "I think I know what's going on."

"You do?" Aiden sighed in relief.

"Do you mind waiting for a few minutes? Then I can explain. Maybe over lunch? My treat."

Food. Yes. Now that he thought about it, he was starving. "Sounds good."

"Great. I'm Claire, by the way. Claire Duncan."

Now the boat's name made a lot more sense. "I'm Aiden Stone."

"Brinley."

"Nice to meet you. Let me write a quick letter, and I'll be right with you." She took off into the boat. "Make yourselves at home," she called over her shoulder.

"A letter?" Aiden whispered. "Wasn't expecting that."

Brinley snickered. "Yeah, who writes letters anymore?" She sobered. "Do you think it's safe hanging around with some random lady?"

"Sure. She's a local business owner." Besides, they'd go to lunch in a public place. It wasn't like they'd let her lure them back to her house.

"And she seems nice."

Aiden would agree, except their interaction with Jack left him doubting his sister was a good judge of character. "She says she has answers. What choice do we have but to hear her out?"

A few minutes later, Claire strode off the boat. No letter in hand. And that purse she carried was too small to fit anything but Tic Tacs inside. Strange. Hopefully, she wasn't a lunatic.

~

One look at the clothes folded neatly on the bed in Marina's new room, and Ugly Hair Lady tsked. "Nothing appropriate at all." She rummaged through the tank tops and shorts. "Why on earth would you bring only underthings on a steamboat?"

Underthings? Marina looked down at her current ensemble. No wonder the crowd had gasped. They thought her half naked.

Ugly Hair Lady straightened and gave a little shake of her head as she studied Marina. "I'll have to see if one of the ladies has an extra frock. Mine would never fit you. And I'll fetch you a bonnet. No one need know your hair is sheared." She bustled to the door. "I'm Mrs. Martha Winthrop, by the way. I'll return shortly."

Marina nodded numbly. She scooted the pile of clothes over and sat on the edge of the bed. What a nightmare. This would be a great time to wake up.

Her room had a red velvet couch that matched the one in the saloon. Two paintings of rivers hung on opposite walls. What was that thing in the corner? She'd seen one before in a movie. A washstand. That was it. A gilded mirror hung directly above it. A glance behind her showed thick red curtains. What lay behind them? She'd explore more later.

Her gaze trailed to the corner where her suitcase stood. The suitcase she'd left in the hotel in South Haven. In fact, the clothes were from her drawers and closet there too. And the parenting book that had been on the bedside table there now sat on the bedside table here. All her things were here, but her children were not. When would Dr. Duncan come to explain?

A sharp knock sounded, then Martha let herself in, burgundy *frock* in hand. "I believe this will do nicely." She held the dress out, a pleased smile on her face. "Miss Greenbough felt so bad for you, she said you could keep it. Mr. Greenbough is quite wealthy, I've heard."

What was Marina supposed to say to any of this? She must look woefully out of place.

Martha didn't seem ruffled by her lack of response. "I also brought you a corset. I hope you don't mind. The one you're currently wearing is hardly effective." She eyed Marina's tank top. "I must say, I've never seen such an outlandish style of corset, nor such … unusual bloomers. Where do you hail from?"

Marina blinked. At least that was one question she knew the answer to. "St. Louis."

"Oh, you've just left home, then. Splendid. I'm entirely curious as to why you have no appropriate clothing, but I told myself I wouldn't pry. Let's get you dressed, shall we?"

Marina's cheeks heated. "Oh, I'll dress after you leave."

Martha's mouth formed a perfect *O*. "But how will you tie your laces?"

"I'll manage."

"As you wish." She laid the dress, corset, and petticoats on the bed. An envelope remained in her hand. "Oh, and this is for you."

"A letter?"

Martha nodded. "I found it outside your door."

Someone knocked, and Martha opened the door before Marina snapped out of her daze enough to move. A male voice spoke from beyond the threshold. "I believe this belongs to Miss Stone. We found it on the floor near where she collapsed."

"What is that contraption? A small trunk of some kind?"

"I don't rightly know. Just came to deliver it to the lady."

"Thank you, Mr. Reed."

Marina stepped toward the door, curiosity over what they were talking about compelling her. Martha shut the door and spun around with Marina's cooler in hand. She'd forgotten about it. "Oh, good." She could go for a Gatorade about now.

"What is it?" Martha placed it on the floor and studied it, frowning. "Is it some sort of small crate?"

Uh … "Yes." She had no desire to explain and had a feeling she ought not to.

"You sure are a strange bird."

Sure, *she* was the strange one. Now to get Martha out of her room so she could read the letter that burned in her palm. "Thank you for everything. Have a lovely evening." What time was it, anyway?

Martha's brow furrowed for a moment before her expression smoothed. "I'll leave you be. If you need anything, I'm in room 20."

Marina nodded her appreciation, and Martha scooted out the door.

Alone at last, she ripped open the envelope, unfolded the letter, and read.

Time travel? Yeah, right. What kind of crazy prank was this? Someone might be filming her right now, zeroing in on her reaction to this ridiculous letter. She schooled her features and glanced around for a camera. None in sight, but of course, it'd be hidden somewhere. She continued reading.

Time travel. How could anyone expect her to believe this? Quite an elaborate prank, though. Everyone perfectly in character. Why would they go through such effort? Outlandish. The time travel explanation fit with everything she'd experienced, but she couldn't allow someone to dupe her for social media views.

A knock sounded at the door. She opened it to find Dr. Duncan, his neck scarf loose, and his hair in even more disarray than before.

"May I come in?"

"Please." She stepped back.

"I apologize for the delay. I've been quite busy with the cholera epidemic. I couldn't explain your predicament among eavesdropping ears."

Marina put her hand on her hip. "Let me guess. I got sucked back into time and must complete a mission before I can go back?"

Dr. Duncan's eyes widened. "Yes, indeed. You've time-sailed to 1849 on the *White Cloud.* How did you know?"

"I received a letter."

"Ah, yes." He nodded. "The mailbox allows you to communicate with people in your time."

This was all too strange. Unbelievable that a cast of characters could pull off a stunt this elaborate. "This is all a crazy dream. I'll wake up soon." She wiped her sweaty palms on her capris and sat again on the edge of the bed.

"The longer you deny what's happening, the longer it will take to complete your mission and return."

Return. To her children. If this was an act, how could she call it off and get back to her teens? If it was the truth … She massaged her forehead. Aiden and Brinley were alone in South Haven. No telling what trouble they could get into unsupervised. What if they got sick? Did something dangerous and hurt themselves? Got mixed up with the wrong crowd? So many things could go wrong.

If this was a dream, she'd wake up, and all would be well. But what if it wasn't? What if, for some unexplainable reason, what Claire and Dr. Duncan said was true? No way. Couldn't be. But what if…? She needed to get back to Aiden and Brinley as soon as possible.

"What kind of mission am I supposed to accomplish?"

"I can't say. Each time sailor's purpose is different. You'll find out sooner or later."

"What do you mean you *can't say*?" Later wasn't an option. Aiden and Brinley needed her. If this crazy time-sailing thing was true, they were probably worried sick. And scared.

"I have no way of knowing what your mission is. *You* must discover it."

Great. She'd add that to her list of concerns. Figure out some mysterious mission. Find where she'd misplaced her sanity. Figure out what to tell Claire.

Claire wanted to call someone to take care of them, but there was no one. With Adam gone and her estranged from her family, there wasn't a soul who would do such a thing. Her parents hadn't approved of her marriage. Called Adam reckless and swore he would hurt her. Not that warm fuzzy feelings surrounded her relationship with her parents before she got married. But afterward? Even soft embers snuffed out.

Would Claire take the teens in? Surely, she would. It was the Duncans' fault Marina was in this mess. Something must be wrong with the stairs on that boat. That's why she'd slipped and fallen.

"The boat left from St. Louis?" If Martha was right, maybe it'd return there, and she'd be somewhere familiar. Was she actually going along with this nonsense?

"Indeed. Though this boat normally travels the circuit back and forth between New Orleans and St. Louis, she's currently making a short trip up the Illinois River to Peoria. Nearly there. Then, we'll head back to St. Louis."

Dr. Duncan surveyed the room. "I see your things followed you just fine."

Another part of the prank? Somehow, the time travel explanation was beginning to seem more plausible than a group of people tricking her for laughs. She patted her empty pockets. "Where's my phone?"

"Ah. I've heard this question before, though I don't understand the contraption you speak of. It seems the device must be in your hand to travel with you."

"But it was." She stood. She clearly remembered holding the cooler in one hand and her phone in the other … unless … "Wait. I dropped it when I fell."

"It wouldn't work in this time, anyway."

That made sense, but what she wouldn't give to look at a picture of her children right now. She'd have to scroll far back to find one of them smiling, but even a grumpy *Mom, you're seriously taking a picture right now?* one would lift her spirits.

She had to get back to them.

"Let's say I believe you. I find my mission, complete it, and then I can go back. Any rules I need to follow for this to work?" She could kick herself for never having read any time travel novels. Instead, parenting podcasts had consumed her free time. Time travel had guidelines, right? Was she the only one without a clue as to what they were?

He tilted his head thoughtfully. "Try to blend in as much as possible. It will go easier for you if you do."

So, she needed to wear that ridiculous dress. Play along. "Okay." What would it hurt? As long as there was even a minute possibility this could be true, she should go along with it.

"If you need me, ask the steward or chambermaid to fetch me."

She nodded, even though she had no clue what those were. If only Adam were here. He'd always known what to do and could take charge of any situation. He'd been more of a mountain to her than a mere rock. How could she keep pressing forward without him?

No use dwelling on such things. She'd figure it out. Complete her mission. Return to normal life. All of it as quickly as possible. Her teens needed her.

~

Claire's body hummed with nervous energy. How was she going to explain this? When Dr. Rodney Duncan described time-sailing to her and Wendy, they'd thought for sure he'd lost his mind. Would Aiden and Brinley believe her? What could she say to convince them?

They crossed the street and made their way to Clementine's.

"Looks good," Aiden said as they entered. "I'm starving."

Her stomach flopped at the scent of fried onions. Hopefully, she could make it through this meeting without getting sick. Would they feel awkward if she just ordered a Sprite? Not the best move, offering to pay for their lunch as tight as her finances were. Clementine's wasn't exactly cheap, but McDonald's was too far away to walk to, and food was the way to a teenager's heart. Of that much, she was confident. And she needed them to hear her out.

Once the hostess seated them at a booth, and the waitress took their drink orders, Claire made eye contact with the teens and splayed her hands on the wooden table. "This is going to sound crazy, and I know it will be hard to believe, but please listen to the whole spiel."

Brinley raised a brow at Aiden. "Ooookay."

"I know what happened to your mom because the same thing happened to my friend Stella a couple of years ago."

The waitress interrupted to place their drinks on the table and take their appetizer orders. Tater skins *and* Mexican nachos? Man, teen boys ate a lot. *Lord, let this baby be a girl. Or triple our finances.*

Claire smiled sweetly at the waitress. "Give us a few minutes to figure out what else we'd like." Hopefully, they preferred burgers to steak or seafood.

"Sure thing, honey." The waitress sauntered away.

"You were saying?" Aiden gulped his Coke.

"There's this thing called time-sailing. It's when another time in the past calls to someone. That person unintentionally slips back to that time so they can complete a mission. Whenever they finish the mission, they return home."

Brinley snorted. "Like time travel?"

"You're kidding, right?" Aiden narrowed his eyes.

Claire took a long sip of Sprite. This wasn't going well. "Yes, like time travel."

Aiden shook his head. "I knew you were a kook."

"Listen, your mom time-sailed. I'm sure of it. It happened just like it did for Stella. She was there one minute and gone the next, right? All her things disappeared because they followed her to … whenever she is." She gasped as a revelation struck her. "That must be her phone. Did she have a red phone?"

"Yeah …"

Claire smacked the table. "I found a phone that day, and no one claimed it, despite the announcement. That's hers." Although Stella had carried a phone with her into 1856. Why wouldn't Marina's phone go with her?

Minor detail. No one claimed the phone because its owner had sailed back in time. It made complete sense.

"Wait, where's her phone?" Aiden asked.

"On the boat in the lost and found. Behind the bar."

"Look, lady." Brinley scooted to the edge of the booth. "I think you need some kind of therapy or something."

Aiden scooted after her.

Were they about to run out of here? "Wait. Stay."

The waitress deposited Aiden's appetizers onto the table. Aiden gave his sister a meaningful look and tilted his head toward the tater skins. See? Food. Claire knew at least one thing about kids. The two settled back into their seats and dug in.

"Your mom is gone, which means you have nowhere to stay, right?"

Brinley picked up a nacho. "I'm pretty sure she paid for the hotel until the end of the week."

Two teens alone in South Haven did not sit well in her gut. "Got money?"

Aiden's mouth twitched. "A little."

"Enough to survive on your own for a week?"

"Probably." He averted his gaze. Liar.

"I wrote your mom a letter. She'll get it and write back. I'm sure of it."

Brinley burst into laughter. "A letter." She dabbed the corners of her wet eyes with a napkin. "Right."

"A letter, of course! Because they didn't have texting or email in the olden days." He nudged his sister to get her to move out of the booth.

They had to think she was a lunatic and possibly dangerous. Her stomach clenched, nausea bubbling up. She could not get sick now. "I know it sounds impossible, but letters can go back and forth between the time periods through these antique mailboxes."

"That's our cue to leave." Brinley stuffed one tater skin into her mouth and stood. "Thanks for the snack."

Aiden followed her, taking skins to go.

Ugh. They'd hardly touched the appetizers, and now she needed to chase after them. What a waste. She dug through her wallet and threw two twenties on the table before rushing out the door. They'd made it halfway down the street before she stumbled onto the sidewalk.

"Wait," she called, but they didn't even turn to acknowledge her.

Fine, then. She'd follow them. She couldn't in good conscience leave them to their own devices when their mother had time-sailed from Bearett's boat. She was partly responsible, being a Duncan and all.

Bearett had always hoped this would happen—hence, why he'd installed the mailbox on the upper deck. Duncans had been guides to time sailors throughout the centuries. "Wouldn't it be amazing if someone was called to the past from our boat?" he'd said. Yeah, so amazing. Only, they'd never thought through what it would mean for the family or friends left behind. Teenagers. How could the past have called a mom away from her teens?

God, You do know what You're doing, don't You? Because this seems like a bad plan.

They turned left, so they had to be headed toward the marina or the beach. Out of breath, she slowed her steps. They might need a minute to process. She could give them a little space.

When she approached the marina, there they were, boarding *Duncan's Delight*. Should she call Bearett and let him know what was going on? No time. Way too hard to explain, and she needed to catch up.

By the time she stepped onto the boat, they'd already found their mom's phone. It seemed they were trying different number combinations to unlock it. She took a deep breath before approaching. She couldn't scare them off any more.

"Who's the guy?" She nodded to the screen saver.

"Our dad." Aiden's voice held a pinch of sorrow.

Oh. If she could find him, at least she wouldn't need to feel responsible for two teenagers, even if he didn't believe her story. "Where is he?"

"Dead," Brinley deadpanned.

Claire sucked in a breath. Okay, so no father was coming to the rescue. "I'm sorry."

Brinley shrugged and turned her attention back to Aiden. "Try Dad's birthday."

Aiden's fingers tapped the screen. "It worked!"

"Any clues?" Brinley crowded closer to him.

"Give me a minute, would you?"

They weren't likely to find any clues on that phone, but it was possible … "Why don't you check the mailbox upstairs?" She gave a slight shrug.

"Yeah, sure." Brinley's voice was cloaked in sarcasm.

Aiden sighed. "Couldn't hurt. Where is it?"

Claire pointed up the stairs. "Right at the top." She followed them up.

"Weird." Aiden brushed his hand over the engraved lion on the mailbox. Its rusty hinges squeaked as he lifted the lid and peeked inside. "There's something here."

Claire held her breath. Was it the letter she had written or a response from their mom? He took it out, unfolded it, and read out loud.

> Aiden and Brinley,
>
> Are you okay? I'm so sorry to leave you like this. My foot slipped as I was going down the steps of *Duncan's Delight*, then I woke up here. I'm on the river steamboat the *White Cloud* in 1849. We're almost to Peoria, then we'll return to St. Louis. I have no idea how this is happening. Maybe I'm dreaming. But just in case this is real, I need to know that you're okay.
>
> Just as Claire predicted, this man named Dr. Duncan told me I need to complete a mission before I can go back home, only I don't know what that mission is. He said I'll find out in time.
>
> Please be careful there in South Haven. The owner of the boat, Claire, wrote to me to explain things, and I have no choice but to trust her. I must trust her with my dearest treasures, you. Listen to her and do what she says. She'll take care of you since I can't. Tell her there's no one else to call.
>
> Love,
> Mom

She'll take care of you. Talk about pressure. "What's your mom's name?"

The letter trembled in Aiden's hand. "Marina."

Claire nearly laughed. Marina. How fitting. "Write back and let her know you're all right. You guys can stay with me and Bearett until she gets back." It was the least she could do, since their boat was responsible for this mess. How long had Stella been gone when she'd time-sailed? Nine days? Surely, Claire could keep two teenagers alive for nine days. Marina might accomplish her mission even sooner. It'd be fine.

She'd take care of them.

Chapter Five

If Marina was going to discover and complete her mission, she needed information. Once she managed to get into the blasted dress—no easy feat—she slid into a pair of flats—those had to be less conspicuous than flip-flops. As she exited her room, that old mailbox stared back at her. She glared at it. The stupid thing had gotten her into this mess. Had given her the shock that made her insane, apparently, because she was going along with this time-sailing nonsense. What other choice did she have?

A whistle shrilled, piercing her ears. She covered them and stumbled a bit as the boat rocked slightly to the left side. Lake travel had been far smoother. The couch she'd woken up on stole her attention. It sat directly ahead of her in the open interior someone had called a social hall. Or was it a saloon? Close to it, a man sat in the barber chair as a bald man with a thick mustache cut his hair. At the same time, a Black man in an apron shined the man's shoes. She peeked inside an area sectioned off with thick red curtains to find several women sitting on couches. A piano stood near an unlit fireplace. An ornate rug decorated the floor. Far more luxurious than the *Duncan's Delight.*

"Come in, dear." One woman with long, dark curls patted the adjacent spot on her couch. "Are you feeling better?"

She offered a polite smile. "Yes. Thank you." She crossed the area and attempted to maneuver her skirts so she could sit. So much fabric. How'd the other women make it look natural?

"We haven't seen you in the ladies' cabin before." Another woman with that same ridiculous, looped hairstyle paused from her knitting to meet Marina's eyes.

Each woman introduced herself. The only name that stuck in her brain was Christina's, the dark-haired woman who'd first greeted her.

"It's nice to meet all of you." As long as there wasn't a quiz later.

Christina angled toward her. "My husband, Lewis, is in the fur trade."

"My Charles is a banker." The woman with that hideous dog-eared hairstyle beamed.

"As is my husband, Thomas." The third woman spoke up. Two blonde curls draped the sides of her face, while the rest of her hair was pulled back.

"What does your husband do, dear?" Christina asked.

A pang hit Marina's chest. "I'm a widow." Could she leave it at that?

"My condolences." Mrs. Dog-Eared made the sign of the cross.

The other ladies echoed her sentiment. Adam's handsome face flashed in her mind. Time to change the subject. Only, how to broach the subject of her mystery mission?

"Do you ladies know of anything that needs to be done?"

"Done? On this boat?" Christina's laughter trilled like a wind chime.

Mrs. Dog-Eared looked up from her knitting with a twinkle in her eye. "That's what the steward and chambermaids are for."

So much for that line of inquiry. She worried her lip as she stumbled for another way to get the women talking.

"Terrible about the cholera epidemic, isn't it?" Mrs. Dog-Eared asked without looking up.

Blondie tsked. "Dreadful. Thomas insisted we remain in St. Louis only a few days. Thankfully, we were able to steer clear of the bad air and emerge unscathed."

Did she mean … Would the boat be headed directly back into an outbreak? Cholera killed people, didn't it? At least, that's what she'd learned from playing Oregon Trail as a child. "Is it …" She bit the inside of her cheek. "Is it bad?"

She could smack herself upside the head. What kind of question was that? The terms *cholera* and *epidemic* were answer enough.

"Oh my. You must still be suffering from confusion." Christina shook her head. "I heard over the past couple of weeks, nearly one hundred people perished of the disease."

"I heard ten people a day in the city limits alone." Mrs. Dog-Eared sighed. "Fine and dandy one day. Dead the next. That's how it goes with this plague."

Definitely bad. What would happen if she caught cholera? If she died in 1849, would her body return to her time, or would she lose the life she loved? Her children couldn't lose *both* parents. Unthinkable. Maybe she should get off in Peoria and stay there. She pulled at her gown's collar. She needed some air. "Which way to the deck?" No harm in asking since they already thought her confused.

"The hurricane deck?" Christina looked at her with pity. "You'll find a stairwell in the back of the boat."

Marina stood. "Nice meeting you all. I'm sure I'll see you again soon." Without waiting for a reply, she rushed out of the curtained area and turned toward what seemed to be the rear of the boat.

She nearly collided with a young Black woman wearing a black dress and crisp white apron. Her hand flew to her chest. "I'm sorry. I wasn't paying attention."

"Not a problem, miss. I'm Alanda, your chambermaid. Is there anything I can help you with?" Alanda's gaze remained near Marina's shoes.

"I just need some air. Where can I find the deck?" She pointed in the direction she'd been headed. "That way?"

"The hurricane deck?"

Was there another option? Marina nodded.

"Follow me, miss." Alanda led her past several rooms, then out a door and up a stairwell. When she reached the top, she gestured to the open area with rocking chairs around the perimeter, facing the river. Two black smokestacks towered on either side of the deck, belching gray smoke. Perched on the other end of the deck were two other enclosed areas, stacked like a cake with the top layer smaller than the bottom. "You can also access the promenade deck from your stateroom's back door."

Oh. That would have been easier.

"Anything else you need, miss?"

Marina shook her head, gaze traversing the murky river. Nothing but farmland as far as she could see, with a dotting of cows here and there. What river was this again? *The Illinois River*, Dr. Duncan had said. How long was a short steamboat trip? When would they arrive in Peoria? If she returned to St. Louis, how long would that take? She should have asked more questions. Earlier, she'd reveled in the view of Lake Michigan. Clean, crisp morning air had filled her lungs. Here, the fishy air seemed thick enough to choke on. Talk about muggy.

"Were you the lady who fainted earlier?" A clean-shaven man in a suit and neck scarf moseyed toward her.

"That'd be me." She leaned against the railing. "Marina Stone."

"The name's George. George Randolph." He stuck out his hand.

She kept the handshake brief. Though he looked to be around ten years her senior, she didn't want to give him any ideas.

"Feeling better?"

"A little."

He broke into a wide grin. "That's good. Everyone was worried. I prayed for you. The Good Book says to pray instead of worry, so that's what I did."

Tension coiled around her shoulders. A praying man. He seemed nice enough, but experience told her such people reeked of judgment. Growing up in church, she'd tried to pray a few times, but it had never resonated. She'd spent much of her Sunday school years in trouble because she could never sit still. No matter how hard she tried, she couldn't be good enough for those people. For God.

Still, she managed a polite smile and a thank you. Now, to veer the subject away from prayer. "What do you do, Mr. Randolph?"

"I'm a traveling Bible salesman." He pointed to a messenger bag sitting on a bench. "After a short stop in Peoria, I'm headed back to St. Louis to try and reach the forty-niners before the love of mammon swallows them whole."

So much for steering the conversation away from churchy things. "Forty-niners?" She'd heard of them before. Were they a football team?

He tilted his head to the side, as though confused by her question. "Those headed to California to mine for gold. Gold fever is sweeping the country, Miss Stone, and my soul is burdened for those who dream that striking it rich will cure all their problems."

Ah. Gold diggers. But California was a long way away. "Why St. Louis?"

"It's the Gateway to the West. Overlanders pass straight through St. Louis on their way. What better place to sell a Bible than while they're gathering supplies for the trek?"

She nodded as though this made sense, but how many gold diggers would purchase a Bible when their eyes were set on wealth out West? Poor George Randolph had a hard job ahead of him. Maybe her mission was to purchase a Bible from the guy. Might be the only one he ever sold.

Ridiculous. She didn't have any useable money, anyway. If she was supposed to blend in, she'd need to keep her modern currency tucked in her wallet.

"I wish you the best," she said, and meant it. She'd heard the Bible could bring great comfort to people, and it sounded like people needed a lot of comfort in 1849.

As for her, she needed answers.

~

Aiden hoisted his suitcase up Claire's front step and waited for her to unlock the bright-red door. The simple gray ranch house wasn't much to look at. Wouldn't a boat captain be able to afford a nicer place? At least it was only two blocks to walk to downtown and another few blocks to South Beach.

Brinley fidgeted beside him as the door swung open, and Claire motioned them forward. "Come in. Come in. Make yourselves at home."

At home. Right. Mom was forcing them to stay with complete strangers, and they were supposed to ignore the weirdness. "After you." He nudged Brinley forward.

The two of them stopped right inside the threshold. White couches with navy blue pillows surrounded a square white table. He blinked. Everything was blue and white. The curtains. The walls. The bar stools tucked up against the island. The tablecloth and place mats on the dining room table. "Very … nautical."

"Nautical?" Brinley whispered. "You nerd."

"Yeah, well." Claire breezed to the kitchen island and dropped her keys into a blue bowl on the counter. "It fits." She pulled a 7UP from the fridge and took a few sips. "I'd give you a tour, but there's not much to the place. Two bedrooms and two baths." She pointed. "That's the room Bearett and I share." Her finger moved slightly to the right. "And that's the guest room. Sorry, you'll have to share. That's probably weird at your age, huh?"

Brinley shrugged. "We were sharing the hotel room."

And they would have been perfectly fine continuing to do so. Why couldn't they have stayed there? Mom didn't trust them at all. She probably never would.

Claire gestured to the guest room. "I was planning on making tacos for dinner. Sound good?"

"Sure," they mumbled in unison.

An uncomfortable dinner with strangers who thought they were the boss of him and his sister. Joy. How could this be happening? They'd taken a family vacation to Crazy Town.

"Bearett will be home in a couple of hours. He's searching for a new caterer."

"Does he know about our … situation?"

"Not yet."

Great. This was sure to be a blast.

Maybe he should have told Mom the truth in the letter he wrote back to her, instead of trying to make it seem like everything was fine. But what was the truth, anyway? If this whole time-sailing thing was true—and he had no better explanation—it wasn't like she needed to rush back to rescue them. Still, even Mom was better than two bystanders. Why did Mom trust them? They could be psychopaths for all she knew.

"Come on." Brinley rolled her suitcase across the living room to the guest room. He followed and shut the bedroom door behind him.

"Ready to ditch this place?" he whispered.

Brinley plopped onto the bed. "I swear Claire looks familiar. I can't place her, though. It's bothered me all day. I'm sure I've never met her before, but I can't get over it."

Familiar? He pictured her face. Nope. "Never saw her before in my life. Before the cruise, I mean."

"Well, I have. I just don't know where."

"Hopefully, not on a true crime show."

Brinley swatted him with a pillow. "She's not that bad."

Whatever. "Did I do the right thing in my letter to Mom?" He sat on the edge of the bed.

"What do you mean?"

"You know, playing it down. *Don't worry about us. We're fine. We're having a great time.*"

"Of course. The last thing she needs is to worry about us. She'll never complete her mission if she's busy freaking out." She shook her head. "This is lunacy. We've all lost our minds."

"Yeah." He palmed his face. "I can't believe we're actually going along with this craziness."

"I know, right? My friend Clarissa believes all these crazy conspiracy theories, and I've always thought she was nuts. Yet, I don't know what else to believe about Mom."

Neither did he.

~

With the teens settled and watching an Avengers movie in the living room, Claire retreated to her bedroom and pulled out her laptop. Time to research. Bearett lay with his arm strewn over his eyes, the nightly news playing on the television.

"You said she slipped?" His voice slurred from grogginess.

"Yep." They'd already been over this, but it'd do no good to point that out.

"That's not good. She could sue."

Claire bit her lip. "I don't think she will. We're watching her children after all." Hopefully, that would earn her favor.

"I've waited for years for this to happen. Couldn't wait to see time-sailing in action. Now I'm worried about the repercussions."

She patted his leg. "It'll be fine." Apparently, she'd adopted that as her new mantra.

"God forbid one of her kids gets hurt on our watch." He sighed long and deep. "We don't know the first thing about raising teenagers."

Gracious. Negativity seeped from his pores. This wasn't like him. The business must weigh heavily on his shoulders lately. "We don't have to raise them, honey. Just look after them for a few days." She swallowed down the lump in her throat. "Besides, we *were* teenagers not that long ago." If only she believed the trite assurances she dished out.

Another heavy sigh was his only response.

She opened her laptop, pulled up the search bar, and typed in *The White Cloud*. Nothing about a steamboat. She added *1849* to her search. The results populated, and she gasped.

"What?" Bearett sat up and angled toward her.

"Marina's boat is where the Great St. Louis Fire of 1849 started."

"How?"

She read on. "A mattress caught on fire while the ship was docked, then the wind spread the fire to other steamboats, and then to the levee and the city. It burned for eleven hours, destroying twenty-three steamboats and four hundred and thirty buildings. Hundreds were homeless. Thousands out of work."

"Great. We're responsible for her time-sailing straight into a disaster zone."

Claire eyed him. What was going on with him? Her hopeful dreamer had transformed into Eeyore. "You know we're not responsible for this."

He scoffed.

As her heart rate gained speed, she grappled for something to say that would allay his worries. How could she make this better? Make *him* better? The ground seemed to shift under her. "What's this really about?" She braced herself for an answer she'd rather not hear.

Clasping his hands in his lap, he let out a bone-weary groan. "We're going to lose the boat, Claire. All my dreams are about to go up in smoke, just like with that fire."

"No." Money was tight, obviously, but they'd weathered ups and downs since their wedding. This was just another wave. Right?

"I can't see another way around it." He pressed his fists to his eyes. "I'm telling you, if anyone lays one more thing on me, I'll snap like a twig."

She resisted the urge to touch her stomach. *One more thing.* She had to keep her pregnancy to herself until things turned a corner. She could not break her husband.

Chapter Six

Marina awoke to find someone had slid a letter under her door. Her kids? She jumped from bed and snatched the envelope. Were they okay? They'd written her back yesterday, assuring her they were completely fine. Claire had written as well, reiterating their well-being and saying she'd host them until Marina returned. But what if she'd changed her mind?

She devoured the words from the page as if they were her first meal in days.

> Marina,
>
> Aiden and Brinley are settled at my home. We are happy to have them here and will take good care of them. Don't worry about anything here.
>
> I researched the *White Cloud* and discovered some disturbing information. What's the date there? If it's May there—

May? The date? Wouldn't it be the same month and day here as in South Haven, just a different year? Or did Claire's question mean it could be any month, that time here didn't necessarily correlate with the time she came from? She needed to find out *when* she was.

Rushing from her room, she nearly plowed into Alanda. She clasped the woman's upper arms to steady her. Alanda flinched.

After dropping her hands, Marina took a step back. "Sorry. I just … Can you tell me the date?"

Alanda stared at her shoes. "It's May 12, ma'am."

May 12. Not the end of June. Crazy. "Thank you." Marina dashed back to her room to read the rest of the letter.

> If it's May there, you may be headed straight for one of the most devastating fires in St. Louis's history. I don't want to scare you, but on May 17, between nine and ten at night, the *White Cloud* is going to catch fire. Wind will spread that fire to other steamboats and then to buildings. It will start with a mattress on your steamboat.
>
> Of course, you won't be on the boat when the fire breaks out. It will be docked, and all passengers will have disembarked. But please be careful. Wherever you happen to be on that night (if you haven't returned before then), the fire will affect you in some way.
>
> I couldn't find any other information about the boat, and I'm not sure what your mission might be. I'll pray the Lord reveals it to you and gives you the strength to complete it. Maybe it's earlier in the year. You could not encounter the fire at all. Did Dr. Duncan explain about snags? They complicate the timing.
>
> Please write back and let me know if you've discovered what your mission might be.
>
> Best,
> Claire

Marina's gaze caught on one word: fire. In five days. Fire. Her pulse raced. *Dear God, no.* It was the first prayer she'd uttered in a decade, and it fell as woefully short as the others. Three words. That's all she could muster in the face of her flashbacks.

Adam had headed off to work after they'd just fought. She'd said, "I love you," as she always did, but her voice had been cold. When sirens blared, the question of if he was headed that way bubbled to the surface. The call telling her he'd been injured. The other call while she was on the way to the hospital informing her he hadn't made it. The funeral where she'd fortified her heart from displaying grief. She'd had to be strong for her children.

Her husband had died in a fire, and she was headed straight into one.

If this was part of an almighty God's plan, what kind of sick game was He playing?

The letter shook in her hand. A bell sounded. Had to be breakfast. They'd rung a similar bell to signal dinner last night. She should go out there and mingle. Attempt to gather as much information as she could. But there was no way she could stomach food right now.

She burrowed under the covers again, pulling them up to her chin. She couldn't face a fire. Not when it was her fault Adam had died. If only she hadn't pressed him to continue firefighting. To think, she'd been nervous about finances. What she wouldn't give to weather a financial rough patch with Adam. If she could go back in time …

Wait. She *had* gone back in time. Just not to the time of her deepest regret. She couldn't change what happened to Adam, but she *could* change something. That was the point, right? The universe—God?—had sent her back in time so she could right a wrong.

How much more obvious could it be? She'd been sent to stop the fire. Why else would fate have dropped her here right before this catastrophic event? She didn't need to have read up on time travel to figure this one out.

Catapulting up, she threw off the covers. No hiding from this. It was her destiny. Perhaps she knew more about fires than other people in 1849. Adam had relayed so much information over the years. She could do this. She could face her fears and save St. Louis. There was a poetic justice about it. A redemption of sorts. If Adam looked down upon her now, he'd be proud. What a way to honor his memory.

Now, to figure out *how* to prevent the fire. With a five-day lead, surely, she could come up with a plan. Claire had said it started from a mattress. Perhaps she could throw all the mattresses overboard the morning of the seventeenth. No mattress. No fire. No devastation.

How would she gain entrance onto the boat when it was docked? Perhaps she could get rid of the mattresses while still on board the ship. But how would she gain entrance into everyone's staterooms and convince them to not stand in her way? She needed to earn their trust. And if Claire could narrow down where the offending mattress was located, she could be strategic.

Fresh purpose propelling her, she dressed for the day and rushed out her door to breakfast. She needed allies. Good thing being social was her superpower.

~

Aiden didn't bother to look up from his phone as he rode in Bearett's passenger seat. He and Brinley had been given a choice. Go to work with Claire or with Bearett. Brinley had chosen to tag along with Claire. Apparently, she taught some kind of exercise classes at the YMCA. He'd rather die than spend a day with a bunch of women doing aerobics. So, here he was, going back on the dumb boat.

Why were Claire and Bearett treating them like they were little children? It wasn't like they couldn't be trusted to hang out on their own for the day. What trouble could they cause?

Flashing police lights came to mind. But seriously, the whole jail thing hadn't been their fault. Stupid Jack had set them up.

He scrolled Instagram as Bearett drove. Something about needing to run an errand before they went to the *Duncan's Delight*. Oh, great. There was another picture of Stacy and Brad. They were all over each other. Definitely a couple. Aiden rubbed at the burning in his chest.

Had Stacy seen the picture he'd posted of him and Nevaeh? Maybe she had, and they were now in a war to make each other jealous. Ridiculous. He should move on. No use chasing after a girl who wanted nothing to do with him.

Except her dad had said …

Could he make it into the force on his own merits? Clumsy and plagued with asthma, wouldn't he fail the physical fitness test? They'd laugh him out of the training. His mind went to the plot of *Paul Blart: Mall Cop*. Would that be him? A pathetic loser who couldn't make the cut. Not if he remained in the good graces of Stacy's dad. That man was his ticket.

"Everything okay?" Bearett's gaze bore into him.

"Yeah." Just stuck hundreds of miles from home with complete strangers while the girl of his dreams cuddled up to another guy. Couldn't be better.

"So, you're going into your senior year? Got any plans for after you graduate?"

Great. The guy wanted to chat. "I'm going to be a cop." If only stating it like it was a definite would make it true.

Bearett nodded, as though impressed. "Sweet."

"Wish my mom thought so."

"Not on board with your plan?"

Aiden scoffed. "Not at all. She says I'm too smart to waste my life."

Bearett whistled. "Well, that's a … strong opinion. Are you smart?"

"I guess." His cheeks warmed. "I've never gotten a grade lower than an A. Mom thinks I should become a doctor or scientist or something. The smart thing is an excuse, though. The truth is, she doesn't want me to put myself in danger."

"Ah. I can understand that."

"My dad was a firefighter. He died on duty. Suddenly, Mom turned into a control freak. She'd wrap us in Bubble Wrap if she could."

Why was he talking so much to this guy? He'd never mentioned any of this to anyone but Stacy and Brinley. Something about Bearett made him want to open up.

Bearett parked in front of a bank. "Hang tight. I'll only be a few minutes."

"'Kay." More time to obsess over Stacy's pictures. Only, he couldn't keep torturing himself. After a few minutes, he stuffed his phone in his pocket.

Out of the corner of his eye, black hair caught his attention. Nevaeh. She sauntered toward a coffee shop, long hair blowing in the breeze. Gorgeous. And alone. Might she want company?

Before he could question himself, he stepped out of the car. "Nevaeh!"

When she turned, a smile lifted her lips. "Hey, Aiden. What are you up to?"

Hard to explain. "Waiting for Bearett Duncan to come out of the bank. He's taking me on his boat and showing me the ropes." Yeah. That sounded way better than *He's babysitting me.*

"That's cool. I didn't know you knew the Duncans personally."

He gave a noncommittal shrug. Wind whipped her hair in front of her face. His fingers itched to tuck the strands behind her ear.

She flung her hair behind her. "How long will you be in town for?"

"Not sure." One hundred percent true. "Awhile."

She checked her pink watch and grimaced. "I've got to go, but let me give you my number. Call me if you have time to hang out later this week."

"Sounds good." He pulled out his phone and entered the number she rattled off, then he watched her walk away and enter the coffee shop.

He'd just ducked back into the truck when Bearett emerged, frowning. One look at Aiden, and the corner of Bearett's mouth lifted. "Why are you grinning like a fisherman who caught a ten-pound bass?"

He was? He covered his mouth with his hand. "No reason."

"Right." Bearett backed out of the parking space and headed toward the marina. "Bet it has to do with a girl."

No use denying it. Best to change the subject. "Are you going to teach me how to man the boat?"

Bearett's eyebrows shot up. "If you want to learn."

"Why not?" If he was stuck with a babysitter for the day, he might as well learn something useful.

~

Claire stopped by the boat before Pilates class to check the mailbox. Two letters. One for Aiden and Brinley. One for her. She opened hers right there on the top deck. Best not to read it in front of Brinley, who waited in the passenger's seat of her car, in case it contained sensitive information. And heaven knew, she couldn't wait until after class.

> Claire,
>
> I found out what my mission is. I'm supposed to stop the Great St. Louis Fire. Not sure if the teens mentioned this, but their dad was a firefighter. I'll save the city of St. Louis in his honor. Thanks for the tip. I'll keep you updated.
>
> Oh, and can you figure out where on the boat the offending mattress was located?
>
> Marina

What? No! Didn't everyone know you can't knowingly change history. *Back to the Future* proved that. Of course, someone's life course would shift due to Marina completing her mission, but nothing that would alter the history books.

She needed to warn Marina. And Bearett.

But first, she had to get back in the car with Brinley as if nothing were amiss and teach a Pilates class.

Brinley's phone held her captive. If only Claire could shake her. Warn her about the effects of social media on today's youth. But she certainly hadn't earned the girl's trust yet. Brinley wouldn't give her advice a second thought. Maybe after they developed a relationship.

"Hey." Claire slid into the driver's seat and handed Brinley her envelope. "Letter for you."

"Thanks." Brinley didn't make a move to open it. Instead, she angled toward Claire. "I finally figured out where I know you from."

A sinkhole opened in Claire's stomach. Uh oh.

"You're that Pilates star. Claire-ity Fitness Channel." The girl grinned like she'd won the lottery. "You changed your hair color. That must have been what threw me off."

Busted. "That's me." She shrugged. "Or that *was* me. I don't have that channel anymore."

"Yeah, but your videos are still everywhere. You had a million followers. Fans aren't just going to forget about you."

Claire cringed. Surely, they would, given enough time. "Look, I stepped away from that lifestyle for a reason. It wasn't healthy for me. It came with a ton of pressure to keep upping my game."

"Yeah. Insta is like that too. I have an account for my dog, Frankie. I dress him up in crazy costumes and make reels like he's talking. I'm up to seven hundred thousand followers. People can't get enough."

No. Brinley couldn't be caught up in that madness at only sixteen years old. Claire's throat tightened. She was too young.

The social media game had no winners. It could destroy her life.

Brinley flashed her phone screen at Claire. Yep, there it was. FunnyFrankie with 702K followers.

Wait, FunnyFrankie? She'd followed that channel once upon a time. Before she'd banned all social media from her life.

How to approach this situation delicately? Claire nibbled her lip. "So, is it hard to keep up? I mean, is it a lot?"

Brinley sighed. "Yeah, for sure. But it's fun too, you know. I like doing it, and I'm making money with it. Though I like to shop, so it never stays in my account long. But at least I've never had to flip burgers. It's a great gig for me."

"I can see that." Such a level of success had to be tempting for someone so young. But she could see the dangers far more clearly than Brinley could. The sleepless nights. The demand for more, more, more. The greater the success, the heavier the demand. Pressure to be perfect … or to *appear* perfect on the outside. She'd nearly broken down under the weight.

"So, you teach Pilates at the YMCA now?" Brinley scrunched her nose as if she smelled skunk. Clearly, she wasn't nearly as impressed with Claire's current career.

"Yep. I love it." She pushed extra enthusiasm into her voice. "I get to see the people I impact. Actually interact with them instead of performing for a screen. It's life-giving." Even if her income had taken a huge hit. Even if it wouldn't be sustainable with a baby. A sinking feeling traveled through her like a Plinko chip.

"But right now, you only affect a handful of people when you used to reach a million." Brinley straightened and looked at Claire with wide eyes. "Why don't you video your classes? It would be the best of both worlds."

Huh. She'd never considered that. "You're pretty smart, you know it?" But the idea wouldn't safeguard her heart from the pressures of social media. If only there was a way to protect her mental and emotional health and increase her income. She couldn't stand the thought of Bearett losing his boat.

Brinley beamed.

Marina couldn't change the future. If only Claire could change hers.

Chapter Seven

The boat docked in Peoria, but Marina stood rooted in her stateroom, watching from her back door. Passengers disembarked, one after another, strolling into safer circumstances. She could get off too and avoid facing a fire and an epidemic. Toss the terrifying possibilities aside. The memories. The grief. She could avoid it all if only she'd step off this boat.

But she had to return to St. Louis if she was to get back to her teenagers. Aiden. Brinley. She couldn't abandon them. Her mission wasn't in Peoria.

The boat set off again the next morning with her, Dr. Duncan, George, and Christina on board. Marina had tossed and turned all night. Nightmares of flames licking her stateroom walls had frightened her awake. With those vivid images emblazoned in her mind, she could only force down a handful of berries for breakfast. She had just returned to her room and plopped on her bed, intent on a nap when screams reached her ears.

"Fire! Fire!"

She sprang into action, jetting to her purse and grabbing the mini–fire extinguisher she'd carried with her since Adam's death. A glance out her window showed they were still chugging down the river. Wasn't the fire supposed to happen when they were docked? Maybe Claire had the wrong information. Not everything on the internet proved accurate.

Tension coiled around her muscles as she rushed out her door toward the shouting. Christina nearly charged her. The lady who'd seemed so poised previously now grasped Marina's forearms with white knuckles. Several curls dangled loose from her chignon. She looked how Marina felt inside, but fear couldn't win today.

"Where's the fire?" Marina attempted to pry herself free from the frightened woman's grasp.

"In the ladies' cabin."

Really? There were no mattresses there. Marina sidestepped Christina and barreled toward the curtained-off area they'd met in yesterday, pushing past a few other hysterical women.

Smoke billowed both above and below the curtain. If she'd had time, she'd have wet a piece of clothing and tied it around her mouth and nose. Instead, she pulled the top of her T-shirt over her mouth. With her Prepared Hero Fire Spray primed at the ready, she pushed past the curtain barrier between her and the fire.

Hungry flames licked the couch. Burning wood and fabric popped and sizzled with the inferno, releasing an earthy, sickly-sweet smell. Smoke stung her eyes. She blinked rapidly to clear them. George stooped over the area, smacking flames with a blanket.

"Here!" she shouted above the crackling. Heat pressed into her, along with memories of Adam in his gear. As much as her feet begged her to flee, she had to press forward. She squeezed the nozzle, and white foam shot out. It wrestled with the blaze until the flare's screams died down to whimpers, then at last it was extinguished.

A charred circle stared back at her. Her chest heaved. She'd done it! She had stopped the Great St. Louis Fire. She sucked in a breath only for smoke to strangle her lungs. She bent over and coughed.

"Miss Stone, are you all right?" George peered at her.

She nodded but couldn't manage to push out words. He stared at her another moment until she managed a smile. Then he released a sigh and slouched against the fireplace, sliding to the floor.

Someone pulled back the curtain. A Black man in uniform waved a paper fan in the air. The steward, most likely.

"I daresay, what is that substance? I've never seen anything like it." George gestured toward the extinguisher in her hand.

So much for blending in. A glance down showed she wore a T-shirt and shorts. She'd been in too much of a hurry to even think about dressing for the era. Her cheeks heated. "It's a new invention."

"Fascinating. Where did you—"

"I need fresh air." She rushed from the room before he could finish his question. And before anyone could gasp at the scandal of her state of undress. As she ducked into her stateroom, she kicked an envelope across the floor. Another letter? How had she missed it?

Lungs still burning, she crossed to her room's back door that led to the promenade deck and cracked the door open. She wasn't ready to venture outside yet, but the warm breeze soothed her lungs from where she stood. Breathing deeply, she opened the letter.

> Marina,
>
> As a time sailor, you can't knowingly change the future. I mean, you can't do anything that would alter history books. Your true mission won't be as dramatic as rescuing an entire city. Please don't try to reshape the account of the fire that way. I'm not sure what will happen if you do. We've never encountered that situation. Bearett was told from a young age that time sailors were not to try. The results could be catastrophic.
>
> Take care,
> Claire

Marina scoffed. Too late. Besides, what did Claire know? Not much, apparently, since she couldn't even name a consequence. So, what if Marina had altered history books? She might not have any idea how that would work, but it didn't take a genius to understand that history would be better off without a fire destroying a city. She'd just saved twenty-something steamboats and hundreds of businesses. History would thank her.

She tossed the letter onto her bed. She should get dressed so she could enjoy time outside. Once in her burgundy *frock*, she stepped out her back door and stood at the railing. The murky river drifted by. A mosquito buzzed by her ear and landed on her hand. She smacked it off, then craned her neck from side to side. St. Louis wasn't anywhere in sight. Only miles of farmland. She waved her hand in front of her face, circulating muggy air.

How could Claire have gotten the story so wrong? It didn't make sense that putting out the fire in the ladies' cabin would save the city of St. Louis. Claire had said the fire spread from the *White Cloud* to other steamboats—only there were none close enough for that to be logical.

It didn't have to make sense to her. The important thing was that she'd done it, and now she could return home to her teens who needed her. They *did* need her, didn't they? Their letters overflowed with assurances that they were doing well without her. A twinge zinged through her chest. Why did children have to grow up? What a cruel job motherhood was. Raise a child to be independent, and if successful, they can leave you behind.

"Quite a bout of excitement, don't you say, Miss Stone?" George's voice invaded her pity party.

Her hand flew to her heart. "You startled me, Mr. Randolph."

"I apologize. 'Twasn't my intention." He dug his hands into his pockets and rocked back and forth on his heels.

"No worries." She studied the horizon again, searching for any sign of St. Louis. Water lapped the boat. Steam hissed from the boilers.

"You were quite heroic back there. The rest of the ladies fled from the fire, while you ran straight toward it."

Hadn't she said something similar to Adam once? Adam. Her brave, hero husband. Worthy of every honor. Worthy of far more respect than she'd given him. If only she could go back, tell him how much she appreciated and admired him. If only there was no such thing as *too late*. Her eyes stung again, this time not from smoke. "I did what I had to do." What she'd needed to do so she could return home. Heaven knew she would never have faced a fire otherwise. Only love for her teens propelled her.

"'When thou passest through the waters, I will be with thee; and through the rivers, they shall not overflow thee. When thou walkest through the fire, thou shalt not be burned, neither shall the flame kindle upon thee.'"

She lifted a brow. "A Bible verse?"

He smiled. "Isaiah 43:2."

See, that's why she couldn't trust God or His Bible. Adam walked through the fire, and he *did* get burned. So much for petty assurances.

"I'd like to offer you a complimentary Bible, Miss Stone. In honor of your bravery."

She started to shake her head, but the hope in his eyes halted her movement. The poor man hadn't been able to sell his Bibles. How would he feel if he wasn't even able to give one away?

"Thank you, Mr. Randolph. That's kind of you."

He grinned and handed over a pocket-sized book. She trailed her finger over the gilded lettering. *Holy Bible.* She slipped it into the pocket of her jean shorts under her dress. Sure, she'd hold on to this if it'd make George feel better. She wouldn't be in 1849 much longer anyway. Any minute now, she'd return home.

~

Claire and Bearett sat in navy Adirondack chairs on their back patio, watching the sunset. The teens remained inside, likely scrolling on their phones. That was all they ever did, it seemed. If only she could be a positive influence on them. Get them to ditch, or at least severely lessen, their time on social media. But she'd need to build a relationship with them first, and that had proved difficult thus far.

Bearett sipped his Coke, staring at the flames leaping up from their fire pit. The night was unusually cool for summer, but the heat made it cozy. He seemed to be in a better mood today. Less ho-hum. But still not his usual optimistic self. "I had a nice time with Aiden. He's a good kid. Opened up a little."

Claire angled toward him. "Yeah? Brinley did too. She recognized me from my channel."

"No way. Wouldn't think a teen would be into a Pilates channel."

She scrunched her nose. "I don't think she's interested in Pilates as much as influencers. She's got an Instagram account for her dog."

Bearett lifted an eyebrow. "That's a thing?"

Claire laughed. "Yes, apparently a big thing. I'd heard of her dog before."

"She's doing well, then?"

"Yeah. FunnyFrankie has close to a million followers." Claire grimaced. "I'm worried about Brinley. She's too young to get sucked into all of that."

"It's natural for you to feel that way, but maybe it's not the same." He shrugged. "Maybe she enjoys it. Might not be so pressure-filled for her."

She did seem to enjoy it, but no pressure? Doubtful.

He sighed low and long. "Did you know their dad died in a fire?"

She straightened in her chair. "Aiden and Brinley's dad?"

He nodded.

"No. I had no idea." They'd told her he passed away, and in the picture on Marina's phone, he'd been wearing a firefighter uniform, so perhaps she should have surmised.

"Ironic, isn't it? That Marina would time-sail to a fire when her husband died in one."

Claire covered her mouth. "That's horrible. Those poor kids."

"I know." A muscle in his cheek twitched.

"We definitely shouldn't tell them, then."

Bearett swiveled to face her, brow lifted. "About?"

"About how Marina is headed into one of the worst fires in St. Louis's history. I was going to mention it tonight, but that's too much for a kid to take in."

"You think? They're pretty mature for their age."

She shook her head. "I thought about telling them, then asking them to pray for Marina. But I have no idea if they even believe in God. And if they don't, the prospect of losing both of their parents to fire is too scary."

"Hmm." Bearett took another sip. "Maybe they'll figure it out on their own. They know she's on the *White Cloud*. It'd only take a simple Google search."

"Well, if Marina has her way, there won't be a devastating fire anyway."

"What?"

"She plans to stop it. Save the entire city."

Bearett groaned. "She can't change the history books."

"I know. I told her as much. Not sure if she believes me." She chewed her thumbnail. "What happens if she *does* change the history books?"

"I don't know. I was only told to warn time sailors not to try."

"You don't think she'll die, do you? Never return? I mean, how bad could the consequences be?" She shuddered.

"I hope I never find out."

~

Aiden let the sheer white curtain on the back window drop back into place. Icy tendrils crept up his back as the words "losing both of their parents to fire" continued to squeeze his heart. His day at the helm next to Bearett had turned out pretty sweet. Aiden thought the owner of the *Duncan's Delight* was a decent guy. Even if he chose a ridiculous name for his boat. Not as cool as Dad, but good. And then the guy betrays him? Not cool.

Brinley stomped away, face pinched. "What right do they have to keep information about our mom from us?"

His question exactly. Who did they think they were? Sworn protectors of the Stones? He joined Brinley in pacing. He'd heard enough.

Brinley's face flushed. "We should just leave. Find somewhere else to stay. We can't trust these guys."

"But then we'd lose our only connection to Mom. How would we know what was going on?"

"They don't tell us anything anyway."

"But the letters …"

"We can sneak onto the boat and check the mailbox ourselves."

Not a bad plan. They'd likely find out more that way. But where would they stay? Would Nevaeh's family take them in? He didn't have enough money for a hotel. Besides, Bearett was the one who knew about time-sailing. He was the only one who could answer their questions.

The back door creaked open, and Brinley pounced. "You shouldn't tell us that our mom is in danger, huh?"

Both Claire and Bearett blanched.

"What did you hear?" Claire pressed her lips together.

"Enough," Brinley said.

At the same time, Aiden said, "Not enough."

They stared at each other. What?

Brinley huffed. "We heard enough to know you're keeping things from us. And that Mom might die in a fire."

Bearett shook his head. "Your mom won't die in the fire."

Brinley propped her hands on her hips. "How do you know?"

Open hostility wouldn't get them any answers. Best to tone it down. Aiden tried to signal his sister with his eyes, but she wasn't looking at him.

"But can you die when time-sailing?" he asked.

Claire and Bearett exchanged glances. What were they communicating?

Claire took a tentative step forward. "It's unlikely."

Aiden crossed his arms. "But not impossible?"

Bearett sighed. "There have been a few time sailors over hundreds of years who never returned. We're not sure what happened. It's not like we can ask them. Did they die? Or did they just never accomplish their mission? We'll never know."

"So, Mom *could* die in a fire."

Bearett tilted his head back and forth. "Possibly."

Claire shot her husband a glare. "But not likely."

Brinley threw her hands in the air. "Look, I get that you don't want to scare us, but we're not little kids. We can handle the truth. We need to know."

Claire's shoulders sagged. "The truth is, we don't know much for certain. Your mom *might* be in St. Louis during the Great Fire of 1849. Or she might not. Very few lives were lost in that fire. It mostly devastated property and buildings. So, even if she's there when it happens, she'll probably be fine."

"I can't imagine Mom facing a fire." Aiden shuddered.

Brinley snorted and mumbled, "I can't imagine Mom *facing* anything."

When Claire's forehead wrinkled, Aiden filled in the blanks. "Mom's more of an active avoider with most things." Like grief.

"We're not allowed to talk about our dad," Brinley said, then mimicked Mom's voice. "'Time to move on. Put the past behind us. It's a new day.'"

"Oh." Claire frowned. "She must have loved him very much."

Yeah, she did. So why, then, did she want to erase him from their lives? From their memories? They hadn't just lost their father once. They'd lost him a hundred times. Each time Mom said, "Leave your father out of this," it was another loss.

As if reading Aiden's mind, Bearett said,

"Everyone deals with grief in their own way."

He could scream. Wasn't that the point? Mom didn't *deal* with her grief at all. She ignored it.

Claire and Bearett both tossed them a look of pity. Those downturned mouths and slightly pouty lips made him nauseous. "You're not our parents, and we're not your charity project." Aiden crossed to the guest bedroom and slammed the door behind him.

Chapter Eight

Marina groaned and turned on her bed. Why wasn't she back in South Haven? And why did she feel like someone had raked her insides? If this was an effect of the "traveling sickness," she wanted to beat Dr. Duncan over the head with a broom for not warning her.

She rolled out of bed and crawled to her back door. She'd never make it to the women's bathhouse in time. Better she expel the contents of her stomach overboard than in her stateroom.

As soon as she opened the door, muggy air slapped her face. She barely made it to the railing before she could hold it in no longer.

A woman jumped up from a nearby rocking chair. "Oh dear, not another one." She covered her face and mouth with a floral-patterned scarf. "Cholera!" she shouted. "Fetch Dr. Duncan."

Cholera? No, she couldn't have cholera. She'd been fine hours before. Now she felt like death.

Murmurings came from farther down the promenade deck. "She's as pale as a sheet."

"That makes seven on this very boat."

"Best sequester in our cabin. She's filling the deck with her contagion."

Marina laid her forehead on the railing. She should have written to Claire and asked about cholera. Right now, she hadn't the strength to pick up a pencil.

Everyone fled from her like she carried the plague. Quiet blanketed the deck. Perhaps she did have cholera. Her mouth and throat might as well have been covered in sand. She needed a drink. The cooler still had Gatorade, right? She'd only consumed one bottle of the twelve pack, so there should be plenty left. She slunk back to her room, gulped some down, and then … Oh, great. She needed to get to the bathhouse. Quickly.

Her legs quaked as she stood. In five wobbly steps, her hand clasped the doorknob. Suddenly, a bell clanged. Then the boat lunged to the right. She stumbled into the wall and crashed to the floor. Darkness crowded her vision. With no strength left to fight, she succumbed to it.

~

When Marina opened her eyes, the sun burst through her window. She squinted toward it. Why did it seem to be higher on the horizon, not lower? Surely, she hadn't slept until the next morning. She fingered the blanket covering her. How had she gotten into her bed?

A knock banged on her door. "Come in," she croaked.

Alanda stood at the threshold, twisting the end of her apron, eyes downcast. "Miss? You must disembark now."

Disembark? Were they kicking her off because she was sick? She forced a swallow down her parched throat. "Why?"

The maid studied the floor. "We're in St. Louis, miss. This boat is scheduled to undergo repairs before embarking again. All passengers must exit."

"How are we in St. Louis already? What day is it?" The return trip couldn't be that much faster than the trip to Peoria. She sat up and swung her legs over the side of the bed. The room tilted. Her head swam, and she dropped it into her hands.

"Are you not feeling well?" Alanda asked.

"Not well at all."

"Oh, dear. Dr. Duncan has already left the ship. You're the last passenger here. Shall I ask the captain to call a doctor for you?"

Marina shook her head. "No need." She was here to save 1849, not languish in a primitive hospital. She could summon her strength and make it off the boat on her own.

"Let me help you pack." Alanda emptied the dresser of Marina's clothes and stacked them, along with her other belongings, on the table next to her bed.

"You can put them in the suitcase."

Alanda cocked her head to the side as though confused.

Marina nodded to her rolling Samsonite.

The maid examined the suitcase like it were a spaceship. "How does it open?"

"The zipper." Had those not been invented yet? She leaned over to demonstrate.

"Mighty fine." Alanda played with the zipper a bit before fully opening the case and tucking the items inside. A smile spread across her face as she zipped it up and set it upright.

If Marina had felt better, she would have found it amusing. For now, she needed to focus all her energy on not keeling over.

"Would you like me to carry this for you?" Alanda's ebony fingers trailed the suitcase as if reluctant to part with it.

"It rolls. I can push it." Marina stood, extended the handle, and braced herself on its steadiness. "Actually, if you hand me the cooler, I can set the suitcase on top of it and my purse on top of them both."

The maid pointed to the cooler and lifted an eyebrow. "This?"

"Yes. It rolls too." She'd forgotten that coolers were also nonexistent in this time. "And my purse." She nodded to where her ginormous handbag lay on the plush, velvet chair. As Alanda handed them over, she stacked them. Now, she just needed to balance them as she rolled forward. "Lead the way."

With slow, staggering steps, Marina followed her out the door and through the empty saloon, past the bar and barber shop, and out into the fresh air. She halted at the view of the St. Louis riverfront.

She'd visited downtown St. Louis many times, but never could she have imagined the sight before her. Dozens of steamboats bobbed at the wharf, banners proclaiming unique names. On the boat next to them, a handful of men unloaded crates and barrels and sacks, hefting them on their shoulders. Sweat glistened on their foreheads and slid down their backs. Massive piles of wood stacked half as high as a building stood near the levee, some covered with tarps. Buildings that must be warehouses sat with yawning mouths ready for their next meal. It looked like some kind of humongous open-air market. A hive filled with buzzing bees.

What had to be hundreds of horse-drawn buggies and mule-drawn wagons thronged the streets, as did men with pushcarts and women with parasols. Dust coughed up from the street under wheels and shoes. Brick and wood buildings stood next to what looked to be older, colonial structures. A steeple towered proudly above the skyline of the city. The old cathedral? The chattering of different languages reached her ears. German? French? Irish? Poorly dressed, barefoot children ducked and dodged between the crowd. Bells clanged. From churches?

If her hands had been free, she would have covered her ears to shield them from the tumultuous noise. Or perhaps she'd choose to cover her nose from the accosting scent of manure. Without the Arch, this looked nothing like her home city.

She was here, not back in South Haven, which must mean she hadn't accomplished her mission. Might this beautiful city still be in peril of burning? And if so, how could she save it when she could barely muster the strength to walk? Right now, what seemed to be in the most danger was *her* life.

~

Claire had really screwed up this time. The teens had sequestered themselves in their room for three straight hours. They hadn't even come out for a snack. What had she been thinking, keeping information from them? Hadn't she been furious when Wendy had done the same thing to her? It was their mom. They deserved to know everything she knew.

"Stop beating yourself up." Bearett sat beside her on the couch and picked up the remote to turn the volume down on the television. The nightly news now played mutely in the background. She hadn't been paying attention to it anyway.

"I should have known better." She rubbed her temples.

Bearett shrugged. "It was an innocent mistake. One you made because you were trying to look out for them. It's not the end of the world."

"But they were just starting to open up to us. Now they hate our guts."

"They'll get over it."

She rubbed her hands on her leggings. "I have to make it up to them."

He placed his hand over hers, stilling her movement. "No, you don't. You can apologize, but I'm telling you, Claire, you don't have to wallow in guilt over a *mistake*. When we become parents, we're bound to mess up a ton."

The hair at the back of her neck stood up. He knew. He had to know. Why else would he reference becoming parents?

"You look like you're going to be sick again. Are you sure you're over whatever that was?" He placed the back of his hand on her forehead.

He didn't know. She released a shaky breath. Or was he baiting her? Trying to get her to tell him? Time to change the subject.

She shook his hand off. "Do you think I should write Marina and tell her we're having trouble with the teens? She might have some advice as to how best to handle them."

Bearett shook his head. "We're not having trouble, honey. They're teenagers. This is par for the course. They're fine. We're fine. And Marina needs to focus completely on her mission. No distractions."

"Yeah, but ..." How could Bearett not feel like he'd been tossed in deep ocean waters without a raft or life preserver? She was floundering. How was she supposed to take care of teenagers or any children, for that matter? She could master nutrition and exercise, but parenting hovered way over her head. She stood so abruptly that Bearett rocked back with the couch cushion's shift. "I'm going to go for a run."

His forehead dimpled with his frown, but he simply said, "Okay."

She slid on her tennis shoes, then jogged out the door. Darkness blanketed their street, interrupted by shimmering streetlights. Party music emanated from the next block, and the television blared through her next-door neighbor's open window. Still, the atmosphere proved far more peaceful than the tug-of-war she felt in Bearett's presence.

Her feet found a steady rhythm as she crossed into downtown. Her lungs were burning with blissful exertion while she wove around scatterings of people on the sidewalk. How long would she be able to run like this? Her belly would grow. And grow and grow. She could still do Pilates throughout her pregnancy, but probably not high-impact aerobics. And afterward? Would she purchase a jogging stroller and run with the baby to get back into shape?

She slowed at a corner and braced her hands on her knees, catching her breath. Her life was about to drastically change. She wasn't ready.

Oh, God. Is it true You won't give us more than we can handle? Because it sure feels like You have. I don't think I can do this.

What was she praying? It wasn't like she wanted to lose this baby. She only wanted to live in a world where birth control worked one hundred percent of the time. One where she felt fully equipped for every challenge placed before her. One where, before she conceived, she had the confidence that she had what it took to be a mom. More maturity. More examples of what good parenting looked like. Something *more*. Her lack loomed before her.

If she could successfully take care of Aiden and Brinley, it would prove she could be a good mother. They were only a few days in, and she'd already failed miserably. Her poor baby was probably destined to spend years in therapy.

She had to fix this. Jaw clenched, she sprinted forward again, faster and faster. Racing past the *Duncan's Delight* bobbing in the moonlight. Pushing herself toward the beach until her lungs screamed and her side burned. Maybe Bearett was right. Her relationship with the teens wasn't beyond repair. She'd won Brinley over once. She could do it again. She just needed to befriend the girl. Surely, Aiden would follow suit.

Her feet sunk into the soft sand, steps slowing as she approached the moonlit water of Lake Michigan. She stretched her arms behind her head. Graceful waves lapped in rhythm with her heartbeat. The lighthouse beaconed. Solid. Sure. Hopeful.

She was not a failure. Not yet.

~

The morning sun sliced through the bedroom window, taunting Aiden. He stopped pacing for a minute and ran a hand through his hair, pulling at the ends. He had to get out of this house before he went insane. Enough with babysitters. He was nearly eighteen, a legal adult. He didn't have to stay here, enduring more judgment, pity, and control.

"Let's head to the beach."

From where she lay on the bed, Brinley set her phone down and looked at him. "You want to sneak through the window or ask our wardens?"

With their luck, if they snuck out, Claire and Bearett would call the cops, and they'd end up back in jail. "No need to go through the window. We don't need to *ask* them to go to the beach. We'll just *tell* them that's where we're going. They're not the boss of us."

Brinley sat up. "You're right. They're not our parents, and they can't keep us here against our will." She threw items into a canvas bag. "Got any sunscreen?"

He sniffed a T-shirt to make sure it was clean. Good enough. He pulled it over his head. "No, Mom has it." Mom always had everything they could possibly need.

"Guess we'll have to pick some up from the corner store."

They took turns getting dressed in the en suite bathroom. Brinley emerged with a tank top and jean shorts over her swimsuit. Aiden wore teal trunks that matched his shirt. He slung a towel over his shoulder. "Ready?"

"Let's go."

They marched out of their room. Bearett was nowhere in sight, but Claire looked up from a bowl of yogurt. "Oh, hi, guys." Her voice squeaked. "Hungry for breakfast?"

"Nah," he lied. They'd pick something up. Wouldn't want to live on the Duncans' charity. "We're headed to the beach. Catch you later."

Claire stood. "O-okay." She stepped forward, as though she would come try to talk them out of it but stopped. "Have fun."

As soon as they were out the door, Aiden smirked. "That was easier than I thought." Claire probably felt bad for yesterday. He could capitalize on that. "I forgot I have Nevaeh's number. Let me text her and ask her to meet us."

> This is Aiden. We're headed to South Beach. Meet us there?

His palm tingled, waiting for her reply.

> See you in thirty.

Why did her text send a thrill through him? He wasn't into her. He'd been holding out for Stacy to realize what she was missing.

Brinley scoffed. "You're grinning like an idiot. I assume that means she's coming."

"She's coming." He tried to rein in his smile.

"Good. You two look good together."

He rolled his eyes. "We're not together."

"Yet," she teased.

They grabbed muffins from a coffee shop on the way. Even though they'd probably still beat her there, when they set foot on the soft sand, Aiden scoured the area for Nevaeh. Instead, his gaze landed on Jack, lounging in a beach chair. He hooked his arm through Brinley's and steered her to the other side of the beach, away from the creep.

"Where are we going? It's more crowded over here."

Ignoring her question, he spread his towel on the sand. Brinley followed suit, eyeing him with suspicion.

"It's a great spot." He sat, arms resting on his knees.

"Shoot. We forgot to grab sunblock."

"I'm sure Nevaeh will let us borrow some of her sunscreen." Squinting against the sun's glare, his gaze searched the beach for her again. Mom probably carried his sunglasses in her huge purse too.

"Look who it is." Jack stepped in front of a beam of sun, giving their eyes a temporary reprieve.

"Jack." Brinley sounded breathless. Oh brother.

He wasn't about to chat with the guy who'd landed them in jail. "Get lost, will you?"

Jack threw his hands up. "Hey, man, I understand why you're upset, but it was all a misunderstanding."

Aiden stood. He couldn't stomach this weasel looming over him. They were about equal in height, though Jack was more muscular. "You're joking, right? We're supposed to forget about spending the night in a cell because you say it was a misunderstanding?"

Brinley stood and put a hand on Aiden's shoulder. "Let him explain."

"Look"—Jack locked eyes with Brinley—"I borrowed the bike from a friend. I had no clue his dad would report it as stolen. It was just a miscommunication."

Brinley tilted her head to the side. "I guess that makes sense."

Had she lost her mind? Apparently, from the way she twirled her hair around her finger.

"I'm sorry you got mixed up in that." Jack looked far too polished. Did he superglue his hair in place? Because it wasn't budging in the wind.

This guy was fake, and they needed to steer clear of him. Aiden crossed his arms, flexing his barely-there biceps. "Fine. Whatever. You can go on your way now."

"Actually." He flashed a slimy smile. "I was hoping to make it up to you. Why don't we gather some people for a volleyball game, and then I'll take you out for ice cream." His gaze clung to Brinley's as if pulled by a magnet. Apparently, this offer was for his sister alone.

"Not interested."

"Sure."

Aiden and Brinley spoke at the same time. He glared at his sister, but she didn't seem to notice. She was going to ditch him for some smooth-talking thief? Not cool.

Brinley batted her lashes and toed the sand. "Do you have any sunblock? We forgot ours."

"Yeah." His cheesy grin widened even more. "Come over to my spot, and I'll get your back."

He started in the direction of his beach chair, and she followed blindly. Did she forget Aiden was there? He was wrong. Apparently, Brinley *did* need a babysitter, but it wouldn't be him. He wasn't about to waste a perfectly good beach day watching those two make heart eyes with each other. He'd keep her in his range of sight, though, in case creepy Jack tried something.

"Hi, Aiden."

He turned to find Nevaeh looking even more gorgeous than he remembered with her pink one-piece and jean shorts and her hair pulled back into a long braid. Tanned skin. Rosy cheeks. Perfect heart-shaped face. He couldn't help but grin.

"Mind if I settle next to you?" She tilted her head toward her black-and-white-striped beach bag.

"Not at all."

Jack who?

Chapter Nine

Marina stumbled past a herd of pigs that were scavenging through the contents of a busted sack of wheat on Front Street. Newsboys shouted from all directions, drab hats partially shielding their dirty faces. Every step she took kicked up a cloud of dust. There must be at least an inch of dirt on the street. More bells, nearly continuous. Did they ever stop?

If she hadn't needed both hands on her suitcase to keep balanced, she'd have covered her nose. Heaps of manure sat in the middle of the streets, reeking of ammonia. The alleyway to her left was piled high with rotting garbage. Then she passed a slaughterhouse and couldn't keep from getting sick right there in the dingy street. Noxious fumes emanated from the building. The odor of hot fat mixed with feces and death.

Some people claimed the modern-day city was dirty. They hadn't a clue what unsanitary truly looked like. It was a wonder that every single person wasn't dying from cholera. Was she? Her body shook with chills despite the warm temperatures.

The farther she got from the levee, the thinner the crowd until she barely passed a soul. Where should she go? She stumbled past houses and businesses. A dry goods store. A barber shop. A flour mill. A hotel stood directly across the street, but she had no money for a room. Not unless they'd take her modern-day currency. Doubtful. Would a hospital take her in without payment? No telling. At least the farther she staggered, the less the sights and smells turned her stomach. Bells rang again, the sound emanating from two different directions. Did they signal a church service? Where in heaven's name was Dr. Duncan? The nerve of that man to abandon her like this.

Her legs wobbled like melting wax as her surroundings spun. She couldn't go much farther. Perhaps she *was* dying. Adam. She could finally be with Adam again. Not the worst thing in the world. Her knees buckled, and she plummeted face-first into the dust.

Darkness pulled at her. She could barely turn her head and catch shallow breaths. No strength to stand. Not even to sit. Her body lacked the will to move. Sleep dragged her down, down, down into black nothingness.

No telling how much later, the clomp of slowing horse hooves and squeak of rolling wheels nudged her into consciousness. She barely managed to open her eyes as black boots approached. A sigh.

"Another one," a man with an Irish accent said. He sounded nearly as tired as she felt. He lifted her as though she were a rag doll.

Her dry mouth tasted as though someone had stuffed it with cotton. She tried to tell the man to stop, but only a groan came out.

The man gave a small cry, then plunked her to her feet. She swayed and would have collapsed had he not caught her around her waist.

"Ma'am? You're alive?"

"I think so." Her words slurred.

"Jiminy! I nearly put you in the funeral wagon. My apologies."

Her blurry gaze slid over to the wagon filled with dead bodies. She dry-heaved and slid back to the ground.

"Need help to the hospital, miss?" His Irish accent curled around his words.

She shook her head. No way would she ride in that wagon with him and the dead. "Just point the way." She'd summon the strength to walk there.

"The common schools have been turned into hospitals. There's one two blocks thataway." He pointed.

Two blocks. Could she make it two blocks? She'd have to. "Thanks," she mumbled, her eyes growing heavy again.

"I'll have someone there come check on you." He hopped into his buggy and snapped the reins.

She licked her dry, cracked lips as he rode away. What was cholera anyway? She'd never known a sickness that could turn someone from normally functioning to a pile of goo so quickly.

With a start, it occurred to her that she still had Gatorade. Her sandpaper throat testified to her dehydration. Surely, electrolytes would help. She crawled the few feet to where her belongings were strewn and pried open the cooler. It took all her strength to twist off the bottle's lid, but when she did so, refreshing liquid rewarded her. She gulped it down greedily, then grabbed another.

She couldn't give up. Couldn't allow herself to die in 1849. She may no longer be a wife, but she was a mother, and her children needed her.

~

Even as Claire led her class at the Y in the shoulder bridge, her thoughts spun like a dog chasing its tail. Should she have let the teens leave like that? Surely, they were old enough to enjoy a day at the beach unchaperoned. But maybe she should have given them a curfew. Or at least told them to check in with her a few times during the day. Had her parents given her that much freedom at sixteen? Not that it mattered. That relationship wasn't one she'd ever choose to emulate.

"And now, let's roll up." She had plenty of experience with keeping her voice perky even as thunder clouds loomed in her mind. "And down. We're going to do six reps of this one."

What would it be like to try and do this exercise with a big belly in the way? It still didn't seem real. There was a life growing inside her, doing its own little stretching routine, but she couldn't feel it. Though her pants fit tighter than they used to, the naked eye couldn't discern the difference. If not for nausea and fatigue, she could almost forget she was pregnant.

As she led her class of mostly women over fifty in their closing stretches, she forced a smile. Lolla and Dottie grinned back. Those two were always profusely grateful for each class. How would they feel when her pregnancy forced her to quit?

"And that's it for today. Great job, ladies." She stood and swigged water.

Dottie came up to her and clasped her hand. Purple veins showed through the older woman's papery skin. "Thank you, dear. I haven't felt this good in ages. I know it's because of this class."

"You're welcome." Now Claire's smile proved genuine. "I'm so happy to hear that."

See? She *was* making a difference, even in this smaller version of her life. She might not reach the masses, but the ones she did impact found her service invaluable.

She turned and startled. Bearett stood in the doorway. What was he doing at the YMCA?

He swaggered toward her. "Hey, beautiful."

Her cheeks heated. "Hi, handsome. What brings you here?"

"I thought I'd take my lovely wife on a lunch date. You game?" His eyes held a mischievous twinkle.

She didn't currently feel sick, but her stomach was as precarious as a tightrope walker. One aversive smell or taste could throw it off-balance. Still, she couldn't exactly turn him down. Such romantic gestures deserved cooperation. "Sure." She nearly asked if there was a special occasion but stopped herself. If he had news to share, he'd share it in his own time. If not, such a question could put a damper on his joyful mood.

"Clementine's?"

They couldn't afford to eat there often, but they did whenever they could. The chandeliers with frosted glass globes and the golden patterned ceiling added to the elegant ambiance, while the brick walls declared everyone welcome.

Some wore swimsuits with cover-ups. Others dressed up. She never felt out of place.

But she held back a gag at the remembrance of the fried onion smell. "Sounds good." She pulled on a T-shirt over her sports bra and threaded her fingers through Bearett's. They took his car, wrangled a coveted parking spot, then strolled hand in hand inside the restaurant.

Once seated at a booth, Bearett said, "You're good at what you do, you know."

She glanced at the menu while breathing through her mouth to avoid the wafting scents. What could she stomach? Something bland. A salad without any dressing?

Under the table, Bearett nudged her foot with his. "You know it?"

Oh. "You're good at what you do too."

He lifted a brow. "Why're you so distracted with the menu. You always get the salmon."

Just the thought made her stomach lurch. "I want to try something different today."

"You go right ahead. I'll stick with my usual."

A burger topped with onion rings. Great, that atrocious onion smell would dance right before her nose.

"I'm going with the farmer's market salad."

"Good." He slid her menu from in front of her and placed it to the side. "Now that you've settled that, will you listen to me?"

"Of course. I'm sorry." She held up a finger. "Actually, I need to run to the restroom first."

Another fun sign of pregnancy. She rushed off, ignoring Bearett's curious expression. The sign in the stall said *Please do not flush paper towels, baby wipes, sanitary products, goldfish, or hopes & dreams.* She chuckled, but her chest squeezed. Bearett had hopes and dreams. She couldn't flush them. Needed to be supportive. Had to help him get his own boat. Return to annual mission trips. She couldn't be the one to douse his enthusiastic spark.

She returned to their booth with new determination. "Sorry about that."

"It's fine. I only want to tell you about this idea I have."

"Go ahead."

"Remember how the Pilates class you led on the cruise boat was such a success?"

"Yeah." It'd been her last big hurrah before phasing out her channel. Unforgettable.

"What if you taught classes on the *Duncan's Delight*? We wouldn't even need to take her out and use fuel. It could remain docked, and people could come on board for exercise classes. We could keep the entire amount we charge, no giving a cut to a gym."

She leaned forward, excitement building. "The locals wouldn't have to drive to Grand Haven. They could have classes right here."

"In nice weather, you can use the open-air top deck. When it rains, or even throughout the winter, you could use the bottom deck."

"It'd be great exposure. People seeing the class on their way to the beach might want to get in on the action."

His ever-widening grin seemed full of promise. "And if it didn't catch on, we wouldn't lose anything. What do you say?"

"I love the idea." She beamed back at him. "I'm not sure how it will work once the baby comes, but at least for now, it seems like the perfect solution."

Bearett's brow wrinkled, and his smile vanished. "When the baby comes?"

Oops. That had slipped out. Her smile wobbled. "Surprise."

"We're … Are you telling me we're having a baby?" He sat back, looking gut-punched.

"Yes."

"That's why you—" He ran a hand through his hair. "I can't believe I didn't catch on. When were you going to tell me?" His wide eyes filled with hurt.

"Soon." She rubbed her sweaty hands on her leggings. "I just needed to come to terms with it first."

"But why? How come you kept this from me? We're a team, Claire. It's my baby too." His face smoothed as awe overtook his features. "I'm going to be a father."

She fiddled with her straw.

"Didn't you know I'd be thrilled?"

She bit her lip, eyes welling with tears. "No, I didn't know. We'd agreed not to start a family yet. And finances are so tight. How will we afford a baby?"

"Honey." He stretched out his hand to take hers. "We'll figure it out. Sure, this wasn't our plan, but it seems that God overrode our puny agenda. How could I not be happy?"

Tears slipped out and tracked down her cheeks. She swiped them away with her free hand. "But Bearett, *I'm* not happy. I don't want a baby, not now. I haven't a clue how to be a mother. What if I—" She sniffed. "What if I botch this all up? What if I don't have what it takes?"

"Oh, honey, you'll be an excellent mother. I know it."

But his assurances failed to douse the fire of panic raging inside her.

~

Aiden strolled beside Nevaeh as they dipped in and out of local stores. When she dared him to purchase a hot-pink touristy South Haven T-shirt, he bought two. One for each of them. Maybe not the wisest financial move, but the way her face lit up at the gift made it more than worth it.

"Hungry for ice cream?" He pointed to a Pepto-Bismol-pink ice cream shack ahead.

"Is that really a question?" She grinned. "There's always room for ice cream."

He nearly said *That's my girl* but stopped himself just in time. Nevaeh wasn't his girl. Not even close. So, why did this feel like a date? And why did his fingers itch to weave themselves with hers? Ridiculous.

They sat across from each other at an outside table and raced to finish their ice cream before the heat turned their treats into puddles. A trail of vanilla trickled to her chin.

"You've got a little something right there." He pointed to his own face.

Her laugh danced in the breeze. "We should have grabbed more napkins."

"No need." He brushed it away with his thumb.

Her breath caught. Electricity buzzed between them. He lowered his gaze. What'd he do that for? Pretty forward of him. And now he had the strange feeling he was cheating on Stacy.

Ludicrous. Stacy had broken up with him. He was more than free to move on. But did he want to?

What had been easy conversation between them stilted. Nevaeh blushed and averted her eyes. *Great job, Romeo.* Way to make things awkward. He scrambled for something to say, some way to sway them back to comfortable waters.

She spoke first. "So"—she tucked a strand of hair behind her ear and tentatively lifted her gaze—"tell me more about you. Are you involved in any sports? Do you go to church or a youth group?"

He took a big bite of his Death by Chocolate parfait to delay his answer. How important were athletics to her? Would the true answer to both questions disappoint? He might be friend-zoned. Hard. But it was no use pretending. She'd find out eventually. Better now than before this spark of attraction grew into a full-blown flame.

"I'm not into sports. I have a lethal combo of asthma and incoordination." He winced. "Basically, I suck at anything athletic. In gym class, I spiked a volleyball onto my foot."

Nevaeh burst into laughter, and somehow, in the process, got a dab of ice cream on her nose. He sat on his hand to keep from touching her face again. She wiped it off with her forearm. "At least you have a good sense of humor about it."

Did he? He hadn't intended to be funny, but he'd tell a hundred lame jokes if it meant he'd make her laugh again.

"Okay, then." She licked the side of her cone where some ice cream had gone rogue. "What about the other question?"

"Church?" He polished off his parfait. "Nah. My family has never been into religion."

"Oh." Her smile disappeared.

"Don't get me wrong. I believe in God. And I try my best to be a good person."

Her nod lacked enthusiasm. "I see."

His stomach sank. It'd been the wrong thing to say. With one confession, he'd ruined things between them. Might as well end this not-date and put her out of her misery. He gathered up two soggy napkins and dunked them in the trash. He wiped his sticky fingers on his trunks.

Nevaeh licked her fingers and stood. "Thanks for the ice cream."

"You're welcome. Ready to head back to the beach?" He should probably check on Brinley and creepy Jack. He took a step in that direction but stopped when Nevaeh didn't budge.

"Look." She blew out a breath that fanned her hair away from her face. "My faith is very important to me. I don't want to … I can't … get involved with anyone who doesn't feel the same way."

Had she wanted to get involved with him? Heat crept up his neck. "I understand." Not really, but it sounded like the right thing to say. They started to walk back in companionable silence. He'd never met anyone who cared much for religion. Curiosity pulled at him. "Tell me what faith means to you."

The way her eyes lit up proved his question pleased her. "It means Jesus is my best friend. I talk to Him all the time. I know He's always with me. And I want to follow Him because I know He'll never lead me wrong."

He stared at her, dumbstruck.

She chuckled. "What?"

"I've just never heard anyone talk like that."

She shrugged. "Get used to it if you want to hang around me."

Did he ever.

They passed a pet store he hadn't noticed on their way to the ice cream shop. Several dog costumes hung in the window display. Frankie. For the first time during their trip, he missed his sister's celebrity dog. "Mind if we stop in?"

"Sure."

He headed straight toward the costumes. "My sister has an Instagram account for our dog. *Her* dog, really. FunnyFrankie. Ever heard of it?"

Nevaeh shook her head. "I'm not on Insta much."

"She dresses him up in all kinds of costumes and makes these hilarious videos. She's got a huge following."

Nevaeh tilted her head and offered a sweet smile. "So, you and your sister actually get along? I thought siblings that close in age were supposed to hate each other."

"Nah. Brinley's cool." He flipped through a dozen options. A shark. A lion. A UPS driver. A … fireman. He held that one up. "I'm getting this. I don't care what Mom says." It'd be a perfect way to honor his dad.

Her forehead crinkled. "Why would your mom have a problem with a costume?"

Oh, yeah. She didn't know. He was used to everyone knowing what had happened. When the papers touted your father as a hero, it wasn't like you could keep your situation under the radar. "My dad was a firefighter. Died on duty."

Nevaeh's hand flew to her heart. "Oh gosh. I'm so sorry."

He nodded. "Yeah, it sucks. It's been almost two years, but we're still not really over it. Even if Mom thinks we should be."

"Why …" Her mouth twisted, as if she were trying to figure out how to ask her question.

"Mom wants to push through. Move on. Pretend like nothing ever happened. She took down all his pictures. Won't even mention him. The only time she allows us to talk about him is on the anniversary of his death when we put flowers on his grave.”

She frowned. “Everyone grieves in their own way, I guess.”

He scoffed. “No, Mom doesn’t grieve at all. That’s the problem. Why can’t she just admit that it bites and we’re all sad?”

He took the costume to the register and paid. On their way out, Nevaeh put a hand on his arm. “Your mom is hurting too. She just might be afraid to show it.”

He shrugged a shoulder. “Yeah, maybe.”

When she removed her hand, his skin screamed for its return. He sucked in a breath. “Could I …” His face heated. “Would it be okay if I held your hand? Or would that be … too involved?”

Her cheeks looked like two red apples. “I think that’d be okay. As long as you promise not to go stealing my heart.”

His free hand found hers. He wove their fingers together. He’d promise no such thing.

Chapter Ten

Marina felt life entering her body with each sip of Gatorade. She remained sitting on the street corner in front of a few houses and a blacksmith, slowly working through one bottle of precious electrolytes after another. Thank goodness she'd brought her large cooler on vacation.

A fire station stood across the street with its brass bell perched on top. Ironic. Was God mocking her? Or reminding her of her mission? No movement in or around Missouri No. 5. Alanda had never answered her about the date. When would the Great Fire take place?

Every so often, someone would pass by, but for the most part, the streets remained eerily empty. What would she do after she regained her strength? Where could she go?

She'd have to take things one step at a time. Maybe her next step would be to keep some food down. She opened her cooler and pulled out an apple, pear, and some cherry tomatoes. Her stomach flopped just looking at them. Didn't she have crackers in her purse?

When she checked, her hand grazed an envelope. Another letter from Claire or the teens? Her pulse ratcheted up a notch. Maybe they'd be able to continue to communicate with her even without the steamboat and mailbox. But as she pulled out the letter, hope leaked from her at the unfamiliar handwriting. Strange coins tumbled onto her lap.

She opened the letter and read.

Miss Stone,

Enclosed is some money to finance your stay in St. Louis. I'll meet you at the pier three days hence, first class ticket to the *White Cloud* in hand. Once you step back on the boat, no one will remember you from your previous trip. Time resets.

I apologize for not giving you this in person. You snagged forward in time, and we missed each other. If you need me for anything, simply dream-summon me.

Sincerely,
Dr. Duncan

Snagging forward in time? Dream-summoning? What was he talking about? Her head ached from attempting to comprehend his cryptic language.

Wait. What was today's date? She checked the letter. May 17. If he'd written it this morning … Her stomach sank. The date of the fire. She wouldn't meet Dr. Duncan in front of the *White Cloud* in three days if she didn't manage to stop it. She *had* to get better. No other option. At least he'd given her much-needed money. For that, she was grateful. She examined the change. A handful of coins with *one dollar* engraved on them. Interesting. She deposited them into her purse.

A scraping noise stole Marina's attention. A woman in raggedy clothing with an eye patch approached, leaning heavily on a cane. She stepped with her right foot, then dragged her left forward. Wrinkles covered her face, folding in on each other. Instinctively, Marina clutched her purse to her chest.

"What's that you have there?" She stooped over and studied Marina's produce.

Poor old beggar. A wave of empathy rose within her. "Are you hungry? Would you like an apple? Or some tomatoes?"

"Them small red balls are tomatoes?"

Marina nodded. "Yeah, cherry tomatoes. Would you like some?"

"I've never seen tomatoes that small. I would love to try them."

Warmth spread through Marina's chest. "Here. Take the whole carton." It wasn't like she was going to eat them any time soon, and they were liable to go bad before she could stomach such flavors.

The woman grinned as she took them.

A whistle sounded from across the street. A man stomped toward them, scowling. He wore a long jacket with shiny buttons down the front and a derby hat. He clenched a club in his fist.

The old woman startled. "The police. I best be going." Keeping her head down, she hurried away. Stomp, drag. Stomp, drag. What was her hurry? Was she running from the law? Perhaps Marina's first purse-clutching instincts had been right.

The policeman pointed a finger at her. "What did you sell that woman?" He peered at her through narrowed eyes.

"Tomatoes. But I didn't sell them. I gave them to her." What was the big deal? Marina's head felt fuzzy, and her thoughts were like trains barreling in different directions, never connecting. Nothing made sense.

"Just as I thought." He pulled out handcuffs. "You are under arrest for selling vegetables within the city limits."

A laugh burst out of her. "What?" This had to be a joke.

His glower deepened. "You heard me." He yanked her up and pulled her wrists behind her, snapping on the cuffs.

"Wait." Her knees wobbled, but she forced strength into her voice. "There must be some mistake. I didn't do anything wrong."

"People like you are the reason the whole city's infected with cholera. No regard for others. Despicable."

The world around her spun as the officer shoved her to get her to move. She stumbled forward a few steps, head reeling. "Where are you taking me? What about my stuff?"

He whistled again, and another officer raced toward them. "What do you need, Bert?"

"Can you carry this woman's things to the station?"

"All right."

The police station? How was giving an old lady tomatoes a crime? What kind of craziness did she time-sail into? Certainly, tomatoes had nothing to do with cholera. She was like Alice stumbling down the rabbit hole into Wonderland.

What she wouldn't give to go home.

~

Claire sat on the couch, picking at her cuticle as she waited for the teens to come home. Well, not *home* but the closest thing they had right now. Her stomach had tied itself in knots all day. First, when they left for the beach. Then, when she accidentally spilled her secret to Bearett. Again, when she checked the boat's mailbox and found no letter from Marina, despite Claire sending two letters the day before.

And now, as she waited for Aiden and Brinley to return. What if something happened to those two? It'd be her fault for not keeping a better eye on them. How would she explain her blunder to Marina? The woman trusted her to keep them safe in her stead. And she'd let them walk out.

When they came back, maybe she should lay down the law. Insist they ask her before leaving the house. She knew next to nothing about these kids. They might need strict supervision. Or … perhaps she needed to develop a closer relationship with them. Would they respect her more if she became a cool mentor figure instead of an authoritative parental substitute? She'd be far more comfortable acting like a fun aunt.

Chatter and laughter filtered in through the open window. She peeked between the blinds. *Thank You, God.* Here they came. Safe and sound. She had only a minute to choose which path to take.

They spilled inside. "You're right. It's perfect," Brinley said.

Claire jumped to her feet. Way to be cool. She slid a hand into her pocket for a more casual air. "What's perfect?"

Brinley smiled and held up a bag. "Aiden bought Frankie a new costume. I love it." She pulled a firefighter ensemble out. "Aw. Looking at it makes me miss my baby so much. I hope he's doing okay."

"I'm sure he's—"

Brinley cut Aiden off. "Fine. I know. You keep telling me that. I wish I knew for sure."

What had she been afraid of? They hadn't gotten into trouble after all. Aiden obviously cared for his sister and looked out for her. They were fine. She'd worried over nothing.

"Hey." Claire shifted her weight. "Wanna go out for ice cream?" Apparently, she was going with the cool aunt option. And using the lure of food to do it.

"Nah." Aiden waved her off. "I just want to veg. It's been a day."

"I'll go," Brinley said.

Aiden shot his sister a look Claire couldn't decipher, but after some kind of sibling telepathy, he shrugged and plopped onto the couch, dropping a shopping bag at his feet. "Have fun."

Brinley smiled at her. Such a different vibe from what she'd been giving last night or that morning. Claire should capitalize on the change for sure.

"I'll grab my purse." Claire stepped toward her room.

Brinley motioned to the costume. "I'll put this away."

A minute later, they met at the door and headed to Claire's car. The sun was beginning to set, splaying brilliant colors on the horizon.

Brinley sighed deep and long. "Beautiful."

"It is." Claire glanced at Brinley's profile. What a beautiful girl. Did she find her self-worth in her appearance, or was she more mature than Claire had been at that age? The urge to know her houseguest rose within her. Maybe she could be a mentor to her. A positive influence. As a teen, Claire had desperately needed someone to fill that role for her.

"So, what'd you do today?"

Brinley shrugged. "Just hung out at the beach. Played volleyball."

"Cool. You made some friends, then?"

One side of Brinley's mouth twitched up, then she pressed her lips together. "Yeah."

Okay. How to keep the conversation going? Time to ask more questions.

"You like volleyball?"

"Yeah."

Claire waited for her to say more, but she didn't. Goodness. If she wanted to pull teeth, she'd have become a dentist. At least Brinley seemed content in the silence between stilted conversation. She wasn't stewing. Probably just thinking.

They arrived at Kilwins ice cream shop and entered.

"Order whatever you want." That was something a cool aunt would say, right? It was kind of fun to pretend she had all the money in the world.

Brinley ordered two scoops of chocolate peanut butter in a waffle bowl, and Claire purchased a vanilla cone—the cheapest thing on the menu. She needed to get the girl talking if they were going to establish a rapport. They settled onto a bench outside.

"Tell me more about Frankie."

Brinley's eyes lit up as she dug her phone out of her pocket. "Oh my gosh, he's the cutest dog ever."

For half an hour, the two of them watched videos from Brinley's channel, at times laughing so hard they couldn't breathe. The connection between them wove a thicker, tighter cord with Claire's response to each video. A rapport. Exactly what they needed. She pushed down a niggling worry that Brinley was sinking fully into social media quicksand. Watching these videos together was the perfect way for Claire to earn the right to speak into Brinley's life. The ends fully justified the means.

"How do you come up with all this stuff?" Claire wiped the corners of her eyes with a napkin. The hilarity had nearly brought her to tears.

"I don't know. It just comes to me. Frankie's such a good sport."

"He's adorable, for sure, but the scripts are magic." The girl had major creative talent and a delightful sense of humor.

"Well, well, well. If it isn't Mrs. Anti–Social Media fawning all over Instagram."

Claire looked up to see Betty Sue, the receptionist at City Hall, looming over them. She suppressed a groan.

Brinley's mouth twisted. "What do you mean, anti–social media?"

Betty Sue planted a hand on her hip. "Miss Claire's done several talks at schools and churches, warning people of the dangers of social media and how it impacts today's youth. Thinks kids shouldn't have social media accounts. She's pretty convincing too." She pointed a finger at Claire. "But it looks like she's got a secret obsession."

Claire's stomach sank to her toes.

Brinley's gaze snapped from Betty Sue to Claire and back again. "That's … interesting."

"Mm-hmm." Betty Sue's snarky chuckle seemed to linger in their space even after she wandered away.

Claire attempted to redirect her attention back to the phone, but with a click of Brinley's finger, the screen went dark. The connection that had seemed so solid moments before snapped like a thread.

"If it was up to you, I wouldn't be allowed to have an Instagram account, huh?" Brinley shook her head, disgust written all over her face. "You've been playing me this whole time. Why?"

"I wasn't playing you. I truly enjoy your channel. I wasn't lying when I said you have talent."

"Talent you think I should waste." Her eyes narrowed.

"No, not waste. Redirect, maybe? Look, I care about you and don't want—"

"Oh, please."

"I do."

Brinley rolled her eyes, picked up her trash, and stood. "Ready to go?"

"Yeah."

What had started out so promising turned out to be a disaster. What more proof did she need that she was going to fail at this parenting thing? Every other step with these teens ended with a stumble.

~

When Bearett asked Aiden if he wanted to join him on the sunrise cruise the next day, Aiden didn't hesitate. "Yeah, sure." He'd been too hard on their hosts. Bearett was a cool guy, his company far superior to Brinley's sullen, grumpy self. She never said what happened during their ice cream run last night, but she came back in a horrible mood. Best to give her space.

Now, with the crisp morning air ruffling his hair, he listened to Bearett's directions on how to navigate the boat. Which was awesome. Almost like a father teaching his craft to his son. He could nearly pretend Bearett was his dad who would pass down the business to him someday.

That thought both soothed and sliced. But it wasn't like he was forgetting about Dad. If he could have things his way, he'd wish his father back with them. No contest. No one could replace Dad. Bearett, though, wasn't a horrible runner-up.

He squinted against the sun's glare off the glistening water.

"Didn't bring sunglasses?" Bearett asked.

"Nah. I think Mom has them in her purse." His shades had apparently time traveled with her. Wild.

"I've got an extra pair you can have." He fished them from a small shelf at the front of the boat. "Here."

Aiden's palms warmed as he took them. Dad had bought his last pair before teaching him to drive. But it wasn't like he was replacing them. Not replacing Dad with Bearett. He needed shades. Bearett had some. The end. So why did a twinge spread through his chest? He was allowed to look up to other men. Needed to.

Stacy's dad had filled the spot inside him that yearned for a man to guide him, but not perfectly. It was like a puzzle piece that didn't quite fit, but if you pounded it hard enough, it mostly worked. Did Mr. Mazoni still think about him? After yesterday, the appeal of being back together with Stacy had dimmed. The feel of Nevaeh's hand in his nearly made him forget his mission to win his ex-girlfriend back.

"Go ahead and grab breakfast," Bearett said. "You'll have to let me know what you think of our new caterer."

"Okay." Aiden had taken a few steps toward the buffet when he turned around. "You want anything?"

Bearett's smile warmed him. It reminded him of the look Dad gave him when he brought home a report card or won a chess tournament. Like he'd done something right. "Grab me whatever looks good."

"Will do."

Aiden returned with two plates filled with chocolate hazelnut crepes. He handed one plate to Bearett.

"Looks amazing," Bearett said.

"Doesn't it?" Aiden forked a bite into his mouth and moaned. "Don't tell anyone, but this is even better than the kind my dad used to make."

"He made crepes?"

"Crepes. Pancakes. French toast." He spoke around another bite. "Breakfast foods only, but he slayed them. The best I'd ever had." He tilted his head toward his plate. "Until now."

"That's a positive first review for our caterer. Looks like I'll keep her." He took a bite and nodded. "Definitely, keeping her."

They ate in companionable silence for a few minutes. Memories swarmed Aiden's brain. Dad wearing the ridiculous quilted apron Mom gave him for Christmas. He'd danced around the kitchen singing U2 songs.

Bearett set down his empty plate. "Tell me about your dad."

Really? No one had asked him that before, and Mom shut down any conversation about him in her presence. What would it be like to freely remember? He finished his last bite, then asked, "What do you want to know?"

Bearett took the wheel and turned his attention toward the horizon but cast a glance over his shoulder, proving he was still listening. "Anything. What was he like?"

"Fearless." Aiden couldn't help but smile. "To him, everything was an adventure. He wanted to soak it all up, you know? Live life to its fullest." As he spoke, it was as if a tightly wound coil loosened in his chest. His lungs could fully expand.

Bearett looked over at him again, his interested expression encouraging Aiden to continue.

"He always wanted to go skydiving. Never did, but he did take Brinley and me bungee jumping once."

"How was that?"

"Exhilarating. Skydiving's got to be a hundred times as amazing. But I'll never know for sure."

"Why not?"

Aiden scoffed. "Mom would never let me. And even though I could do it when I turn eighteen, I'd have to hear her badger me about my 'reckless choices' every time I saw her. It'd spoil the fun of it."

"She's not much of an adventure seeker?"

"Not now. She didn't used to mind, but ever since Dad died, she's freaked out about every little thing."

Bearett frowned. "I can understand that. Can you?"

He shook his head. "I get that she wants to protect us, but come on. We're going to suffocate."

"At least you know she cares. There are a lot of teens out there who would trade a kidney to know someone loved them that much."

Aiden grew quiet. He'd never questioned Mom's love for him. Only her sanity. Of course, Mom cared about him and Brinley. Her entire world revolved around them. Maybe that wasn't always a bad thing. He'd still give anything to be able to breathe in her presence.

"Mom's always been super involved. PTO president, room mother, things like that. After Dad died, she needed a job, so what did she do? Applied to be our school's secretary. She's literally lurking twenty-four seven. She's buddy-buddy with all our teachers. We can't catch a break."

It seemed like Bearett was holding back a smile. "I can see how that would get annoying."

"So annoying. And she's got this loud, excited voice, and an even louder laugh."

Bearett chuckled. "Moms. Can't live with them; can't live without them."

Aiden sobered. What would he do if Mom never returned?

Chapter Eleven

arina pressed her temples. How had she managed to get into this mess? If she'd have done something to stop the Great St. Louis Fire, she'd be home by now. Instead, the officer dragged her into a white-bricked building smaller than a modern gas station. She sweated in the jail cell. They'd stuffed her in a walled cage. The box was so small she could stretch out her legs and touch the opposite wall. Poorly lit. Permeated with the smell of mildew. A stain marred her thin mattress. Gross. The fire would probably start tonight, and she was powerless to stop it. How could she complete her mission from here?

Though she felt far stronger than she had earlier—perhaps thanks to the Gatorade or snagging forward in time past the worst of her sickness—exhaustion still pulled on her eyelids. She gave in and lay on her cot. She didn't know anyone in this time and place, so there was no one to bail her out. If only she could get ahold of Dr. Duncan. This was where a cell phone would come in handy. As it stood, no one at the jail knew of him, let alone how to contact him. She was utterly alone.

Her eyes stung, but she wouldn't give in to pity. She'd comfort herself with memories of her children. She'd have to go years back for good ones. Most recent memories involved fights or cold shoulders. How had her relationship with them disintegrated? Had it happened all at once or gradually?

There'd been good times, but not many since Adam died. If she flipped back through the pages of her mental scrapbook, though, there she was, taking her two- and three-year-olds to the pet store to see the animals. Aiden jumped up and down with excitement over the snakes. Brinley was mesmerized by the bunnies. Back then, all she had to do to make their day was to go through a car wash. They'd erupt into giggles when she yelled, "The cleaning monster's going to get you!" Easy entertainment. Baking cookies at Christmastime. Watching them jump in puddles after a summer rain shower.

And the crafts. Always the crafts. From stringing beaded bracelets to weaving pot holders to making bird feeders by coating pinecones with peanut butter, she used to delight in leading them in messy, creative endeavors. She used to be a fun mom, right? Adam's death had changed everything. Changed her.

Sleep grappled for her. She must have nodded off because she startled awake, attempting to remember the details of a strange dream. In it, she'd worn a cape and dashed around at super speeds. But why? Flames. There'd been flames and … fire hoses? Yes, that was it. She'd been a superhero, putting out a raging fire.

She sat up and rubbed her eyes. What time was it? Darkness shrouded the small, barred window in her cell. She must have slept a good while. She certainly felt more refreshed than she had since leaving for vacation. Covering a yawn, she stood and strode to the window. Though she stretched onto her tiptoes, she couldn't make anything out. Black. Just like her circumstances.

Heavy footsteps. She paced to the cell door and grasped the bars. If only she had superhero strength to bend the bars far enough to climb through.

An officer approached, keys in hand. "Miss Stone, a Dr. Joseph Duncan is here to see you."

A sigh rushed from her. Thank goodness! How had he known where she was? No matter. The important thing was that he was here now. To rescue her.

The guard unlocked her cell and opened the door. "Come with me. The doctor has paid your bail."

Oh, she could hug Dr. Duncan. She'd never been so thankful for a familiar face as when she rounded the corner.

There he stood, hands in his pockets, a worried line marring his brow.

Another officer gave a distracted smile. "You are free to go."

Dr. Duncan simply turned on his heel and walked out the door.

She followed. "Thanks."

They'd made it four steps before he spun around and lifted a brow. "Time sailors have dream-summoned me before, but never have I seen such ridiculousness. What did you think you were, Miss Stone? A bat? Flying around the city like that." He brought his hand up to his chin and tapped it. "No, a bat can't run like you were in that dream. Some kind of nimble bird, perhaps?"

Her mouth fell open. "What are you talking about?"

He tilted his head back with an exasperated huff. "Your dream, Miss Stone. Your dream."

"You had the same dream?"

"Heavens, woman. That's what dream-summoning is. You called out to me for help. Here I am. Now, do you plan on flying or racing through the streets?"

What in the world? Could this time-sailing thing get any stranger? She certainly hadn't meant to summon him through a dream. At least, not consciously. Subconsciously, maybe.

When she didn't answer right away, he started off at a fast clip, stirring up dust with each step. "There's some commotion at the wharf. I heard shouts on the way here but didn't stop to investigate."

Her stomach plummeted. The fire. It had to be.

Steps slowing of their own accord, she wavered. The small fire in the ladies' cabin was one thing, but could she truly face a full-out blazing inferno after what happened to Adam? Perhaps she could run the other way. It was too much. Too hard. In real life, she was no superwoman.

But Aiden. Brinley. If she didn't complete her mission, she'd never see them again. They'd enter adulthood without a father or mother. How would they navigate it all? If they'd acted out after Adam's death, how much more trouble could they get into without any parental influence? She pictured them behind bars. Surely not. They'd become well-adjusted adults, right? She couldn't take the risk. Besides, her heart ached for them.

Whatever lay ahead, she'd have to face it. She quickened her steps.

An alarm bell clanged. "What's that?" she asked.

He cast a glance over his shoulder to where she lagged behind. "What?" The bell rang again. "Oh, bells ring at all hours. I hardly pay it any mind anymore. Church bells when a funeral concludes. Fire station bells when they lose a company member."

"But … a funeral at this hour?" She managed to catch up to him.

"It *is* unusual, now that you mention it."

A strong wind whipped her hair into her face. She brushed it away, only for the same thing to happen again. Forget it. When she'd cut her hair, Adam had gotten her a dragonfly barrette. She dared not carry it in her purse and risk losing it. It sat on her dresser at home. If only she had it with her, maybe she could summon strength from it. From her husband's lingering touch. But no. She'd have to face this on her own.

As they turned a corner, an eerie glow emanated from the direction of the riverfront. A shiver tingled her spine.

Dr. Duncan broke into a jog. She followed suit. More bells. Frantic shouts. People rushing about.

And then, there it was. The stuff of her nightmares. A raging inferno spit fire from what remained of the fully engulfed *White Cloud*. A spark flung onto the neighboring steamboat. The name painted on its white front proclaimed it to be the *Edward Bates*. Those aboard hollered and scattered about like ants on an anthill that was targeted by someone's boot. Some rushed to douse the growing flame with water, while others loosened her moorings. Getting the boat away from the blazing furnace next door seemed a wise move, but they weren't quick enough.

Wind slapped the boat's face and spread the fire farther and farther. The upper deck caught flame. The men aboard scrambled off, some jumping overboard, while others navigated to shore. Dr. Duncan stood frozen next to her, mouth agape, as the *Edward Bates*, now a ball of fire, floated from its place and spun out of control. It crashed into nearby steamboats, spilling burning cinders and chunks of charred wood onto their decks, setting them aflame.

As if he'd snapped out of a daze, Dr. Duncan sucked in a breath and said, "Hurry. Let's assist before the entire city goes up in flames."

~

Brinley was still moping around when her phone rang the next afternoon. Aiden checked his texts for the fifth time in an hour and sighed. Still no response from Nevaeh. Didn't she want to hang out with him again? He had texted her that morning with a beach day invite. Hopefully, their time together the other day hadn't scared her away.

"But I can't. I'm out of town." Brinley's voice rose as she paced the kitchen.

"Can't what?" he whispered.

"I don't know. You've got to keep him there until I get back." She gasped. "No! He's going to be okay, isn't he?" Her lip wobbled.

Aiden stood and moved closer. "What's up?"

She waved him off. "Take him to a vet. We'll pay."

A vet? "Is something wrong with Frankie?"

Her eyes filled with tears. "I'll be there as soon as I can, but I'm kinda stuck here." A pause. "No, my mom is unavailable right now."

Bearett came out of his room, frowning. He cast a glance at Aiden, who shrugged. Walking up to Brinley, he placed a hand on her shoulder.

"Hold on a minute," she said into the phone. After pressing a button, she turned her attention to Bearett.

"What's going on?" Bearett's hand dropped from her shoulder, but the look of concern on his face never wavered.

Brinley sniffed. "Frankie is sick. The boarding place says I need to come and get him. Something about their policy saying they can't keep him any longer."

"Let me talk to them." He held his hand out for her phone.

She passed it to him, then hugged herself tightly. A single tear trekked down her cheek. She locked eyes with Aiden. "He's never been sick before. What if he … if he—"

Aiden shook his head. "Don't say it. He's going to be fine."

"But—"

"No buts. Just have faith." Faith in what was anyone's guess. Faith in fate? In the dog himself? Nevaeh would probably say faith in God. Easy for her to say. She hadn't lost her dad.

Bearett's voice leaked frustration. "Her mom can't come get the dog. Don't you have a vet on-site? Or at least on call?" A long pause. "What are you going to do with him if he isn't picked up by tomorrow afternoon?" Another pause. Bearett groaned. "We'll call you back."

Claire entered the front door, laden with two canvas shopping bags. "The farmer's market was buzzing with activity this morning. So many people. Great fruit and veggie selections. Lasagna with homemade sauce for dinner. Keto berry cookies for dessert." She glanced from person to person. "What's wrong?" She set down the bags.

"You mean besides keto cookies?" Bearett massaged his forehead.

Brinley rushed up to her. "Frankie is sick. The boarding place says he can't stay there."

Bearett crossed his arms. "I tried to reason with them, but they told me someone has to pick up the dog by five p.m. tomorrow, or they're taking him to an animal shelter."

"What? No!" Tears freely flowed down Brinley's cheeks. "They can't do that to Frankie."

Surely, it was just a threat. Frankie was a dog celebrity. They had to treat him well.

"What's the matter with him?" Claire asked.

"They suspect the dog flu. He has to be picked up because it's contagious, and they don't want their other boarders infected."

Dogs could get the flu? Weird. Aiden asked, "It's not fatal or anything, though, right? Frankie will recover?"

Bearett nodded like he had full confidence. "Of course." Was he trying to make Brinley feel better, or did he truly know about dog sicknesses?

Brinley slumped onto the couch and cradled her head in her hands. "My baby. What are we going to do?"

~

Claire's heart leapt toward Brinley, whose sobs flooded the house. The poor dear. Never having owned a pet, Claire could only imagine how helpless the girl must feel. "I'll drive you to pick him up." The words flew out of their own accord.

Aiden narrowed his eyes at her, as if daring her to take it back. "It's like a six-hour drive."

"It's fine. I love road trips." Mostly true. Long car rides were a blast when traveling with Stella and Wendy.

Brinley peeked through her fingers, still covering her face. "Really?"

"Really?" Bearett echoed.

She didn't make eye contact with him, lest he talk her out of it with nonverbal cues.

"Of course. Someone needs to pick him up. No way I'm letting him end up at a shelter." Maybe this would get her on the teens' good side. She could be the hero for once.

Brinley wiped her damp cheeks with the backs of her hands. "We could get him before closing time tomorrow?"

"If we leave in the morning, it will be no problem." Six hours of quality bonding time. Maybe they'd open up to her.

Bearett's hand found his chin, the other arm crossed. "What about your classes? Aren't you supposed to teach three of them?"

"No big deal. I'll ask Donna to sub." She picked up the bags and went to the kitchen to unload. She had lasagna to throw together and keto cookies to bake.

The teens spoke to each other in low tones as she unbagged grass-fed ground beef.

Bearett came up beside her, leaning against the counter. "Are you sure about this?"

"Of course." Noodles. Tomatoes. Onion. Garlic. Olive oil. What else did she need? Oh yeah, cheese and an egg. She grabbed them from the fridge. "I'll see if Wendy can meet me for lunch. It's been too long since I've seen her."

Connecting with one of her besties would be a highlight of the trip, for sure. Plus, Wendy was a mom. Perhaps she could give Claire much-needed advice on what to expect and how to navigate this new territory.

"You plan to drive there and back in one day?"

"Yeah."

"Might be best to spring for a hotel."

She lowered her voice. "You know we can't afford that. Especially since I'll lose income from missing my classes."

"That's a lot of driving."

"I'll have good company."

He burst into a laugh.

She shot him the stink eye. "What?"

"Nothing. You have fun with your *Leave It to Beaver* road trip. I'll stay here in the real world."

She bumped him with her hip. "Oh, stop."

He tossed his hands in the air. "Just sayin'. It might turn out differently from what you expect."

Why'd he have to be a downer? "They have their licenses. We can take turns driving. I'll pack snacks. It'll be great."

"I'm sure they'll love your celery sticks and hummus." He snickered as he walked to the bedroom.

Once the lasagna was in the oven, she stepped onto the back porch and called Wendy.

Her friend answered on the second ring. "Hey, girl. What's up?" A sweet little voice giggled in the background. Bryce must be two already. What were two-year-olds like? She'd find out soon enough. "Hey. I'm going to be in your neighborhood tomorrow. Are you free for lunch?"

"You're coming to St. Louis? Why?"

"It's a long story."

"Might as well tell me now so we can talk about other things tomorrow."

Claire relayed the story of Marina's time-sailing escapade and the two teens left in her wake.

"Oh, my goodness. How wild. Did you tell Stella?"

"Not yet." Though she had no reason not to. Her time-sailing bestie would get a kick out of it. Her stomach churned. She hadn't even told her friends she was pregnant. They'd likely be thrilled for her. Would they understand her apprehension?

"Oh, I wish she could come to lunch too. Wouldn't that be fun?"

"Yeah." If only Stella lived closer. With two young children and a demanding career in the Kansas boonies, she wouldn't be able to make a spontaneous road trip. "I might need to bring the teens with me. Maybe they could sit at their own table." She had burdens to unload on Wendy only.

"I'd pick up the dog and meet you halfway if I could, but Layla has a dance recital after church. Maybe I could do it later in the afternoon. No, wait. Grayson leads Bible study, and I can't bring the kids along. Bryce gets super carsick."

"It's no trouble. I'm looking forward to lunch with you at The Screaming Peach."

"Same. You should drop the teens off at home for a while. They weren't planning on such a long trip. They might want to pack other clothes and things."

"True." It'd be nice to have an afternoon without worrying about them. But she couldn't stay and chat for too long. Who knew when Marina would return? They needed to be in South Haven when she did.

"So, what's this dog's Insta handle? I've got to check him out."

The two chatted for another twenty minutes before Wendy had to go make dinner. "See you tomorrow around noon at The Screaming Peach." Then she sang a couple of lines from "Meet Me in St. Louis, Louis."

Claire couldn't hold back her smile. The three friends had bonded over musicals.

"Will do." Claire needed to get to work as well. They'd need plenty of keto cookies for their trip.

Chapter Twelve

Once Marina got her feet to move, they didn't stop. Adam had run headlong into a blazing inferno. How could she not do the same? He'd taught her that action conquered fear. Said that once he moved forward, did something to help, he was back in control and anxiety took a back seat. She had to act, to *do* something, lest memories of the night he died render her frozen in place.

Someone among the mayhem handed her a bucket. She bailed river water to toss at the spreading sheet of flames before her. Intense heat pushed against her, stinging her skin like a sunburn. Sweat plastered her hair to her forehead. The heavy dress did her no favors. Her sweaty legs itched to run far away from this nightmare. She clenched her jaw and kept moving.

Firefighters lined the riverfront with primitive hoses, and many residents helped alongside her. Still, they were no match for the monstrous fire. It advanced down the line of steamboats. One by one, she watched them disintegrate into wooden skeletons. The *Montauk, Red Wing, Eliza Stewart, Timour, Alice, Alexander Hamilton* ... Helplessness enshrouded her. How could she have ever imagined she could accomplish this mission?

The light from the fire blazed brighter and brighter, only black smoke masking the glow here and there. The *White Cloud* broke free and entered the river's current, sparking the steamboat on her other side, the *Eudora*.

Whistling wind took the boat's flaming cinders and flung them to shore. Eyes stinging from the smoke, Marina snapped her gaze to the bales of dry hemp and piles of lumber stacked on the levee. No, no, no!

They ignited in flames too.

What would Adam have done in the midst of such pandemonium? Would he move forward in confidence, or would helplessness render his arms wet noodles? She used to wipe his sooty face with a washcloth when he'd returned home from fighting a fire. He'd smiled at her as she'd done so, his eyes full of admiration. But the grooves in his forehead and around his eyes had deepened with each encounter. He must have carried burdens he dared not unload on her. Seen things he'd never spoken of. If only he could speak to her now.

Rows and rows of lard and bacon sat nearby. Suddenly, they burst into a grease-fueled inferno. A wall of flames separated her from the firemen on the other side. Above the blockade, a tower of black smoke coughed into the sooty air.

Stumbling a step, she dropped the bucket and watched it plummet to the dusty ground. This Goliath wouldn't fall on account of her measly stone. Useless. She was powerless against the seething giant raging in front of her.

Powerless. Just as she'd been the night Adam hadn't come home. The night that flaming claws had ripped her life to shreds. Adam's blue-green eyes. The night he'd dropped to one knee on the shore of Creve Coeur Lake, golden sunset hues shimmering on the water, he'd promised to love her for the rest of his life. Never had she imagined tragedy would cut it short.

The bridge of her nose burned. She clamped her jaw. This was no place for tears. No place for memories. Action. She needed to take action.

More bells clanged, from boats, fire stations, churches. The incessant tolls might ring in her mind for the rest of her life. How could she band with the firefighters to help in a more efficient way? Though every muscle screamed, she rushed from the riverfront, searching for a fire truck. Blasted dress. The heavy skirts weighed her down, making every step difficult. This would have been so much easier in shorts and a tank top.

She found a few men struggling to pull their engine—a horse cart without the horse—over the rough stones of Cherry Street. She wasn't built of muscle, but surely another person would prove beneficial. "I'll help."

They grunted and strained as she joined them. One firefighter flashed a small, grateful smile. "Thanks. Our company left to join the Liberty men."

Liberty men? Must be another company of firefighters. From the snippets she'd heard, several volunteer fire companies normally competed against each other. But not tonight. Now, everyone joined forces to defeat a common enemy.

She heaved with all her strength, muscles trembling under the strain. Together, Marina and the firemen dragged the engine closer and closer to the levee. "How much does this thing weigh?" she asked between panting breaths.

"Around five hundred pounds, not including the hoses."

Her mouth fell open, allowing a fresh coating of soot to enter. She spit into the dust. Over five hundred pounds? She probably wasn't much help at all against such weight.

As they approached the riverfront, flames punched through the roof of a two-story warehouse. A group of firefighters managed to extinguish that blaze. Thank heavens.

"What's the plan?" she asked, as though she were one of them.

He didn't hesitate. "Douse the roofs of the buildings along the levee."

She nodded. Made sense. "Where's the nearest fire hydrant?"

"Huh?"

"The nearest fire hydrant? Where is it? I can help hook your hose up."

"You mean fireplug?" He pointed down the street. "There."

Fireplug. All right then.

"But you'll need a wrench." He pointed to the tool inside the engine.

She took it and dragged the heavy, leather hose in that direction, only to find another fireman hooking up his hose. Her heart pounded in her chest as if attempting to leap free. The fire that surrounded her felt like it'd taken residence in her muscles. Her entire body burned.

Between gasps, she asked him where the next nearest *fireplug* was, but apparently, he couldn't hear her over the chaos. Her gaze frantically searched the street. There. In the opposite direction. With strength that could only be born of adrenaline, she heaved and tugged the hose to it. After several fumbling attempts to figure the contraption out, a bystander rushed to help her with the wrench. Together, they hooked up the hose. In the process, water sprayed her dress. Blessed, cool relief, but within mere moments, all was dry again.

More plumes of smoke appeared over a large building.

The bystander pulled his hat from his head and swiped soot with his sleeve. "Heavens! The foundry."

Whatever that was. As she dashed back to the fire engine, several more buildings erupted into flames, pummeling her with searing heat. Why were all these buildings made of wood? Hadn't they learned anything about fire prevention? If Adam could see this disaster, he'd shake his head.

Adam.

No, she couldn't think about him. She had a mission to accomplish.

She returned to the fire engine and helped hold the hose as the fireman directed the flow onto the flames. Smoke invaded her nostrils and mouth. Each cough sounded more and more hoarse as her parched throat cried out for relief. Her eyes stung. Grime coated her skin. Heat licked at her. How were these firemen standing so close to the blaze without protective gear?

Hours must have passed, and though they managed to put out small pockets of flames, more erupted by the minute. Cinders landed on the roofs lining the next streets. She watched in horror as those buildings surrendered to the inferno.

The fireman looked at her with wide, helpless eyes. "Go find more help. Any able-bodied man you can find. Take my fire trumpet." He tossed it to her.

She started off, trumpet in hand. When she came upon a group of men gawking in the street, she tried to blow it. No, it didn't work like that. More like a megaphone. She shouted into it, "Help! Everyone, help!" She waved them toward the levee and started off again.

Up and down burning streets, she ran. Thick smoke clouded her view. Where was she, anyway? Had she come from the left or right? Her brain fogged. Whenever she stopped to catch her breath for a moment, her legs wobbled. If she didn't keep moving, she'd collapse.

Coals of fire larger than her hands cascaded from above, landing in yards and on sidewalks. Was this the end of the world? Of course, it wasn't. She knew that better than anyone else. But, man, did it feel like it.

Walls bellowed as they crashed to the ground. Buildings groaned as they succumbed to the flames. People scrambled through the streets, streaming away from the riverfront with armfuls of goods in hand. Rescuing possessions even as flames devoured their homes. Men pulled wagons of goods away from the inferno.

She passed a clothing shop where the owner called out for a cart. One stopped in front of him. "I'll get all that to safety for a hundred dollars."

"A hundred dollars! Why, it typically only costs thirty."

"You want my help or not?"

Despicable. Even in the 1800s, extortioners took advantage of crises.

She couldn't linger. She continued to call for helpers, though most people paid her no mind, intent on saving their livelihoods. One man threw clothing down a well. That was one way to save it.

When she reached Fourth Street, piles of furniture dotted her path as far as she could see. Some men scurried around inspecting the pieces, eventually making off with a trunk. Looters? A policeman rounded the corner and chased them down. Yep, looters.

She made her way back toward the levee, shouting for help through the trumpet. When she neared a warehouse by the river, a boom erupted, stabbing her ears. It vaulted her from her feet and flung her onto her back. Pain sliced through her ribs, stealing her breath. An explosion?

"You okay, miss?" A man with an Irish accent extended his hand to help her up. "The fire reached a cache of gunpowder below *Martha*'s deck."

A mushroom cloud dominated the sky. Splinters and debris rained down on the riverfront. She rose, arm raised to shield her face. "I'm okay." She panted in smoke-tinged air.

Shouts arose around her. "The cathedral! She's burning!"

Her gaze swung to the golden cross that topped the steeple, obscured by smoke. She'd been inside it once, along with the newer, more opulent, Cathedral Basilica, on a school tour. Wasn't it the first church in St. Louis and the oldest standing building in the city? Far too historic to let it burn. Muscles screaming, she headed in that direction. On the way, she came upon a fireman spouting curses at a fireplug.

"Everything okay?" she asked. Stupid question. Nothing was okay tonight.

"The water supply gave out."

No. What were they going to do? Even with a full supply of water, they were losing the battle against the spreading fire. How could they battle the flames without water?

Another fireman approached. "Go to the ferry landing on Market Street. We're pumping directly from the river."

She stopped, looking up and down the street. Should she join the firemen at the ferry landing? Or head to the cathedral? No matter where she went, it hardly made a difference. She was a little speck in the scheme of things. How laughable that she'd ever envisioned being the hero of the hour. There was nothing she could do to save the city.

Exhaustion, and maybe discouragement, turned her limbs into putty. She sat on the side of the street, gulping in sulfur-singed air. Why try to fight it? The city would burn, but history proved St. Louisans would rebuild.

A woman scrambled past her from the direction of the river, blanket in hand. A trail of water followed in her wake. A wet blanket?

Marina called after her. "Can I help?"

A wave of gratitude passed over the lady's face. "Please. My sister's house has caught fire."

Following the woman, she asked, "Got any more blankets?"

"Found this one in the street."

Ah. The spilled contents of trunks and carpetbags littered the streets. Which reminded her, where had she left her suitcase and cooler? She'd never taken them from the police station, had she? If the station still stood, hopefully her things would remain undamaged. Marina rifled through a heap of fabric and emerged with a quilt. Good. Maybe she could prove useful after all.

She made it only a few steps before another explosion boomed, shaking the ground beneath her. "What was that?"

The woman turned and gazed into the distance. "Must be the fire wall. Heard some men talking. They mean to blow up buildings to stop the fire."

Strange, but hopefully effective. She followed the woman to a nearby house where flames licked the right side. A tub full of water sat in the yard. Children dumped buckets of water into it, then rushed back toward the river. Marina dunked the quilt into it and flung the blanket onto the flames.

After what seemed like hours, they—with the help of five other women—managed to extinguish the flames. Half of the house remained intact, while the other half was charred beyond recognition. They all collapsed, sitting in the grass and staring vacantly ahead until another woman called for their help down the street. After dragging themselves to stand, they went to assist, wet blankets in tow.

When dawn broke over the horizon, the smoke that had coated the sky now filled only sporadic patches. The worst had to be over. She'd faced her fear. Rushed into danger like Adam had done. Would he be proud of her? Or not, since she obviously had little impact on the outcome? Blocks and blocks stretched out around her, mere rubble where there used to be houses and stores. How many buildings had the fire destroyed? Hundreds, surely.

She stumbled through the streets in what was, hopefully, the direction of the police station. Everything looked different with charred and broken walls and debris scattered throughout the streets. The cathedral appeared unharmed. But of course, it would be. It remained in modern times, with the Arch towering nearby. It's octagonal light-blue steeple stood like a stubborn child with its arms crossed, daring anyone to defy it. She hadn't done a thing to contribute to that miracle.

Men, women, and children sat on the edges of the streets. Their homes had likely been destroyed. Dust and soot covered their clothing and skin. Little ones cried out for food. She had some in her cooler, if it hadn't burned. She'd best eat and drink herself before she collapsed.

As adrenaline drained from her body, putting one foot in front of the other seemed impossible. Her eyelids drooped. Just a few more blocks. She forced herself to keep moving. There were people far worse off than her who needed help.

She coughed out an exhale when the police station appeared in her line of vision. With no place to call home, this was as close as she could get to something familiar. As she neared, the silhouette of a man stood against the sun's flare. He took off his hat and passed it from hand to hand. She drew closer to find a bedraggled and dirty Dr. Duncan.

~

Twenty minutes into their drive, Claire debated about turning around. What crabs. Maybe Aiden's and Brinley's sullen attitudes had to do with waking before dawn. Once they sloughed off their sleepiness, surely, they'd be better company.

She tried again. "Do you like to play road games, like finding each letter of the alphabet on license plates and billboards?"

In the passenger's seat, Brinley lifted both brows. "Yeah, that was fun when I was six."

Claire was a decade too late. Fair enough.

With a sigh, Brinley put her earbuds back in. Both teens had tuned into their music as soon as she backed out of the driveway. They only took the earbuds out when Claire continued to ask questions and only with huffs and groans as if she was the most annoying person in the world. Aiden returned to his own world within two minutes. Brinley indulged her a bit longer.

Perhaps she should have brought headphones of her own. She could be listening to an audiobook—maybe Sherry Shindelar's latest novel—instead of driving in uncomfortable silence. But no. She'd envisioned them having meaningful conversations for the duration of the trip. Bearett was right. *Leave It to Beaver* expectations indeed.

After another half hour, keeping silent seemed like torture. "So …" She raised her voice so they could hear her over their music. "Do you guys have significant others?"

Brinley yanked out her earbuds. "Huh?"

"Do you have a boyfriend?"

"No." The headphones went back in.

"What about you, Aiden?" she nearly shouted to the back seat. "Got a girlfriend?"

"Nope."

One word. Stellar. So much for conversation. Didn't they realize she was doing them a huge favor? They should cut her some slack.

"Cookie?" she asked.

"No thanks," Aiden replied. Then he mumbled, "Not if they're the ones that taste like Styrofoam."

He probably didn't think she could hear that.

"Do either of you want to take a turn driving?"

"Nah. I'm good," Aiden said.

Brinley shuddered. "I don't drive on highways."

"And that's for the best if you want to get there alive," Aiden teased.

"Shut up." Brinley's fingers flew across her phone. Every thirty seconds, the device chimed. Apparently, she was having a conversation with somebody. Just not Claire.

"Who are you texting with?"

Brinley ignored her. Should she press? Of course not. She wasn't the girl's mother. And Brinley was making it quite clear she wasn't her buddy either.

Would it be this way with her own child? Or would they develop a close-knit relationship, one that encouraged sharing and trust? If only she knew how to draw them out. Maybe they should stop for ice cream. That seemed to work before. She nearly rolled her eyes at herself. Was she going to spring for a treat every time her child didn't adore her? They'd need a bigger budget and perhaps a diabetes consultation.

She couldn't always use sweets as a reward. If her child was successful, unlike Clarie had been when her parents did the same with her, it'd create an unhealthy relationship with food.

A ding resounded from the back seat. Great. Now both of them were having a good old time texting with friends, and Claire was left to endure hours on end of silence. She turned on the radio to the contemporary Christian station.

"Can you turn that down?" Aiden asked. "I can't hear."

She slapped the radio off. No problem. She wouldn't want to disturb his bubble of happiness.

Only four more hours until she would meet Wendy. The thought lifted her spirits a smidge. Funny how there'd been a time when she couldn't stand being around her friend. They'd both grown so much, and their bond had strengthened.

Aiden groaned. "I'm starving."

Seriously? "There's a bag of snacks right next to you."

Rustling came from the back seat. "There's nothing good in here."

Deep breath. A glance at the fuel gauge. "I'll need to stop for gas soon anyway. You can grab something then."

When they left the gas station, both Aiden and Brinley had armfuls of junk food. If she was their mother, would she allow such unhealthy eating habits? Surely, a road trip was an exception. An exception that depleted her bank account unnecessarily. Oh, well. At least they wouldn't complain for a few hours.

"Thanks," Aiden said around a mouth full of Cheetos.

At least that was something.

At the intersection, a handful of firefighters stood at the corners, boots in hand. Collecting money for some charity. The crunching and munching sounds ceased as they sat at the red light.

"Dad used to do that," Aiden said.

Her heart squeezed. What must it be like to lose a father in such a horrific way? Every time a fire truck passed, they'd remember. And likely grieve.

"Hand me my purse." She put her hand back to retrieve it from Aiden. They didn't have extra money to give. The cash she offered wouldn't even go to a cause relevant to Aiden and Brinley. Not to victims of fire or any such thing. Still … She pulled out two twenty-dollar bills, rolled down her window, and stuck them in the boot. "God bless you."

"Thank you, ma'am." The man smiled at her.

When the light turned green, Brinley said, "That was a lot of money."

"It's the least I can do." To show these surly teens she cared. That she empathized with their pain. That if she could, she'd heal their grieving hearts. But she wasn't anyone's healer. That job belonged to God alone. Would they let Him?

~

Aiden smiled as he shifted in the back seat and returned Nevaeh's text.

Dangerous flirting. Then again, he *was* currently unattached. Maybe he didn't need Stacy or her father. He could move on and leave that heartbreak in the dust. He pictured Nevaeh's sweet face, his imagination zeroing in on her lips. What would it be like to kiss her? Stacy was the only girl he'd ever kissed. The only one he'd wanted to … until now.

From the driver's seat, Claire's chipper voice carried. "So, what was the best vacation you've ever been on?"

He'd been ignoring her questions for hours, feigning not being able to hear her. This time, though, he mumbled under his breath, "Not this one."

Claire was reminding him more and more of Mom with her incessant chatter. She was trying way too hard. She needed to chill.

What if he could make a go of it with Nevaeh? What started out as a nightmare might become a dream come true. Only, what were the odds they could make it work, even if she was into him? They lived in different states. Long-distance relationships never turned out well. Besides, he couldn't kiss her from hundreds of miles away.

Brinley spoke up. "My favorite vacation was when Dad took us surfing. Do you remember that Aiden?" She turned in her seat to look at him.

"Like I could forget." He'd fallen off his board more times than he could count, but Dad never seemed discouraged. It was always *Get back on and try again*. He hadn't mastered it during their three-hour board rental. Dad promised they'd try again the next summer. Except that summer, he was dead.

Brinley went on about the thrill of mounting waves, but Aiden tuned her out. Some memories—even good ones—hurt too much to think about. Was that how Mom felt? No energy to ponder that. Instead, he texted Nevaeh.

He pictured her lying on the beach, tanned skin glistening in the sun. Or maybe …

> Playing volleyball in a minute. Wish you were here.

He rubbed the back of his neck. So did he, but not so he could get in on the game.

She sent a selfie of her wearing the hot-pink shirt he'd bought her.

> Like my outfit?

He laughed and snapped a picture of himself in his matching shirt. Looked at it. No way. Tried again, this time with a peace sign and not such a goofy grin. Better. He sent it.

> What a coincidence. Great minds think alike.

The shirt looked way better on her.

> Lookin' good.

Heat crept up his cheeks. Was she only talking about the shirt, or did she think he was attractive? Could he … Should he …

He typed fast and hit send before he could second-guess himself.

> Not as good as you.

Definitely flirting. And he felt lighter than he had in a month. She'd said she didn't want to get involved with someone who didn't share her religious views, but she hadn't backed off. Perhaps he was a decent enough guy to pass her religious test. Maybe she'd forget about her standards. Or lower them a little. It would be so easy to dive into a relationship with her. For him to forget about everything that bothered him and just enjoy her company.

"Earth to Aiden." Brinley waved her hand in front of his face.

He pushed it away. "What?"

"I asked if you remembered the time Dad put inserts in your shoes to make you tall enough to ride that roller coaster at Six Flags."

Ah, yes. He'd been dying to ride it and ended up being slightly too short. Dad ran to the nearest store and bought shoe inserts to push him over the minimum height requirement. Mom had rolled her eyes but hadn't stopped him. What a day that had been, riding over and over again, with his heart dropping to his feet every time they came out of an upside-down loop.

"Dad was the best." He cleared his throat from the croak in his voice. It was a happy memory. Why'd sadness follow on its heels?

"Who have you been texting anyway?" Brinley made a kissy face. "Nevaeh."

He swatted at her shoulder. "Shut up."

"Is it her?"

"Yeah. So?"

"You like her," she said in a singsong voice.

"And you like Jack. Big deal." Only her stupid crush was a delinquent. Not the same thing at all.

"Wait," Claire said. "Who are Nevaeh and Jack?"

He rolled his eyes. Why'd Brinley bring them up in front of Claire? "Just some people we met at the beach." No need to go into details.

"Oh. People from South Haven, not from home?"

Nevaeh was from Nebraska, but whatever. "Yeah."

"Hmm." It sounded like she wanted to say more but held herself back. Good. She didn't need to pry into their lives.

He pulled Nevaeh's picture up on his phone. Just the sight of her eased the tension in his shoulders. Could he win her over? It was worth a shot. When he got back, he'd start Project Sweep Nevaeh off Her Feet.

Chapter Thirteen

Marina staggered up to Dr. Duncan. Her gaze dropped to his feet where her things sat, seemingly unharmed.

"How did you—"

"I figured you'd come back here. Quite a dream you had, wasn't it? Almost as though you knew what would happen."

She shrugged. What could she say?

A policeman dragged a cursing man, covered with soot, into the station.

Dr. Duncan followed her gaze. "Looters. Over sixty arrested so far."

"How horrible."

"I protected your belongings." He nodded toward her suitcase.

"Thank you." Her legs nearly gave way right there on the side of the street.

Dr. Duncan took her arm. "There's a bench right there." He led her to the wooden bench a couple of yards away, then returned for her things. She plopped down with a sigh. A glance down the streets showed the fire hadn't affected this area. Things here almost looked normal, except for wisps of smoke in the air and a lingering scent like charred feathers.

"Rest for a spell and then help me assist the burn victims."

Burn victims? She hadn't thought about such things, but now that he mentioned it … She riffled through her purse, searching for bottles of aloe vera gel. Her hand grasped something else, though, and she retrieved it first. Aiden's sunglasses. Her chin quivered. How was he doing without them? Maybe he'd bought another pair. Or not. Adam had gotten him these, glasses that matched his own. She'd laughed at those two posing in them, the blue tint of the lenses making them look like they were trying too hard to be cool.

"What's that?" Dr. Duncan leaned in to see.

Ignoring his question, she quickly stashed the glasses back in her purse and fished for the aloe vera.

"Ta-da. I've got just the thing. They were buy two, get one free."

"What is it?" He took a bottle from her and studied it.

"It's aloe vera gel."

"Remarkable." He held the bottle up to the sunlight. "Where did you find the plant? And what is this moldable glass?"

She stifled a laugh. "I bought it from the store, and it's plastic, not glass." Apparently, plastic hadn't been invented yet.

"Extraordinary." He handed it back to her. "Why is it green?"

"Is it not supposed to be?"

He shook his head. "It's clear when extracted from the plant."

"Hmm. Must be a marketing tactic."

His brow furrowed. "At any rate, it will prove most helpful."

"And I have a little food for the displaced who are hungry."

"Very good."

But was it? She could have sworn her mission was to stop the Great Fire, but she'd obviously failed at that. Maybe if she hadn't been in jail, she could have caught it at the first sparks and doused the *White Cloud* before the fire had a chance to spread. Then again, her firefighting skills had proven abysmal. Chances were, she wouldn't have been able to stop it even if she'd been there at just the right time.

Maybe stopping the fire wasn't the mission. Maybe providing aid to those in need afterward was. Could history have called out to her because she carried aloe vera in her purse? Ludicrous. Far too small of an impact. But what could her true mission be?

She puffed out her cheeks. "Let's go." No use sitting here doing nothing. She wouldn't return to her children by lounging on a bench.

He narrowed one eye. "If you're sure you're up to it." With a grunt, he picked up her cooler and suitcase.

She nearly told him the suitcase could roll, but she stopped herself, not ready for him to marvel at that technology. She slung her purse over her shoulder. "Ready as I'll ever be."

Except she wasn't prepared. Not to see the destruction in broad daylight. The burned hulls of twenty-three boats gleamed in the sun. The acrid scent of smoke still overpowered the air. She hurried past Dr. Duncan to a commotion at the riverfront and sucked in a breath as her shoe sank into a slimy substance nearly up to her knee.

Dr. Duncan wrinkled his nose. "Grease from the lard and bacon." He had to walk nearly a block to sidestep it.

Her stomach lurched. The grease must have been two feet deep. She clomped through the sludge. When finally free of it, she shook her feet, but it did little to extricate the residue. If only she'd minded her own business. A group of men pulled a burned, broken body from the *White Cloud*'s wreckage. Burned beyond recognition. A man or a woman? No telling. She looked away, hiding her face in her hands. A memory slammed into her. Identifying Adam's body. Burned. Scarred. Broken.

Bile climbed her throat. She was going to be sick.

She stumbled forward a few steps, knees shaking.

Dr. Duncan came up beside her again and steered her in the opposite direction. "Oh, look, it's Miles. I've been meaning to introduce you two."

"Miles?"

In the distance stood a muscular young man. Very young. Aiden's age? Ash covered him from head to toe, making him almost look black, except for a stripe across his forehead, likely where a hat used to be.

Dr. Duncan lowered his voice. "Miles Sutton is a time sailor too."

She perked up. "Really?"

His gaze roamed their surroundings. "We can't talk about it here. Let's see if he needs assistance."

They neared where Miles and others hauled blackened wreckage from charred ships out of muddy-brown waters. Miles's eyes lit up when his gaze landed on Dr. Duncan. "Heya, Doc!" He wiped beads of sweat from his forehead, then wiped his palm on his dirty pants.

"Miles, this is Marina."

She nodded a greeting, and he returned it in kind.

Dr. Duncan lifted his brows. "You two have much in common."

"She's a—" Miles snapped his mouth shut.

Dr. Duncan rocked onto his heels. "A fellow traveler."

"Welcome to St. Louis, Miss Marina. What's left of it." He frowned.

She counteracted it with a smile. "I have no doubt it will be a thriving city again someday soon."

He nodded. "You're right. I shouldn't grow so discouraged." Turning his attention to Dr. Duncan, he asked, "You heard about Captain Targee, didn't you?"

"Yes. Poor man. A tragedy." Dr. Duncan's gaze fell as he shook his head. "A shame."

"Who?" Marina looked back and forth between the men.

"Head of the Missouri Company," Miles explained.

Ah, another volunteer firefighter.

"Suggested blowing up surrounding buildings to create a firebreak," Dr. Duncan said.

"He hoisted a barrel of gunpowder onto his shoulder and ran into the music store, only to be blown to bits." Miles winced. "They found his head nearly a block away."

Marina gasped. How awful.

"He gave up his life to save the city. A martyr of sorts." Dr. Duncan's eyes misted.

"A true hero." Miles sighed. "At any rate, can I help you with something?"

Marina clasped her hands together to keep from smoothing down an errant strand of hair near Miles's forehead. Aiden always hated it when she did that to him. Miles reminded her so much of her son that a pang shot through her. How was Aiden? Did he miss her? Was he thinking about her even now? Not likely, but she could hope.

Once again, she forced a semblance of a smile. "Actually, we're here to help you."

He tilted his head quizzically.

"Is anyone around here in need of treatment for burns? Or food?"

He held out his arm. Underneath the grime lay an angry red welt.

She held back a cringe. "Let's get that cleaned up and treated with aloe." Wasn't there a small travel washcloth somewhere in her purse? She dug through the mess, found it, and held it up. "Where can we find clean water?"

Miles's face brightened. "You're like Mary Poppins."

She nearly laughed in delight at the reference to something ahead of this time. "You have no idea."

"Who?" Dr. Duncan asked.

Miles chuckled. "Never mind."

As she treated his burn, she held back questions about whether he had a passion for being a first responder, like Aiden. She couldn't stand to know. Dangerous work. She shuddered. Best not to think of her new acquaintance rushing into perilous situations.

Over the next two hours, Marina and Miles helped Dr. Duncan treat burn victims. They also managed to share all her non-produce food with those whose houses had burned down. The children staring at her with wide, soulful eyes broke her heart. Goldfish crackers and Teddy Grahams had them gasping in awe and drew a delighted chuckle from Miles.

He lowered his voice, directing his words to her alone. "I used to love those as a kid."

"My teenage son still enjoys them."

The look they shared over those modern snacks sang with camaraderie. Funny how such a simple thing could thicken the bond between the time sailors.

When most of her snacks and aloe ran out, Miles headed back toward the docks. She looked around at the blackened, gutted buildings. Ash covered the street. Remnants of torn clothing and broken dishes lay in heaps here and there. How could so much change in a matter of hours? A familiar question haunted her. It was the same question she'd asked herself after Adam died. One minute, she had an intact, happy family. The next minute left her a widow and single mother struggling to connect with her grieving children. One never knew how fast life could change.

A pathetic whine stole her attention. A bedraggled basset hound with a coat of what surely used to be white fur looked up at her and whimpered. Her hand flew to her heart. Frankie? Could dogs time travel too? She bent down and scratched the pup under his chin. Hmm … one of his ears was larger than the other. Couldn't be Frankie. But man, if it didn't make her miss Brinley's prized dog.

"Hi, sweetie. You're so cute. Are you hungry?" She had nothing left but a few Goldfish crackers. She placed them in her hand and stretched them out to the dog, who scarfed them down. "Poor baby. You're starving."

Dr. Duncan came up beside her. "A stray, I take it?"

She shrugged. It had no collar, but had those even been invented yet? "I assume some animals were displaced right along with their owners. Someone might be looking for him." Too bad she couldn't upload a picture of him to the lost animals Facebook group. How did one go about finding a lost dog in the 1800s? "I'll keep an eye on him for now." She'd do it for Brinley. A small way to remain connected to her daughter across time.

Dr. Duncan's blank expression didn't reveal how he felt about the idea. "You must be exhausted. Let's find a boardinghouse that didn't succumb to the fire."

Exhausted didn't begin to describe it. How long had it been since she'd slept? Time had melted together since she left the boat. The boat that no longer existed. The bridge of her nose burned as she blinked back tears.

"How am I supposed to get home now? Without the boat?"

Home. Their cozy four-bedroom in modern-day with its gas fireplace and cabinets full of corny mugs. Silverware drawer forever devoid of spoons. Brinley's music vibrating through the walls. Aiden's dirty socks littering the hardwood floors. The mirage beckoned her to return, but how?

"You don't need the same vessel to return. You only need to be on water."

"But have I accomplished my mission yet? Was I supposed to help fire victims? Or is there something else I need to do?"

"You'll know when you complete your mission. The water will call out to you. An irresistible force." His mouth twisted into a scowl. "Well, nearly irresistible. Miles managed to fight it."

Or did he miss it? The waters calling to him. What did that even look like? She didn't trust herself to know, to be in tune to some magical siren call from the water. If only she could ask Claire more questions about how it all worked.

The fire had destroyed the mailbox, severing the only link to her children and Claire. It hit her like a punch to the gut, the sudden yearning for familiar faces. Aiden. Brinley.

She followed Dr. Duncan with dragging steps past blocks of debris until they entered a section of the city untouched by last night's disaster. Her newfound furry companion didn't need much coaxing to join her. A simple click of her tongue and "Come here, boy," did the trick. He probably hoped for more food. "I'll find you more to eat soon." What she would feed him remained a mystery. Had bagged dog food been invented yet?

"Ah, Miss Woodhouse's place was spared. I'll go in and inquire if she has a vacancy." He walked up the elongated steps of a towering brick home with matching turrets on both sides. Shrubbery lined the walkway. Vines wove through the metal balcony railings above the rounded archway hosting the front door. The house stood in stark contrast to the wooden shambles mere blocks away. Brick. A far wiser building choice. Remnants of a song she used to sing in Sunday school flitted into her mind. *The wise man builds his house upon the rock.* Where had that memory come from? Regardless, it made sense.

A few minutes later, Dr. Duncan emerged from the stately building. "She has one room left." He came and carried her suitcase and empty cooler to the front door.

The pup panted at her feet. She gave him another scratch behind the ears. "Will she allow a dog?"

"Not usually, but considering the circumstances, she'll make an exception."

Good. The two of them could comfort each other as she waited for whatever would come next. Her throat burned as she swallowed down self-pity. She would not—could not—break down. Giving in to a wave of emotion wouldn't help her discover her mission. And she *had* to discover it. Soon.

Dr. Duncan tipped his hat to her as he turned to leave.

"Wait," she called out.

He turned.

"How am I supposed to get ahold of you? What if I need you for something?" He might be a crummy guide, but he was all she had.

"You'll find me when you need me."

She nearly growled at his cryptic answer. Not an answer at all. Did he expect her to simply trust this crazy process? Fat chance. Trust didn't come easily for her in normal circumstances. And this? Far from normal.

Frankie II's whine redirected her gaze away from Dr. Duncan's retreating form. "Okay, buddy. Let's go in and come up with a plan."

As soon as Claire put the car in park in front of the pet boarding place, Brinley jumped out and ran in the front door. "Guess she really misses her dog," Claire mumbled.

"She's been super worried." Aiden exited the car at a normal pace.

Wow. This wasn't just a standard kennel. It was a pet hotel. The sign in the window boasted large suites with raised beds and TVs. Access to a swimming pool and all-day play. Talk about pampering.

Claire fell into step beside him. "After we pick Frankie up, I was planning on dropping you guys off at your house for a bit. You can grab whatever you need for an extended stay in Michigan, plus supplies for Frankie."

He shrugged. "Sure."

Well, that was an easy sell. Claire opened the front door, and they entered.

Brinley stood at the front desk. "But I don't have a credit card. Didn't my mom prepay for everything?"

The receptionist shuffled through papers, then waved her hands as though flustered. "It says here she paid the deposit and would pay the rest upon pickup."

Claire came and stood next to Brinley. "Did Mrs. Stone leave a card on file?"

The receptionist shook her head. "The record states she paid the deposit in cash."

Brinley's mouth twisted. "That's right. I remember now."

"What do we owe you?" Claire nearly winced at the use of *we*. She didn't owe them anything. She'd gone out of her way to come and get the dog. She sure didn't have money to pay for his boarding. But what choice did they have? Hopefully, Marina would pay her back when she returned.

"Six hundred and fifty-two dollars."

Holy moly.

"Couldn't my mom pay you later?" Brinley hugged herself.

"I have almost a hundred and fifty dollars in my account. Can you take a rain check for the rest?" Aiden asked.

The receptionist's mouth puckered. "We cannot release the animal to you with an outstanding balance."

Brinley's breaths came short and shallow.

Claire put a hand on her shoulder. "It's okay. I'll lend you the money. Your mom can pay me back." She retrieved a credit card from her purse. The credit card they'd only recently paid off. The one they'd sworn never to use again. She'd nearly cut it up, but Bearett had insisted she keep it on her in case of emergencies. Like if her car broke down. What would he say about her using it now? What choice did she have?

"Thank you." Brinley's response came as a choked whisper.

"No problem."

A few minutes after the receptionist swiped Claire's card, a woman with short, cropped hair brought Frankie to them.

Brinley took him in her arms and smothered him with kisses. "How's my baby? How's my sweet boy?"

Frankie lay limply in Brinley's arms, emitting a whine, followed by a cough.

The woman offered a sad smile. "I suspect it's the dog flu, but a vet will be able to tell you for sure."

A vet. Another expense. How would they afford the monthly credit card payment, much less pay off this balance? Worry wrapped around her chest, squeezing. *Oh, Lord, You are my provider. Surely, You'll supply this need.* She needed to trust Him and move forward in love. "I'll make an appointment for tomorrow at the vet by my house."

Brinley snuggled her face on the dog's floppy ears.

"If that's all, we best be going." She had a lunch date with Wendy in forty minutes.

The woman handed Claire Frankie's crate and leash. "Come again."

"Fat chance," Aiden murmured.

Twenty minutes later, Claire pulled up outside the Stones' modest split-level home. Its blue siding and front flower bed gave a peaceful feel. As if all it needed was a white picket fence, and it'd be the epitome of perfection for an ideal family. One would never guess the heartache it housed.

"I'll come pick you up in about two hours. I'll text when I'm on my way."

The teens shuffled out of the car without a word, Frankie still cradled in Brinley's arms. She watched them until they were safely inside.

"Thanks so much for driving all this way, Claire. We appreciate you. You're the best," Claire murmured to herself. She probably shouldn't expect teenagers to show gratitude, but it'd be nice to receive at least some appreciation. Well, Brinley had thanked her for paying. That was something. Why didn't it seem like enough?

On the drive to The Screaming Peach, she called Bearett and updated him. She didn't mention the credit card charge. No need to worry him. He'd find out soon.

Claire pulled into a metered parking space outside The Screaming Peach and paid. Other restaurants and shops lined the city block. The scent of burgers, seafood, and Indian spices mingled in the air. Only a few shoppers strolled the patterned sidewalks. A flower box in front of the restaurant boasted a few red canna lilies.

Wendy waited for her at an outside table shaded by a red umbrella. The wind whipped her curly hair into her face. She waved and half stood when her gaze landed on Claire.

Claire rushed to her friend and wrapped her in an embrace. "It's so good to see you. I've missed you so much."

"Ditto." Wendy hugged back, infusing strength into her. "You look great." She pulled back and studied Claire. "You're glowing."

Claire's hands flew to her cheeks. "Really?"

"Wait." Wendy's eyes narrowed. "You're not pregnant, are you?"

She hadn't meant for the news to tumble out like this, but … "I am."

Another hug. "Oh, my goodness. How exciting! I'm ecstatic for you."

The two sat. Claire tried to smile.

"What? Are you not happy?"

"I want to be."

"But …" Wendy eyed her.

"I'm scared."

Wendy burst into laughter, then covered her mouth. "Sorry. I'm horrible. I'm not making fun of you, I promise."

"Oookay …"

"It's just, welcome to motherhood, dearie."

"Oh, that's comforting."

A waitress approached and took their orders. Upon her recommendation, Claire ordered the harvest peach salad. Wendy, a burger and fries.

Wendy continued once the waitress left. "I meant, no one has this gig figured out. Trust me, we're all winging it."

"You're making things worse."

Wendy placed her hand on top of Claire's. "No, it's comforting." She squeezed, then took a drink of her water. "You're not behind or lost or anything. At least, not any more than anyone else. I don't know how people do this parenting thing without Jesus. I have to rely on Him for everything. Everything. But the good news is He's there, walking with us, giving us strength and courage and wisdom."

"Okay, but you're a teacher. You have some kind of gene that makes you naturally good with kids. I don't have that gene. Plus, I didn't have amazing parents. I'm flying blind here."

"Didn't you hear anything I said?"

Claire huffed out a breath. "I heard you but—"

"Girl, God's got you. He's going to lead you through this."

Claire buried her head in her hands.

"And, for the record, I'm not a teacher anymore."

Claire snapped her head up. "What?"

"I quit. I had every intention of returning after Layla was born, but my heart wasn't in it anymore. Everything I want and need is at home. Bryce will turn two next month. I have two incredible children, and I want to spend as much time with them as possible."

"But you loved your job."

She shrugged. "I did. It was a wonderful season. Now, the season has changed."

How could someone give up their career like that? Claire could never. Not fully. Not for an extended period of time. But things *would* change when the baby came. What would life look like?

She pictured Aiden and Brinley absorbed in their phones with her surrounded by silence. "Things aren't going great with the teens."

"How so?"

Claire gave Wendy a rundown of the past week. "I can't seem to make them happy."

One corner of Wendy's mouth lifted. "Good thing that's not your job."

"What *is* my role, then? How can I be a good parent if I can't keep an eye on two teenagers for a couple of weeks?"

Wendy tented her fingers on the table. "Love isn't about giving someone everything they want. It'd be a disaster if God did that with us. Love gives what is best for that person, whether they like it or not. You've got to be unmovable, rooted and grounded in love, as Scripture says. If they appreciate what you're doing, you love them. If they throw a hissy fit, you love them. It won't always feel good, but it *is* good. Love never fails."

"So, you're saying …"

"Don't let them walk all over you. Don't bend over backward to win their approval. God's opinion is the only one you need to be concerned about."

If only she could hear Him clearly. Wendy made it sound easy.

Their food arrived, and the two continued chatting between bites. How wonderful to spend time with someone who'd known her for years, through highs and lows, and loved her anyway. She winced as she checked her watch. "I need to go. The teens will be waiting on me, and we have a long drive ahead of us."

"You're free to stay the night at our place."

"Thanks, but we need to get back." Before Marina returned. Which could be any minute or … days? Weeks? Heavens, no. But when she did get back, they had to be there, waiting for her.

~

Once Aiden finished packing, he wandered the house. How strange for Mom not to be here. She was always home. Always hovering. And now …

Brinley sat in the recliner, Frankie in her lap. A sitcom played in the background, but she didn't seem to be paying attention. Instead, she scrolled Instagram. Aiden threw some pizza rolls in the oven and continued to meander aimlessly.

He ended up in the hallway, looking at pictures. Each of their school photos were displayed in golden frames, from pre-K on. Aiden's on the top, Brinley's on the bottom. Cheesy smiles. Until the last couple of ones, which displayed stiff smiles and dull eyes. Dad's death had snuffed the life out.

He came to their last family picture. Dad and Mom beamed. He'd smiled more from the promise of ice cream afterward. No matter. The photographer had captured a perfect family. Happy. Together. Whole.

Aiden clenched his fingers into a fist and punched the wall next to the picture. It wasn't fair. He needed his father. It wasn't supposed to be this way.

"What the heck?" Brinley appeared next to him with Frankie in her arms. "You scared the dog."

"Sorry."

"Feel better?" She lifted a brow.

The half-moon of cracked plaster mocked him. Broken. Just like them. "No."

The timer went off. He stomped to the kitchen and slid the pizza rolls out of the oven, placing the pan on the kitchen island.

Brinley set Frankie on the couch and blew on a roll before biting into it. "Hey, Mom's not home. We can explore Dad's office."

She was right. What a perfect opportunity to spend time in a place Mom had declared off-limits. "Yeah. Okay."

Aiden's heart pounded as he creaked open the office door. What if they found some secret? A letter addressed to them or … no, certainly not evidence of a double life. But when he flipped on the light, the sight that greeted them was clean and kempt. Almost sterile. No papers littering his desk. No pictures adorning the walls. No lingering smell of his cologne.

"Mom must have purged everything." Brinley set Frankie down and opened desk drawers. "Empty. They're all empty."

"It's like she erased him from the whole house. You'd think she'd leave this room untouched." He ran a finger across the desk. Only the faintest trace of dust.

Brinley crossed her arms. "Why doesn't she want us in here if there's nothing of his here?"

"No clue." Man, he missed Dad. If only there was a place he could feel free to remember the good times. This office could be a showcase for Dad's memory.

"I don't get it. Don't get her." She plopped into the desk chair and spun back and forth.

"Yeah. I can't figure her out." She had to have her reasons, right? He'd burst a blood vessel trying to figure out what they were.

From his back pocket, his phone chimed. Nevaeh? He took it out and stared at the screen. It was Stacy.

> Just drove by your house and saw a light on. You must be back. Can you come over?

A fresh, full breath entered his lungs. She wanted him to come over? Why?

"What is it?" Brinley asked.

"Stacy invited me over. Do you think she wants to get back together?" This could be what he'd been hoping for.

Brinley blinked back at him. "Maybe, but what about Nevaeh?"

He shook her question off. Stacy lived just down the street. Nevaeh lived a world away. She didn't even want a relationship with him, as far as he could tell. Stacy was here and now. And everything he'd set his future on.

"I'm going over there. See you later." His fingers grazed the broken plaster fist hole on the way out.

Chapter Fourteen

Marina fed Frankie II a few scraps of meat Miss Woodhouse had given her and scratched him behind the ears. The filthy hound tilted his head to the side and leaned into her touch, thumping his leg on the bed. Adorable. She'd never been much of a dog person. That was Brinley's thing, not hers. Yet, this stray tethered her heart to her daughter. How could she not love him?

"We've got to figure out our mission, boy. What do you think it could be?" Of course, there was a possibility she'd already accomplished it. She'd aided burn victims as well as displaced people. Dr. Duncan had told her that in order to return to her time, she needed to be on water. Perhaps she could use the rest of her money to board another steamboat, one not destroyed in the fire.

And go where?

If that wasn't her mission, she'd be off to another destination. Hadn't fate deposited her in St. Louis for a reason? She wouldn't be here if her mission was somewhere else.

No, leaving posed too much of a risk. Assisting fire victims wasn't enough. Her mission had to be bigger.

Distant bells clanged. Likely another funeral. How many bells had tolled since she'd arrived? Thankfully, only three people had died from the fire. But there were so many dead and dying from cholera. And they thought vegetables were to blame. How backward.

What this city needed was a modern understanding of hygiene. They didn't get the importance of handwashing and germs. Or how vital clean water was. But she did. No wonder 1849 had called to her. She could save St. Louis from cholera.

All she needed to do was go to a hospital and explain to the doctors what she knew. Enlightened, they'd approach the epidemic differently. No need for hundreds, much less thousands more, to perish from this disease. It didn't torment society in modern times for a reason. Knowledge was power, and she held scores of it.

Fueled with a burst of energy, she changed into a clean *frock*—one Miss Woodhouse had lent her that didn't reek of smoke—and used the washbasin and a towel to scrub soot from her face. As she combed out her tangled hair, bits of ash rained onto the hardwood floor. She needed a hot bath, but this would have to do for now. She finally understood her mission and needed to hurry and accomplish it. Brinley. Aiden. Their faces floated in her memory. A perfect mix of both Adam and her. Oh, how she missed them. When she returned, she'd hug them long and hard, no matter how much they protested.

"Come on, Frankie. Let's go." A cluck of her tongue and he sidled up to her like she'd been his owner for years.

On her way out, she asked Miss Woodhouse where the nearest hospital was. Armed with directions, Marina scurried to the Sisters of Charity Hospital with Frankie II trotting at her side. The streets wept with an eerie silence. Though she was blocks from where the fire took place, the scent of charred wood lingered in the air. At least she wasn't close enough to the riverfront for the melted lard to turn her stomach. A wagon rumbled down the dirt street. Its driver's face sagged with a frown so deep it appeared permanent.

Marina looked away. No need to see dead bodies today. She'd had enough of death and destruction.

As she neared the corner of Fourth Street and Spruce Avenue, the three-story building with six massive white pillars in front came into view. A low fence surrounded the structure. How different it appeared from modern hospitals. If she didn't know better, she'd have assumed it an art museum or government building.

"You'll wait for me, won't you, boy?" The dog licked her outstretched hand. If only she didn't have to leave him, but no way would they allow a dog inside, especially one so filthy. "I'll be back as soon as I can."

Frankie II whined as she left him at the gate. Poor guy had grown attached to her already. The affection was mutual.

She opened the heavy wooden door and strode to a nun sitting behind a desk. Instead of the usual scarf-like head covering of a modern nun's habit, this woman wore a large white one on which the sides rose up and out like a bird in flight, turning her head into the shape of a *V*.

"May I help you?" The sister met her gaze with kind eyes, but dark bags hung under them.

"Hello. May I please speak with a doctor?"

The sister's brows rose. "Are you ill?"

"No. I have information a doctor might find useful. About cholera."

"You don't need to be admitted. You only came to chat?"

Marina's neck warmed. It sounded ridiculous when the nun said it. "Yes."

The sister's lips pursed as she studied Marina. "You must understand, our doctors are very busy, as are our nurses. We work around the clock, giving exceptional care."

"I *do* understand, but if there's any way I can snatch even a minute of someone's time. What I have to say will prove useful in treating your patients more efficiently."

A small grunt. "You can speak to Sister Francis Xavier Love. She's in her office now." The nun stood and motioned for Marina to follow her down the hall.

"But is Sister Xavier Love a medical professional? I really need to talk to a doctor."

The sister's steps slowed with deliberate clomps. "Did you know this is the first hospital to be run by women, as well as the first Catholic hospital in the United States?" She enunciated each word. "We've gained quite the reputation and have extensive experience."

Heat spread to Marina's earlobes. "I'm not questioning that. I only want—"

"You may speak to our hospital administrator, Sister Francis Xavier Love, or no one at all. Which do you prefer?"

Surely, this Francis nun was better than nothing. Marina bowed her head. "I'll speak with her. Thank you."

The front desk nun led her to a room where she knocked on the doorjamb. "Sister Francis, a … woman wishes to speak with you."

Marina peeked her head in.

Sister Francis sat behind a desk, wearing the same ridiculous hat. Stacks of papers filled both sides of her desk. She looked up, removed the wire-rimmed glasses from the bridge of her nose, and ran a finger across her forehead, as if to smooth out the deep crease there. "Very well."

Marina took a seat across from her. "Hello. Thank you for agreeing to meet with me. I won't take much of your time."

"How may I help you, Miss …?"

"Stone. Marina Stone."

"How may I help you, Miss Stone?"

Marina cleared her throat. "It's come to my attention that you … I mean, the medical community believes that vegetables are to blame for cholera. That's simply not true, not unless the vegetables are washed in unsanitary water. You see, there are these things called germs. Bacteria. And you can't see them with the naked eye, but they are what cause disease. The way to—"

"Excuse me, Miss Stone. Do I understand that you mean to inform *me* about the cause of cholera? Are you aware that we work tirelessly around the clock to treat these victims and that we've set up a hospital expressly for that purpose on Quarantine Island?"

"No, but … I mean, I am trying to inform you, but—"

"We have seen large, strong-bodied men suddenly struck and expire in a few hours, and before we could remove one corpse, a second, third, and fourth were ready. We've seen life after life expire before our eyes. I dare say, not many know more about this dreadful disease than our sisters."

"But the cause—"

"The cause, Miss Stone, is well-documented. The miasma theory states that cholera comes from bad air. St. Louis's swampy, unkempt streets and alleys full of rubbish contaminate the air. When people breathe it in, they become sick. The Committee of Public Health, though only just formed, plans to implement measures to remove waste from our streets and alleys, as well as drain flooded cellars and privies. We will do all we can to combat this plague and eradicate it from among us."

"I see how those sanitary measures would help, but there are other considerations. It's not caused by bad air, but by—"

"Where did you obtain your medical training, Miss Stone?"

She pursed her lips. "I don't have any training. However—"

"How many patients with cholera have you nursed?"

"I haven't, but—"

"Then I suggest you leave the care of our patients to those trained to do so." She picked up her glasses from the desk and perched them back onto the tip of her nose, then directed her attention to the papers in front of her.

Infuriating. If only Sister Francis would listen. Weren't nuns supposed to be the soft, compassionate types? This one grated with hard edges. Then again, didn't there used to be school-teaching nuns who would rap children's knuckles for the slightest infraction? Perhaps this sister should have gone into education.

Continuing to plead her case would waste her breath. Perhaps she could find someone to listen to her at a different hospital. "I'll see myself out." Her words came out sharp. Not the most respectful way to talk to a nun.

Sister Francis didn't even look up. "Good day, Miss Stone."

Marina marched out, steam fueling her steps. She'd find another hospital. She'd go to every medical building in the blasted city until someone took note. When she stepped into the muggy sunshine, Frankie II waited for her on the other side of the gate. At least, someone listened to her. She bent to pet his dirty fur. After this errand, she'd figure out a way to give him a bath.

All day long, she trekked from one hospital to another, each with similar results. Little attention given to what she had to say. Doctors and nurses touting "bad air" as the source of the problem. No matter how she attempted to explain bacteria, no one paid her any mind. Even when she dropped the whole germ theory thing and simply urged them to boil their water, they wrote her off. If they'd only listen …

The sun had begun to set by the time she and Frankie II trudged back to the boardinghouse. Her feet throbbed. How many steps had she walked today? Nearly the entire city's worth. The sweat that had trailed down her shoulder blades earlier in the day left a sticky residue. She needed a bubble bath. What were the chances Miss Woodhouse could provide one? That and some good, dark chocolate. Unfortunately, that was one thing she'd neglected to cram into her purse.

Maybe if she could have a good cry in a soothing bath with chocolate reinforcement at the ready, she'd be able to figure out what to do next. Because right now, it looked as though she'd be stuck in 1849 forever.

~

When Aiden walked through Stacy's front door, warm welcomes greeted him.

Her mom hugged him. "We've missed you around here."

Her dad clasped his hand. His dress shirt was rolled up to his elbows. "Good to see you, son." He gestured to the kitchen. "We're making ice cream. Want some?"

Did he ever. Dad used to make ice cream in his little churn. Nothing like it.

"Later, Dad." Stacy looped her arm through Aiden's. "We'll be in my room." She tugged him toward it.

Once inside, he surveyed the bedroom. Cheer posters everywhere. A picture of Stacy with her friends. Her shoes tucked underneath her bed. Everything neat and tidy. Odd how nothing much had changed on the walls, yet everything between them had.

Stacy turned to him and pleaded with her big blue eyes. "Look, I made a mistake. I never should have broken up with you."

Was this seriously happening? He'd dreamt that those exact words would come from her mouth. Too good to be true, and yet, this was real. He opened his mouth to speak, but no words came.

"I got scared of how close we were getting and panicked. It was dumb of me. I could never love anyone but you."

Suddenly, her arms wrapped around his neck, and her lips pressed against his. So familiar. He drank her in, and she melted against him. A perfect fit. Stacy. His forever. He moaned in delight, exploring her mouth with his. Oh, how he'd missed this.

Nevaeh's face flashed in his mind. Stupid thoughts. He deepened his kiss, clinging to Stacy, trying to push all visions of Nevaeh out of his mind. After all, she'd never expressed interest in dating him. Plus, she lived far away. Stacy was in his arms. Real. True. Solid. She wanted to be with him. He'd be an idiot to throw away a sure thing for a mirage.

They pulled away, breathless. She smiled up at him sweetly. "I missed that."

He leaned his forehead onto hers. "Me too."

Taking his hand, she swung their arms between them. "So, I was thinking you could help me study for my math test. Summer school sucks."

"Okay." They plopped onto the beanbags at the foot of her bed. She pulled out her textbook.

As he helped her through problems, worry pinched at the back of his mind. Did she only want to get back together with him for his brains? For what he could do for her?

If only he could ask, "Do you really love me or are you just using me?" But of course, he wouldn't dare. A true answer might kill him. So what if she was using him. Wasn't he doing the same to her? Did he truly love her, or did he only want to be with her because of the advantages her family offered? Best not to dwell on such questions. The answers wouldn't make him feel any better.

His stomach was so jumbled, when Stacy's mom came to offer them ice cream, he declined. Is this who he wanted to be? A guy who used his girlfriend to get what he wanted? But giving this relationship up would be ludicrous.

Stacy's mom entered again. This time, her hands were empty, and she shuffled her feet, avoiding eye contact with Aiden. "Stacy, Brad's on the landline. Said you weren't answering your cell." Brad Bonville. The creep who'd been all over Stacy in those pictures.

"Oh." Stacy chuckled nervously. "It's on silent." She stood, offering Aiden a sheepish smile. "I'll be right back."

Had she not ended it with him? Maybe she'd kept him in her back pocket in case Aiden hadn't responded as she'd hoped. She could be ending things with him now or—

His phone chimed. Brinley.

> Frankie seems worse. He's wheezing. I don't know what to do.

He stood and barreled out of the room, colliding with Stacy in the hallway. He put a hand on her arm to steady her.

"Where are you going?" What was that look washing over her face? Guilt?

"Frankie's sick. I need to get back to Brinley."

"Tell her to bring him here. Mom can take a look."

He folded his arms across his chest. "Your mom's a nurse, not a vet."

"Yeah, but she knows stuff. She can at least tell if it's an emergency."

"Okay." He fired off a text, then stared at his phone, waiting for a reply. A few minutes later, his phone lit up. "She's on her way." Good thing Stacy's house was just down the street.

"Great." Stacy took his hand, intertwining their fingers. "Are we good?" Those soulful eyes gazed up at him.

What could he say? Her mom was about to help their dog. He couldn't call their relationship off now. Did he want to call it off at all? No, but something didn't feel right. Like a pebble in his shoe, it rankled. What should he do?

~

Claire pulled up in front of the Stone residence and honked. Her lunch with Wendy had run longer than she'd anticipated. She covered a yawn. They needed to get a move on, or she'd fall asleep while driving. Pregnancy fatigue was a beast.

When no one came out, she knocked on the front door. No answer. Eerie quiet surrounded her. She tried the doorknob. Locked. Were they not here?

She retreated to her car and texted them both, asking where they were. Tapping her foot against the floorboard, she tried to quell her rising panic. She'd promised Marina she'd look after these guys, and she … what? Lost them?

A dozen scenarios flitted through her mind, from a kidnapping to them hiding out in the house, purposefully ignoring her. Did they not want to return to South Haven? Maybe they thought they'd be better off staying here. Maybe they were right.

She laid her head on the steering wheel, eliciting a honk. She startled, then tried again in a different spot. She was horrible at this. Wendy's words swirled around her heart, but she barred their entrance. The Lord might have perfect wisdom, but she certainly did not. She had to be defective, unable to hear and follow God's guidance.

Tears stung her eyes. *Lord, what do I do?*

No answer. See? Defective.

She called Wendy.

"Hey, what's up?" A baby fussed in the background.

"They're gone. What should I do?" At least her friend wouldn't respond with silence.

"Gone? As in …"

"As in they're not here."

"Did you call them?"

"Texted. I've never seen them talk on the phone. Only text."

"Try calling them. If they don't answer, I'd wait there for them to get back. Maybe they went on a walk or something."

A walk? Not likely with a sick dog. "Okay, I'll try." She so did not have time for this.

"Let me know what happens."

Both teens' phones went to voicemail. She left desperate-sounding messages. Pathetic. Rubbing her belly, she tried to imagine her baby as a teenager. Nearly impossible. What if this little bean one day ran away from home? How would she respond? The idea of her with a teenager was so preposterous, she couldn't fathom what it'd be like.

She sat in the silence for a few minutes. Slowly, her ears attuned to birds chirping, a breeze softly blowing, a dog barking in the distance. It wasn't silent at all. There was a host of soft sounds when she took time to listen.

An idea struck her. Maybe they'd posted an update on social media. Instagram might show where they were.

She didn't have the Instagram app on her phone anymore, so she used the browser and searched for their names. Her breath caught as a picture of Brinley holding Frankie appeared on her screen.

> Send Frankie your best wishes. I'm at the animal urgent care with him now.

In the picture's background, she made out the name Gateway Pet Urgent Care on a sign. She plugged it into her GPS and set out.

Was the idea to check Insta an answer from God? Had He given her wisdom? Perhaps just when she'd thought He was silent, He proved otherwise. She only had to be still enough to listen.

She arrived in less than ten minutes and strode up to the front desk, asking for Frankie the dog and the Stone children.

"I'm afraid there are already too many people back there, but you can have a seat in the waiting room."

She nodded and sat in a stiff plastic chair. At least she was in the right place. How had they gotten here? It was too far to walk. Had they driven in one of their cars? If they even had their own cars. She knew so little about them, as closed off as they'd been.

Two cats, one dog, and a hamster came through the doors before Brinley emerged with Frankie in her arms and Aiden right behind her. Another woman exited with them, curly blonde hair bobbing with her steps.

Claire jumped to her feet. "Guys, you scared me half to death. Why didn't you answer my texts or calls?"

Brinley's eyes went wide, as if she just remembered Claire existed. "Oh, sorry. I haven't checked my phone in a while."

"Me either," Aiden said. He had to be lying. Neither of them could go five minutes without checking their phones.

The curly blonde stepped forward and stuck out her hand. "Hi, I'm Bridgett. Stacy's mom."

Claire smiled like she knew what that meant and returned the handshake. "I'm Claire. I've been looking after Aiden and Brinley." That didn't sound right, but there didn't seem to be a better word. Babysitting sure didn't fit. "Their mom is on a … trip."

"Oh." A slight line appeared between her brows. "Nice to meet you."

"You as well." She turned her attention to the dog. "How's Frankie?"

Brinley nuzzled her cheek on the dog's fur. "He needed IV fluids, and the vet prescribed an anti-inflammatory and cough suppressant. He's going to be fine. Just needs to rest."

"Excuse me?" The receptionist waved at them from the front desk. "You can settle your bill here."

Bridgett looked from the receptionist to Claire and back again. "Well, I guess I'll head back home. I hope he feels better soon." She hugged Aiden. "And I hope to see you around more often. We've missed you."

The corner of Aiden's mouth twitched. "Thanks for your help."

"No problem." She waved at Brinley and Claire, then left.

Guess she didn't want to get stuck with the bill. As if Claire did. Sighing, she made her way to the front desk. "How much do we owe you?"

The receptionist consulted her computer. "Four hundred and fifty-two dollars."

Claire coughed. "Any chance you could put it on their mom's tab?"

The woman shook her head. "Sorry, no. Will you be paying by cash or card today?"

"Card." Claire slid the credit card across the counter. These kids were breaking her bank account. Marina had better reimburse her. She bit the inside of her cheek. That was a selfish thought. No telling what Marina had to endure in 1849. Claire needed to drum up some compassion and stop worrying about finances.

"Thanks for paying." Brinley's voice was uncharacteristically soft.

"No problem." A small lie.

A glance at her watch showed it was nearly five o'clock. Her vision blurred as she returned her card to her wallet. There was no way she could drive six hours tonight.

As they left, she said, "I'm going to call my friend Wendy and see if we can stay the night at her house. We can drive back in the morning."

Brinley cast her a look that said *Seriously? We have to stay with more strangers.* "Why can't we crash at our house?"

"I don't feel comfortable sleeping at your home without your mom's permission. And I'm not leaving you there by yourselves." Not after what had just happened. "You'll like Wendy. She's a middle school teacher." *Was* a teacher. Crazy to think of Wendy not doing the thing it seemed like she was born to do.

"Fine." Brinley sighed.

At least Aiden didn't protest. "Okay, but I left the bag I packed at home. We'll have to run by and get it."

"Sure." But she wouldn't let them out of her sight again.

Chapter Fifteen

Marina sat at Miss Woodhouse's table, shoveling beef stew into her mouth. She hadn't realized how hungry she was until the savory aroma hit her nostrils. No breakfast. No lunch. No wonder she was famished. After a day of pleading with a host of people who wouldn't listen, what a relief to pile her burdens onto Miss Woodhouse's willing shoulders.

"The first person I talked to was a nun at that Sisters of Charity Hospital. She wouldn't even let me get a word in. Kept cutting me off. So rude." She spoke around a potato chunk. *Ugh.* Now who was the one who lacked manners? Frankie II whined by her feet. She slipped him a piece of beef, then wiped her fingers on a napkin.

"That must have been frustrating for you." Miss Woodhouse rested her folded hands upon the table, her gray bun far looser than it'd been that morning. "However, I can't help but think of how overworked and weary those sisters must be. First with cholera, then with the fire. It'd be a wonder if they've gotten a good night's sleep in ages. They truly have advanced medical opportunities in this city, and they've proven that women can be competent nurses."

Marina's chewing slowed. Had that truly been up for debate? Most nurses she encountered were female. Did males use to dominate the field?

"Truly remarkable to see women working outside the home. Only the ones without families to tend to, of course."

"Of course." She hadn't just stepped back into a different year. She'd stepped into an entirely different paradigm.

"I hope you will give the sisters some grace."

The gentle rebuke stung like rubbing alcohol to a scrape. Not fun, but probably needed. She'd rushed to judgment and hadn't considered the hospital workers' circumstances or predicaments. She washed down another bite of stew with a glass of tepid water, then winced. What if the water here was contaminated? Too bad she didn't have any more bottled beverages in her cooler.

Miss Woodhouse stood and took Marina's bowl. "What are your plans for tomorrow, dear? Do you intend to visit more hospitals?"

Marina shook her head. No way would she waste her time like that again. "I think I'll try to track down Dr. Duncan. See if I can be of any assistance." Maybe he would listen to her, knowing she was from the future.

"Splendid idea. I'll have Ida bring a washtub to your room and fill it up so you can have a bath."

Could the woman read her mind? Marina offered prayer hands. "Thank you. You're a godsend." The phrase slipped out before Marina could consider whether she believed it or not. Did God send gifts to people? More likely, there were all kinds of characters in the world. Some mean-spirited, some kind. She'd happened upon a kind one.

After a warm bath—no bubbles, but at least soap—Marina bathed Frankie II, then settled beneath her sheet and sank into slumber. The next morning, she felt like a new woman, ready to face the world and find her mission. Surely, Dr. Duncan knew more than he'd let on before. He'd help her figure things out. Only, where could she find him? He acted like her intuition would lead her right to him, but he gave her far too much credit. Perhaps she should take a nap and attempt to dream-summon him again.

Miss Woodhouse suggested asking some of the druggists if they'd seen him. Armed with the names and addresses of several, she set out with Frankie II at her side.

What gorgeous homes sat on Miss Woodhouse's block. Were any of them available to tour in modern-day? There was something impressive about buildings in this era, the ones that didn't burn down. The ones made of brick. Stately with exquisite detail on the pillars. Rounded balconies. Stained glass windows.

At the fourth house down, her steps stalled. On the front door hung a wreath. Red ribbon intertwined the branches. What used to surely be fresh sprigs of holly drooped, wilted and listless. Was this wreath left over from Christmas? Perhaps the owners had meant to take it down with the changing seasons, but tragedy distracted them.

Marina used to love making and decorating wreaths. She'd gotten quite good at it, selling her creations at craft fairs, earning spending money that she, of course, spent at craft stores. That seemed so long ago. Another life. Her before-children life. When Aiden and Brinley came along, her entire trajectory had shifted. But that creative spark … Did it still lie dormant inside her? Perhaps it could be resurrected with a simple project. A painted pot. A spool of ribbon. A wreath.

She shook her head, dislodging such impractical thoughts. Her mission. She had to focus on her mission, on things that truly mattered.

On to the drugstores.

The staff at Edwards and Francis drugstore hadn't a clue where Dr. Duncan was, and neither did those at D. Moritmore or L. Wesbrooks. But at the Canton tea store, she found him at the counter, purchasing Dr. Cannon's cholera preventative.

His gaze swept from the druggist to Marina. "Miss Stone, how do you do today?" Apparently, he wasn't surprised she'd found him. He probably thought it her intuition, not Miss Woodhouse's hand-drawn map.

"I feel much better after a hot bath."

"Well and good." He neared the doorway. "Walk with me for a spell?"

"Yes, please." She had so much she wanted to ask him. Mystery shrouded her future. How ever could she get home?

He gestured for her to precede him outside, then they moseyed toward the riverfront. "I'm bringing this to Miles. You met him, remember?"

The sweet teen who reminded her so much of Aiden. How could she forget? "Yes. You said he time-sailed here?"

"Indeed." Displeasure dripped from his tone.

"When did he arrive? Prior to me, I'm guessing."

"Much."

"Much?" Her steps slowed. "Has he been unable to complete his mission?" She braced herself for an answer she didn't want to hear. How long would she remain stuck in 1849?

"He's not unable. He's unwilling."

"Huh?" She hurried to catch up to his long stride.

"He refuses to return to his time. Says he has nothing to go back for."

"You can do that? Stay in the past?" A shudder slipped through her as they passed what appeared to be the last undamaged house before entering the district ravaged by fire. It was like entering a war zone. Blackened brick. Pieces of splintered wood scattered here and there. Inches of ash swirling in the street with each breeze. A chipped China cup lay on its side next to a gutted building.

Dr. Duncan stopped abruptly, and Marina nearly tripped over her own feet. Frankie II scrambled to a stop as well, cocking his head at her.

"A time sailor must be on the water to return. Miles doesn't wish to return, so he refuses to go on the water." He ran a hand through his already disheveled hair. "I can't seem to talk sense into the young man. Perhaps you could try."

Her? Why would he listen to a stranger? More importantly, "Why doesn't he want to go back?" Perhaps he loved this foul-smelling city. She wrinkled her nose. Not likely.

"Both of his parents, as well as his sweetheart, perished in his current time. Something about a building collapsing. A terrorist attack, he said."

Marina gasped. "Nine-eleven?"

He frowned. "Sounds familiar. Whatever that means." He waved a hand and resumed walking. "I wish every time sailor would restrain themselves and not tell me of the future. It's dangerous, you know. Giving me information that could change history. Some people can't seem to help themselves, despite the possible consequences."

She sucked in the side of her cheek. Dangerous? Surely, it wouldn't hurt anyone to enlighten him about cholera. Such information could only help mankind.

But back to Miles. "So, Miles lost everyone he cared about in his time and then time-sailed here. And he wishes to stay?" How tragic.

"That sums it up."

She didn't blame him. And Dr. Duncan wanted her to persuade the poor guy otherwise. But why? If he was happy here, and his time would only bring him heartache, why would Dr. Duncan care if he chose to stay?

As though he could read her mind, Dr. Duncan said, "Time sailors belong on the water. They need a vessel like they need air."

"But why? Why can't Miles make a happy life here?"

Dr. Duncan growled. "Blast it, Miss Stone. That's the way of it. The way of a time sailor. If he wishes to stay here, for the rest of his life, he must never step upon any boat, whether large or small. He lives right next to a river, but he can't partake of it. What kind of life is that?"

A dry one, apparently. But it couldn't be that hard to stay off boats. Had trains been invented yet? If not, travel would prove difficult. But one could have a satisfying life without ever leaving home. If she didn't have Aiden and Brinley to think of, she might consider the same thing.

"Please, Miss Stone. Attempt to reason with the young man. It's not proper for him to remain here. He knows too much. Many people could get hurt through his knowledge."

Oh, so that was it. If Miles slipped up and told others about the future, it could mess up some kind of time continuum.

He stopped again, brought his face close to hers, eyes wide. "He could perish."

"Perish?" Was he being overdramatic for emphasis?

"If a time sailor alters history books, they perish in both times. At least, that's what I've been told." He shook his head. "I've never lost a time sailor. I don't intend to start now."

"Who told you that?" Maybe his source was unreliable.

"It's a story for another time. But I implore you not to test it."

Her scalp prickled. That meant if she changed history, she would … die? What would happen to Aiden and Brinley? It didn't make sense. "How can I complete a mission if I can't change history?"

"History *books*, Miss Stone. History books. Each time sailor's mission changes someone's life or perhaps the lives of several in a family. But they can't change major events. No actions that change cities or people groups. The waters will rise against them if they come close to doing so."

Her jaw unhinged. "What? The waters will rise against them?" And that meant …?

"They will perish in the waters' wrath." His straight face didn't crack in the least. He must not be joking.

Which meant if she *had* managed to stop the Great St. Louis Fire, or even come close, she would have died. She rubbed her clavicle. It was all so unreal. She'd been in danger and hadn't had a clue. She should have listened to Claire. Thank goodness for those tomatoes. They landed her in jail before the waters' wrath—whatever that meant—could take her life.

"I don't get it. I've got to make a difference in this time to go back to my life, but if I make too much of a difference, I die. Can't you give me some clue about what I'm supposed to do?"

He pinched the bridge of his nose. "I can't tell you your mission."

"So you've said. You don't know what it is. I don't either. Apparently, I'm supposed to guess. Only if I guess wrong, I'm a goner." She flung her hands in the air. "How is any of this fair?"

"Every time sailor is led toward his or her mission, Miss Stone. It's not guesswork."

"Led? By who?" Her gaze whipped around the blackened streets. "I don't see anyone leading me. Except for you, and you're leading me right into a brick wall."

"Time sailors are led by the Time Holder."

"Oh, good. That's something. Can you take me to him? Or is he like the Wizard of Oz?"

Dr. Duncan's forehead bunched. "Who? There's no wizardry involved, I assure you."

Right. What else was she supposed to attribute this crazy time-traveling fiasco to?

"Please, Miss Stone, speak to Miles. Urge him to get back to the water. For his own safety."

At Frankie II's whine, she bent to scratch the pup behind his ears. If Miles died and she could have done something to prevent it … wait. Maybe *that* was her mission. Convince Miles to return to his time. Save this teenager. Perhaps 1849—or the Time Holder—called her because she was a mom of a teen boy. Sure, she hadn't had much success talking sense into her own children. But maybe this was a second chance.

She straightened and met Dr. Duncan's steely gaze. "I'll talk to him."

~

Aiden scarfed down the meat loaf Wendy had served as he listened to Claire and her friend tell the story of Stella, their former college roommate, disappearing while on a cruise. Stella's mission had been to get some runaway slaves to safety. What was Mom's mission? Maybe she didn't even know, because if she'd accomplished it, she'd be back already.

What if she'd returned while they were gone?

"So, you both met your future husbands on that cruise?" Brinley asked.

"Yep." The two friends exchanged a look, then grinned.

"That settles it. If I end up old, like late twenties, and I'm unmarried, I'm going on a cruise."

Wendy snorted. "I wouldn't recommend it as a way to meet a great guy. It just sort of happened for us. But there are a lot of creeps too."

Another knowing look exchanged.

"Huge creeps." Claire's lips pressed into a thin line.

There must be a story behind that, but Aiden wouldn't ask. He had too many other things occupying his mind. Stacy wanted him back. Her family was amazing. He always felt welcome at their home. Her dad understood his passion for police work. And Stacy … well, he liked kissing her. But if he was honest with himself, she came in second to her family. And what was with her and Brad?

"And then they served a mermaid tail on a platter," Wendy said.

He nodded.

She waved a hand in front of his face. "Hey, there. You didn't hear a word I said, did you? You zoned out."

"Oh." He scrubbed his hand over his face. "Sorry. A lot on my mind."

"Girl troubles." Brinley munched on another piece of garlic bread.

Claire pointed her fork at her friend. "Wendy's quite adept at helping teens navigate relationships."

Wendy rolled her eyes. "Oh, stop."

Aiden put his hands out. "I don't have girl troubles. It's kind of the opposite."

"Two girls to choose from. Whatever will he do?" Brinley teased.

The question wasn't really about which girl he wanted more, but about who he wanted to be—the guy in Stacy's pictures, while they both used each other, or the guy who opened himself up to Nevaeh and her faith. "I think I know what I need to do. I just need the guts to do it."

He excused himself from the table and made his way to the guest bedroom Wendy had offered him. Well, really it was the baby's room with an inflatable mattress on the floor, but at least he had it all to himself. Wendy said the baby would sleep in a Pack 'N Play in her room for the night. He needed silence to think. Maybe even pray.

Yeah, he should pray. That's what Nevaeh would do. But how? Wasn't there some prayer you were supposed to recite?

He texted Nevaeh.

How do you pray?

Then, he dropped his head into his hands. Stupid question. She was going to think him an idiot.

Just talk to God like you would a friend. You don't need fancy words.

Just talk. He could do that. He kneeled next to the mattress and folded his hands. He'd seen that somewhere. "God," he whispered. "I don't know what I'm doing, but could You help me? I've wanted to be with Stacy for so long, but now it doesn't seem like the right thing to do. Can You help me let go? And could I get to know You like Nevaeh does? Can I have the joy she has?"

What now? Was he supposed to cross himself or something?

Without a clue how to finish, he just said, "Amen." Hopefully, that was good enough.

On the drive home the next morning, he and Nevaeh texted back and forth. He asked questions about her faith, and she answered. He could imagine the light in her eyes, the life in her voice.

According to her, all he needed to do was confess Jesus as his Savior and the Lord, or boss, of his life and believe in Him. Seemed far too easy, but surely she knew what she was talking about. Was he ready to take such a big step? His friends wouldn't understand. Mom might not either.

If I do this, I'll be all alone in it.

Maybe that was his biggest fear. Being alone.

> No, you won't. You'll have me and Claire and
> Bearett.

Yeah, but …

You all live far away from me.

Once again, she replied quickly.

> God's people are everywhere. You'll find them.
> You can go to a youth group. There are Christians
> who go to your school, and there will be
> Christians at college.

That's right. Wendy said she, Claire, and Stella met at some Bible study in college. Were there really so many people who believed in Jesus?

Brinley turned around in the passenger's seat to face him. "Are you texting with Stacy or Nevaeh?"

"Nevaeh." But he did need to send Stacy a text. He couldn't string her along.

He clicked on her text thread, studying the picture of the two of them. He'd thought he was happy with her, but he'd never had the joy that Nevaeh radiated. Blowing out a long breath, he composed a message to her.

> I don't think things are going to work out
> between us. Tell your mom we're very thankful
> she helped with Frankie.

Should he write more? Words escaped him. This would have to do.

She replied five minutes later.

> I understand. Mom says you're welcome.

He stared at his phone. She understood? What did that mean? She wasn't going to try and change his mind, beg him to take her back? Maybe she knew as well as he did that something was off in their relationship. That, or she might already be back in Brad's arms. *Ugh.*

"If you're tired of driving, I can take over," he offered to Claire. It was time to move on.

~

When Claire pulled into her driveway, Bearett was standing on the front porch, arms open. She rushed into them. She had so much to tell him. Her simple texts hadn't conveyed the turmoil the past forty-eight hours had put her through.

Gently, he rubbed her back and kissed her hair. "I'm so glad you're home."

"Glad to be home."

Aiden dragged his suitcase past them, followed by Brinley. Claire couldn't pry herself from Bearett's arms to follow, so she remained on the front porch, a gentle breeze teasing tendrils of her hair.

Bearett pulled back and searched her eyes. "You okay?"

She nodded. The teens were safe. She'd made the trip back without incident. She'd had extended time with her friend. All was well … except for her shaken-up heart. The ordeal of not knowing where Aiden and Brinley were had rattled her so thoroughly that her hands still trembled. Perhaps pregnancy hormones exacerbated the experience.

A couple of minutes later, Aiden stepped back out of the door. "I'm headed to the beach. See you later."

Brinley followed. "Me too."

They were? No. They weren't. She'd let them walk all over her for too long. She'd thought she'd lost them only yesterday. No way were they going to gallivant around the city without supervision. She summoned all the confidence she could muster. "No. I want you both to stay here for the day."

They turned, question marks written on their faces.

"What?" Aiden asked.

"I said no." She crossed her arms for emphasis. Or to hold herself together so she didn't break down and beg.

Brinley huffed. "Why not?"

Bearett put his hand on her shoulder, but she didn't look at him.

"We've just been on a long trip. We need to recoup."

"Long trip?" Aiden scoffed. "We left yesterday."

"*Early* yesterday." She straightened her spine. "And a lot has happened since then."

Aiden shifted his weight, as though trying to decide whether to take the path back to the house or the one leading to the beach.

"Plus, what about Frankie? Are you really going to leave him all alone as sick as he is?" She lifted an eyebrow at Brinley.

"He needs to rest." Brinley's tone rang defensive.

"He needs *you*."

The teens exchanged a glance. A world of meaning behind that single look.

Brinley's hands found her hips. "You can't tell us what to do. You're not our mother, and we're not little children."

They both turned and walked away down the path to the street.

"You're not grown yet." Her voice took on a whine. "You can't do whatever you want."

Aiden tossed a hand up in a wave.

She turned to Bearett. "Why are you just standing there? Do something."

"You want me to chase them down and hog-tie them?" A trace of humor crossed his features.

"Yes!"

He took both of her hands in his. "Let's go inside and talk about where this is coming from."

She stomped into the house and dropped onto the sofa. He followed a minute later, her suitcase in tow.

He wheeled it into their room, then sat beside her. "What's really bothering you?"

"They don't listen to me. Wendy said not to let them walk all over me. That I should give them what they need instead of what they want."

"And they need to stay cooped up in this house?"

"They need supervision. They shouldn't be left to wander around South Haven unsupervised. What if something happens to them?"

"I'll be heading to the boat in less than an hour. I'll check on them then." He wrapped an arm around her shoulder.

"That makes me feel a little better." Her voice sounded small, almost childlike.

"What's really bothering you?"

She laid her head on his shoulder. "Am I going to be a good mom? Or am I going to screw this kid up?"

"You're going to be a great mom. No doubt about it."

"But what if I mess up horribly?"

"You will."

She lifted her head and studied his face. He was serious.

"I will too," he continued. "Your parents were far from perfect, yet look at how you turned out. Far from damaged beyond repair."

"Thanks to Jesus."

"Yes, thanks to Jesus. The Savior. The One who does what we can't. The One who will watch over this little one." He placed a hand on her belly. "We have to trust Him to heal whatever we hurt because it's inevitable. Neither of us will be perfect parents. We're only human."

"But—"

He put a finger to her lips. "God is stronger than your weakness. Let's put more faith in His ability to redeem than our ability to not fail."

Faith in God's strength. In His redemptive power. Truth saturated Bearett's words. If only she could soak them up, but she was more of a rock than a sponge. She could nearly feel the truth sliding off her. Her head returned to his shoulder. She had no more words. Spent, she dozed until he roused her.

"I've got to go to work now."

She stretched. "It's been an hour?"

"Nearly. I'll let you know how the teens are doing."

She yawned. "Have a good day."

When he vacated his spot on the couch, she lay down, pulling an afghan over her. She could sleep for hours.

Her phone rang half an hour later. Bearett.

"Aiden's hanging out with some girl."

"Must be Nevaeh. What about Brinley?"

"She's with some guy. I don't have a good feeling about him."

She sat up. "What? Does he look sleazy?"

"It's just a gut feeling."

Not good. Bearett's intuition was normally spot-on. "I'll drive over there to check on them." Not like she could do much. Would she take Brinley by the ear and march her back home? Ground her to her room? Helpless. She was completely helpless.

But no, what had Wendy said? That God would guide her every step of the way. Where was that guidance now?

Fifteen minutes later, she parked in the lot and scoured the scene for Brinley and her mystery guy. There was Aiden, wearing a goofy grin, looking completely smitten with a beautiful black-haired girl. She continued the search. There they were, hitting a volleyball back and forth. He didn't look familiar.

She got out of the car and walked up to Brinley, sand tickling her toes through her sandals. "Brinley!" she shouted when she got closer.

Brinley turned. Frowned. "What are you doing here?"

"Can I talk to you for a minute?" Claire waved her over.

Brinley dragged her feet but neared, volleyball in hand. "Yeah?" Annoyance doused her voice.

"Be careful around that guy."

Her face scrunched. "Jack? Why?"

"We have a strange feeling about him." No telling whether the squirm in her gut came from her own intuition or Bearett's suggestion.

Brinley rolled her eyes. "Would you back off? You sound like Mom, and she's paranoid."

She sounded like a mother? A smile attempted to twitch its way onto her face, but she suppressed it. "Just be careful, okay?"

"Sure. Whatever."

She'd count that as a victory.

Chapter Sixteen

Marina smiled as Miles appeared in her line of vision. That same errant curl dipped across his forehead. He looked up from where he was stacking rubble into a pile. "Hey, it's Mary Poppins!"

Dr. Duncan sighed. "I don't understand." He put out a hand. "But don't explain. Please."

Miles's grin spread.

When was the last time Aiden had smiled at her like that? She itched to wrap her arms around the young man. She pinned her hands to her sides as she neared. "That's me." She gestured to her purse. "What do you need? Sunscreen? An umbrella? I've got just about everything in here." She winked.

"Ha. I'd love to see you pull an umbrella out of that thing." He wiped a soot-covered hand across his forehead, leaving a trail of grime.

She dug through her purse and produced a hot-pink travel umbrella. "Ta-da."

A laugh bellowed from him. "Wonders never cease."

Frankie II stood on his hind legs and sniffed at her purse. "Sorry, buddy. I don't have any treats." She scratched behind his ears.

Dr. Duncan rubbed his hands together. "Miles, I thought it good that the two of you get better acquainted." He handed Miles the bottle of cholera medicine. "I also brought you this."

Miles took it. "Aw. Thanks, Doc."

"Does it really work?" she asked. It seemed like something from a social media ad touting a miracle cure. A scam, most likely.

Dr. Duncan shrugged. "You never can tell. After witnessing the devastation of cholera, how could we not try?"

Marina nodded. He couldn't lose a time sailor. Understandably, he'd do just about anything to prevent it.

"Well, then." He clapped his hands together. "I'll leave you to converse. If you need anything, I'll be at The Screaming Peach."

"The what?" she asked.

"It's a restaurant," Miles said.

"Ah. Creative."

After they bid Dr. Duncan farewell, Frankie II went off to explore what was likely his much-altered old stomping grounds. Marina turned to Miles. "So, what do you do here in 1849? Besides firefighting?"

He swiped a curl away from his left eye. "Well, I *used* to work at this warehouse." He pointed behind him to the charred remnant of a wooden building. "Not sure what I'll do now. Help rebuild the city, I guess."

She lowered her voice, even though no one appeared to be within earshot. "You're from 2001?"

His countenance fell. "Yeah."

"Nine-eleven?" she whispered.

His Adam's apple bobbed as he nodded. "I lost everything. Everyone."

"Oh, sweetie." She couldn't help it. She wrapped him in her arms, rubbing his back with gentle strokes. And the crazy thing? He let her. Even leaned into her embrace. "I'm so sorry that happened to you."

His breath shuddered. "I haven't been able to talk about it. Not here."

"That has to make it a hundred times harder."

"Yeah."

"Do you have a few minutes to tell me about them? The people you lost?"

He pulled back and cast a look over his shoulder at the piles of charred wood and ash. "I guess it wouldn't hurt."

The scent of fish mingled with that of charred wood as they settled onto a boulder by the river, and he told her of his parents and girlfriend. "We were going to get married. I had the ring picked out and everything." He pulled a velvet box from his pocket and snapped it open. An emerald-cut solitaire shimmered inside.

She sucked in a breath. "Beautiful." Tragic.

"I was going to propose that day at the restaurant in the Twin Towers. I was running late." His voice faltered. "They all died while waiting for me."

"You know it's not your fault, right?" That much seemed obvious, but guilt wasn't logical. It couldn't be reasoned with.

He nodded. "I only wish I had been there. At least then, I'd have died with people I loved rather than reliving the nightmare over and over."

She draped an arm around his shoulders and squeezed, then released him. A show of affection but not smothering. She sensed it was what he needed. Unimaginable what he'd been through. "So, you got on a boat and ended up here?"

"A ferry. Just needed to get away for a bit."

"Well, you certainly did that."

He chuckled. "Who would have guessed I'd get *this* far away." He spread his hands out.

She bumped his shoulder with her own. "Crazy, huh?" They sobered, gazing out over the river where the shattered remains of dozens of burned boats bobbed with the current. Pieces of blackened wood drifted on the water. Several items had washed ashore. A trunk. A splintered sofa. A barber's comb. "Isn't there anyone who's missing you? Anyone to return for?"

He shook his head. "My grandma was still alive at the time, withering away in a nursing home. She had dementia and couldn't remember me anyway. I'm guessing she's passed on by now, but even if she hasn't, she wouldn't know me from the doctor. Besides, how could I return after being away for so long? It's been almost a year. There's no way to explain that." He dabbed at the corner of his eye.

"Oh, Miles." She pressed her hand against the searing in her chest.

What was that about? No time to ponder. She needed to convince Miles to return. "Go home, Miles. Dr. Duncan says it's not safe for you here."

He groaned. "Not you too."

"I only want what's best for you."

He blinked rapidly, like a fluttering of hummingbird wings. "You sound like Mom."

"That's because I *am* a mom. Just not yours."

Frankie II trotted over to them. She put her hand out, and he licked it.

"Who's this?" Miles scratched Frankie II's back.

"I call him Frankie II. My daughter has a similar dog back home named Frankie. At first, I thought he'd time-sailed too."

"Hi, Frankie II," Miles cooed.

Frankie II's tail wagged.

Watching the two of them sent a pang of homesickness through her. "He likes you."

"He probably likes everyone."

Possibly, but … "I think he knows decent people when he sniffs them."

She stood and stretched. Down the riverfront, a ferry pulled up to the wharf. "It's nice to see a semblance of normal. The night of the fire, it seemed the blaze had destroyed every existing boat."

"That's the ferry to Arsenal Island. They're calling it Quarantine Island now."

"Oh." She straightened. "That's where they're taking care of cholera patients."

"Yep. Any ship that comes to St. Louis has to stop there so they can check for cholera victims. No one can dock unless they give the all clear."

Trying to stop the spread of the dreadful disease. "Good idea." Though, obviously, the efforts hadn't eradicated its presence from the city.

A ferry to a nearby island. An idea sparked. She'd tried to reason with staff at many city hospitals, but she hadn't tried Quarantine Island. What if she took the ferry there? If she'd already completed her mission—if it *did* have to do with providing relief for fire victims—she should return to her own time when on the boat. Either way, she'd know for sure.

And if she remained in 1849, perhaps she could quietly convince a doctor or nurse on the island to hear her out regarding the cause of cholera. Secretly. Could it be done in a way that didn't change the history books? It was a small island in the middle of a river. One she certainly had never heard of, even though she lived in St. Louis. Could she save a life or two and not risk the waters' wrath? She had to do *something* to get back.

Her gaze trailed to Miles. Maybe she could convince him to go with her. He'd likely return to his own time. If *that* was her mission, she could check it off as accomplished.

"Why don't we go? See if we can help the sick there?" She brushed off the back of her dress.

 His mouth pressed into a firm line. "You know I can't."

"You could."

"I won't."

She planted her hands on her hips. Why'd he have to be so doggone stubborn?

He stood and took a step away from her. Distance. "It's not happening."

The way the edge of his mouth quirked up melted her resolve. He was such a sweet boy. A bit headstrong, but in an endearing, not irritating, way. She could … she could stay too. Guide Miles through life. Make a home here with him and Frankie II. Her children didn't need her—or want her—anyway.

Traitorous thought. No matter what Aiden and Brinley said or how they acted, they had to need their mother … unless Claire had taken that role like Marina could easily do for Miles. No. They needed *her*, not some stranger, no matter how kind.

Miles's lips inched upward on the other side. "Besides, what about Frankie II? They won't let him on the ferry."

Hmm. Good point. What to do? She couldn't leave Miles after the connection she'd made with him. And how could she abandon Frankie II? But she'd only known the two of them for such a short time. She needed to return to her children. Nothing could replace the history they'd built over the years.

"There she be." A stocky man with bulging muscles pointed straight at her.

What in the world? He marched up to her and stuck his finger in her face. "It was you, wasn't it? You poisoned my mother with your tomatoes. She told me all about the woman with short brown hair who gave her the dwarfish vegetables. We knew they were odd, we did."

The son of the old beggar woman? "There was nothing wrong with those tomatoes."

"Wasn't there? Then why did she perish yesterday?"

Her jaw fell open. The old lady had died? How much death and destruction could one city hold? "I don't know. I'm sorry for your loss. But it wasn't my fault."

"I wouldn't normally lay a hand on a lady, but you best watch your back. Murderer." He punched a fist into his other hand and seared her with a heated glare.

She gulped. Miles sidled up next to her and crossed his muscular arms. "Leave her alone."

The man ground his shoe into the dirt. Surely, symbolic of what he wanted to do to her. "I'll be back, and next time, I'm bringing me friends." He stalked off.

Goodness. A whoosh of air escaped from her lungs. Her arms and legs trembled. Miles took her by the arm and led her back to the boulder to sit. "Don't worry about him. I'm sure he's all talk."

But what if he wasn't? Her teeth chattered.

"Stick with me. I'll look out for you."

She shook her head. She couldn't stay here. Not on the mainland. It would accomplish nothing, and she'd forever be looking over her shoulder. Arsenal Island was her best bet …

even if she had to leave her two closest friends in this time to get there.

"I have to go." She stood. Too fast. Her knees wobbled.

Once again, Miles took her elbow, steadying her. "Go?"

"To Arsenal Island." Her heart cracked as he frowned. He'd lost everyone, and now she was leaving too. "You might not have a reason to return to your time, but I have a reason to return to mine. I've got two teens around your age. They need me."

A muscle twitched in his cheek. "I understand."

"Take care of Frankie II for me?"

"Of course." He enveloped her in a hug. Oh, the sweetness. His shirt still smelled of smoke, but no matter. She savored the feel of this boy in her arms, hugging her the way she wished Aiden would.

When she pulled back, it was like rubber bands stretching, then breaking. A connection that could be strong and good was severed.

She should give him something to remember her by. Besides the dog. She dug into her purse. Aiden's sunglasses? Guilt twinged her chest at the thought. No way. Sunscreen? Yes. Perfect. She pressed the bottle into his hand. "Here, take this."

"Oh, wow. It's been so long since I've seen this. And the spray kind. A bonus."

"Enjoy." Her smile quivered. "I might be back."

"For your children's sake, I hope not." He offered a weak attempt at a smile. "I'll miss you, Mom. Can I call you that? You're the closest thing I've got."

Oh, to be a mom to this boy. He needed her, accepted her help, in a way her own teens hadn't in years. "Of course." But now he'd lose two mothers instead of one. Because she couldn't stay. Her heart stretched toward him even as she walked away.

Aiden spread his towel out next to Nevaeh's and lay down on his stomach. She looked up at him from her position, lying on her back with her hands behind her head. Her long hair splayed around her shoulders like some kind of sea goddess.

"Did you read that passage I suggested?" Her eyes lit in … expectation? Eagerness?

Good thing he wouldn't disappoint her. "I don't have a Bible, but I googled it." He pulled out his phone. "I'd heard John 3:16 before but had never heard verse 17. 'For God did not send his Son into the world to condemn the world, but in order that the world might be saved through him.'"

Nevaeh rolled to her side and nodded for him to continue.

"So, I guess this means God's not standing over us with a hammer?"

She laughed. "That's one way to put it."

"Like, He's not looking to find all my faults and punish me for them?"

"He doesn't need to *find* your faults. He already knows about them all, even ones you don't realize yet."

Could she see his weaknesses so clearly? "Gee, thanks."

She playfully shoved his arm. "No, it's a good thing. You've got nothing to hide from Him. He knows it all, and you're right, He's not out to punish you for it. Jesus already took that punishment on the cross."

Nothing to hide. Throughout his relationship with Stacy, he'd always felt like he needed to display the best version of himself and hide anything unappealing. Because maybe she wouldn't still love him if she knew everything about him. Or her dad wouldn't continue to support him. He hadn't realized how exhausting it had all been until yesterday.

They continued chatting about what different verses meant. How different was this God from everything he'd assumed.

Nevaeh winced. "Am I getting sunburned?" She turned her back to him to inspect.

"Yeah, right here is red." He drew a gentle circle on the shoulder that had faced the sun during their conversation.

"Ugh. I knew I forgot something."

"If my mom were here, she'd have some aloe in her purse."

"You miss her, don't you?"

He hadn't told Nevaeh about the crazy time-sailing. He'd only mentioned that she had to go do something and had left them with Claire and Bearett. "Yeah. I guess I do." Strange. He hadn't realized how much until she mentioned it. "My mom is over-the-top, but she's cool too."

Nevaeh smiled like his answer pleased her.

"Tell you what." He sat up. "Let's go find some aloe."

"Okay. There's a surf store right over there." She pointed to a souvenir shack at the edge of the beach. "I bet it has aloe."

"Sounds good." He stood and extended a hand to her.

"Do you need to find your sister and tell her where we're off to?"

"Nah. She's a big girl. She can take care of herself."

Abandoning their towels, they walked hand in hand. Her fingers were slender and smooth, except for the callous on the side. From playing volleyball, most likely. He rubbed his thumb over hers. He'd done the right thing, breaking things off with Stacy. Even if he and Nevaeh never had a future, he'd treasure this moment.

At the store, he found the green aloe vera, the kind Mom always got, and paid for it, along with two Cokes and a package of Skittles to share. Back at the beach, he sat behind her and carefully rubbed the green goo onto her burn, then sunscreen onto the rest of her back and shoulders. Her skin was soft to his touch. The urge to kiss her shoulder blade, her neck, her cheek beckoned him, but he resisted. He wouldn't scare her away. Wouldn't jeopardize this relationship. Maybe it could turn into more. Perhaps, one day, he'd have a right to kiss her like he longed to.

He flipped the cap closed on the aloe. "Do you want to get out of the sun? We could go get ice cream again."

She sighed and leaned back against him, wetting his chest with green glop. "I just want to stay here with you."

He wouldn't argue.

~

Once again, Claire found herself waiting for the teens to come home. *Home.* She had to remember this wasn't *their* home. But though she wasn't their mother, she had promised to keep an eye on them. She hadn't completely failed in that regard, had she? They were both alive and healthy. They'd traveled hundreds of miles together, and there'd been no disasters. But would Marina see that as a victory? Not if Brinley developed feelings for a thug. Then again, adults couldn't control teenage love. It had a life all its own. That much had proven true from her horrendous failed relationships when she was younger.

Brinley must have returned to the house while Claire taught at the YMCA, because when she came back, Frankie was gone from his spot on the teens' bed. It wasn't like the dog had a means to escape, even if he had the energy. Plus, his leash had disappeared as well. It wasn't likely he'd be up for a walk or time at a dog park. Maybe Brinley had just wanted to show him off to her new *friend.*

At eight, Bearett returned from his last cruise of the day.

"Beef stew's keeping warm in the Crock-Pot," Claire said absentmindedly.

He bent down and kissed her cheek. "That's a treat. My favorite."

She attempted to smile back, but worry fought her effort. When would Aiden and Brinley return? Were they okay? "I didn't have the energy for anything more. Still worn out from traveling."

He put a hand on her belly. "And growing our baby."

"That too."

He eyed her. "What's wrong?"

She opened her mouth to answer, but rustling at the door stole her words. Aiden breezed in with a goofy grin on his face.

190

"Hey." He threw his towel on the love seat. Grains of sand scattered onto the floor.

Claire stood and peered out the window. "Where's Brinley?"

"Dunno. Haven't seen her all day."

Her insides spun as if in a blender. If what Aiden said was true, she'd been the last to see the girl. And what she'd seen hadn't exactly set her at ease. She texted her for the second time, though she'd be shocked if Brinley responded.

Aiden rubbed his hands together. "Something smells good."

Bearett and Claire spoke at the same time. "Beef stew's in the Crock-Pot."

"Cool." He sauntered to the kitchen, leaving bits of sand in his trail.

She should sweep. She needed something to keep her mind occupied. She retrieved the broom and dustpan from the closet.

"Have you already eaten?" Bearett asked.

She shook her head. "Not hungry."

"Babe—"

"I'll eat when Brinley comes home." She wouldn't be able to stomach anything until then.

The boys dished out stew and slathered French bread with butter. While she swept, Bearett asked Aiden about his day. The girl she'd seen him with was Nevaeh, like she'd thought. His cheeks reddened as he spoke of her. Man, he was falling hard. Hopefully, that wasn't a mistake. She hadn't gotten any weird vibes from the girl, though. Only from Brinley's ... *acquaintance*.

Five minutes later, there was nothing left to sweep. She returned to her spot on the couch, waiting. An hour later, the boys had finished eating, and Aiden had retreated to his room. The TV blared from behind his closed door. Another hour later, and Claire couldn't stand it any longer.

She paced in the living room. "Will you drive to the beach and see if you can find her?"

Bearett glanced out the window to the dark street. "Sure." He must have been growing worried, too, for him not to argue.

If he couldn't find her, then what? Should she call the police, or was that overkill? She'd had a late curfew when she was that age. Another call to Brinley went to voicemail. A scan of her social media showed no updates. She knocked on Aiden's door, then let herself in.

"What's up?" He lay on top of the comforter, hands behind his head. Like he hadn't a care in the world.

She had to be overreacting. "You sure your sister didn't say anything to you about where she'd be? What she'd be doing?"

"Nah."

"What time's her curfew normally?"

"Ten, but Mom's not here, so …"

So, she likely figured she could do whatever she wanted. Great. "Will you text her? She's not answering me."

"Yeah, sure." He yawned, then reached for his phone. "Don't freak out, though. Brinley never gets into trouble." He shifted his jaw. "At least, not any trouble she deserves."

Whatever that meant. "Let me know if she replies."

"Will do."

She left his door ajar so she had a better chance of hearing him if he called out. Needing something for her hands to do, she washed the dishes, wiped down the counter and table, and placed the rest of the stew in the fridge. She could always heat up a bowl for her and Brinley.

When her phone rang, she jumped, heart hammering. Brinley? No, Bearett. "Did you find her?"

"No. She's not at North or South Beach, and I drove up and down nearly every nearby street. No sign of her."

Her throat constricted. "What do we do? File a police report?"

"I'm going to drive around a little longer, then I'll come home, and we'll talk about what to do."

"Okay." Her eyes filled as she ended the call. Why wasn't he more concerned? Bearett's carefree personality usually put her at ease, but not tonight. Maybe pregnancy hormones were making her irrational. But no. She'd *lost* a child. If anything deserved a freak-out session, this was it. Marina would kill her. She had every right to.

"Brinley texted back." Aiden ambled into the kitchen, grabbed a glass, and poured some chocolate milk.

Claire's breath caught. "What'd she say?"

He gulped half the milk before replying. "She's on a trip with her new friends and don't worry."

"She's what?" Claire's voice exploded.

He crossed his arms. "That's what she said. I didn't know she made any friends, except for Jack, who's a sleaze ball."

A tremor shot up her spine. "Jack?" That must have been the boy she'd seen earlier.

"Yeah. I don't like him, but she didn't listen to me when I told her to steer clear."

Myriads of questions swirled in her brain. "A trip where?" She'd ask more details about Jack later.

"Didn't say." His frown showed he was worried, if even a little.

She leaned her elbows on the counter and focused on taking deep breaths. She couldn't melt down, not now. They had to find Brinley. "Try to find out. Please."

She called Bearett and relayed what she'd learned. He promised to head home. Together, they'd formulate a plan. Once again, she checked Brinley's Instagram. No new posts. Not a hint as to where she was.

When Bearett entered, he strode directly toward her and wrapped her in a hug. "It's going to be okay. We'll figure this out together. But first, have you eaten?"

Eaten? Was he crazy? No way could she think about food at a time like this. Her expression must have relayed her thoughts.

He rubbed her arms. "Stress isn't good for the baby, hon. Sit down and eat something."

His eyes shone with such sincerity, such concern for her and their child. She acquiesced and sat at the table, allowing him to heat her up a bowl of stew. She texted between bites.

> Brinley, please come back. We're worried about you.

Finally, a reply.

> Don't worry about me. I'm fine. Promise.

That tempted her to ease her worry, but what if it wasn't really Brinley replying? She could have been kidnapped. Anyone could have typed out those words.

> I need proof. Send me a photo of you safe and sound.

A minute later, one appeared. Brinley held Frankie's face against her own. She wasn't quite smiling but didn't appear distressed. Content was more like it. Claire handed her phone to Bearett.

After scanning the thread, he sat back and sighed. "Not much we can do at this point but wait."

Seriously? "Shouldn't we go to the police?"

"We're not her legal guardians. There's nothing to say we have any right to know her whereabouts. And how would we explain where her mother disappeared to? Plus, I think there's a twenty-four-hour rule. She probably hasn't been gone long enough to file a report."

Claire's leg bounced at rapid speed.

He pointed to her phone. "Look at the picture. She's fine. Not in danger. Didn't you ever run away from home as a kid?"

"No, of course not. I'm guessing you did?"

"Before the Lord got ahold of me, I did a lot of things that drove my parents crazy."

Aiden peeked his head around the corner. "She won't tell me where she is but insists she's fine. Says she's with a group of people, not just Jack, which makes me feel better."

"Thanks, Aiden. Let us know if she tells you anything else," Bearett said. He took her hand in his. "Nothing left to do but pray."

For the first time, that didn't seem like enough.

Chapter Seventeen

Marina waved to Miles as the ferry pulled away from the mainland. Frankie II barked his farewell. She blew him a kiss. "Be a good boy."

She'd meant it for Frankie II, but Miles replied with "I will. Take care, Mom. I'll miss you."

Her heart warmed. When her children were young, they'd told her they would miss her whenever she stepped out of the house. She'd return to eager hugs and vibrant accounts of what she'd missed while she was gone. She'd always known she was appreciated back then. Now? Well, it'd been a long time since they'd expressed as much. That didn't mean they weren't grateful for her, right? It just wasn't cool to express it.

Despite her internal pep talk, her spirits sagged. Here she was, leaving the one person on earth who saw her as valuable. And for what? So she could return to two people who couldn't care less about her, despite the fact that she loved them fiercely.

She had to shake off this melancholy. Look on the bright side. Push past the pain. She'd become quite adept at such things since Adam's death. Keep on keeping on and all that. Wallowing in self-pity didn't do anyone any good.

She took a deep breath of slightly fresher air. A hint of smoke lingered, but the more distance that grew between the ferry and the rubble, the more the smell of dampness and fish replaced it. She gripped the railing. Would she return to her time now that she was on the water? She waited with stilted breath, but the only movement was the boat bobbing underneath her. No dramatic zaps through time. Maybe she needed to touch a mailbox first, like she'd done when she'd traveled here. Was there one on board?

Her hand trailed the railing as she meandered toward the pilot house. Much smaller than the *White Cloud*, this ferry boasted an open deck that was filled with passengers, as well as horses and buggies. No cover from bad weather if such arose. Thankfully, only puffy white clouds dotted the sky. Two nuns huddled together on the other side of the deck. Likely nurses on the island. Marina could join their ranks as a nurse. She'd likely make more headway as one of them instead of as an outsider claiming superior knowledge.

After taking a step in their direction, she remembered her original destination. A mailbox. Was that one hanging from the side of the pilot house?

Yes. She drew near and braced herself before touching the cool metal. No shock. Unlike the two previous mailboxes, there was no engraved lion. Only smooth metal and slightly rusty hinges. She waited with trembling limbs. Nothing. With an exasperated sigh, she kicked the white wood of the pilot house. She must not have accomplished her mission. What if she never did? She could be stuck in 1849 forever.

Would that be so bad? Miles. Frankie II. Miss Woodhouse. Even Dr. Duncan. It wasn't like she'd be alone. Maybe she could do more good here than she ever could at home.

No. Ridiculous. Not returning would mean never seeing Aiden's and Brinley's faces again. The kids she'd seen grow and change every day of their lives. They were also her only remaining tie to Adam. She couldn't give up on them. On returning to them. She took a determined step toward the nuns, then stopped again.

A mailbox. She could send a letter home. They deserved an explanation as to her delay. What if they were worried about her? Even if they weren't, she needed to let them know what was going on. It was only right.

She dug through her purse until her fingers closed around a notepad, then a pen. She leaned against the pilothouse and slid to a seat on the hard deck. What should she say? She puffed out her cheeks. Something hopeful. Nothing that would worry them. She had to remain strong.

Dear Aiden and Brinley,

I hope you are well. I'm safe and good. I'm sorry it's taking me longer than anticipated to get home. I have important work to do in St. Louis in 1849. Cholera is running rampant here, and they need my modern perspective. Don't worry about me. I'll be back as soon as my job is finished.

I found a stray dog here that reminds me so much of Frankie. I named him Frankie II. He's a sweetheart. I bet you miss your Frankie. As soon as I get back, we'll go get him.

Be good for Claire and Bearett. Please stay safe and out of trouble.

Love you,
Mom

There. That sounded positive, yet informative.

She folded the letter and tucked it inside the mailbox. As she did, her hand brushed something. Envelopes? She pulled them out, and her breath hitched. Four letters addressed to her. Sliding back down to the deck, she sat and devoured each one.

One from Claire once again urging her not to try and change history. She shuddered to think that she had nearly ignored the last warning. She could have died. At least she knew now. But what if informing 1849 of the benefits of sanitary measures changed the history books? If the doctors took what she said to heart, wouldn't it only make a difference for the people on the island? But if word spread … Of course, word would spread. She'd have to take precautionary measures herself—washing her hands and boiling water if possible—without trying to convince anyone to follow her lead. She might make a difference to a few patients that way, but was that enough? It seemed too small of an impact to be her mission. The Time Holder, as Dr. Duncan had called him, probably wouldn't go through all the trouble of dragging someone to a different era for something so trivial. But what else could she do?

She moved on to the next letters, all in Aiden's handwriting but signed Aiden and Brinley. Each assured her that all was well in South Haven. They'd made friends and were having fun at the beach. Claire and Bearett were treating them well. Not a hint of needing her or missing her. *We'll see you when you get back.* Hadn't they been worried when she hadn't returned their letters?

Well, then. Apparently, she could take all the time she wanted. No need to rush. She stood, placed the letters into her purse, and sighed. They might not miss her, but man, she missed them.

A groan rasped from the other side of the pilot house. Did someone need help? She rounded the perimeter. There, writhing in a heap on the deck, lay George the Bible salesman. She dropped to her knees beside him. "What's wrong?"

A hand to his clammy forehead proved him unwell. He clutched his stomach and moaned.

Cholera? Most likely. Hopefully, she was immune now that she'd already contracted it. Or was that not how this disease worked? No matter. She couldn't ignore the man. Water. He needed water, only she no longer carried any with her. She'd left the empty cooler at Miss Woodhouse's place. The only liquid available here would come from the river and might be contaminated.

"How can I help?"

He grasped her arm. "'I have called thee by thy name; thou art mine.'"

She shuddered. "What?"

"'Fear not.'" His lips quivered on his cloud-white face. Glassy eyes bore into her.

He must be delirious. Spouting nonsense. Possibly hallucinating.

His hand dropped from her arm and clutched his stomach again. Then his cheeks puffed out, and he stumbled to the railing to expel the contents of his stomach. He turned to her, swaying. "'Thou art mine.'"

Then he heaved again, leaning far over the railing. She blinked, and he was falling over the side. A splash into the water. "George!" She ran to the railing.

A gurgle at the water's surface was the only response.

~

The next morning, Aiden headed to the beach right after breakfast. Still no sign of Brinley. He hadn't run into Claire and Bearett, only heard their muffled voices from inside their bedroom. He shot a text on his way, telling them where he was at. No need for them to worry about him too.

He could wring Brinley's neck for pulling a stunt like this. If Mom knew, she'd have a heart attack. He could picture smoke coming out of her ears like in the cartoons he'd watched as a child. This would be enough to send her over the edge, for sure. Good thing she had no way of finding out.

Thankfully, Claire hadn't called the police. The officer might have recognized them as the hoodlums who'd snuck out of the station. That would have caused more trouble. No, it'd be better to find her himself. He just needed a lead. Someone there had to know something. A group of teenagers didn't just leave the beach for some random trip without anyone noticing.

Jack had to be behind all of this. Next time Aiden saw him, fists would fly. The jerk needed to stay away from his sister.

Nevaeh met him at the beach as he'd requested. "What's up? It sounded important."

Aiden filled her in.

"Oh, man. My mom would kill me if I pulled something like that."

"Our mom too. Claire's sick with worry. Will you help me ask around?"

"Of course." She slid her hands into the back pockets of her jean shorts and tilted her head. "But can we pray first?"

"Yeah. Sure."

She bowed her head but didn't fold her hands or kneel. He followed her lead.

"Heavenly Father, we ask that You'd help us find Brinley and that You'd keep her safe. We don't know where she is, but You do. You see her even now. Please surround her with Your angels and bring her back unharmed. Amen."

Unharmed. For the first time, it occurred to him that Brinley could get hurt. He swallowed down the lump rising in his throat. "Amen."

Nevaeh slapped her hands together. "Should we split up, or ask around together?"

He scanned the area. Not too many people yet, but that would change quickly. "Let's split up."

"Deal. I'll ask around on the beach. Why don't you ask everyone on the marina?"

"Good idea." He grabbed her hand and squeezed. "Thanks for your help."

"Of course." Her smile sent a zing through his chest. He pulled away, lest he grow distracted.

Holding out his phone, he flashed Brinley's picture in front of three men who were working on their pontoon boats, asking if they'd seen her. No luck. A woman scrubbed down the interior of her sailboat. Upon asking her the same, she replied in Spanish, shaking her head. He thanked her and moved on. The more people he asked, the more desperation clawed him. How could no one know where she might be?

Shielding his eyes from the blinding sun, he headed back toward the beach, scanning the area for Nevaeh. When he got close enough to spot her and catch her attention, she shook her head. She hadn't found out anything either. He pulled at the ends of his hair. What kind of trip had Brinley gone on? A road trip in a friend's car? Had they taken public transportation? Or maybe … maybe they had taken a boat. Or rented one.

That's who he should ask—boat rental places. There were several among the downtown shops. He jogged to Nevaeh. Perhaps they'd have better luck together. *Better together.* Yeah, that sounded right. He told her his idea, and they headed toward the nearest rental company, half jogging, half speed-walking.

"You're brilliant." Nevaeh smiled at him.

"Hardly. If I were so smart, I would have kept a closer eye on my sister."

"Not your job."

He tilted his head. "Kind of is, with Mom gone."

"Where did your mom go again?" She breathed hard, taking two steps to each one of his.

"On a trip." He needed to stop this conversation before it snowballed. But how?

"You told me that. But where? Why?"

He kept his gaze ahead. If he looked at her, she might figure out he was hiding something. "It's a long story."

"I'll listen."

If he could trust anyone with this secret, it'd be Nevaeh. Still, he couldn't stomach her thinking he was a lunatic. What if she pulled away because of it? No. He wouldn't risk it. "Now's not the time." True enough. They needed to focus on Brinley. Mom's *adventure* would only distract from that.

They came to the marine rental place and spilled through the door. Cool air slapped them. The scent of donuts lured Aiden to the front counter where an employee in a light-blue polo stuffed the last of a jelly roll into his mouth. "May I help you?" he asked around the bite.

Once again, Aiden pulled up Brinley's picture on his phone. "We're looking for my sister, Brinley Stone. Did she rent a boat from here by chance?"

"Or have you seen her at all?" Nevaeh added, her voice sugar-sweet.

The man's eyes lit as though he recognized Brin, but he brushed a crumb off his shirt and said, "All customer records are confidential."

The guy had to know something. "Okay, but she's missing, and we're worried about her. I get that you can't give any details, but can you at least confirm she was here?"

Donut Man pressed his lips together and shook his head.

Nevaeh widened her eyes and fluttered her eyelashes. "Not even just a hint?" Was she flirting?

"No can do. Confidentiality and all that."

She pouted and trailed a finger across the counter.

Donut Man stood as solid as a rock. Nevaeh's charm might not work on him, but Aiden wanted to wrap her in his arms and kiss her breathless.

Not the time.

Aiden pressed his palms on the counter and leaned forward. About as intimidating as he could get. "How old do you have to be to rent a boat?"

"Twenty-one."

"Well, Brinley's only sixteen. If we find out you rented to her …"

Donut Man's gaze hardened. "We don't rent to anyone without proper identification showing they're of age." He planted his hands on the counter like he were going to jump over it and thrash both of them. "You need to leave now."

Aiden lifted his chin. "And if we don't?"

"I'll call the police."

Seriously? "A bit extreme, isn't it?"

Nevaeh pivoted and headed to the door. "Thanks anyway."

"Thanks for nothing," Aiden mumbled.

Once outside, she planted her hands on her hips. "She was in there. I'm sure of it."

"Probably. But I doubt she was the one who rented the boat. And Jack's not old enough, is he?"

"No, but I wouldn't put it past him to carry a fake ID. Or it could have been someone else from the group."

"That'd make it harder to track her down. Should I go back in there? Threaten the guy?"

Her mouth twisted. "No, that'd only get you in trouble. We should wait until a different employee comes in and ask again. Just because that guy was a stick in the mud doesn't mean everyone who works there is unhelpful."

Not a bad idea. "I'd better go back to the house and update Claire and Bearett." Maybe they could formulate a solid plan together.

"I'll come with you." She clasped his hand and held on tight.

Hopefully, she'd always stick by his side. *Better together.*

~

Claire huffed as she stormed out of her bedroom and into the kitchen. Bearett still wouldn't agree to involve the police, especially since it seemed that Brinley was safe. If something happened to that girl … A dozen scenarios flew through her mind, from a drunken party that led to an accident to a human trafficking ring. She'd never shed the guilt if anyone harmed Brinley.

Aiden had texted, saying he was headed to the beach to ask around. Maybe someone there saw her and would have a clue how to track her down. She should probably join him. She knew many of the locals and might get further than a teenage boy could.

But first, a quick breakfast. Bearett had insisted, and since her stomach grumbled against her less-than-full dinner the night before, she acquiesced. She wouldn't be able to face this day without some nourishment.

She'd just sprinkled granola over yogurt when the doorbell rang. Her heart jumped into her throat. The police? Had they come to relay news of a horrific accident? She froze in place, unable to force her feet forward.

Bearett emerged from their room, buttoning his shirt. "Who's that?"

She couldn't form an answer.

He swung the door open, then sucked in a breath. "Hi, Mom. Dad."

Mom and Dad? He took a step backward, and Claire's mother and father entered. *Her* mom and dad. Her hand found her throat. No, no, no. What were they doing here? This was almost worse than the police. Horrible thought. Of course, Brinley's safety trumped Claire's sanity.

She forced a smile. Made her feet move toward them. She leaned forward for an awkward, tap-the-back hug and obligatory kiss on the cheek. "This is a surprise." Understatement of the year. "What brings you here?"

Mom clasped her hands in front of her and studied her surroundings with pursed lips. "We wanted to surprise you."

Dad rolled a suitcase behind him. "We've been talking about taking a vacation for months, and since we've never seen your place, it seemed like as good of a place as any to visit."

Claire's gaze zeroed in on the suitcase. Did they plan on staying here, at the house? That wouldn't work. She only had one guest room. "How long do you plan to stay?" Hopefully, that came across as merely curious.

Mom waved a hand. "Oh, since we've retired, we're not on a timetable. We can stay as long as you like."

In that case, it was about time for them to leave.

"Have a seat." Bearett gestured to the couch. "Can we get you anything to drink? Eat?"

"A mimosa would be lovely, thanks." Mom dusted off the couch before sitting.

"An orange juice would suit me fine." Dad sat beside her.

"Orange juice we can do, but we don't have any alcohol on hand." Seeing as how they didn't drink. Never had.

"Oh, well." Mom sighed. "An orange juice for me too, then."

Bearett headed to the kitchen while Claire slumped onto the love seat.

A line formed on Mom's forehead. "Why are you making your man do all the work, Claire?"

As if pouring juice was a chore.

Before she could formulate a response, Dad jumped in. "Guess who we talked to not an hour ago?"

Had to be Julie. "Who?"

"Your sister. She's doing quite well for herself. Already been accepted into a residency."

"Cardiology." Mom beamed. "That has to do with the heart."

"I know, Mom." She would have ended her statement with *I'm not stupid*, but best not to start an argument.

Mom leaned forward as though spreading juicy gossip. "She's dating a surgeon."

"That's great for her."

"Isn't it?" If Dad's grin grew any wider, it might damage his face.

"So—" Time to change the subject. "You'd normally be more than welcome to stay with us." *Lord, forgive me for lying.* "But we have a couple of houseguests at the moment. We can recommend some great hotels."

"Houseguests?" Mom straightened. "What houseguests?"

How to explain?

Bearett handed both a glass of orange juice. "We're hosting two teenagers while their mom is away on a trip."

Dad's eyes narrowed. "Who are these people?"

"They're good kids." Bearett retreated to the kitchen, then returned with two more glasses and handed one to her.

Good kids. Right. She'd aged a decade in the week they'd been here.

Once again, Mom studied the space. "Well, this place *is* smaller than I envisioned. Julie's apartment might be larger. I guess we shouldn't have expected you to have room."

Claire fought an eye roll. Of course, her mother would turn the size of their home into a competition with Julie. Claire never won against her sister. Ever. After downing her juice, she went to deposit it in the sink. "I was just about to head out, actually," she said from the kitchen.

She couldn't stay here and chitchat when Brinley's life might be on the line. Her parents wouldn't like her leaving. She strengthened her resolve and returned to the living room.

Mom's gaze dropped to Claire's middle, and her mouth parted.

No. She couldn't tell, could she? The bump was barely noticeable. Then again, Mom had an uncanny ability to hone in on all of Claire's faults. No doubt pregnancy would fall into that category for her.

"Don't tell me you're pregnant, Claire."

Perfect.

"We're so excited," Bearett offered.

"Excited? Have you gotten a better job, Bearett? One that pays better?"

He shifted his jaw. "I'm still a charter boat captain."

Claire placed a hand on his shoulder. "He has his own business managing the *Duncan's Delight*. He's quite good at what he does."

Dad scoffed. "That's well and good, but it's more of a hobby, not a legitimate business. Isn't it time for you to get a real job? Especially now that you'll have another mouth to feed."

"He has a real job, Dad. He provides well for us." Not well enough, but that wasn't his fault. More like hers for not contributing more to the finances.

"But he's intelligent enough to be doing more with his life." Mom smiled at him as if her words were a compliment.

"He loves the water. Loves what he does." She wanted to proclaim that he was a Duncan, doing exactly what he was called to do, but they wouldn't understand. It's not like she'd divulged the Duncan family's connection to time sailors. Not like they knew about time-sailing, at all. They'd laugh and berate them for the rest of their lives if she spilled that secret.

A muscle twitched in Bearett's cheek. "We thought you'd be happy to be grandparents."

All air seemed to leave the room as silence hung between them for nearly a full minute.

"Grandparents," Mom whispered.

"There could be worse things," Dad said.

Mom's gaze flitted between them. "Well, at least with Bearett's brains and your beauty, our grandchild might have a fighting chance."

Chapter Eighteen

Marina reeled as the ferry approached Quarantine Island.

George lay on a blanket on the far side of the deck, barely conscious. After a man jumped in the water to save him, others assisted in hoisting him back on board. He was alive, thankfully, but in no state to converse. The doctor would care for him on the island, and he'd, hopefully, fully recover. Then, perhaps, he could explain what he'd been saying to her.

You are mine. Way to creep her out. What did it mean? Did she now belong to 1849? Or was George some kind of stalker? Had he grown obsessed with her after she'd accepted his Bible? She never should have taken it. Must have led him on. Poor guy. He was so sickly and helpless. And here he'd set out to do something admirable, at least in his own estimation—save those forty-niners from destruction—only to end up half dead. He certainly didn't seem threatening to her, not like a deranged stalker. But those words …

No use wasting time thinking about them. She had a mission to accomplish, and the boat was nearly there. How should she go about this? She could say she was there to help.

She still hadn't figured out how to do this without changing the history books. If only she could gently infiltrate their archaic health system by spreading a few hints regarding hygiene, but that might endanger her. If she helped to save lives secretly, would the history books take note? An impossible situation. Taking any action was a risk, but not taking any meant staying here forever. Aiden and Brinley didn't seem to need her to rush back. But how long could she go without seeing them?

She readied to disembark, but the boat floated past the island. She turned to a nearby man with a pipe in his mouth. "Aren't we stopping at Quarantine Island?" She motioned to the passing sandbar.

"Indeed. But that is Duncan's Island. Quarantine Island is the next one."

Interesting. Was Duncan's Island named after Dr. Duncan?

Soon, the boat docked at the island farther south. A few passengers disembarked, a couple of men supporting George among them. The nuns set off with purpose. She followed close after them, sand pillowing around her shoes. One of them turned around and studied her. "What do you need, miss? Are you ill?"

"No, not ill. I'm here to help."

She tilted her head. "Help?"

"Yes. I can nurse."

"We're from the Sisters of Charity. We might be advanced in employing female nurses, but the doctors trust our expertise. They won't let just any woman be a nurse here."

Marina implored the woman with her gaze. "I understand, but can't you use all the help you can get?"

A sigh escaped the nun's lips. She continued to inspect Marina as though she could see the jean shorts under her dress and disapproved.

The other sister spoke up. "Come on, Sister Margaret. Surely, we can find something for this lady to do. Emptying chamber pots at least."

Marina fought a cringe. *That* could *not* be her mission. But perhaps it was a foot in the door, a means of finding out what purpose brought her here. "I'll do whatever's needed."

The nuns turned and continued walking without another word. Marina trailed them. Beyond a set of rough-looking buildings, cattle roamed what looked to be pastureland. A stand of trees on one side of the island provided some shade. She squinted as she attempted to gauge the island's size. Maybe a fourth of a mile across, at best. Not quite a mile long.

Were they going to let her help? She wasn't above begging, if need be.

They passed a docked steamboat and continued to a simple wooden building with roughly sawn boards, the edges jagged and uneven. Before the nuns entered, Sister Margaret once again turned to her. "Wait here. I'll talk to my superiors." She took another step, then stopped. "What is your name? Catherine Weber, right?"

What? Why did they think she was named Catherine? She opened her mouth but couldn't seem to force words out. Her name. She needed to tell them her name.

The nuns left before she could get her mouth and brain to work together. Oh, well. What did it matter if they thought she was Catherine Weber?

Sweat pooled between her shoulder blades as she waited in the blistering sun. How could those nuns stand their heavy black robes in this heat? She could barely take being in a long, confining dress. If only she could wear nothing but shorts and a tank top. Wouldn't that cause a stir.

Finally, Sister Margaret returned. "Miss Weber, you can assist."

Wonderful. A chance to escape from the heat. But as she followed the sister inside, no cool blast of air greeted her. Would she ever get used to no air-conditioning? It was a convection oven behind the closed doors.

"Your duties will consist of emptying chamber pots, changing bed linens, and fetching water for the patients." Her gaze sharpened.

"I understand."

"Patricia will show you what to do." Sister Margaret motioned to a young brunette in twin braids. She couldn't be much older than Aiden—twenty at the most. The clomp of Sister Margaret's shoes echoed down the hallway.

Marina took a step toward Patricia. "Hi, I'm … Catherine. Care to show me the ropes?"

The girl's nose scrunched. "We don't have ropes here, miss."

A chuckle nearly escaped. "Then can you show me how things work here? And how to help?"

Patricia nodded. "Dozens of steamboats arrive through here each week. The quarantine officers board and inspect each one coming from the south. Many immigrants come up from New Orleans, you see. They arrive from Europe already carrying the disease. We must stop them before they dock at the wharf and infect the city."

She moved to the window and pointed to a large building on the mainland. "That's Montesano House. There's a yawl tied up there—"

"A yawl?"

Patricia's forehead creased. "A small boat with sails."

"Ah. Of course. Please continue."

"It transports the quarantine officers to the incoming boats, day and night."

"How do boats know to stop here?"

"The yellow flags, miss. See how they're flown from the *St. Louis*?"

Marina looked toward the mainland.

"Not St. Louis, the city. The *St. Louis*. The steamboat moored there." She pointed to the boat Marina had noticed earlier. "Before laborers built these quarantine wards on the island, it served as a floating hospital. Even now, we may use it if we're overrun by cases."

"Interesting."

"They also fly flags from the shot tower near Montesano House, as well as the yawl. At night, they use lights."

"What if a steamboat refuses to stop?"

"They shoot a cannon. See it there on the bluff." She nodded to the bluff near the resort house. An impressive cannon overlooked the river.

"I'm sure that's effective."

"Very. Regulations call for ten rounds. If the boat still doesn't stop, a horseback rider alerts the city, and the fire bells ring the alarm. If they don't turn around, they'll face arrest."

"So, officers inspect all incoming boats. If they're clear of disease, they can pass on to the wharf. What if they're not?"

"Those infected must stay here in the quarantine wards for at least ten days." Her face drooped with a frown. "If they make it that long. The cemetery is already quite full."

"They get better, or they die here." It wasn't a question. Just a sad fact. Those who came to this country to seek a better life might end up dying on a sandy island, bodies piled into an overcrowded cemetery. "How many sick are here on the island?"

"Over a hundred."

Wow. "That many and only two nurses?"

"Before the sisters came, the quarantine crew was severely overworked. Dr. Barr hardly sleeps."

What a sad state of affairs. "How'd you come to be here?"

"My father was one of the carpenters who worked to construct the shanties and hospital buildings. He contracted the disease and passed on. My mother had already died from it." She shrugged like this horrid story was everyday news. "Since I was left alone, I thought I might as well make myself useful. I'm not afraid of meeting my end here."

Heavens, what a tragic story. "You're brave."

"Or perhaps I have nothing left to lose." Patricia turned back to the row of empty beds and sighed. "We must strip these and place fresh linens upon them."

A pang wedged under Marina's ribs. She didn't need to ask what had happened to the patients previously inhabiting those beds. Would she truly be able to handle being around the dead and dying each day? Adam had had a closed-casket funeral for a reason. If she looked death straight in the face, she might not survive.

~

Claire's knee bobbed up and down as she listened to her parents drone on about Julie again. How could she extricate herself from this conversation? She had to get to the beach with Aiden. Ask about Brinley. It was ridiculous to try and make casual chitchat when a girl was missing. She'd tried to excuse herself several times, but her parents kept cutting her off. Cutting her down. Why was it so hard for her to assert herself with them?

"And how is your job going, dear?" Mom asked.

Not as well as Julie's. That was for sure. "I enjoy teaching at the Y. It's rewarding." Though true, her career was far from impressive, especially to her parents. Her gaze trailed to the front door. How to escape?

Dad grunted. "Yes, but when are you going to get a real job? It's far past time."

"Have you considered modeling? I've always thought you'd make a lovely model." Another insult veiled as a compliment from Mom, and a familiar one at that.

"Marge, she's about to blow up like a balloon. No one wants a fat model."

Bearett cleared his throat. Opened his mouth as if he was about to defend her, but Mom beat him to it.

"Magazines hire pregnant models, dear. Someone has to show off maternity wear."

Another grunt. "After she has the baby, she'll have a pooch. Not modeling material."

"I don't want to model." Claire tried to keep her tone calm, but an edge snaked through. They'd been over this a thousand times, but for some reason, modeling was the only career her mother deemed her capable of. "I want to teach fitness classes. And someday, I'd like to be a homeopathic doctor."

Mother's face twisted like she'd bitten into a lemon. "Oh, come on, Claire. That's a nice thought, but becoming a doctor is a lot of work, even if it's one of those natural gurus instead of a real doctor."

Bearett slapped his hands against his legs. "Have you eaten? I could take you out for brunch. Claire has … an errand to run."

Amazing man. She shot him a grateful half smile.

"We're fine, dear." Mom sat stiff and straight, hands folded in her lap. "I had a protein bar before we arrived."

Dad shifted on the couch as though trying to get comfortable. Julie no doubt had nicer furniture. "No need for you to spend money you don't have. Save it for our grandchild."

Footsteps approached, then Aiden burst through the door, the black-haired girl right behind him. "We found out where Brinley might have gone. Or at least, how she got there." He stopped short as his gaze landed on Claire's parents. "Oh, hi."

Claire stood and gestured to their guests. "This is my mom and dad."

Mom tilted her head up slightly. "Mr. and Mrs. Severe."

"Oh. Hello." He offered them a polite smile before turning his attention back to Claire. "We have a lead, but the guy won't talk."

Dad's eyes narrowed. "A lead to what?"

Claire pressed her lips together. How could she explain without admitting her incompetence?

Aiden tossed her parents a glance. "My sister's missing, and we found someone who knows something."

"Missing?" Mom's hand flew to her heart. "Does he mean the guest you're supposed to keep an eye on?"

"Yes, but—"

"It's not Claire's fault Brinley snuck off." Aiden crossed his arms. Sweet of him to stick up for her.

"Don't you have any control over these hooligans?" Dad huffed.

The dark-haired girl's eyes widened.

Aiden's jaw dropped. "We're not—"

"Wait outside, please." Claire motioned Aiden toward the back porch. "I'll be right there, and we'll come up with a plan."

"Yeah. Sure." He let himself outside, his *friend* nearly stepping on his heels to get away from the indoor chaos.

"And you think you have what it takes to raise a child? Goodness gracious, Claire." Disappointment dripped from Mom's words.

Claire's face flamed.

Bearett jumped to his feet. "Claire is going to be a wonderful mother. Speak to my wife with respect, please."

Mom raised her hands. "I meant no offense." She turned to Dad and mumbled, "Someone is touchy today."

"Mom, Dad, please." Her neck muscles tightened. "This is important."

"Obviously," her mother mumbled.

Once Claire closed the sliding glass door behind her, she turned to the girl. "And who's this?"

"Sorry, this is Nevaeh."

Just as she'd thought. "Nice to meet you, Nevaeh. You look familiar."

"I've been on several of your cruises." She smiled sweetly.

"That explains it."

"Nevaeh is helping me track down Brinley." He went on to explain their suspicions from the employee's odd behavior at the marine rental shop. "She must have been there. Probably rented a boat or was with people who did."

Nevaeh tucked her hands into the back pockets of her jean shorts. "I think we should wait until that worker leaves and someone new comes on shift, then ask again. We might have better luck with someone else."

Smart girl. "Great idea." She glanced through the door to where her parents sat stiffly on her couch. Bearett was once again sitting across from them. "How can I help?" She had to do *something*. Try to hunt Brinley down some way.

Aiden shook his head. "If the next person won't talk, maybe you could try prying information from them? You might have better luck being older and part of the community."

"Sure thing. I should go try now. Maybe the person who brushed you off will talk to me."

"Doubt it," Aiden said. "And if we tick him off too much, we might make things worse. He could tell the other workers to keep their mouths shut. Or call the police for harassment."

"I won't harass anyone. Just politely ask questions."

"I don't know. Might be best to wait."

She held back a growl. How horrible to feel so helpless. She placed her hand on the door handle. "Sorry about my parents. They're … a lot. I've been trying to brush them off for over an hour."

"Not your fault." Aiden took a step away from the door. "But I think we'll walk around the house so we don't have to talk to them again."

Good call. If only she had that option.

Nevaeh reached out, as if she was going to put her hand on Claire's arm, but then she tucked her hand back into her pocket. "Children aren't responsible for their parents, and vice versa. Everyone makes their own choices."

With that, they rounded the house and disappeared from sight. If only *she* could get away that easily.

Everyone makes their own choices. Claire wasn't responsible for her parents' atrocious behavior. Same with Brinley's. But surely, she'd be responsible for her own child. It was her job to train her children up in the way they should go. If they strayed, didn't that mean she hadn't done her job well enough? The weight of that responsibility hung so heavily on her shoulders that her knees nearly buckled.

Lord, where are You in this mess? Would You truly give me a child if I didn't have the ability to raise him or her right? Oh, God, I need You. I can't do this on my own. Her thoughts turned to Brinley. *And keep Brinley safe. Bring her home, Lord. Show us where to find her.* Because this was another problem too big for her small hands.

~.

Aiden peeked through the window of the marine rental shop. "He's still there." The man who wouldn't tell them anything leaned against the counter, phone in hand.

Nevaeh lifted a tanned shoulder. The sunburn had faded, leaving beautiful sun-kissed skin. "There'll probably be a shift change around lunchtime. We'll come back."

"What should we do until then?"

Nevaeh scanned the beach. "Looks like a group is playing volleyball. We could ask to join?"

Aiden shook his head. "No, thank you." He'd pass on completely humiliating himself in front of his growing crush.

His gaze landed on a poster plastered to the shop's window. "What about jet-skiing?" Another thing Mom was too afraid to let him try, though it didn't make sense why not. It wasn't like the news warned of deaths from jet-skiing accidents.

"Oooh. That sounds fun. Let's do it!" Her smile dimmed. "How much does it cost?"

He glanced at the fine print. A hundred dollars an hour, plus fuel. Spending an hour with Nevaeh's arms wrapped around his waist would be worth draining his bank account. But should he really be having fun when his sister was missing? It would only be for an hour, and there wasn't much else they could do but wait. "No worries. I'll cover it."

Her eyes danced. "Looks like we'll pay Mr. Tight-Lipped another visit."

He held out his hand, and she took hold. Together, they reentered the shop and strode to the counter.

The man frowned. "You again? I told you to scram. I can't give you any information."

He lifted his hands in innocence. "I heard you. I'd like to rent a Jet Ski."

The man eyed him. "How old are you?"

"Seventeen."

"Must be eighteen to rent. Sixteen to drive one. You'll have to have your parent rent it for you."

His shoulders slumped. Even if Mom were here, there was no way she'd do such a thing.

Nevaeh bumped her hip into his. "Ask Claire."

The worker perked up. "Claire Duncan?"

"Yeah. She's a … family friend."

"My girlfriend takes her yoga classes." All traces of defensiveness fell away.

"Pilates," Aiden corrected. Where had that come from? "She's busy at the moment. Probably can't come down here." Although this might be the perfect excuse for her to flee from her awful parents.

"Whatever. Tell you what. If you can get her on the phone to give me verbal permission, I'll sign off on it." He winked.

So, this man was willing to bend the rules. Did he do so for Brinley, or had her group included someone old enough to rent a boat?

After a quick phone call to Claire, Aiden left the shop with keys in hand. Mr. Tight-Lipped led them to the marina across the street where their Jet Ski waited and explained operating instructions. "Have fun."

No *be careful*? Maybe that mantra belonged only to his mother. Aiden hopped on and scooted forward to make room for Nevaeh. She straddled the Jet Ski and wrapped her arms tight around him. Sweet heavens. The one-hour rental would hardly be enough.

He started the engine. "You ready?"

"Absolutely." Nevaeh's breath tickled his ear, sending shivers down his spine. Her coconut scent teased his senses.

It took him a few seconds to reorient himself, then he throttled the gas. They took off, sputtering at first, then flying through the waves. Water misted his face and splashed his legs. Nevaeh's laugh resounded behind him. Almost like music. Could there be a better sound? If only he could listen to her laugh forever.

Forever?

There he went, rushing ahead again. He needed to dial down his growing feelings for her. This was a summer fling, at best. No way it'd ever turn into something serious. Nothing that warranted the word *forever*.

The hour seemed like minutes as they zipped across the lake, hooting, hollering, and laughing. Loving. Woah. There he went again, making far too much of this experience. He wasn't in love. Couldn't be. And yet, there was nowhere he'd rather be than with her.

When he puttered to the dock, a few teens stood in front of the shop, vaping. Did they hang around here often? They might know where Brinley went. He dismounted and crossed the street to their haze of smoke, trying not to cough. Nevaeh followed.

"Hey, do any of you remember seeing a girl named Brinley a couple of days ago? She's about two inches shorter than me, same color hair and features. My sister."

Two of the guys exchanged a look before one with a tattoo of a surfboard on his neck spoke up. "Yeah, maybe. Jack had a group of losers with him—no offense to your sister."

Jack. Of course. "Did they rent a boat?"

Tattoo Guy angled his head toward the shop's entrance. "Not positive, but they all went in there and came out hyped up."

A girl by his side shuddered. "That Jack's bad news. A real jerk."

Tattoo Guy scoffed. "You don't know that."

"I do."

"How?"

Aiden put out his hands. No need to get involved with their disagreement. "You're sure Brinley went with him?"

"Not positive," the guy said.

The girl crossed her arms. "Pretty sure."

Nevaeh stepped forward. "Any clue where they went?"

"Said something about a trip. Brought a ton of beer."

Great. Just what he needed to hear. He stepped away from the smoke-filled haze, running his hand through his hair. Why hadn't he kept a closer eye on his sister? Some brother he was.

Nevaeh put a hand on his arm. "It'll be okay. We'll find her."

But how?

An idea struck out of nowhere. How come he hadn't thought of it before? "I have a plan." Or at least, the start of one. "We need to go back to Claire's."

Chapter Nineteen

Days passed, and Marina was no closer to accomplishing her mission than when she'd first stepped onto the island. Once again, the medical crew spouted outdated conclusions and solutions regarding cholera. She'd heard them all. Some thought it resulted from sauerkraut or beer. And, of course, they thought fruits and vegetables were at fault for being "excitable" to the digestive system. No mention of contaminated water as the cause or clean water and electrolytes as the cure. She had to clench her jaw to keep from arguing with them and risking death.

When she turned to leave a room, whispers of "insane" followed her. With each chamber pot emptied and linen changed, her heart folded in upon itself. She couldn't stand doing such menial tasks. People. She had to interact with people.

And so, gradually, she abandoned her assigned tasks to sit next to patients and offer comfort. She visited every bed, lingering with those who were the sickest. Those on the brink of death had sunken eyes and pale cheeks. Dry, cracked lips and glazed expressions made it obvious when death was imminent.

She hadn't been with Adam when he died. Hadn't gotten to the hospital in time to hold his hand as he passed. Would regret forever dog her? These poor souls had no one to comfort them in their last hours. The overworked staff could do little more than administer tonics to those they thought had the best chance of making it. Two nuns couldn't possibly provide adequate care and counsel to so many. Those who appeared to be lost causes were often left to die.

She sat by one such man, Edwin, as he faded. His blonde hair lay pasted to his forehead with sweat, his lips cracked and pale. Though she offered sips of water, ladling them into his mouth with a spoon, he didn't improve. Perhaps the very water she offered was contaminated. No way to boil it. She might be hastening these patients' deaths by attempting to quench their thirst.

She took Edwin's hand as his labored breaths barely lifted his chest. He had an hour maybe. Perhaps far less. Nothing more could be done. She should say something, but what? What possible comfort could she offer? She had no wise words. What did he need to hear, anyway?

Maybe a song. She racked her brain for one. Something hopeful. Something churchy. She hadn't set foot in a church in ages, but one song she heard at Adam's sister's funeral flitted to the top. All the exact words proved elusive, but she bumbled her way through "I Can Only Imagine." At least she likely got the chorus right. Or mostly right. He took his final breath before she finished the song.

Tears pricked her eyes. Ridiculous to cry for this stranger. She hadn't allowed herself to shed more than a few tears for Adam. But then, she had to be strong for her children. Here, there was no one to be strong for. No need to bury her grief. She allowed the tears to come, to make trails on her cheeks, to pool at the base of her neck.

The man who collected the dead and transported them to the graveyard came and stood next to her. "He's gone?"

"Yes," she choked out.

With a solemn nod, he lifted the frail man from his bed and carried him outside. She followed, singing the chorus again. These words she didn't believe thrashed in her chest. Had that man truly gone to be with Jesus? Was he right now standing before God? What if the talk about heaven was real?

When the man deposited Edwin's limp body into a cart, Marina ducked back inside. Maybe she could sing to another patient. Her voice wasn't Grammy-worthy, but she could carry a tune. It might prove comforting to these poor souls.

Edwin wouldn't have a funeral attended by loved ones. The gravedigger would bury him quietly and without ceremony. Would they even mark his grave? How unimaginable to be laid in an unmarked grave on an island in the middle of a river. Far from home. Far from loved ones. No one to visit and lay flowers.

If only she had some flowers to bring to the island cemetery. Trees and bushes flanked the buildings, but hardly a trace of a flower. Maybe … maybe she could make wreaths. That long dormant creative spark lit within her. Her pre-mother life. When she'd spent every free minute designing all kinds of crafts. Decorating baskets with Mod Podge and ribbons. Creating stylish centerpieces from whatever happened to be on sale at the craft supply store. And, of course, wreaths.

Outside the quarantine ward, the groundskeeper piled broken tree and vine branches. She might be able to weave them into something resembling a wreath. While there were no true flowers on the island, dandelions grew abundantly. They wouldn't last long for a decoration, but at least it was something. These people deserved honor in their deaths. She could provide a touch of dignity.

Suddenly energized, she rushed outside and began the tedious work of manipulating branches, twisting them together until they formed a circle. When she finished one, she started on another. Then another. She was no Martha Stewart, but they turned out decent. She took off to the field to gather dandelions. When she completed her projects, she carried them to the cemetery.

She stilled and looked out upon a sea of graves, the earth mounded in waves. So many bodies. The scent of dirt mingled with decay. She shivered. Could she do this? Draw near to such sorrow? She'd spent so much of the last couple of years avoiding grief. Avoiding the thought of death. And now she approached it with a measly three-wreath offering. Pathetic. Still, she took a deep breath and stepped forward.

Aiden barreled through the Duncans' front door and made a beeline to his bedroom, Nevaeh on his heels.

"What in heaven's name?" This from Claire's mom. Best to ignore her. "Such uncouth behavior. Claire, you really must rein these children in."

Whatever. No time for polite greetings. Brinley might be in danger.

That Jack's bad news. A real jerk. A ton of beer.

He entered his room and flung open the top dresser drawer.

"Are you going to tell me what's going on?" Nevaeh stood on her tiptoes to look over his shoulder.

Claire stepped into the room. "Yes, please enlighten us."

He dug under socks and underwear until his hand clasped Mom's phone. He pulled it out and powered it on. "Pretty sure Mom has GPS tracking on both of our phones. She's paranoid like that."

"Smart." Claire shut the door and came closer. "You think you can access it on her phone? It will tell us where Brinley is?"

"That's the idea."

"Genius." Nevaeh held prayer hands up to her face. "Please, God, let this work."

"Amen," Claire said.

"Amen," he echoed.

Mom's phone lit up with the picture of Dad. Aiden keyed in Dad's birthdate, then navigated to the correct app. "Bingo." Only, could that be right? "It says she's in Chicago."

"Chicago!" Claire's voice exploded through the room. "How'd she get to Chicago? And why?"

"She must have sailed there. That's possible, right?"

Claire tugged her hair from its ponytail, ran her hands through it, then put it up again. "Well, yeah, but it'd have to take over ten hours." She frowned. "Depending on the boat. You think she rented one? What kind?"

Nevaeh's expression pinched. "We're not positive, but a group of teens said they saw her with Jack, renting a boat." She pressed her lips together. "They said he had a ton of alcohol with him."

"Oh, my word." Claire plopped onto the edge of the bed. "This is a disaster."

Aiden stared at the icon. If only he could use mind control to move it to another location. Like in this house. "Brinley doesn't drink." At least, if she did, she'd hidden it from him well. And they didn't have secrets from each other.

Claire rocked back and forth. "What if this Jack's plan was to get her drunk and … take advantage of her?"

Oh, heck no. He'd beat the jerk to a pulp if he so much as touched Brinley without permission. She wouldn't … give him permission, would she? No. She wasn't that kind of girl. But what if she *did* drink? Alcohol might lower her inhibitions and cause her to do things she'd normally balk at. "We have to find her."

"Of course." Claire stood. "I'll get Bearett. We can take his boat."

She left the room. He studied Nevaeh. Her eyes held compassion, and what else? Determination? "Will you come with us?"

"I'll have to ask my parents, but if they're game, then I will."

He grasped both of her hands in his, then brought them to his lips. He kissed each knuckle.

Her cheeks turned a delightful shade of pink. How easy would it be to fall for her completely. If he gave himself the barest nod of permission, he could. He would. He lowered her hands from his lips.

She swung them side to side. "I had no idea meeting you would be such an adventure."

Despite everything, he couldn't help but smile. Oh, how he wanted to kiss her. He inched closer. Their gazes danced, hers dropping to his lips, then climbing back up. Her mouth parted ever so slightly. Did she want him to kiss her? Her chest rose and fell in rhythm with his own.

He angled his head. She leaned in. Mere inches away. She closed her eyes. Yes, she had to desire this as much as he. She certainly wasn't pushing him away. His heart banged in his chest. He wrapped his arm around her waist and lowered his mouth to hers.

Sweet heavens.

The door banged open, and they jumped apart.

"Bearett said—" Claire's eyebrows shot up as she surveyed the two of them.

He crossed his arms, uncrossed them, crossed them again. Nothing felt natural. How could it, with Nevaeh no longer in his embrace? She bit back a smile and twirled a strand of hair.

"Um." Claire pressed her lips together, then continued. "Bearett said he'll be ready to go within the hour."

"Great." Aiden nodded. Did he appear nonchalant? Or could she tell she'd interrupted what was sure to be the best kiss of his life?

"I'll call my mom." Nevaeh pulled her phone from her back pocket and wandered to the corner.

"Is she coming too?" Claire asked.

"If she can."

Claire pointed two fingers at her eyes, then back at him.

He lifted his hands. Sure, she could keep an eye on them. It wasn't like they'd done anything wrong. He was seventeen years old and allowed to kiss a girl. His neck heated. When they could sneak another moment to themselves, he'd finish what he'd started.

~

Great. Claire was in charge of a runaway *and* a lovesick boy. A *teenage* lovesick boy. All those hormones. She was powerless against such a pull. Yet, somehow, she needed to keep Aiden out of trouble while rescuing Brinley from disaster. And her parents were in town. No pressure.

She spun around and reentered the living room. Sitting across from her parents, she threaded her hands between her knees. Bearett had excused himself to their bedroom to make a few calls. "Mom, Dad, I hate to be rude, but something came up, and both Bearett and I need to go out on the boat for … a while." How long would this rescue mission take? Maybe her parents would just mosey on back home.

"Something came up." Mom scoffed. "You've got to chase down that girl you're supposed to keep an eye on, don't you?"

No use denying it. "Yeah. We know where she is now, and we need to go get her."

Dad tsked. "My, my, Claire. How'd you manage to get yourself into such a pickle?"

She shrugged. "Bad luck?"

"More like lack of common sense," Mom mumbled.

Ouch. Did the two of them have to berate her at least ten times per hour? Was there some kind of quota? And they wondered why she'd moved. If only she and Bearett had settled in Europe instead. She couldn't get far enough away.

"We came here to spend time with you." Dad shook his head, making it clear she'd disappointed him. "We've only just arrived."

"I know." She clenched her hands. "Some things can't be helped. If you choose to stay awhile, I'm sure we could have lunch or something tomorrow. But if not, I understand." No way they'd hang around for hours on end, waiting for her to return.

"Why don't we join you in your little escapade?"

Claire about choked on her saliva. She cleared her throat. "Join me?"

"Yes, dear. We wanted to see Bearett's boat anyway. It's a beautiful day to go out on the lake."

"But it might take a while. A long while."

Dad shrugged. "We've got time."

Bearett exited their bedroom, white ball cap in hand. "I had to cancel the next cruise. I don't know when we'll be back, but surely not in time. Antone said he'll call the customers and offer them a voucher for another cruise or a refund."

"Honey, my parents volunteered to go with us, but wouldn't it be faster to drive?" She attempted to signal her distress through widened eyes.

"It would, but if they take off in their boat, how would we catch up to them?"

"Okay." Apparently, he didn't understand her distress signal. His reasoning made sense, but spending multiple hours on the boat with her parents? She'd rather take her chances swimming across the lake. "How long will it take?"

He settled the hat on his head and folded the brim. "I think we could make it there in a little over three hours."

"Oh." That was much better than ten. "Where'd I get ten hours?" She must have heard it somewhere.

"If they took a sailboat, it'd take that long or longer. We've got a good-sized boat with a decent engine." He rubbed his hands together and directed his gaze toward her parents. "You two up for at least a six-hour adventure?"

Please say no. Please say no.

Dad smiled. Actually smiled. "Sounds refreshing."

Nevaeh exited Aiden's room, sliding her phone into her pocket. "My mom said I can go."

Wow, really? Her parents would let her accompany virtual strangers on a rescue mission to Chicago?

Aiden stood beside her, goofy grin proving his delight at the prospect of more time with the girl. Kind of cute, actually. Young love. Sweet. Maybe she didn't need to worry about him at all. What would Marina think?

Marina. What in the world was going on with her? Would she ever return? She had to eventually, but not hearing from her for so long left much to the imagination. If she tried to change history … No. Claire couldn't allow her mind to go down that path. Aiden and Brinley needed their mother, and they'd get her.

Please, God, let her return soon.

Bearett turned to Claire. "Any chance you could throw some sandwiches and snacks together?"

"Yep." Would they be good enough for her picky parents? Probably not. At least Aiden and his girlfriend would likely enjoy them. She went to work putting together veggies and dip and assembling turkey sandwiches.

"Make mine with Dijon mustard, dear, if you have it," Mother called.

She didn't have any, and Mother would never abide yellow mustard, but she didn't say anything. No use arousing her displeasure before they even set foot on the boat.

"Ready." She looped the cooler bag around her shoulder.

Bearett put on his ball cap "Does everyone have what they need? There are beverages on board."

"I'm not comfortable leaving our car at the beach after dark, and we might not be back by then," Mom said.

When everyone confirmed they were ready to go, Bearett led them out the door. "We'll be a little squished in our SUV, but it's a short drive."

Six people in a five-seater? Great. Claire allowed her father to take the passenger's seat and sidled next to her mother in the second row. Too close for comfort. Aiden sat on her other side, and Nevaeh planted herself in his lap. Would Marina freak out about this? Hopefully, she'd never find out.

Mom rolled her eyes at the lovebirds' arrangement, then patted her knee. "Don't worry, dear. I'm here to help you straighten this whole mess out." Oh joy. "Do you think you'll need me to move here when the baby's born? It's a lot for someone like you to handle, you know."

Someone like her. Brainless and incompetent, apparently.

Nevaeh's gaze swung in her direction. "Wait, you're pregnant? That's great."

"Yeah, congrats," Aiden chimed in.

Mom huffed but said nothing.

Great. Yeah, that was the word for it. She placed her hand on her stomach. If only she could drum up some excitement for this baby. Maybe it'd come in time. If her parents didn't squash her last seed of hope.

Chapter Twenty

"Helfen Sie mir bitte."
The anguished cry beckoned Marina to the last cot in the row. There, a pale, skeleton-thin blonde woman fisted her sheets. She looked like a ghost. Likely only a shell of who she used to be.

Marina searched the archives of her brain for the German phrases she'd learned while helping Aiden with his high school class. This is where it helped to be *over-involved*, as Aiden had put it. *Helfen.* Help. *Bitte.* Please. Oh, dear. If only she *could* help. *"Wie kann ich helfen?"* How can I help? Hopefully, she'd gotten that right. She held up a glass of water. *"Das Wasser?"*

"Nein." The woman shook her head vehemently, but a spark of something like hope broke through her gaze. *"Meine Kinder."*

Her children? It was as if an electric current shot from the German woman's heart straight to Marina's. This lady had children, and she was dying. Steely determination solidified within her. *"Wo?"* Where?

A pearl-shaped tear beaded in the corner of her left eye. *"Ich weiss nicht."* She didn't know.

Marina grasped the woman's limp hand. "I'll find them. I'll take care of them." What were the German words? *"Ich finden. Ich ..."* She grappled with bits and pieces from her memory of Aiden's course material. Nothing. "Care."

Even without the correct German words, the woman nodded, like she understood perfectly. *"Du erziehst meine Kinder. Sei du ihre Mutter."*

Erziehst? What did that mean? *Mutter* was obvious. *Du*? You. Marina sucked in a breath. Was this woman asking her to take over for her as the children's mother?

No, she couldn't do that. She had her own children to care for, as soon as she could return to them. But she could ensure these children were taken care of before she left 1849 for good. Hopefully. She certainly didn't know enough of the language to argue. "*Wie heissen Kinder?*" She winced as she said the words. That wasn't right. But probably close enough for the woman to understand her meaning: What are the children's names?

"*Frieda und Heinrich.*"

Marina squeezed her hand. "*Ja. Gut.*"

Nothing about this situation was good, but how in the world did one say *Okay, random lady, I'll search for your children and ensure they're cared for after you die*? Now, if she could only get the woman to drink.

She held out the water glass again. "*Wasser. Trinken bitte.*" Or was it *bitte trinken*? Close enough.

When the woman shook her head again, Marina softened her voice even further. "*Bitte.*" She brought the liquid to the woman's lips. Only a sip, but better than nothing. What she wouldn't give for modern medicine. IV fluids could save so many lives.

She set the cup within reach and rose. She had no more words. Her brain hurt from trying so hard to find the ones she'd already used. She dared not speak the only German word that held fast in her mind. *Auf Wiedersehen.* Goodbye.

She approached Patricia, who hustled to tuck in fresh sheets. Readying a bed for a new patient. The old man who'd occupied the spot was gone forever.

"Do you know where two German children might be? Frieda and Heinrich."

"How old? Are they sick?"

"No idea. Their mother is in bad shape. She's asking after them."

"In that case, try the southmost shanty. Sister Margaret put an older girl in charge of the younger orphans there."

Her heart crumpled. There were more of them? Children without parents. And here she was a parent without her children. Perhaps they could find comfort in each other. She set off.

She opened the shanty's door and gasped. There had to be over twenty children stuffed in that small space. They huddled together, knees to their chests, faces streaked with tears, foreheads damp with sweat. Some cried. Some screamed as though she were the grim reaper coming to take them away. Marina could hardly breathe in that stuffy room. Only four cots, far too few, with barely any light seeping through the lone window. A dozen pairs of wide eyes searched hers, while the other children slept. Such fear. Such uncertainty. Their need crashed into her with the force of a tidal wave.

When Patricia had said an older girl, Marina had pictured a sixteen-year-old. Instead, the tallest among them couldn't have been more than twelve. She bounced a baby on her hip, dirty hair tangled around her shoulders. "Yes, miss?"

"Are you in charge?"

The girl nodded. Oh, for shame. This was far too much for someone so young to handle.

"They should go outside. Play in the field." The island boasted of wide spaces. There was no reason the children shouldn't utilize them.

"They're afraid of catching the cholera. This island is full of bad air."

"No, not at all." The whole theory was ludicrous. "The fresh air will be good for them, and the sunlight provides vitamin D, which will strengthen their immune systems. They're far more susceptible to sickness cooped up together in here." Could the young girl even comprehend her explanation? Before the girl could protest and lecture her about preventing cholera, Marina shooed the children outside. "Go play. Go. *Schnell.*"

When they were slow to respond, she picked up a child and set him on his feet outside the door. "Run. Play."

Once that child found his feet and ran off, others followed until the room emptied. The young leader's expression clouded.

"Don't worry. It's fine. I promise."

She frowned. "I hope you're right."

Oh, the German children. She'd forgotten the reason she'd come in the first place. "Which ones are Frieda and Heinrich?"

"There." She pointed to a girl of maybe eight, wearing a crown of platinum blonde braids and holding hands with a boy who was little more than a toddler.

So young? *Oh, Lord. Help them.* Another prayer. She was on a roll.

The boy waddled down a slight slope, hair blowing this way and that in the breeze. Adorable. It wouldn't be hard to find adoptive parents for these precious ones, would it? Only, with an average of one hundred people a day dying throughout St. Louis, the number of orphans left behind might prove staggering. Would enough willing adults be left to care for them?

She approached the children, picking dandelions on the way. Kneeling before them, she wove the weed-flowers into some semblance of a crown and set it on Frieda's head. If only she knew the word for princess. But she did say, "*Schön.*" Beautiful.

The corners of Frieda's mouth inched upward, then dropped again. "*Mutter?*"

How did one break the news to children that their mother was dying? She wouldn't be able to do so with grace in English, much less with her limited German.

"*Ist Mutter noch krank?*"

Krank? Not a clue what that meant. "*Sie hat Bauchschmerzen.*" She has a belly ache. A woefully inadequate explanation, but all she could weave together.

The boy's lower lip wobbled. Oh no. Was he about to cry? Her heart might shatter if he did. She needed to distract him. How did one challenge someone to a race in German?

"*Laufen?*" The word for run was all she could come up with. She bent into a runner's pose and pointed to a tree several yards away. "To the tree."

Heinrich cocked his head.

"On your mark, get set … go!" She took off. A glance behind her showed that both Frieda and Heinrich had caught on. They chased after her, faces no longer bent in frowns. She slowed, allowing them to catch up. She and Frieda reached the tree at the same time, little Heinrich a few strides behind. Frieda giggled, her dandelion crown now askew. Marina straightened it.

"*Wieder,*" Frieda said.

Again. Sure, she could manage another race. This time she pointed to a shrub. "There. On your mark, get set … go."

Shrieks of laughter buoyed her. Foreign sounds in this place, yet so needed. What light children could bring.

She wouldn't be able to run forever. How else could she entertain them? Surely, she had something in her purse. She mentally cataloged its contents, then broke into a smile. Balloons! She had a few left over from Brinley's last birthday party. Man, were they going to love that surprise. For the first time since she'd landed in 1849, her chest felt light. The air swirled with the promise of a future beyond tragedy. Was this hope?

~

Claire slid her sunglasses on. Bonus: Now her mom wouldn't be able to tell when she rolled her eyes. The sun glared down on the six of them as Bearett guided the *Duncan's Delight* into the open waters. Sweat had already gathered between her shoulder blades. The air-conditioned deck below would be nice right about now, but her parents insisted on the view from the top deck. So, she stood, back to the railing, surveying the motley crew.

Dad lounged, sporting his fisherman's hat and draining a beer as though this trip was the height of relaxation. Mom wandered, likely inspecting every corner for dust or something. Aiden and Nevaeh sat bow side, chairs scooted as close together as they could possibly get.

Mom circled back to the mailbox, studying the outside like there'd be a test later. Why couldn't *she* time-sail? Claire covered a snort at the thought of her mother stuck in the primitive past. She'd pay good money to see a film detailing that adventure.

"Why ever would you have such an ugly thing on your ship, Claire? It's atrocious."

"It's an antique."

"It's junk."

If only Claire could mask her facial expressions as well as she could her eye roll.

Mom lifted the lid and peeked in. "There's something in here."

Claire's chest tightened. "There is?" She'd checked a couple of days ago, and it had been empty. She hadn't thought to check again. Marina had somehow received their letters. Had she now written one in return?

Mom could *not* read it if that was the case. She nearly sprinted to the box. "I'll take it." She snatched the letter from her mother's hand.

"For goodness' sake, Claire. What is all this about?" She waved her hand toward the letter.

What to say? Her pulse thrummed. "Sometimes, passengers leave notes for us. Nothing to worry about."

"Like a comment box?"

"Mm-hmm." Something like that.

"You really should have a sign explaining what it's for. How do people know to take advantage of it?"

"We tell them."

"A sign would be more convenient."

"Good idea." She'd hang one up tomorrow. *Attention passengers: If you happen to time travel to the past from this boat to another, please utilize the mailbox.* That would earn them a great Trip Advisor rating.

She took the letter to the far side of the boat to read. The paper flapped in the breeze. Marina said she was well—*safe and good*—and that she was doing important work. The good news? She hadn't died. The bad? She seemed settled there. Almost content. She'd even named a dog. Was she still trying to change the future by solving the cholera pandemic? If so, she might still be in danger of never coming back.

A niggling worry twisted Claire's gut. Was it because of Marina's stubborn insistence to bring dynamic change to 1849? No. What bothered her more was the fact that Marina didn't seem to understand that she was needed here. In the present. With her children. What work could be more important than raising the son and daughter she'd birthed into the world? Couldn't she see that was her highest calling?

What about you? Do you see it?

The gentle whisper encircled her heart. It was the Lord's still, small voice, without a doubt. She sucked in a long breath of fresh air. What was God trying to teach her? Could it be that her greatest contribution to this big, beautiful world was the life her body was nourishing undercover? But she'd never questioned whether motherhood was important. Only if she was up to the task.

Bearett had spouted off a quote once. Something about God qualifying those He calls, not the other way around. If this baby was her high calling, wouldn't God equip her for the task?

"Um, Claire?" Aiden neared, face in a grimace. "I screwed up."

"How so?" She lowered her shades.

"I texted Brinley, letting her know that we were coming to get her, and she disabled the GPS tracker. I can't locate her." He rubbed his forehead. "It was stupid of me to give her a heads- up. I'm sorry."

Poor guy. It's not like this mess was his fault. Brinley had made her choices. "It's okay. Let me talk to Bearett and see if he wants to continue on to Chicago."

"She said they were about to set sail. She might not be there when we arrive."

Nevaeh came up behind him, typing on her phone. She glanced up. "Sorry. My mom." She pocketed the phone. "So, what's the plan?"

"Let me find out." Claire bounded down the stairs.

"What's going on?" Mom called behind her.

Claire ignored her and strode to Bearett.

"Trouble in paradise?" The left side of his mouth crooked up.

"Brinley disabled the GPS on her phone. Should we risk trying to find her at her last known location or head back home?" Claire bit her lip. If they continued and didn't find her, Mom would have a grand ole time berating her for the wild goose chase. But what were the other options? Just wait for her to return?

"Hmm." Bearett swiped the hat from his head and rubbed his brow with his arm before returning it. "I'm not sure what the right thing to do is. Let's pray."

Prayer. Of course. Much better than freaking out.

He kept his hand on the wheel and his eyes ahead as he prayed. "Lord, You said that if anyone lacks wisdom, they should ask, and You'll give it. We're asking for wisdom now. Lead and guide us, God."

"Amen." She puffed out her cheeks. Now would be a great time for a booming voice to break in from on high. Nothing.

Bearett sighed. "If she doesn't want to be found, we're not going to find her."

"Thanks, Mr. Positive. You're blowing me away with your optimism."

"I'm serious. I don't think it'd be beneficial to keep going. Besides, what are we going to do if we *do* find her and she refuses to come home? Should I throw her over my shoulder and bind and gag her? She'd only run again the first chance she got."

"Then handcuff her to the boat, for goodness' sake. She's too young and vulnerable to be on her own."

"I agree this is a horrible situation, but I can't see how going after her now will solve anything."

Claire rubbed her temples. "Does this mean I have to go back up there and tell my parents I failed yet again?"

"You didn't fail, sweetheart." He kissed the top of her head. "None of this is your fault."

Her eyes burned. She pinched the bridge of her nose. "Will you explain that to them?" Not that she believed it. She could list a dozen *what-if* scenarios where she might have prevented this disaster.

"Absolutely. As soon as we dock."

Which meant, she'd have to be the one to let them know. "At least I won't have to stay on this boat with them for six more hours."

"And our guest room is taken. You'll get a break."

If only that meant she'd be immune to their insults.

~

Aiden nearly growled as the *Duncan's Delight* drifted into South Haven's harbor. He'd been an idiot, texting Brinley like that. He should have listened to Nevaeh, who had questioned the idea. But no. He'd thought his close relationship with Brinley would be enough to draw her back to him, back "home."

This was all his fault.

Claire's parents kept griping about how Claire didn't know what she was doing and how she never should have volunteered to keep an eye on his sister and him. As if she'd signed up for this mess. Aiden had to nearly bite his tongue to keep from shouting at them that none of this was Claire's fault. If he lost it and gave them a piece of his mind, they'd only blame Claire more for not being able to control him.

Nevaeh placed her hand over his on the railing. "You're still blaming yourself, aren't you?"

His hand tingled with her touch. They'd never gotten around to finishing that kiss. And now he was in a foul mood. "Maybe."

"Don't."

As if it were that easy. He smirked. "You're a bossy one."

She smiled. "Hey, my church is holding a prayer meeting tonight. We're just in time to go if you want. That's what I was chatting with my mom about. I asked her to put Brinley on the prayer list."

"I don't know." He'd do nearly anything to spend more time with her, but a prayer meeting? He'd stick out, for sure. He didn't know the first thing about prayer. Plus, it sounded more boring than watching paint dry.

Please come with me, her gorgeous eyes pleaded.

His resistance melted like the ice cream they'd consumed on their non-date. "If you're sure I'm allowed. Not being a member of your church or anything."

She laughed. "I'm not even a member. I don't live here, remember? This is just the church we go to whenever we're in town. Of course, you're welcome."

"Okay. If you say so."

The pleasure written on her face buoyed his spirits. He'd become a pastor if it'd mean she'd look at him like that forever.

When the boat docked, he followed Claire and Bearett off. Their slumped shoulders caused another wave of guilt to rise. Way to ruin everyone's day.

"This would be a nice boat with some improvements," Claire's mom said behind him.

The only improvement needed was to ban obnoxious people.

He left Nevaeh's side to catch up to Claire. "Hey, I'm going with Nevaeh to a prayer meeting at her church. If that's okay with you, I mean." After the day she'd had, he wouldn't demand his way. Plus, if she said no, it'd give him an excuse to skip the awkwardness.

"That's fine." She lifted a weary smile.

Okay, he was doing this. Going to a prayer meeting. He halted his steps, waiting for Nevaeh.

"Claire said it was fine."

"Great. The church is within walking distance."

He took her hand, threading his fingers through hers. "Lead the way."

She fit beside him like a puzzle piece. With her next to him, nothing could defeat him. Not even his mistakes. They walked at a leisurely pace. He was in no hurry to trade Nevaeh's presence for that of some stuffy religious people.

Only, Nevaeh wasn't like that. She seemed to have a special relationship with God. She called Him her friend. Intriguing. This meeting might not be that bad if the other attendees were like her.

When they arrived at South Haven Christian Church, Aiden hesitated on the top step. This was crazy. Why did he think it was okay to crash a prayer meeting? He wouldn't know anyone here. They might all be ninety-year-old grandmas. They'd probably sense that he didn't belong and send him judgy looks.

Nevaeh, a couple of steps ahead, gently tugged his hand. "It'll be fine. Don't worry."

It was like she could read his mind. He'd made it this far. As long as Nevaeh was beside him, he could force himself to follow through. He trudged forward.

She entered as if she belonged and led him to a staircase. "They meet downstairs."

Great, a prayer meeting in a creepy basement. Nothing better than that.

But as they came down the last few steps, they entered a well-lit atrium, surrounded by windows on all sides. Not creepy at all. Blue cushioned chairs formed a semicircle around a low platform where a young woman played background music on the keyboard. More than a dozen people sat in the chairs, with a few more standing around the perimeter. Only two of them had white hair.

A lady who appeared to be around his mom's age came up to them and wrapped Nevaeh in a hug, causing her to let go of his hand. "So glad you came, sweetie. Who'd you bring with you?"

"This is my friend Aiden."

"Nice to meet you, Aiden." The woman stuck out her hand. "I'm Gloria, the pastor's wife."

"Nice to meet you," he said as they shook hands.

"We've just gotten started." She pointed to the microphone on the platform. "Anyone can go up to pray at any time. We'll all agree with you."

"Okay, thanks." No way would he go anywhere near that stage.

They sat in the back row just as some guy stepped up to the mic. "Hey, everyone. I want to pray for my grandma who's in the hospital. She suffered a stroke last night. The doctors don't know if she's going to regain movement in her left side."

Compassionate murmurs came from several in the room. The guy bowed his head and prayed for his grandma to be healed and for the doctors to have wisdom. He didn't use big words or religious lingo. Much like Nevaeh, he acted like God was his friend. Someone he could talk to. Aiden tried not to stare. He was probably supposed to bow his head and fold his hands. But Nevaeh's hands remained at her sides. Her eyes were closed. Her mouth moved, but no sound came out. Several people said, "Amen," even before the guy finished his prayer.

Was there really a God listening to this little gathering? A God who cared about the old lady with a stroke? Someone you could just talk to anywhere at any time? Sounded too good to be true. But what if …?

After that guy stepped down, an older woman came forward and prayed for her daughter, who was having a tough time in her marriage. Then, a man prayed for the homeless. Guess anything was game here.

When Nevaeh stood, Aiden tensed. She was going up there? He grasped her hand.

Lines creased her forehead. "What?"

He opened his mouth but couldn't formulate words. Why'd he want to stop her? Was this secondhand embarrassment?

"I'm going to pray for your sister."

He nodded and dropped his hand to his lap. Stupid of him to try and intervene. She was doing this for him.

She explained the situation with clarity and confidence, then closed her eyes to pray. "Lord, we ask You to keep Brinley safe, wherever she is, and that You'll bring her back home. Please move on her heart and cause her to want to return."

Amens resounded. He uttered one himself. Nevaeh continued to pray, her words simple, yet clear and confident. At one point, her voice cracked. Did she truly care this much about his sister? How could a girl she barely knew move her to almost tears?

Affection swelled in his chest. Nevaeh was the real deal. Stacy had often appeared fake, as if she had a different mask for each person she encountered. Pretty masks, all of them, but fake all the same. There wasn't a hint of pretending in Nevaeh's tone. How could seeing her pray attract him to her even more?

There was nowhere else he'd rather be.

Chapter Twenty-One

Marina's heart soared as Heinrich snuggled onto her lap. She sat on the grassy slope outside of the orphans' shanty, soaking up the sun. The light breeze proved a welcome relief from the muggy heat. The island had only patches of trees and shrubs here and there. Not much for shade.

Frieda giggled as she chased another girl, one with flaming red hair. Likely Irish. So many German and Irish on the island. Immigrants who came to forge a better life in America. How many of them had died trying? She shook her head. No use thinking on that somber thought. There was little she could do to stop this deadly plague. Not when even the doctors in St. Louis wouldn't listen to her. Those on the island thought her strange, labeling her as insane but harmless. The whispers were hard to ignore. She'd always been a good eavesdropper.

None of that mattered so much anymore, though. She had Frieda and Heinrich, and they needed her. Sister Margaret had informed her that their mother had passed away two days prior. Marina had fashioned a wreath and cried alongside the children as they bid their mother goodbye.

Now, she was all these poor children had in the world. They needed her, and she needed them. They alternated between periods of sadness—weeping or staring quietly into the distance, as if their mother would come walking toward them at any moment—and delightful childishness. Running, playing, singing, clapping.

Marina couldn't help but hug them tight, savoring their soft hair against her cheek. They needed baths. Badly. But she'd grown so used to the stench of 1849 she could more easily ignore it. Nowhere to bathe except for the river, and its murky brown depths didn't seem sanitary or safe. If only she could whisk them away to her time and delight them with a tub full of bubbles.

Her heart squeezed. She couldn't take these precious children with her. How could she bear to leave them? They'd bonded so quickly to her, and she to them. Maybe she could stay. Should stay. Aiden and Brinley were fine without her, but Heinrich and Frieda needed her. Perhaps Miles had the right idea … only, she couldn't live on the island forever, and there were no bridges to the mainland. She'd have to get on a boat eventually. Would her time whisk her back?

No. She couldn't have accomplished her mission. Nothing she'd attempted thus far had gone as planned. She'd be safe to sail back to the city.

But then what? Where would she work with two children to look after? Where would they live? Surely, Miles would help her navigate things. Miles. She couldn't help but smile at remembering him. Another person who valued her greatly. Life in 1849 wouldn't be so bad. Sure, she'd lack modern conveniences, but if Miles had learned to do without them, she could too. They could be a family, the four of them.

Heinrich patted her cheek, snapping her out of the daydream. "*Du bist schön.*"

Aw. This precious boy thought her beautiful. "*Danke. Du auch.*" Though handsome would probably be a better word, she couldn't come up with the German word for it. Aiden used to tell her she was the *prettiest mama in all the earths*. Oh heavens, Aiden. How could she have thought, even for one minute, about abandoning him? A ridiculous notion. She couldn't forsake her family, even if they claimed not to need her. They'd forged a history together, and that was no small thing. She had to return to them.

Eventually.

Ingrid, the young girl in charge of the orphans' shanty, rang a bell, and the children scampered off for their noon meal.

She'd joined them yesterday but needed to stretch her legs and gather her thoughts today. How could she care for these beautiful children and not allow her heart to grow attached? She'd created a whole fantasy of mothering them long-term in her mind. Best to do something else to clear her head. She hadn't set foot in the quarantine ward since she'd discovered the children, except to talk to the doctors. Perhaps someone there needed her comfort.

She entered to stuffy heat and pulled at her collar. Spending a couple of days in the fresh air had caused her to forget this suffocating feeling. How could the patients stand it? So many of them had fevers.

She ambled from bed to bed, offering smiles and greetings. Hardly anyone responded, their glassy eyes likely unseeing as their bodies cramped with dehydration. She offered water to one man and a cool rag to another's head.

She stopped abruptly at the rasp of a semi-familiar voice.

"'I have called thee by thy name. Thou art mine.'"

Turning, she searched the beds for its source. George. Propped up on a pillow, eyes bright. Far less pale than he'd been on the boat. "George, you're recovering." She rushed to his side, his friendly face a beacon for her in the lonely ward.

"'To every thing there is a season, and a time to every purpose under the heaven: A time to be born, and a time to die; a time to plant, and a time to pluck up that which is planted; a time to kill, and a time to heal; a time to break down, and a time to build up; a time to weep, and a time to laugh; a time to mourn, and a time to dance.'"

She swatted his arm. "What nonsense are you spurting now?"

That was a song, right? "Turn! Turn! Turn!" But how would George know it? Sure, it was an oldie, but not *that* old.

He grasped her hand, his gaze burrowing into hers. "Marina, a time to mourn."

She shook off his hold and looked toward an empty bed. He saw too much. "Yeah, okay, but apparently, it wasn't your time to die, so I'm *rejoicing* in that." She forced a smile. Now she had that song in her head.

"Perhaps he saved me for this purpose, to tell you that even mourning has its season."

What was he talking about? He was clearly still delirious. She offered him a drink from the cup at his bedside. "Here, drink more water." Hopefully, it would help and not harm him further.

His Adam's apple bobbed with his swallow. "'Inasmuch as ye have done it unto one of the least of these my brethren, ye have done it unto me.'"

"That's a Bible verse, right?" She'd heard that before. Maybe at church or maybe at some volunteer function.

"Indeed."

"Good thing cholera didn't knock Scripture out of you. You've still got it." And her insides still squirmed with each verse. Thankfully, he was alive … but that didn't mean she had to sit here and listen to him spout Bible verses all day. "Rest now. The Sisters will visit later and see if there's anything else you need." At least, they would if they could, if they weren't overwhelmed with new patients.

She'd taken three steps away from him when his feeble voice crashed into her back.

"Marina, don't be afraid to mourn."

Afraid? Of course not. She harrumphed as she made a beeline for the door. She needed to get out into the fresh air. That stifling atmosphere muddled her mind. *A time to mourn.* Why would she waste her time dwelling on what was sad? What she couldn't change?

She wasn't afraid of mourning. She'd held Miles as he wept. She'd comforted Frieda and Heinrich. When Adam had died, she'd brushed Brinley's tears away. Given Aiden a pat on the back.

Her steps slowed. A mosquito buzzed by her ear, and she swatted it away. She *had* offered comfort to Miles and the German children. But had she done the same with her teens? Or had she tried to push away their grief because it hit too close to home? She'd focused on being strong for them. Was that so wrong?

What of the other strange things George had said? Why had he spouted the Bible verse about the least of these? And the whole *you are mine* thing creeped her out. Wait … was that another Scripture? Perhaps, instead of being an insidious stalker line, it meant *God* had called her by name and she belonged to *Him*. Only, that didn't make sense. She'd hardly given God a second thought and was certainly not one of His groupies. Why would He want her to be, anyway? She would never fit the mold of a prim and proper church girl.

Better to brush off everything that crazy loon had said. No one thought straight when battling cholera. She might have spouted nonsense as well before she recovered.

Still …

She pulled the small Bible from her pocket and fingered its golden inscription. *Holy Bible.* Maybe if she found the verses George was referring to, it'd all make sense. But how was she to do so—find three little verses in this sea of words? If she waited until she returned, she could google it. A burning in her chest told her not to wait.

With a grunt, she plopped down on a log, flipped the Bible open, and skimmed for George's words. Nothing. An impossible task. Stupid of her to try. But, wait … what was that? The first two chapters of Isaiah 43 caught her eye.

> *But now thus saith the Lord that created thee, O Jacob, and he that formed thee, O Israel, Fear not: for I have redeemed thee, I have called thee by thy name; thou art mine.*

> *When thou passest through the waters, I will be with thee; and through the rivers, they shall not overflow thee: when thou walkest through the fire, thou shalt not be burned; neither shall the flame kindle upon thee.*

The words seared her heart like a third-degree burn. No—she lifted her gaze to the pasture where cattle grazed in the simmering sun—like a cattle brand. She'd thought herself not good enough for this perfect God that her Sunday school teacher had lauded, but what if, for some crazy reason, He still wanted her. What if this promise to be with her through all life's trials was available to her? Maybe there was still time. Perhaps she could still be *His*.

She'd only belonged to one man before, and he'd been taken from her, leaving her heart in tatters. But maybe there was someone who would truly never leave. Who couldn't be snatched from her. Who could manage to love her—all of her—despite her loud mouth and impulsive actions.

Too good to be true. Unless …

She snapped the Bible shut and tucked it back into the pocket of the jean shorts she wore under her dress. Something to ponder at another time. Right now, she needed to get back to the children.

~

Claire slung her purse over her shoulder and headed out the door.

"Where are you headed, sweetheart?"

Drat. Bearett had noticed her almost-departure.

"Errands." She flashed a smile over her shoulder. "See you in a bit." She made it to the bottom step before Bearett responded.

"Wait. Aren't your parents supposed to drop by in"—he checked his watch—"fifteen minutes or so?"

"I won't be long." She hurried her steps.

"I thought you loved me!" Bearett's shout was overdramatic.

She blew a kiss and ducked into her car. If this took long enough, maybe they'd go with him for his afternoon cruise, and she could have more time to herself. Worth a shot.

When she reached the police department, she took a few cleansing breaths before exiting her car and going in. It made no sense why Bearett kept delaying the inevitable. They had to contact the authorities. Everything she'd read online said to do so right away. Anything to ensure Brinley was safe.

She opened the door to a white-tiled floor and white walls. Her footsteps squeaked and echoed as she strode across the lobby to the front desk. "I'd like to file a missing person report." There. She sounded confident and in control. Not at all like she was spiraling.

"Is the missing person a minor?"

"Yes."

"Are you his or her legal guardian?"

"Well, no, but I'm the one who was babysitting her."

"I see. While anyone can make the report, it is usually more effective for the legal guardian to do so since they often know the most about the minor."

How could she explain that Brinley's legal guardian was also missing? "I haven't been able to contact her. She left her daughter in my care."

The woman lifted an eyebrow but said nothing, simply sliding the paperwork to Claire. Okay, good. She browsed the questions. What was Brinley's middle name and birth date? No clue. Address. Social security number. What was she wearing last? Any jewelry? Height. Weight. Uh … She should have brought Aiden along. He'd know far more than she did. She texted him some questions but didn't receive a reply. He was out fishing for info with Nevaeh again, supposedly scouring the beach for anyone who might have seen his sister. Maybe she shouldn't have let him go.

When she finished filling out the sparse information she could, an officer called her back to his office for an interview. Her hands trembled. Why did she feel like she was on trial?

The officer picked her measly paperwork off his cluttered desk. He leaned back in his chair, studying it. Her mouth twisted as she waited. Four foam coffee cups littered the area, as did a McDonald's wrapper. "When was the last time you saw Brinley Stone?"

"A few days ago."

"And you waited this long to file a report because?"

"Well, her brother had contact with her. She said she'd gone on a trip with friends and not to worry. We actually tried to go after her when the GPS tracker showed she was in Chicago, but then she turned the tracking off."

"Where are her legal guardians?"

Claire winced. "Her father is deceased. Her mother is … on a trip."

"And you were left in charge?"

"Yes, sir."

He asked for her narrative of the events of the last few days and pressed for details she couldn't offer. "Okay, then. We'll be in touch."

That was it? "You're going to look for her?"

"We'll do all we can to find her." But his relaxed posture said otherwise. His gaze traveled to the half-eaten McMuffin on his desk. Bet he couldn't wait for her to leave so he could get back to breakfast.

She huffed as she stepped out of the station and into the sunshine, shielding her eyes from the glare. Now what? Whether any good came out of it or not, she'd done what she needed to do. Bearett would understand. Still, she should run by the store. She'd said she was doing errands, plural. Ought not to lie.

Halfway through her shopping trip, Aiden replied with a series of texts. She'd have to call this information in. There would still be gaps, things Aiden didn't know, but at least the police would have a more complete picture.

Should she be keeping a closer eye on Aiden? The last thing she needed was for him and Nevaeh to run away together or something equally scandalous. He seemed like a great kid with a good head on his shoulders, but puppy love could make people do crazy things. Maybe she could lure him to stick close to home via the proven method of food.

She texted back.

I'd love for you and Nevaeh to join us for dinner tonight. What's your favorite dish? I'll make it for you.

She waited as three dots appeared.

Lasagna. What time?

They'd just had that for dinner a few days ago, but no matter. Whatever would make him happy.

6:00

He sent a thumbs-up emoji.

With that settled, she breezed down the pasta aisle. Her parents would likely come too. She needed more of everything, including patience, which wouldn't be found in this store.

~

Sand blew over Aiden's sandals with the breeze, creeping in between his toes. After questioning over thirty people, he'd finally gotten a lead. A guy with shaggy black hair covering one eye admitted to knowing Jack.

"We used to be friends, but we haven't hung out in years." He pulled a cigarette pack from his shirt pocket and proceeded to light up.

Aiden stepped to the left to avoid the smoke. An asthma attack wouldn't be ideal. "Do you know where he lives?"

"Sure. Down the street from me."

Though the dude didn't know Jack's exact address, he gave Aiden the street name and a description of the house. Good enough.

"Do you think he'd ever … hurt someone?" Best not to divulge information about his sister. He didn't know or completely trust this guy.

"Nah. Don't think so. He does like the ladies, though. And he could have changed. I stopped hanging out with him because he was getting neurotic."

Neurotic? That didn't sound good. "How so?"

"I dunno. Could have been the weed, or maybe he was on harder stuff. Mellow one minute, then angry the next. Never knew what was going to tick him off."

Definitely, not good.

"Thanks, man." Aiden left Smoker Guy and searched the beach for Nevaeh. There she was, farther down the beach chatting with a blonde in a bikini. He caught up to her, careful to keep his gaze locked on the black-haired beauty he'd come to … like. Because it was far too early to fall in love, right?

"I found out where he lives." Aiden placed a kiss on top of Nevaeh's head.

She smiled up at him, then gestured to the other girl. "This is Gabby. She knows Jack but doesn't have any idea where he went or why."

Aiden gave a brief, polite nod.

"Thanks, Gabby. Have a great rest of your day." Nevaeh stepped away and motioned for Aiden to follow. "That girl has quite the crush on Jack."

Aiden scoffed. The jerk was probably a player.

"So," Nevaeh continued. "You got an address?"

"Close enough. A street and house description."

"Should we go there and ask Jack's parents where he is?"

They probably should have thought this through. Why would Jack's parents talk to two strangers? Two teenagers? "Maybe Claire should go."

Nevaeh's eyes lit up. "Yeah, that's smart. She's got a better shot."

Smart. Such a simple compliment, but coming from her, it gave him a high. She was looking especially kissable right about now, with a slight blush on her cheeks and a trace of lip gloss on her smiling lips. He trailed a finger on her cheek. Stepped closer. She bent her knee, leaning in.

"Nevaeh, is that you?"

The question stole her gaze away from his. Darn it.

"Gloria, hi." Nevaeh stepped away from him to greet a woman who was at the prayer meeting. The pastor's wife, right? He came up behind her. "You remember my friend Aiden." She gestured in his direction.

"Of course. Hi, Aiden. Any progress in finding your sister?"

"Not much."

"We'll keep praying until she's safely home." She took his hand, patting it like a grandma might. Not that he knew anything about grandparents.

"Thank you."

"So, are you and Pastor Tim enjoying a day at the beach?"

"Yes. Much-needed. Been so busy lately." A man clomped behind her, carrying two folding chairs. "Aiden, this is my husband, Tim."

Aiden nodded. "Nice to meet you." This guy was a pastor? Hard to envision when he wore striped swim trunks and a sleeveless shirt.

"You as well. Join us, will you?" He positioned the chairs in the warm sand. "We've got more chairs in the trunk."

Nevaeh searched his face as if asking permission.

He'd do just about anything to make her happy. "Maybe for a little while." Claire had texted him from the store, so it probably wasn't the time for her to track down Jack's parents anyway.

"Great. I'll get two more chairs." Pastor Tim headed back toward the parking lot.

"I can help." He caught up to the man in two strides. Dad had taught him to help whenever possible, especially with elders and women. This guy didn't look super old, but certainly, Dad would tell him to assist.

When they reached the white sedan and the pastor popped the trunk, Aiden grabbed both chairs.

"Thank you, son."

Son. A strange burning filled his chest.

"Are you here for vacation, or are you a local?" Pastor Tim lifted a friendly smile.

"Vacation."

"How long are you here for?"

No easy answer. "Awhile."

He placed the chairs beside the others, and they each found a seat. Nevaeh was deep in conversation with Gloria. Okay, then. He'd have to brave awkward conversation with a pastor. Could the guy tell he wasn't one of them? He didn't treat him any differently than he did Nevaeh.

"Tell me about yourself," Pastor said. "Where are you from? What are your interests?"

Aiden gave him the basics, divulging his dream of being a cop.

"A police officer. Your folks must be so proud."

"My dad passed away a couple of years ago. He was a firefighter."

Pastor put a hand over his heart. "I'm so sorry to hear that. Losing your father at such a critical age must have been heartbreaking."

"It was. There was no one like him. No one as brave. Or …" What was the word? Did the right word to summarize Dad even exist? "Good."

That didn't cut it. Dad was so much more. A burning sensation spread from the bridge of his nose to the corners of his eyes. A dam of suppressed memories and grief poured out in a flood of tangled emotions wrapped in insufficient words. Memories of his father. Frustration with Mom. The desire to prove himself worthy of Dad's legacy.

Pastor listened intently, nodding and asking questions every so often. Man, it felt good to unload two years' worth of gunk. Who would have thought he had so much to say?

"You've been through quite the ordeal. When those kinds of trials happen, a person can either run to God or away from Him. Which have you chosen?" The question lacked judgment. Pastor's compassionate expression said no matter how Aiden answered, he'd understand.

"I've never given God much thought to do one or the other." He shrugged. "My family has never been religious."

"And yet, you came to my church last night."

"That's Nevaeh's influence." He leaned closer and lowered his voice. "I've never met anyone like her. She speaks about God like He's her friend or something."

A grin split the man's face. "Ah. You're smitten."

No use denying it. "Completely."

"There's no better girl to fall for. She's been attending our church every summer for years. Her faith truly appears genuine."

"I want that. That … fire. That joy."

"It's yours if you want it. All you have to do is ask."

"Ask what?"

Pastor explained how Jesus died and rose again to pay for everyone's sin and how having a relationship with God was as easy as asking Jesus to be his Savior and Lord. "Not that being a Jesus follower makes life simple. Surrender means exchanging your will for God's, and He won't stop trials from coming into your life. But you don't have to *do* anything to make Jesus approve of you. He already loves you fully and completely. Nothing you can do will make Him love you more or less. With Him, you have nothing to prove."

Nothing to prove. What would that be like? He was always trying to prove himself to someone. Exhausting. Stressful. Because, more than half the time, he didn't measure up. Something inside him yanked and pulled at this pronouncement, begging him to take that step. Pray that prayer.

But no. That was ridiculous. Dad was a great guy. A hero. And he didn't go to church or pray. Aiden didn't need to go crazy and get religion to be a decent human being. He could follow Dad's example.

Chapter Twenty-Two

Marina lay on a blanket in the patchy grass next to Frieda as the two of them found shapes in the clouds. She pointed to another white billow. "That one looks like a car. *Ein Auto.*"

Frieda's nose scrunched as she turned to her. "*Was ist das?*"

Oh, shoot. "Never mind. *Macht nichts.*"

"*Ein Hund.*" Frieda pointed to a smaller cloud.

"That *does* look like a dog. *Ja, ein Hund.*" Which turned Marina's thoughts to both Frankies. Her heart twisted. How were Brinley and Frankie? What was Aiden up to? Hopefully, the trip had snapped him out of pining for Stacy. Longing for home swept over her. If only she could wrap her children in her arms right now.

Soft footsteps approached, and Marina craned her head to find Sister Margaret looming next to her. "Hello, Sister."

"Good afternoon, Miss Weber." The nun motioned to the side. "May I have a word?"

"Sure." Marina scrambled to her feet and dusted off her dress. She might never get used to being called by a fake name. Why ever had she spurted it out in the first place?

She walked next to Sister Margaret until they were a few yards away from the children, and the nun stopped to face her. "I wanted to inform you that we've found homes for all of the orphaned children."

Marina sucked in a breath. "All of them?"

"Yes. Of course, there will be more. There are always more with this dreaded disease. But the current children are spoken for. We'd like you to inform them and to help them ready to meet their new guardians tomorrow. We wish them to look presentable. Clean faces and hands and whatnot." One of Sister's eyes narrowed. "Can you manage that?"

"Yes." Marina bowed her head. "I'll see to it."

"Very well. Good day to you." With that, the nun strode toward the quarantine ward.

So much for Marina's fantasy of raising Frieda and Heinrich herself. It was better this way. She couldn't abandon her family to create another in 1849. Still, she pinched the bridge of her nose to ward off tears.

Please, Lord, let them go to good parents. Give them a happy life.

An honest prayer. Maybe George's Bible-thumping had rubbed some religion onto her. Goodness, she'd miss those kids. Beyond precious. So hard to let go. She wrapped her arms around herself, chilled despite the oppressive heat.

"Miss Stone, there you are."

She spun around. Dr. Duncan tramped through the grass toward her, hair disheveled as always, shirt rumpled. She waved.

"I've been scouring the city, looking for you. Finally thought to ask Miles. Only, when I got here, one of the nuns told me they didn't know anyone by the name Marina Stone."

She winced. "I go by Catherine Weber here."

He huffed. "I don't know what games you're playing, Miss *Stone*, but you need to put an end to them."

"It's not a game. I—"

"You must return to the water. Don't let Miles dissuade you from doing so."

The excuses for her alias died on her tongue. "Pardon?"

"You're landlocked, Miss Stone, and it's a dangerous place to be. A time sailor needs the water like birds need the sky. I don't know what nonsense Miles has fed you, but I insist you not partake of it."

"Miles has nothing to do with it." Of course, she'd been tempted to follow his example. Best not to admit as much. "I

can't leave yet. I haven't accomplished my mission."
Whatever it was.

"Don't you feel the pull?"

"The pull?"

"Yes. The pull of the water."

"I don't know what you're talking about."

"Gracious. What's happening? They always feel the pull," he mumbled to himself, tugging at the ends of his hair.

She planted a hand on her hip. "I thought I couldn't go back until I accomplished my mission."

"Yes."

"Well, I haven't. At first, I thought I needed to stop the fire, and I failed at that. Then, I figured I needed to inform 1849 about cholera prevention and treatment, only no one will listen to me. I've botched everything."

He shook his head. "Thank goodness they didn't listen. What if you'd changed time?" He huffed again. "It wouldn't take this long. It never has before."

She shrugged. "Your other time sailors must be more adept at this mission thing."

Pacing, he mumbled to himself again.

"Excuse me?"

He let loose a growl, then pawed the ground with one shoe, a bull ready to charge. "Find a boat, Miss Stone—any boat—and get yourself on it before it's too late." He twisted around and stomped off.

"Okay." What an odd interaction. He hadn't listened at all to her predicament and hadn't offered any suggestions as to what her mission might be and how she could accomplish it. It was like talking to a wall.

Yes, of course, she'd board a boat … just as soon as she did something worthy of being called to 1849. The Time Holder—God, maybe—wouldn't go through all the trouble of transporting her to the past unless there was a good reason. Something she could do that no one else could. Yet, what had she accomplished? Changing a few sheets and emptying bedpans? Anyone could do as much.

"*Frau Weber, sehen!*" Frieda ran up to her and pulled on her skirt. "*Ein Schmetterling.*"

An unfamiliar word, but the bright blue butterfly flittering in the direction of Frieda's slim finger explained her meaning.

"*Schön.*" Beautiful.

Time to gather the children together and attempt to explain their new circumstances. New lives awaited them. New families. New dreams. How would these young ones balance grieving the parents they once had and embracing those who'd stepped forward to care for them? Would they carry loss in the pit of their stomachs for the rest of their lives? Or would they heal and move forward?

Lord, be with them. Comfort their crushed hearts. Hold them in Your everlasting arms.

Another prayer. Look at her go.

She put two fingers in her mouth and whistled as loud as she could. Heads swiveled in her direction. "Come here, children." She motioned them closer. "I have something to tell you."

~

Dinner was not the ordeal Claire had expected. Still, it would have been nice to not have her parents listen in to all the details of how she'd failed. She wanted to appear strong and capable, not like she floundered with every step. And yet—here they were.

Nevaeh hadn't been able to make it, unfortunately. The girl was growing on her. And she might have helped diffuse some of the tension. Oh, well. Aiden filled her in on where Jack lived. They developed a plan for Claire to go and speak with his parents to see if they might have an idea of where he was and assist her in getting Brinley home.

"Should I go with you?" Aiden asked. Good thing he'd swallowed his bite of lasagna this time. Mom might faint if he spoke with his mouth full one more time.

"Nah. I'd better go alone. Don't want it to seem like we're ganging up on them."

"What if they're psychopaths?" Bearett reached for another slice of garlic bread. "I should at least drive you and wait in the car. You can text if someone pulls out a gun."

Mom's hand flew to cover her heart. "Bearett!"

"I'm joking."

"That's nothing to joke about. Is South Haven crime-laden? Do you have reason to suspect they'll be armed?"

"No, ma'am." He chuckled under his breath.

Claire kicked him under the table. He might enjoy getting Mom riled, but she'd be the one to hear about it for the next few days.

Mom cleared her throat. "Perhaps Dad and I should accompany you."

"Why?" They'd never met Brinley and weren't from here.

"The influence of two respectable people might be to your advantage."

Oh. Because she *wasn't* respectable. Got it.

"Plus, your father could protect us if they did turn violent."

Claire groaned. "There's not going to be a shootout, Mom. Bearett was only kidding. They're probably just as worried about Jack as we are about Brinley."

Bearett lifted a brow as if to ask *You sure about that?* She sent him a mock scowl.

Mom huffed. "What?"

"Nothing," Claire and Bearett said at the same time.

But Mom was right. This was serious. The first lead they'd had since the GPS thing fell apart. She needed to make the most of it.

"So, it's settled. I'll head over there as soon as I clean up the dinner dishes. Bearett will drive me but wait in the car." Not for protection, but so they could have a few minutes alone to commiserate about her mother's ridiculousness.

"Oh, I'll clean up, dear." Mom scooted back her chair.

"You sure?" She would never ask a guest to do the dishes, but since Mom had offered …

"Absolutely. You never were much for loading the dishwasher correctly anyway. Everything will be spick-and-span when you return."

No use dwelling on that passive-aggressive dig. Let the woman do it her *perfect* way. "Thank you."

The drive to Jack's street was too short. She hadn't had time to finish listing her myriad of complaints about her parents.

Bearett nodded, his expression somber. "Don't get me wrong—they drive me as crazy as they drive you—but I don't think they're really the problem."

Her hackles rose. Was he saying *she* was the problem? He was supposed to be the person who always took her side.

"Hear me out." He pulled up in front of Jack's house—the only two-story on the street—and cut the engine. "It's awful how they treat you, but I think if you stood up for yourself even once, they'd back down. The problem is, I think you believe what they say about you. You absorb every blow because you agree with their opinions."

That couldn't be true, could it? They thought the only thing she'd be good at was modeling, but she was confident that her ability to help other people prioritize their health was valuable. Besides, she'd learned this lesson years ago. Only what Jesus said about her mattered. Bearett's assessment was a stretch. "You're wrong, but there's no time to regale you with the reasons why. I need to talk with Jack's parents."

Though no car sat in the driveway, flashes of illumination from within the house showed someone was watching TV. They were home.

"Text me if you need backup."

Backup. What was this? *NYPD Blue*? She rolled her eyes. "Will do."

She knocked three times before a thin woman with glassy eyes answered the door. Was she high? "Yes?" Dark circles marred the underside of her eyes. A bright purple bruise peeked out from under the shoulder strap of her tank top. A cloud of cigarette smoke emanated from the house.

"Hi. I'm Claire. My husband operates the *Duncan's Delight*." She held back a cough.

"We're not interested." The woman moved to close the door, but Claire put her hand against it. She hadn't come this far for a door to slam in her face.

"I'm not selling anything. I was wondering if you know where Jack is."

The woman's eyes narrowed. "How do you know Jack?"

"Apparently, the girl I'm supposed to be watching is with him. They disappeared a couple of days ago, and I'm worried about her."

"Jack hasn't lived here for nearly a year. No clue where he's staying or what he's doing."

What did she mean? "Aren't you his mother?"

The woman scoffed. "Not according to him. Jack says he has no mother. He disowned all of us. Good riddance." She tried to close the door again.

Claire wedged her foot into the opening. "You don't have any contact with him?"

"Give it up, lady. I don't know nothin' about your girl." The door pinched Claire's toes as it pushed closed.

Claire stood on the doorstep for a minute. Should she try again? Maybe if she was more forceful, Jack's mother would tell her something. Or would it be better to take a softer approach? Inconceivable that a mother could go for nearly a year without much contact with her son. Had he run away? If so, why?

Soft footsteps crunched behind her. Bearett. "I take it you didn't get far?"

She shook her head. "I think that woman was Jack's mom, but she says he doesn't live here, and she hasn't talked to him." Claire wrapped her arms around herself. "She has to be lying, right? That's ludicrous."

Bearett shrugged. "Some families are like that."

Her brain hurt, trying to comprehend it. As nuts as her parents made her, there was no way she'd go so long without talking to them. "Should I try again? Or maybe you could pry something out of her."

Bearett shook his head. "I don't think so. Was she strung out?"

"Maybe." Probably.

"I have a feeling she's telling the truth." He hooked an arm around her shoulders and guided her back to the car.

"She had a bruise." If this was an abusive household, what kind of a person had Jack become? "I'm even more concerned now."

"Me too."

~

Aiden downed three root beers while waiting for Claire and Bearett to return from Jack's house. Claire's annoying parents had dashed away right after she did, like they were afraid to be left alone with him. Not a moment too soon. As the sky darkened, he turned on one lamp, then another. A Cardinals game played on the television, but he wouldn't have been able to relay the details. The time to himself would have been nice if he hadn't been worried about Brinley. His mind spun with what-ifs. What might his sister be doing right now? Or what might Jack be doing? An uneasy feeling swirled in his stomach. He'd known it from the beginning—Jack was bad news.

When Claire got home from Jack's house, she trudged straight into her room, shutting the door behind her. Bearett plopped onto the sofa next to Aiden and sighed deeply. He adjusted a blue throw pillow behind his back.

Aiden muted the TV. "I take it things didn't go well?"

"You could say that."

"They didn't tell you where Jack is?"

Bearett ran a finger across his forehead. "Claire talked to Jack's mom. At least, we think it was his mom. She said she hadn't seen or heard from him in months."

"The guy's been couch surfing for a while, huh?" He took another swig of his soda.

"Apparently. His mom's messed up. Drugs, most likely." Bearett nudged Aiden. "Told you many teenagers would kill to have a parent who cares."

"You're not about to make me feel sorry for the creep."

"Fair enough." But Bearett's frown proved *he* felt bad for Jack. "At any rate, we left without any intel that could help us find Brinley." He rubbed his hands on his khakis.

The two sat in silence for a few minutes. The muted Cardinals game was still playing on the TV. Finally, Aiden broke the silence. "There's got to be something I can do. I hate feeling so helpless."

"You could pray."

Yeah, about that … "Our family's never been much on religion, but Nevaeh's got me thinking."

"You don't say." The edge of Bearett's mouth quirked up.

"When she talks about God … it's different from anything I've heard before. It's like a …" How could he describe it?

"Like a friendship?" Bearett offered.

"Yeah. Like they're tight, you know?"

Bearett's wide smile shone in the lamplight. "Yeah, I know. That's the kind of relationship I have with the Lord too. Even though He's all-powerful and worthy of my respect and honor, He's my best friend."

"But how can you have a friendship with someone who's invisible?"

Bearett shifted his jaw. "Do you still feel close to your dad, even though he's passed on? Do you wish you could tell him things, hear his advice, that kind of thing?"

"Of course, but that's different. I have memories of my dad when he was here. I've never seen or heard God."

"It's not a great comparison, I'll give you that, but it's something. Your dad will always be with you in some way. God is always there, with us, every day. Just waiting to connect."

"I wish He could be as real to me as He is to Nevaeh."

"He can. He wants to be that for you."

"And all I have to do is ask Him to be, right?"

"Exactly."

"Still not sure I buy that." He tilted his soda bottle back, but only a drop fell into his throat.

Bearett shrugged. "He'll wait."

No pressure, really? Weren't all those TV preachers pushing people to "get saved" before it was too late? Bearett's relaxed posture showed he wasn't worried. "Aren't you going to try and get me to turn my life over to God?"

Bearett stood and stretched. "He's obviously begun a good work in you. I trust Him to complete it. When you're ready, He'll be there."

Was he ready? No. He couldn't make such a huge step right now. Both his mom and sister were missing. He obviously wasn't thinking straight. Once they returned and his life went back to normal, he could decide if he wanted to jump off this cliff or not.

Chapter Twenty-Three

Marina hugged Frieda and Heinrich tight, tears pooling in her eyes. Man, she would miss her little German buddies.

Sister Margaret gathered the orphans up like a mother hen and herded them onto the ferry. Their new parents waited for them on the mainland.

Marina couldn't stand to see them go. What if the prospective parents were cruel or rude? Or cold toward these precious darlings. She'd seen these little ones through this far. She must continue to do so until they were safe in loving arms.

She rushed onto the ferry.

Sister Margaret lifted a brow. "Miss Weber?"

"I'll accompany them." She motioned to the children.

"There's no need. I'm perfectly capable." Her shoulders straightened.

"I understand, but I have to do this. Please." How could she explain the nearly feral drive to see this through? It was as though her feet would not—could not—remain on the island.

With a flick of the wrist, Sister Margaret gave her permission to attend to the children. "You're free to come and go as you please."

Way to make a woman feel needed. No matter. This wasn't about fulfilling a duty or being a hero. Her heart had intertwined with those orphans and wouldn't easily disentangle. Frieda's and Heinrich's eyes lit up as she approached the railing where they marveled at a fish jumping from the water. At least they were glad to see her.

Heinrich waved at the trout. "*Hallo.*"

Marina chuckled and waved to the island. *"Auf Wiedersehen."*

"Auf Wiedersehen," the children echoed.

Heinrich's pockets bulged. Marina pointed and asked, *"Was ist das?"* What is it?

Heinrich stuffed his small hand into his pocket and pulled out more than a dozen rocks of different shapes and sizes. Some dull and unimpressive. Some shiny and sparkly.

"Ooh, a treasure." She'd never learned the German word for such, but the light in his eyes proved he understood. A sweet dimple appeared with his smile.

Another little boy skipped past her and bumped into Heinrich. The rocks fell from his hand, clinking on the deck. Heinrich reeled, stumbled, and veered to the edge of the boat, about to plummet into the unforgiving river.

Marina stretched out her hand and grabbed him by the suspenders, yanking him to safety. So close. Heinrich had come too close to plunging overboard. She could have lost him. Her entire body trembled from adrenaline. What would have happened if she hadn't been there?

"Sorry, mate." Looking sheepish, the skipping boy dropped to his knees to help gather up the spilled rock collection. "Glad you're okay. One rock disappeared down there." He pointed to a crack in the deck.

"Nein!" Heinrich's wet eyes widened as he pointed.

How like a child to be more concerned with a rock than with a near-death experience. "I'll get it." Marina kneeled at the spot it'd disappeared. Not just a crack, but a hatch. Had it fallen inside, under the deck? She maneuvered a metal notch and lifted the trap door. Hmm. With the hatch shrouded in darkness, she blinked to help her eyes adjust. Light from above illuminated a stripe of steps and wood. There. The rock sparkled up at her.

She stretched her hand down but couldn't reach it. Frieda and Heinrich gathered around her.

"I have to go down to get it. Keep the cover open for me?"
Again, she didn't have the German proficiency to translate, but
the children nodded like they understood.

She took one step, then another, keeping the rock in sight.
A third step. A fourth. And then … darkness. Oh no. They must
have closed the cover. Her throat tightened. She wasn't afraid
of much, but enclosed spaces topped her list. She sucked in
rapid, shallow breaths as she banged above her. "Let me out.
Let me out!"

Her worst nightmare. Not enough air. Not even a sliver of
light. Was she hyperventilating? Because her head seemed like
it might lift off like a balloon.

God, help me. Help me!

A strangled cry escaped her lips before her knees buckled,
and she tumbled to the floor.

~

Slowly, a beam of light broke through the inky blackness.
Had she lost consciousness? She blinked, squinting against the
brightness attacking her retinas. She lifted her arms over her
head. Nothing but air. She felt around her. No walls.

"Frieda? Heinrich?"

No answer. Only the gentle lapping of water. Pleasant
chatter and laughter in the distance.

Wait. She wasn't in the hold any longer. As her vision
cleared, she sucked in a breath. The light came from an electric
light shining from the pier. This wasn't the ferry. Could it be …

Yes, it was the *Duncan's Delight*. She leapt to her feet and
spun around. Her suitcase, empty cooler, and purse sat next to
her. She was back!

"Aiden? Brinley?"

She stood on the bottom deck. Might they be on the top
deck? She found the stairs and took them two by two.
"Claire?"

No one on the top deck either. What had she expected?
For everyone to wait on the boat for weeks until she returned?
Clearly, it was nighttime, and the boat was moored for the

evening. A light smattering of people dotted the Harborwalk. The marina office sat dark and empty. Hundreds of shimmering stars twinkled overhead in the cloudless, dark sky. Shining like Heinrich's rock.

Heinrich. She must have left him and Frieda as abruptly as she'd left Aiden and Brinley. Were they confused? Upset by another loss? Hopefully, not traumatized. Poor dears. They'd already lost so much.

As she turned to trek back down the stairs, the old mailbox caught her eye. Sneaky thing. Had it started everything? One shock from that box had sent her on the biggest adventure of her life. Temptation to touch it pulled at her, but she clenched her hands into fists. She would *not* risk it catapulting her back in time again.

Her energy waned as she descended the steps. That burst of energy must have been from adrenaline that was now wearing off. Her legs felt like lead. It was as if someone had draped a weighted blanket over her shoulders. Had she ever been this tired? Not since she'd had cholera. She fought to keep her eyes open.

She had to find Aiden and Brinley, only how? It wasn't as though Claire's letters had contained a return address. No telling what time it was, but with the shops closed, who was there to ask for directions to the Duncan residence? It wasn't likely the young people still milling about would have a clue.

Plus, could she even make it to the beach? Her knees wobbled. No, she'd pass out before she reached the sand. She yawned. Nothing left to do but wait for morning, when Bearett or Claire would likely come to the boat, or when she could inquire about their whereabouts. Until then, what would it hurt to surrender to the pull of sleep?

Pull. The word niggled her brain. Who'd said it? Dr. Duncan. He'd talked about the pull of the water, only she'd never felt it. Unless … maybe it wasn't the drive to be with the children as they met their new families that had caused her to jump on the ferry. Perhaps it'd been the pull of the water calling her back.

But why had she returned without fulfilling her mission?

It hurt her brain to ponder as much. She curled into a ball on the deck and drifted to sleep.

~

Voices murmured in the other room, but Claire couldn't make out what Bearett and Aiden were saying. Just as well. All the energy had drained from her after her visit to Jack's house had yielded no help. Now, she lay on her bed, on top of the covers, with her arm slung over her eyes. Despair beckoned her to give in to it, its hands of quicksand clawing for her. She didn't have the power to fight its draw.

She'd done everything she could think to do, and still Brinley stayed away. The girl had probably fled because of her abysmal parenting—or babysitting—skills. When Marina returned—if she returned—she'd blame Claire. And she'd be right to do so.

Failure. Failure. Failure.

The story of her life.

Okay, that couldn't be true. It sounded nothing like God's voice. Satan's fingerprints were all over the chant that echoed in her mind. She wasn't thinking clearly. And yet, her heavy arms couldn't lift the shield of faith.

Bearett seemed to think this debacle with Brinley was just one of those things teens do. Like it came with the territory. As if it would have happened if Marina were here and in charge. Not likely. His optimism usually bolstered her spirits, but right now, it annoyed her. Her faults glared brightly at her. Why couldn't he see them? Or was he just pretending not to?

Tears stung the back of her eyelids. Stupid pregnancy hormones. As though she needed to be any more of a basket case.

Oh, God. I don't even know how to pray right now. Just ... help.

She couldn't even pray well.

Nevaeh and her mom had organized a prayer chain for Brinley. Why hadn't she thought of that? The two of them attended a different church than Bearett and her. A different circle of people. She could ask friends and acquaintances from their church to pray for Brinley's return.

She pulled out her phone and typed a text to those from her church she had numbers for, then asked them to forward the request on to others in the congregation. Hard to explain everything over text, but she managed to relay enough information for her purpose. If only she could ask them to pray for Marina to return as well. If she included a request for a time-sailing mother, they'd no doubt add Crazy Claire to the permanent prayer list.

She hit send, but the anticipated feeling of accomplishment never came. Shouldn't her spirits buoy? But no. A dark cloud shrouded her mind and heart.

Maybe she needed prayer too.

She composed a text to Wendy and Stella, asking for spiritual backup. Only, Stella didn't even know they'd encountered a time sailor. So much to fill her in on and so little mental stamina to do so. She did the best she could. Hit send. Started to doze off.

Her phone rang, startling her awake. A video call request from Wendy. She answered, cringing at the sight of her own red-rimmed eyes. "Hello?"

Wendy's smile relayed sympathy. "Hey, I'm bringing Stella in on this call too."

A minute later, both friends looked back at her. A lump rose in her throat at the compassion in their eyes. "Hey, Stells."

"Hi, friend. It sounds like you can use some support right now."

She nodded. Her throat was too hot and tight to form words.

"That's what we're here for. We want to hold your arms up like Aaron and Hur held Moses's when he was too tired to do it himself in Exodus."

Cue the tears. She couldn't hold them back any longer. Their kindness undid her.

"We're going to pray for you right now, okay?"

She nodded again, face slick, pillow damp.

Wendy and Stella took turns asking the Lord to strengthen Claire's heart, to encourage her, and to let her feel God's presence. "Remind her who You say she is and what's true about her. Expose any lie that's causing discouragement, Lord," Stella prayed.

Lies caused discouragement. Made sense. Wendy had told her once that God is never discouraged, so this feeling couldn't be from Him. What lies was she believing? Probably too many to list. *Oh, God, show me Your truth.*

As they continued to pray, her breathing slowed and peace enveloped her mind. Everything was going to be okay. God hadn't forsaken her. He hadn't left her to figure out how to do everything on her own. He hadn't chosen wrong when He'd planted a baby in her womb or when He'd

transported Marina from Bearett's boat. God didn't make mistakes, and He didn't abandon His children.

After everyone said, "Amen," Claire filled them in on the details. Though Wendy already knew about Marina time-sailing, she hadn't known about Brinley's disappearance until the text.

"Can we pray for Brinley now?" Wendy asked.

They spent another fifteen minutes asking the Lord to move on the girl's heart and bring her home. When they finally hung up, a brilliant sunbeam of light pierced Claire's once-darkened heart. Tomorrow would be a new day with fresh mercies, and she'd awake ready to face it.

~

It was after midnight by the time Bearett headed to bed and Aiden shuffled to his room. His gaze trailed over Brinley's makeup on the dresser, her clothes peeking from drawers, and the costume he'd bought Frankie hanging in the closet. Weird that he could miss his sister this much. She was the only one who truly understood what it meant to mourn Dad, and they'd grown closer over the past couple of years. So, maybe not that weird. Still, his friends would tease him if they knew.

His friends. He hadn't given them much thought since arriving in South Haven. Since meeting Nevaeh. She consumed his mind at all hours, waking and sleeping. Might she still be awake? The desire to hear her voice called to him. Wouldn't hurt to text and see.

He sprawled out on the bed and sent a message asking if she was still awake. She replied in seconds.

Yep. What's up?

What to say? Should he admit that he missed her and wanted to hear her voice? Not that he could truly hear her voice over text, anyway. Admitting it would sound too boyfriend-like. A role he wouldn't object to, but she'd said she couldn't get involved with him, and yet she'd wanted him to kiss her. No doubt about it. If that wasn't involved, what was? Still, he couldn't take the chance he'd scare her away.

I talked to Bearett about God tonight.

Instead of texting back, she called. "Tell me more."

So, he did. He poured out his jumbled thoughts and feelings. Felt good not to hold back, not to hide. "Bearett told me I have another father, a heavenly one. This other dad wants to spend time with me. It doesn't make sense for me to push Him away. I want the close relationship with God that you have."

"So, what's holding you back?" A smile radiated through her tone.

Fair question. He had a list of excuses, but that's all they were. Flimsy excuses. No solid reasons that would hold up to her scrutiny. "I don't know. I guess … nothing."

A delighted giggle proved her pleasure, but then she sobered. "You're not just saying that because you want the two of us to … you know."

"I'm not saying I want to become a Christian so you'll date me, if that's what you're asking." At least, not *just* so she'd date him. A relationship with Nevaeh was no guarantee. They lived in different states. It'd be stupid of him to make a drastic life change, or even to pretend to, for the right to call her his girlfriend.

"In that case …" Something like a muffled squeal came from her end. He could imagine her covering her face with a pillow and letting loose.

He grinned.

Her voice returned. "Asking Jesus to be Lord of your life is simple. You can pray something like this: *Dear Lord, I know that I've sinned and lived separated from You, but I don't want to be apart from You anymore. Jesus, forgive my sin and be King of my heart. I give my life to You. I want to live close to You, always. Amen.*"

"As simple as that? Then it's all blue skies."

She guffawed. "Hardly. I said simple, not easy. Every day, I have to choose His ways over my own. I have to choose to believe His truth over all the lies. But it's simple in that I don't have to do anything to earn His love. I never could." He could picture her face radiating sincerity. "So, if you want, you can pray in your own words, and I'll agree with you."

"Yeah, okay." He took several deep breaths. He was really doing this. Handing his life over to an invisible God, all because that God wanted a relationship with him. Because He loved him. "I won't be as eloquent as you."

"Doesn't matter."

And so, he dove off the cliff. Prayed the prayer. And experienced the rush of flinging all his cares, hopes, and dreams onto God's shoulders.

Chapter Twenty-Four

Marina awoke to a frantic shout.

"She's back? She's back!"

She opened her eyes to find the boat captain looming over her.

He waved his arms. "You must be Marina? Are you okay?"

She could do without that blinding sunbeam attacking her eyes, but yeah. She sat up, patted her head, arms, legs, and the deck next to her. "Yeah, I'm good." And she was home. Well, not *home*, but back in South Haven. "You must be Bearett."

"Yeah, Claire's husband. Thank God. We were beginning to think you might never come back."

Best not to admit she'd considered staying. She pushed herself to stand. "I'm here, safe and sound. Where are Brinley and Aiden?"

His smile wavered. Oh no. Why? "Aiden and Claire are at the house. Let me call them." He pulled out his phone.

He'd mentioned Aiden and Claire, but not Brinley. A chill skittered up her spine. Where was her daughter?

Bearett paced the deck, phone pressed to his ear. "Sweetheart, you're never going to believe who's on my boat … Yes! She was sleeping on the bottom deck when I got here. Is Aiden still there? Both of you come, quick."

He pocketed his phone, then rubbed his hands together, grin wide. "What do you need? What can I get for you? Something to drink? Are you hungry?"

His boyish enthusiasm caused a laugh to bubble out. "Actually, I'm starving. Do you have any junk food? I'd love a donut or muffin right now. Or a candy bar. Have any of those?"

"Let me see what we've got." He nearly sprinted to the back of the boat and rummaged around behind the bar. "Twinkies?" He held up a package of snack cake goodness.

"Perfect."

He tossed her the package, and she downed the contents in six bites. "Time-sailing takes it out of you."

He grinned from behind the bar. "So I've heard. I've got water, Coke, and chocolate milk."

"Ooh. Coke."

He jogged over with the bottle. "They should be here in a few minutes. I'm bursting with questions, but I don't want you to have to repeat yourself. They'll want to hear too."

She took a swig of the soda. "I have questions too. How'd you know about time-sailing?"

"I'm a Duncan."

"Related to Dr. Duncan?"

"Descendant of him, yes. But he's not really a doctor."

"Of course, he is. He provided medical care to burn victims, gave Miles cholera medicine—"

"Miles?"

"Another time sailor from 2001. He's been in the past for almost a year. Refuses to leave."

"Wait. What? How can someone refuse to leave?"

"He won't get back on a boat. He doesn't want to return."

Bearett's mouth parted. "I had no idea that was an option. Maybe that's what happened. To those who never came back, I mean."

"That, or they changed the history books. Apparently, if you do that, you die." Another gulp. How she'd missed carbonation.

"Oh, man. My mind is spinning. I only know what came from stories my father passed down. All Duncans are drawn to time sailors or those the time sailors left behind. And we're all drawn to the water. But there have been gaps in what we know."

"How come you said Dr. Duncan isn't a doctor?"

"He admitted as much to Stella, Claire's friend who time-sailed to 1856. She got terribly sick from cholera, and Dr. Duncan admitted he didn't know how to help her. He's had no formal medical training."

"Interesting." She thought back to their interactions. Had he done anything more than someone with a little experience could have done? He'd bandaged wounds, applied aloe vera, and used a stethoscope. She'd done nearly as much as him, and she was no doctor. "I had cholera too, but he wasn't around to help during it. Something about a snag and lurching forward in time. I think I missed the worst part of the sickness."

Bearett's face paled. "How'd you recover?"

"Gatorade. I had plenty in my cooler."

"Electrolytes. That makes sense. When Stella was sick, Claire gave her a few homemade remedies to try. The purpose of all of them was to get electrolytes into her."

Footsteps thundered on the wharf. Claire and Aiden burst onto the boat.

"Mom, thank God you're all right." Her son ran to her and wrapped her in a hug. She clung to him, eyes stinging with the threat of tears. When was the last time he'd hugged her at all, much less like this? "I missed you so much."

"I missed you too."

Was this the same boy she'd left behind? Bitterness and disdain had filled her last interaction with him. Now, he squeezed her tight. She relished it for a minute before pulling back and studying him. His face and shoulders sported a deep tan, while the tips of his ears and nose showed a slight sunburn. He seemed taller, maybe even more muscular. More grown up.

Claire sidled up next to Bearett, and he put his arm around her shoulder.

But … "Where's Brinley?"

Claire's and Bearett's smiles dropped. Aiden pulled back, frowning.

"What is it? Where's my daughter?"

"I'm so sorry." Claire took a step toward her. "Brinley ran off with some guy she met at the beach. We haven't been able to convince her to return."

"We tried to go after her," Aiden said. "I used the GPS tracker on your phone to find her, but then she turned it off. Last we knew, she was in Chicago."

"Chicago," Marina whispered. She needed to sit down. She sank into the nearest chair.

"I feel horrible," Claire said. "You entrusted your children to me and—"

"It's not your fault. It probably has more to do with me than with you." She'd pushed her daughter away by not listening to her. By shutting down every conversation surrounding Adam. Was it any wonder Brinley would be vulnerable to a guy's attention?

She'd stayed away too long. She'd assumed her children didn't need her, but clearly, they did. She had no right to thrust Claire into the role that was hers alone.

Claire sat next to her. "I filled out a missing person report."

"You did?" Bearett asked.

"You did?" Aiden echoed.

"Yeah." Claire's cheeks bloomed pink. "I wasn't able to give them much to go on. There was so much info I didn't know. But they said they'd look for her. No luck yet."

Marina breathed deep and let out a long, slow exhale. "It'll be hard to find her if she doesn't want to be found. She's going to have to *want* to return." If the cops dragged her back kicking and screaming, how long would she stay? Was this the new role Brinley would play? That of a rebellious teen?

No. That wasn't her daughter. Brinley might be mad at her, furious with the circumstances, but underneath, she was hurting. She needed love. Needed her mother to wrap her arms around her and allow her to cry. To share. To grieve.

"Where's my phone?" It was clear what she needed to do.

He couldn't take his eyes off Mom, as though she might disappear again if he did. She looked … different. But how? Her hair was the same. Clothes the same as the day she'd left. So, what was it?

"Aiden? Your mom asked where her phone is. You have it, don't you?" He'd been so busy trying to figure out what had changed that he'd apparently not heard her ask a question.

"Yeah. It's at the house."

Mom stood and brushed her hands on her pants. "Let's go get it. Lead the way."

The four of them strode off the boat, Bearett and Claire walking hand in hand in front, Mom at his side.

"How've you been?"

He had so much to tell her—about meeting Nevaeh, about God—but now wasn't the time. "Besides being worried about you and Brinley, I've been good. South Haven's not such a bad place. Sorry for giving you a hard time."

"Eh. You're a teenager. That's your job."

He stopped and put a hand on her arm. "No, I owe you more respect. You've always cared so much about us. I took that for granted."

Mom's eyes grew wide. "What happened to you?"

He chuckled. "Bearett talked some sense into me, I guess." Was that all it was? Or had his newfound relationship with God changed him already?

"Way to go, Bearett. I hope I left you in good hands. They're not psychopaths, are they?"

He snickered. "No. They're good people." As much as he'd balked against having to stay with them at first, they'd been great. "Claire makes good lasagna."

"The most important thing."

"Just don't ask her to bake cookies. She makes some healthy ones that taste like sand."

"Hey, I heard that." Claire glanced over her shoulder. "I happen to think my keto cookies are delicious."

"Sand," he said under his breath.

"There were Twinkies on the boat."

"No way. Bearett, you were holding out on me?"

"Sorry, man."

They all laughed. Mom looked all around at the beach, the stores, the street, as if she was seeing everything for the first time.

"Is it weird being back?"

"So weird." She pointed to the people sunbathing. "When I first arrived in 1849, they thought I was in a scandalous state of undress. Imagine what they'd think if they could see all the people sporting bikinis."

"I want to hear all about your time there."

"Me too," Claire called.

"Sure. But I want to get ahold of Brinley first."

The light mood between them dissipated. He could throttle his sister. How could she do this to Mom? Didn't she ever think of what would happen if Mom came back and she was gone? This should be nothing but a happy reunion. Instead, Mom had to be worried sick. If only he hadn't screwed up their rescue mission.

"Hey." Mom nudged his arm. "It's going to be okay. She'll come back."

"I hope so."

"She's got to return so we can get Frankie. She'd never abandon him."

Aiden rubbed the back of his neck. "She took Frankie with her."

"What? How?"

He explained the boarding situation.

"Claire, you drove all the way to St. Louis to pick up Brinley's dog?"

"Of course." Claire shrugged. "That dog means a lot to Brinley. I couldn't stand to see her heartbroken."

"Wow. Thank you." Mom's steps slowed as she rummaged through her purse. "I'll pay you back. For the boarding, the vet, for feeding my kids all this time." She took out a wad of cash and handed it to Claire. "I saved money by not going on all those family excursions. That's what I budgeted for vacation."

Woah. Mom must have planned a lot of activities. Would he have enjoyed any of them? Probably not before all that had happened. But he thought differently now. It might not have been so bad.

They approached the house and spilled inside.

Claire headed straight to the kitchen. "Make yourself at home. Would you like some orange juice or water?"

Aiden went to his room and fished Mom's phone from the drawer. He returned to find Mom sitting on the couch, glass of ice water in hand. "Here." He handed the phone over. "What are you going to say?" He sat next to her and watched her type.

"Mostly, that I'm sorry. I owe you an apology too, but hold on."

No way. An apology?

> Brinley, I'm back, and I miss you. I've made so many mistakes as your mother, especially these last two years. I should have allowed you to talk about your father and given you time and space to grieve. I'm sorry for shutting you down. I thought I couldn't stand to remember your father, that it'd hurt too much. I was wrong, and it wasn't fair to you. Please come back so we can have a fresh start together. I love you so much.

Aiden couldn't help but smile. Mom's texts were always paragraphs long, with proper grammar and everything. Old people were funny like that.

Mom sent the text, then dropped her phone onto the couch beside her and turned to him, her expression sheepish. "I'm so sorry. Your father's death gutted me, and I didn't think I could survive reliving the tragedy each time you brought him up. But there's a time to mourn, and I haven't allowed you to do that.

I'm sure you've had all these feelings ready to burst out of you because I kept stuffing a cork in them."

His lips trembled. Oh, great. He couldn't break down and cry like a wuss. He sucked in a breath and steeled himself against the rising emotion. "I get it." And he did. Mom hadn't been shutting down all conversation about Dad because she didn't love him, didn't care. It was *because* she loved Dad so much. *Everyone deals with grief in their own way.*

"I was trying to be strong for you, but I went about it the wrong way. Please forgive me."

"Of course." He leaned over and hugged her. When he pulled away, he asked, "Does that mean talking about Dad is no longer off-limits?"

She swiped her finger under her dripping eyes. "You can talk about your dad whenever you want."

A boulder of weight rolled from his shoulders. He took a deep breath and blew it out with a raspberry. "Something must have happened to change your mind about all this. What was it?"

~

Claire sat across from Marina, engrossed in the story about her arriving on the *White Cloud* in 1849. How wild. She couldn't wait to tell Stella all about it.

"So after I helped put the fire out in the ladies' cabin, I thought I'd achieved my mission and expected to come back right away. When that didn't happen, I was so confused. And then I got cholera."

Claire gasped. "No."

Marina nodded. "I've never felt so sick in my life, but I think I skipped through most of it. Something about—"

"Snagging forward in time?" Claire guessed.

"Exactly."

The doorbell rang. She glanced at her watch and groaned. "Oh no. It's my parents. They're visiting from out of town. You won't be able to talk about this in front of them."

Marina's mouth twisted. "Do they know my children have been staying with you? What did you tell them?"

"They know about Aiden and Brinley." Claire stood. "We told them you were on a trip and that I was babysitting for a while."

"They're something else," Aiden whispered to his mom. "Makes me glad I got stuck with you instead of them."

Claire held back a smile. Such a teen way of giving a compliment.

She opened the door to her parents' tight smiles. "What took you so long?" Mom stepped inside.

"Marina is back from her trip." Claire gestured to the time sailor. "We were just catching up."

"Ah." Mom removed her gaudy sunglasses and placed them into her purse.

"Come sit. I'll get you some ice water."

They sat on the love seat, and Bearett made introductions. Claire munched on an ice chip. Maybe it would cool her tongue and help her not to say something she'd regret. She emerged from the kitchen, two cold glasses in hand.

"How'd you meet my daughter?" Mom asked Marina.

Marina shifted in her seat. "Um, on one of Bearett's cruises."

Dad snorted. "You got acquainted on a cruise and decided to leave your teens in Claire's hands? Bet you regret that decision now."

Marina's brow bunched. "Actually, no. I think Claire did a great job taking care of my teens while I was away."

Was this near stranger defending her?

"But didn't you hear? She lost your daughter."

"That wasn't her fault. Brinley's dealing with her own stuff right now." She picked up her phone. Likely checking to see if Brinley had replied. "Claire and Bearett have been nothing but a blessing."

Her parents looked at each other, but neither spoke. Someone had finally shut them up. Wonder of wonders.

Marina continued, "Parenting teens has taught me that everyone makes their own decisions. I can't control these guys. My job now is mostly to guide them how I can and trust that what I've taught them over the years will stick."

Aiden studied his mother with a thoughtful expression.

"That's nice that you're so … free." Mom gave a clipped nod. "I'm just not sure Claire, here, is up to the task of being a mother. She's pregnant, you know."

Marina's eyes widened. "No, I didn't know. Congratulations, guys. How exciting."

Dad scoffed.

Bearett opened his mouth, but Claire beat him to it. "Enough!" She stood, hands shaking. "Mom, Dad, I love you and always will, but this has got to stop. I'm sorry if you want me to be more like my sister. I'm not Julie. And that's okay. Just because I have different talents and abilities doesn't mean I'm less than. Sure, I don't know what I'm doing as a mother, but I'll figure it out." She included Bearett in her gaze. "*We'll* figure it out. God gave us this baby, and He'll give us the wisdom to raise him or her. I can trust Him to lead us along the way, bumps and all."

Mom's back pressed into the back of the love seat. Dad mashed his lips together. The absence of their voices made room for birdsong to filter through the open window. As long as she'd stunned them speechless, she should say all they needed to hear.

Straightening her spine, she looked Mom in the eye. "If you don't start showing me respect, you will no longer be welcome in my home. Bearett and I are going to raise this child in an encouraging environment. We will not tolerate insults here."

Mom's mouth dropped open.

Dad leaned forward and braced his hands on his knees. "Insults? We certainly didn't mean to insult you, Claire."

"You probably didn't mean to, but every interaction I have with you contains a few barbs. I've allowed it all my life, probably because I've always agreed with you and thought I was less than. But I'm no longer going to tolerate it."

"*We're* not going to tolerate it." Bearett stood beside her. "If you can't see what an intelligent, kind, generous daughter you have, it's your loss." He threaded his hand through hers. "There's no one else I'd want to be the mother of my child."

"I think we should leave." Mom stood, rigid and wooden. "It seems we've overstayed our welcome."

A pang knifed her chest. She should have expected her mother to respond this way, but the little girl inside her had spun a different ending. One where her parents apologized in tears, assuring her of their love and acceptance. What a fantasy.

Dad hefted himself from the love seat. "We'll come visit after the baby is born." He came to her and kissed her cheek. "Take care of yourself. And our grandchild."

"Bye, Dad." She patted his back. "Bye, Mom."

Her mother offered a stiff nod before they stepped out the door.

When the door clicked shut, Aiden clapped. "Way to go, Claire. You stood up for yourself."

She tried for a smile. "About time." But even if it was years later than it should have been, she'd set a boundary. Good for her.

"I'm proud of you." Bearett looped his arm around her waist and kissed the top of her head.

Marina's bewildered expression made Claire laugh. "Sorry you got caught in the middle of all of that."

"That's okay." Marina smiled. "I'm still reeling. I feel like I have jet lag."

"Boat lag?" Bearett offered.

"Yes. That's what we should call it."

"Please continue, Marina. We want to hear everything about your adventure." Claire sat again, sinking into the cushion's comfort. Pounds of weight had rolled off her shoulders with her parents' departure. A sunbeam burst through the window, haloing her with light and warmth. Maybe God hadn't made a mistake with her after all.

Chapter Twenty-Five

After Marina finished detailing her time-sailing experience, Bearett announced he needed to head to the boat to prepare for the next cruise.

"Want to come with me?" he asked Aiden.

Aiden looked from her to Bearett and back again. "I don't know."

She shooed him toward the door. "Go ahead. I'm worn out. I'll probably take a nap in a bit."

"Promise you won't disappear on me again."

"I'm not the one who's going on a boat. Don't worry about me. And stay away from that mailbox."

He held his hands up. "I'm not going anywhere near it. Promise."

The two guys left, and Claire joined her on the couch. "Quite the adventure, huh?"

"I'll say." She checked her phone again. No response from Brinley. She rubbed the burning spot at the center of her chest.

"I'll have to get you in contact with Stella. You two can talk all about time-sailing. She'll be thrilled."

"I'd like that." Marina didn't have any close friends. When they left South Haven, she'd have no one to talk to about her experience. Even if Stella was a stranger to her, it'd be nice to speak to someone who understood.

The last thought gave her pause. "I still don't understand something. Something in 1849 called me to complete a mission, right?"

"Yeah."

"But I didn't. I never accomplished anything of merit. St. Louis still burned. People still died left and right from cholera. No doctors would listen to me. I failed at everything I tried."

Claire shook her head. "No, you didn't. You loved on those children when they'd lost everything. You provided them comfort while they waited for new families. And you saved Heinrich's life."

Marina waved away Claire's suggestion. "Anyone could have done that. It certainly didn't require someone from present day." If she hadn't been there to rescue Heinrich from falling, wouldn't someone else have done so?

Claire put her hand over Marina's. "It required you. You're a mother at your core, and that's exactly what those children needed. A mother who knew German."

"Not much."

"Enough to communicate what they needed to hear."

Could that really have been her mission? She'd done so little and spent only a few days with those children. "I don't know. It doesn't seem big enough."

"God doesn't need for you to accomplish something great. He just wants you to walk with Him, being who He created you to be. Day by day. Step by step. Loving the people He puts in your life well. Just be who you are, Marina, and let other people be who they are."

Could it be true? "I really wanted to stop that fire. Be the heroine who saved St. Louis."

Claire shook her head, then rose and went to her room. She emerged with a book in hand. "I bought this online. It's about the Great St. Louis Fire." She leafed through several pages. "It points out how St. Louis came out of that catastrophe stronger than ever. Because of that fire, they built stronger structures from brick, widened their streets, organized a professional fire department, and completely revolutionized their sanitation systems. St. Louis grew from that fire. They flourished in the aftermath." Claire passed her the book.

Yep. There it was. The evidence of the fire's benefits.

"If you would have stopped the fire, you would have stopped the city's progress."

By trying to help, she could have hindered an entire city. Crazy to imagine. She handed the book back to Claire.

"Your mission wasn't to stop all the bad things from happening, but to be present with those going through the hard things. All you had to do was be yourself—be who God created you to be—and you offered hope and comfort to the grieving. Snatching Heinrich when he nearly went overboard was a natural instinct born from who you are at your core."

Her mission was simply to love the people in front of her? The truth of that unpretentious assessment resounded within her. She didn't have to do something big, nor stop everything bad from happening. She only needed to love the people God put in her life.

God? The theory that everything that happened was coincidental no longer held weight. There had to be meaning behind it all. And who else could create meaning like God? She'd certainly grown as a person through her experience. Might God have been behind that, too?

> *When thou passest through the waters, I will be with thee; and through the rivers, they shall not overflow thee. When thou walkest through the fire, thou shalt not be burned, neither shall the flame kindle upon thee.*

She'd been weirded out when George had quoted that verse to her. Cynical because of Adam's death. And yet, wasn't this what Claire was talking about? Her mission hadn't been to take the fire away, but to walk through it with people. Maybe she'd emerged from that fire stronger than ever as well.

As Marina contemplated, Claire continued to leaf through the book. She gasped. "What was the name you went by on Arsenal Island?"

"Catherine Weber." She chuckled. "I still don't know why they thought it was my name. I never corrected them, though as it didn't seem to matter."

"Oh, my goodness. Look." Claire placed the book between them so they could both read.

The book stated that a mentally ill woman on Quarantine Island identified herself as Catherine Weber.

"It's me!" Marina read on. *Pitiful. Mysterious. Idiotic.* "Oh, great. I went down in history as a mental case."

Claire snickered. "It says you visited the sick and seemed to know when they were going to die."

"It was obvious who was in their last moments."

"And you made wreaths for their burials?"

"I did. It was tragic for all those people to be buried on a sandy island apart from loved ones who could remember them properly."

"And you sang? This makes it seem like you were singing unusual songs."

She doubled over in laughter. "I sang 'I Can Only Imagine' by Mercy Me. They must have thought I was making up my own hymn."

"This is wild. You didn't change the history books, but you ended up in one. How's that possible?"

"No clue. But can I have a copy of this page?" She couldn't wait to share it with the children. They'd get a kick out of her being the crazy lady in the history book. If Brinley was there to hear it. Her stomach sank. Where was her precious girl? If only she could be completely confident Brinley was still okay. That no one had hurt her. That Brin hadn't given in to the temptation of alcohol or drugs. *Oh, God. Protect her.*

"Take the book. I'm sure it will be an interesting read for you." Claire handed it over.

Marina refocused. *Fire, Pestilence, and Death: St. Louis 1849* by Christopher Alan Gordon. "Sounds like a happy book."

"I'm sure nothing can compare to being there. I'm kind of jealous. I've wanted to time-sail ever since Stella returned."

And yet, God had chosen Marina. Crazy, neurotic, overprotective, and over-prepared *her*. And all because some hurting people needed comfort. Some orphaned children needed mothering. She'd made so many mistakes since Adam's death, and yet none of them had disqualified her. She still had something to give. A spark of hope lit within her.

I have called thee by thy name. Thou art mine.

Could she really be that important to God that He would call her His? Everything within her leapt at the possibility that she might belong to someone who loved her.

If nothing was a coincidence, then there was a reason she ended up on that boat with a Bible salesman. God wanted her to know three things: There was a time to mourn. He was with her when she walked through trials. And He'd called her to be His own.

Instinctively, her hand went to her pocket. No Bible. Of course not. She'd left it in 1849. "Hey, Claire, might you have an extra Bible lying around that I could borrow?" Or keep.

Claire's grin bloomed. "I believe I do."

~

Claire glanced at her watch and startled. "I almost forgot. I've got to teach class in forty minutes." Was it rude to leave Marina here alone? But she couldn't find a sub with this late of notice. "Want to come with me?"

Marina yawned. "What class is it?"

"Pilates for beginners. You're welcome to stay here, though, and take a nap if you want. You can make yourself at home and use the guest bedroom since Aiden and Brinley aren't here."

Marina tilted her head back and forth. "I'll go with you."

"You sure?" She looked like she could fall asleep there on the couch.

"Yeah. It'll give me a chance to get to know you better."

When Claire had her YouTube channel, fans were enamored with her, wanting pictures, an autograph, a few minutes of her time. Since she gave all that up, it didn't seem like she was important enough to get to know. Which was fine. A quiet life had loads of benefits. But Marina wasn't motivated by her fame or clout. Just friendship.

Marina stood. "Plus, I need to do something to take my mind off the Brinley situation."

Claire offered a sad smile. "I'll get ready. Give me ten minutes."

"Can I participate in your class? What should I wear?"

"For sure. You got any leggings or comfortable shorts?"

"I think so."

They disappeared into their rooms to change. Claire tried her usual sports bra and looked in the full-length mirror. She stilled. Her stomach had a little bulge. A far too perceptible bulge dressed like this. She had to change. Something baggy would do.

Marina knocked.

"Come in."

"Will this work?" She sported a cute orange tennis-like skirt. It had shorts underneath. Her eyes dropped to Claire's middle. "Aw. You're showing."

Claire lowered her hands to cover the bump. "I was just about to change into something more appropriate."

"Why? You look so cute."

"I'm supposed to be a model of prime physical fitness." Plus, everyone would know she was pregnant. They'd congratulate her. She'd have to act happy. Awkward. Only … was she happy? A little, maybe.

"It's a baby, not two dozen donuts. Show that bump off."

Claire's insides twisted. Was this pregnancy a good thing? Was her blooming middle something she should show off with pride? She studied herself in the mirror again. Would everyone know she wasn't up to this? No, she didn't have *failure* stamped on her forehead.

"Claire." Marina stepped closer and put a hand on Claire's arm. "It's normal to be nervous about your first baby, but you're going to do great. It's obvious you'll be an excellent mother. This child will be the delight of your life."

Claire's lips trembled as she swallowed down a wave of emotion. "I'm not just nervous. I'm terrified."

"What are you afraid of?"

Another glance at her watch. "We can talk in the car. I've got to go if I don't want to be late." No time to change. Ready or not, today was the day she'd announce her pregnancy to the world, or at least to her clients.

In the car, Claire shuddered out a breath. "How can I be a good mom? I don't have a clue what I'm doing. I've never had experience with children. And you've met my parents."

"I trust you'll not make the same mistakes they did."

"I'm determined not to. But how do I raise my child differently without an example to follow?" As soon as the question left her lips, it wobbled, not steady enough to hold weight. "I can do all things through Christ who gives me strength."

"Is that a Bible verse?"

"Yeah. One that's taken out of context all the time. But I think it applies here. I might not be able to follow my parents' example, but I do have a guide. The Holy Spirit within me can lead me. Will lead me. And I have a perfect heavenly Father, so I do have an example to follow."

"You sound like George."

"The traveling Bible salesman?"

"Yeah."

"The lies bombard me constantly. *You're not good enough. You can't do anything right. You're not smart. You'll never measure up.*"

"Your parents said those things to you?"

"Maybe not those exact words, but the message was clear. But truly, it's not them. It's the devil trying to take me down." She slowed to let a bicycling couple pass. "I have to constantly go to the Lord and replace the lies with His truth."

"Sounds exhausting."

"It can be, for sure. But I must stay in the fight. Otherwise, the devil wins."

"Hmm. Interesting." Marina gazed out her window. Did she think Claire was crazy? "I think I'm believing a lot of lies myself. Do you think God has truth for me to replace them with?"

"I'm positive He does." Maybe Marina was more open to discussing spiritual things than she'd thought. "We all believe lies, but the Bible says the truth will set us free."

"Freedom. The elusive dream."

"It doesn't have to be a dream." Though she'd just shown she had no room to talk. Her insecurities bound her tighter than any physical chain could. Would she ever fully break free? It seemed like her progress was always one step forward, two steps back.

But wasn't sanctification a lifelong process? Getting healed, getting free, becoming whole. God meant it to be gradual. Pieces of a broken heart chafing off bit by bit. Growing into the likeness of Christ. Knowing Him more every day. Becoming more secure in her identity little by little. She had time. And she had a God who was stronger than her weakness. She couldn't put her faith in her ability to do better, only in His ability to love her heart to life.

Marina turned to her. "It sounds like you have great wisdom to share. You have everything you need to raise this baby well."

Everything she needed.

Didn't the Bible say as much? She'd read the verse just the other day.

By his divine power, the Lord has given us everything we need for life and godliness through the knowledge of the one who called us ...

Didn't a godly life include godly mothering?

Whenever she looked at her weakness and inability, panic seized her. But if she looked to His goodness, His strength, His wisdom … the whole thing didn't seem so frightening anymore.

No, she might not be able, but He was. She was enough because He made her enough.

She pulled into the parking lot and cut the engine. "Thanks, Marina. Talking to you has helped."

"Good. Now, let's go in there and show off your baby bump."

Giddiness tickled her stomach. She was going to have a baby! Right now, a child stretched and kicked inside of her. What a miracle—God weaving an eternal soul together in the hidden place of her womb. "I'm ready. Let's go."

~

Bearett guided Aiden as he steered the boat into the harbor. "You've got it. A little to the left. There. Perfect."

He was driving a boat! And not a dinky one either. If only Dad could see him now. What a thrill. Someone wearing a hood waved to him. To him? He smiled and waved back. Maybe it was like the train at the zoo, and everyone waved as the boat passed by. But wait. This wasn't just a wave. More like waving him down. The girl flung her arms back and forth in the air. She had a leash looped around her wrist. The basset hound at her feet panted in the heat. A girl with a dog? He squinted against the sunshine. Brinley!

Aiden grabbed Bearett's arm and shrieked, "Bearett, look! It's Brinley. She's back." The boat veered right.

"Woah. Let me take over." Bearett took the wheel.

Aiden ran to the railing. "Brinley!" he shouted. It was her, all right. In a rumpled, stained hoodie. He'd better keep his eye on her so she didn't disappear again.

As soon as the boat docked, he raced off. When he reached his sister, he crushed her in a hug. "Thank God you're here. We were so worried."

"I missed you like crazy. Mom's back? Where is she?"

He loosened his grip. "Should be at the house."

Tears glistened in Brinley's red-rimmed eyes. Eyes that had dark bags under them. "I already checked. She's not there. Neither is Claire."

Where could they have gone? "Well, she's here, I promise. They must have gone on an errand or something. Let's go to the house and wait for them." He pulled out his phone and texted.

Where are you?

"I already tried texting and calling. No answer."

"Her phone must be on silent. I'll text Claire."

"Tried that too."

Okay, then. Nothing to do but wait. They hadn't been on the boat, so it wasn't like they both sailed back in time or anything. They had to be somewhere around South Haven.

Together, they walked toward the house.

Aiden had a thousand questions for his sister. Where to start? *What were you thinking?* probably wasn't the best way to begin the conversation. "Where'd you go?"

Brinley's gaze fell to her feet. "It was stupid."

"Obviously. But where'd you go? After Chicago, I mean."

She shrugged. "Just around."

He nudged her shoulder. "Did you want to get away from me that badly?"

"It wasn't you." She gave the leash a little tug, and Frankie scurried to keep up. "He's hot and tired."

"But he's okay? I mean, he recovered from the flu?"

"Yeah, I think so. He just wasn't a fan of our trip."

"Neither was I."

Her mouth twitched. "Truth is, it wasn't great for me either."

"Please tell me Creepy Jack didn't … take advantage of you."

She shook her head. "In the beginning, he pressured me, but I only had to tell him no once, and he moved on to other girls. Probably because I was seasick the entire time. What I wouldn't have given for Mom to pull Dramamine from her purse."

He grimaced. "Sounds miserable."

"Yeah, but it kept all the guys at arm's length, so I guess it was good in a way. Stopped Jack from giving me trouble."

"What a jerk."

"Yeah. I guess you were right."

"Hey." He stopped walking and waited for her to look at him. "I'd normally ask you to repeat that so I could record it on my phone."

The ghost of a smile.

He touched her shoulder. "Seriously, I'm sorry. You don't deserve to be treated that way."

She resumed walking. "It could have been worse." She shuddered.

"Why'd you run off?"

"It was my chance for adventure. To let loose while Mom wasn't around to stop me. Can't you understand that?"

"Yeah." But was that the real reason? "She loves you, Brin. You know that, right?"

"Then why'd she stay away for so long?"

Good question. Mom's explanation of not knowing what her mission was and struggling to accomplish something worthy sounded legit, but still. If she'd wanted to, wouldn't she have tried harder to return? Unless … "Maybe she thought we didn't need her or want her back. She did leave right after a fight."

Her expression turned sheepish. "I was pretty terrible to her that day."

"Me too." He couldn't blame her for wanting to stay away after the things he'd said. "She can be so annoying, but she really does care about us. I think she's doing the best she can."

"It can't be easy without Dad."

"No." And now, maybe Mom could admit that. She'd promised to let them talk about Dad. Remember him. "I think things will be different now."

"I hope so." Brinley's eyes lit up. "How are you and Nevaeh doing?"

He couldn't help but grin at the mention of Nevaeh's name. "Good. Great, actually." Except he hadn't been able to talk to her since Mom got back. She'd had family obligations. "I've got to let her know you're back. She was helping us look for you." He shot a quick text.

"Are you in love with her?" Brinley's tone teased.

"I think so." Only, they'd probably leave South Haven soon. Would he ever see her again?

Chapter Twenty-Six

Marina squinted as Claire drove down the street. Someone was at the house, sitting on the front step. Despite the warm temperature, the person wore a rumpled hoodie. A strand of blonde hair stuck out from underneath the hood. As they neared, Marina squealed and opened the car door while Claire was still driving.

"What are you—" Claire slammed on the brakes in the middle of the street. "Oh my gosh, that's Brinley!"

Marina tumbled out and sprinted to her daughter. As Brinley stood, Marina picked her up and twirled her around. "You're back. Thank God, you're back." Marina kissed her head once, twice, three times, then squeezed her daughter tight.

"Mom, I can't breathe."

"Oh, sorry." Marina pulled back and studied Brinley. Streaks of dirt on her face and legs, but no bruises, cuts, or scrapes. Her daughter had returned to her safe and sound. Her vision swam as tears clouded her eyes. She ran her hands up and down Brinley's arms.

Brinley's lips trembled. "I'm sorry I took off. Didn't mean to worry you."

"Don't you ever do that again." She couldn't keep herself from one more tight hug.

"As long as you don't ever disappear back in time again." A tear rolled down Brinley's cheek.

"Definitely not planning on it."

Marina looked to Claire, who was ascending the steps. "I'm not in danger of time-sailing again, am I? It's a onetime thing, right?"

Claire scrunched her nose. "I *think* it's a onetime thing. At least, I've never heard of anyone sailing twice. That'd be a good question for Bearett."

"If I end up on another boat with a mailbox, I'll stay far away from it."

"Good plan."

"I want to hear all about your adventure." Brinley sidled next to her as they entered the house and greeted Aiden and Bearett. How many times would she have to go into all the details? Claire had said her friends would want to hear the story as well. A bit exhausting to relive everything over and over.

"Later. First, tell me where you've been and why."

"Ugh." Brinley's shoulders slumped. "It was stupid. I should never have gone."

Frankie lay curled up on the couch in a little ball next to Aiden and Bearett. Marina went to him and ran her fingers through his soft fur. Dirt smudged his coat, but otherwise he appeared okay. "Aw, sweet Frankie. I missed you. Though I did spend time with your twin." He licked her hand, then set his head back down. "He's doing fine now? I heard he was sick."

"He had the dog flu, but he's better. Although his energy still isn't one hundred percent."

"I can't believe Claire drove all that way to go get him."

"Yeah." Brinley glanced at Claire who was sliding sliced lemon and lime into water glasses. "It was really great of her."

Claire's smile bloomed. She brought the waters into the living room, and they all sat and sipped. Refreshing.

"I'm sorry for scaring you, Claire," Brinley said.

"I'm just glad you're back. I'll have to let the police know."

"You called the police on me?" Brinley's tone registered shock, not anger.

"Of course. We heard Jack is not a great guy and that you guys brought a lot of alcohol with you on the trip. I was afraid you were in danger."

Brinley winced. "Yeah, sorry. A big group of us went, and most of them were drunk the whole time. It was awful."

"But no one hurt you?"

Brinley looked down but shook her head. "I was pukey the whole time. That kept the guys away. But …" Her lip trembled. She removed her hood. "They cut my hair." She turned her head.

A large chunk of hair was missing at the back of her head. Brinley's mournful eyes filled.

"Aw, sweetheart." Like Heinrich more concerned with a rock than with the fact he could have drowned, Brinley's focus on the minor inconvenience was endearing. In some ways, Brinley was still her little girl. "That stinks, but it will grow back. We'll go to the salon soon. You might even like a new, short style."

Brinley's face screwed up as if Marina's claim was far-fetched.

Aiden mussed her hair. "I think it'll look great short."

Brinley smacked Aiden's hand away, but her lips quirked into a smile. "Thanks."

"So, when are we leaving South Haven?" Aiden braced for a slap in the face. Not eager to go home? She'd nearly dragged him here kicking and screaming.

"Soon, but not yet." She looked back and forth between her two children. They'd come for family time, and yet they'd nearly the entire time apart. Though they'd accomplished her goal of making memories, those memories weren't together. "You two have gotten to enjoy South Haven, but I haven't. We need to do something fun as a family."

"Another cruise?" This time, Aiden didn't sound like the idea was a torturous one, but it couldn't be what he wanted. They longed to take risks like Adam had. They'd inherited his thirst for adventure, and she'd stifled it. Prevented it. She couldn't keep doing so, or she'd squash the life right out of them.

"I was thinking something with more of an adrenaline rush. What about … parasailing?"

"You're kidding." Aiden frowned at her like it were some cruel joke.

"Not at all. It sounds fun."

Brinley's brow quirked. "What happened to you in 1849?"

"Yeah, who are you, and what have you done with our mother?"

She laughed, her spirits lighter than they'd ever been before. "A lot happened, but that's in the past."

She waited for them to chuckle at her pun, but both teens rolled their eyes. They couldn't hide their smiles, though. She turned to Claire. "Where can we schedule parasailing for three?"

"I know a place that offers it." Claire pulled out her phone. "Let me see the times."

"Are you sure, Mom?" Brinley chewed her thumbnail. "We don't have to do this."

"I'm sure." Another pat to Brinley's knee. "I don't want to leave here without at least one good memory of us doing something fun together."

"I don't think you have to worry about this trip being memorable," Bearett said with a wry smile.

Very true. "Even so …"

"They can get you in at two p.m." Claire shot her a look that said *Are you sure?* "Should I book it?"

"Yes, please. Is there a place that could get Brinley in for a haircut beforehand?"

"Oh, for sure. I'll make a reservation for both online."

"Hey, weren't you going to take a nap? Where did you guys go?" Aiden asked.

She *had* been exhausted earlier. Not anymore. Energy coursed through her, as if she'd drunk a few Red Bulls. "I went with Claire to her Pilates class."

Claire beamed. "Isn't it rejuvenating? I always feel so good when class finishes."

"It was fun." She couldn't say for sure if the exercise was what woke her up or if the time-sailing effects were wearing off.

Aiden typed away on his phone. Probably texting, but with who? His friends back home? Stacy? That girl had his heart in her hands like putty. Molding him to be who she wanted him to be. Then pounding it to a pulp. Part of the reason she'd scheduled their vacation was to get his mind off her. But his slight blush showed he was still enamored.

"Hey." Aiden looked up, eyes alight. "Can we head to the beach a little early? There's someone I want you to meet."

"Okay …" What was going on? Had he formed friendships while she was away? "Sure."

"Oh, Mom, I've got to show you the costume Aiden bought for Frankie. Let me get it." Brinley jumped up and rushed into the guest room. She came out holding a sweet little firefighter uniform.

A hot knot formed in Marina's throat. She opened her mouth but couldn't speak until she swallowed. "That's …"

What was the word? What could she say? She pictured Adam in his uniform. Handsome. Rugged. Courageous. The costume would be a reminder of Adam whenever Frankie wore it. But reminders weren't horrible. This one could be pleasant, right?

"It's a way to honor Dad." Aiden studied her. Was he looking for evidence that she'd changed? That she'd keep her word about allowing them to talk about Adam?

"It's sweet." Her smile came effortlessly. "Dad would like it."

The entire room seemed to exhale a sigh of relief. She did too. The burning in her chest left a pleasant warmth. She savored it for a moment before leaving this memory behind and heading off to make a new one.

~

Aiden drummed his hands against his legs as they sat on a bench near the pier, waiting for Nevaeh.

"Who is this person we're meeting? A friend?" Mom rummaged through her purse, pulled out ChapStick, and glided it on.

"Yes, a friend."

Brinley smirked but didn't say anything. Her new haircut made her look older. More mature. Or had her experience on the boat done that?

"Male or female?" Mom's raised brow rose above her sunglasses.

"Let's not play twenty questions." Aiden felt his cheeks flush.

"Hmm … so female."

Brinley chuckled.

Mom crossed her arms. "Why won't you just tell me?"

Because if Mom met her first, she'd see how sweet Nevaeh was and not freak out. But … "She's a girl I've gotten to know over the past couple of weeks."

"Aiden's in looove," Brinley teased.

Now both eyebrows showed.

"Not in love, exactly. I mean, I haven't known her long. But there's definitely something there."

"What about Stacy? Over her?"

"Completely." Maybe later, he'd divulge what had happened when he went to her house. Maybe not. Mom didn't need to know everything.

"And this mystery girl lives here?"

"Her name is Nevaeh, and she lives in Nebraska."

Mom nodded slowly. "Do you plan to date long-distance?"

He huffed a sigh. "We don't have plans, Mom. I just thought you two should meet. I told her you've been gone on a trip and that you got back."

"Have you met her parents?"

"No, but I've met her pastor and his wife. Her 'church home away from home' as she calls it."

"Church?"

There she was—Nevaeh—walking toward him, her smile shimmering in the sun. Aiden stood and opened his arms to her.

"Hey, you." How could she grow more beautiful every time he saw her?

She melted into his arms. Soft. Warm. Perfect.

Mom stood, and he forced himself to pull away. Aiden gestured to his mother. "Nevaeh, this is my mom."

"Nice to meet you," Mom said with a slight smile.

Nevaeh stepped toward her and gave her a hug. "You've raised an amazing son, Mrs. Stone. You should be proud."

Mom pressed her lips together and nodded. Emotional?

She flashed Brinley a smile. "Cool haircut, Brinley."

"Thanks."

"Aiden tells me you guys are going parasailing? How fun."

"You want to come along?" Marina asked.

"Oh, no. This is a family thing. I'll be happy to watch from shore."

So sweet. Mom had to adore her.

"Aiden said you're from Nebraska, but you have a church you go to here?"

Of everything he'd said, why was Mom zeroing in on the church thing? She'd never seemed to care about that kind of stuff before.

"Yeah. We come here every summer, so we found a church to attend while we're here." Nevaeh went on, talking about her church, her family, and what they enjoyed about South Haven.

He could not leave here without assurance that he'd see Nevaeh again. "Doesn't that sound like a good idea, Mom? Coming back each summer?" Once a year would hardly be enough, but something was better than nothing.

"Maybe." Mom's mouth contorted the way it did when she was holding back a laugh. She checked her watch. "Time to head over."

Mom and Brinley walked side by side. He and Nevaeh trailed them, speaking in hushed tones.

"You two seemed to hit it off," Aiden whispered.

She playfully slapped his shoulder. "You said she was neurotic and annoying. Aiden, she seems nice."

"I may have judged her too harshly."

"You've got to appreciate your family. There's a lot of people who don't have one, at least not a supportive one."

People like Jack. Yeah, Aiden could have it a lot worse.

"I'm excited to see you fly."

Was she talking about more than parasailing?

As they reached the parasailing boat, he gave her a quick peck on the lips before boarding. When he was up in the air, tandem parasailing with Mom beside him and Brinley on Mom's other side, the view took his breath away. Mom screamed and gripped his arm but then dissolved into laughter. Brinley kept hooting. He waved at Nevaeh, then—what the heck—blew her a kiss. She returned it. This was the life. His life. And he planned to live it fully.

~

Claire was on the phone with Stella when Marina, Aiden, and Brinley returned with windblown hair and shining smiles.

"Oh, good, you're back. Stella wants to talk to you."

Marina's smile faltered, but she took the phone, plugging one ear. "Hello?" She made her way to the back porch.

"How was it?" Claire asked the teens.

"Amazing." Brinley went to Frankie's spot on the couch and ruffled his ears. "I wish you could have come, baby doll. Do you want to fly?"

Aiden's eyes showed awestruck wonder. "It *was* like flying. I can't believe Mom let us do it, much less suggested it."

"People change." Thank God—for change, for growth, for transformation. Truly miraculous. "Did you introduce her to Nevaeh?"

"Yeah." His neck flushed. "I think she liked her."

"I know I do. She's a sweet girl."

A muscle twitched in his cheek like he were holding back the full force of his grin. "She is."

Dozens of questions raced through her mind about the future of the lovebirds' relationship, but it wasn't her place to ask. She'd wait and see what happened. They would all keep in touch, right? This adventure had linked their lives together. She couldn't imagine the chains breaking. She'd redownloaded the Instagram app, created a new account, and followed FunnyFrankie. She'd also set social media limits on her phone. Maybe social media wasn't inherently evil, but moderation was still key, especially with her history.

Marina stepped inside and handed Claire her phone back. "That was a fun conversation. Now I have both Stella's and Wendy's phone numbers. They want the four of us to video chat sometime after I return home. Apparently, Wendy lives close to me."

"She does," Aiden said. "We stayed at her house."

"Her kids are super cute." Brinley continued to run her hands through Frankie's fur. "Maybe I could babysit sometime."

"Great idea." Wendy could be a mentor for her and a shining example of Jesus's love. Aiden's heart seemed to have softened toward God. Maybe Brinley's would in time.

"She invited us to her church," Marina said.

Aiden's mouth dropped open. "Cool."

Marina eyed him. "Really?"

"I have so much to tell you."

Claire checked her watch. "On that note, I need to get ready for my afternoon class. On my way back, I can pick up chicken for dinner. Sound good?"

"Sounds great." Marina dropped onto the love seat with a contented sigh. "I can book a hotel for tonight"

"No need. You can stay here. We have an air mattress we can use for you or Aiden."

"Thanks. We'll head home tomorrow morning."

Silence blanketed the room. Disappointment twinged through Claire's chest. Of course, they needed to go home, but so soon? She'd miss them all. They'd visit, right? And Marina had just said they'd keep in touch via video chat, so that was something.

"I'm so glad I met you." Claire rubbed her hands over her upper arms, warding off a chill that came from nowhere. "If I could pick anyone to time-sail from our boat, it would be you."

She struggled to breathe out of her now-stuffy nose. Crazy pregnancy hormones brought her near tears yet again. There'd be time to say goodbye tomorrow. For now, she needed to show off her baby bump to her afternoon class.

Chapter Twenty-Seven

When Aiden rolled his suitcase to the car, Nevaeh was waiting for him. She wore the hot-pink tourist shirt he'd bought her and jean shorts with lace at the bottom. Her gorgeous hair draped over one shoulder. So beautiful. He could hardly catch his breath.

A peek over his shoulder showed Mom had gone back inside after placing her full cooler in the back seat. Good. They had at least a few minutes alone.

How could he bear to say goodbye?

He stepped close and put his hands on her sun-kissed shoulders. Another glance toward the front door. It was partially open, but they were still alone. He lowered his mouth to hers in a soft, delicious kiss. She leaned into him as his fingers trailed her cheek and jawline.

Inside the house, Mom called for Brinley to hurry. Reluctantly, he pulled away. Not enough time and so much to say.

He ran his thumb over her lower lip. She captured his hand and kissed his palm. A tingle shot up his arm.

"I guess this is goodbye." *Goodbye.* What a terrible word.

Nevaeh pressed her hand against his chest. "What if we see if this thing between us can work long-distance? It's only a year, and then maybe we will end up at college in the same city." Moist eyes blinked back at him. "Don't you think what we have is worth fighting for?"

He swallowed. "Yes, I do." He'd been about to suggest the same thing. Thankfully, she beat him to it. Now, he could be sure she truly meant it and wasn't just going along with the idea to spare his feelings. "I'll call you every night."

She bit her lower lip. "And maybe on some weekends, we could meet in the middle?"

"I'd like that." Very much.

Mom called for Brinley again. Time was running out.

"I have something for you." Nevaeh pulled a small box from her back pocket. "Something to remember me by."

A parting gift? Oh shoot. He hadn't thought to get her anything. "I didn't—"

She placed the box in his hand. "It's fine." Could she read his mind? "Just open it." Now he needed to kiss her again. He leaned close, but she put her hand out to stop him, giggling. "Aiden, come on. Open it."

He lifted the lid from the box. A compass. Why? "Th-thank you," he stammered.

"Look at the inscription." She turned it over in his hand.

On the back were the words *Trust in the Lord with all your heart, and do not lean on your own understanding, Proverbs 3:5.*

"The next verse says, 'In all your ways acknowledge him, and he will make straight your paths.' They couldn't fit the whole thing on there."

Again with the lip. Did she have any idea what she did to him?

"The compass is to remind you to look to God for direction. I'm praying He leads you closer and closer to Himself." A blush colored her cheeks. "And guides you back to me."

Enough with the distance. He let his lips show his gratitude. She wobbled in his arms as if his kiss had made her knees weak. When the front door creaked open farther, he pulled away, feeling dizzy himself.

"Don't stop on my account." Brinley smirked at them.

He rested his forehead against Nevaeh's. "Thank you for the gift."

"Thank you for being you."

Mom banged out the door, gigantic purse over her shoulder and rolling suitcase in her hand.

His heart pulled and stretched as he took a step back. He'd never, ever forget this summer.

~

Marina clunked to the car, averting her eyes from Aiden and Nevaeh in case they wanted to sneak in one more kiss. He was clearly enamored. Super sweet, but would she break his heart like Stacy had? She could caution him against falling so hard so fast. Then again, Adam had broken Marina's heart through no fault of his own, and not for one minute had she regretted marrying him. No matter what, love was risky. Risky and … worth it.

She opened the trunk, and Aiden helped her heft the suitcase inside.

Nevaeh's face showed the strain of holding back tears. "My big sister is taking me for a college visit in September. In case you want to visit your college at the same time."

"Wait, you have a big sister? I thought you were an only child," Aiden said.

She shook her head. "No, not an actual big sister. I'm in the Big Sisters program. Have you heard of Big Brothers Big Sisters?"

Marina couldn't help but insert herself into the conversation. "Is it that mentor program where adults partner with students?" She'd heard about it from someone at the kids' school.

"Yeah." Nevaeh perked up. "Jami has been my big sister since my parents signed me up for the program when I was eight. We hang out twice a month, sometimes shopping or going to a movie. She's been a huge encouragement in my life."

Huh. Interesting. Maybe Marina should look into that program. When the teens were off at college and the house seemed cavernously empty, she could find new purpose by sowing into a child's life. Not the same as raising her own children, but still meaningful.

Maybe she'd been holding on to Aiden and Brinley so tightly because she had nothing else. No vision for the future beyond their presence in her home. Now it was obvious she needed to allow them to grow up. To take risks. To fly. As safely as possible, of course.

But maybe they weren't the only ones who would soar. God couldn't be done with her yet, could He? Surely, He had a reason for keeping her here. A spark lit within her. Oh, the possibilities.

Claire came outside, Tupperware container in hand, Bearett on her heels. "I made cookies for your trip."

Aiden groaned. "Not again." A smile sneaked through his mock exasperation.

"Don't worry. They're not keto. I used good old-fashioned sugar."

"Cool." He took the container from her.

"Guess it's time to say goodbye." Claire wrapped Marina in a hug.

Marina squeezed her tight. "Thank you for taking care of my most precious treasures."

"It was my pleasure." Claire made her way around the car, hugging each of the teens, including Nevaeh, and speaking in soft tones. Marina couldn't make out what she said, but the affection Claire had for them was clear.

Bearett wished them all goodbye as well. They piled into the car. Aiden kept his eyes on Nevaeh until they turned the corner, then he sighed as though someone had gut-punched all the life out of him. She suppressed a giggle. He had it so bad. She didn't have to think back too far to remember what that was like.

Young love was precious. She and Adam had met in college and fallen hard and fast. What a thrill it'd been when he'd held her hand for the first time. And that first kiss … A tingle raced up her spine at the thought of it. Had she ever talked to the children about those early days? They might be interested to hear how their parents fell in love. Had they ever seen the wedding video? She'd have to dig it out of the attic when they returned. Adam deserved to be remembered.

On that note … She dug through the glove box and found Adam's old U2 CD. She slipped it in and turned up the volume. "Ready for a sing-along?"

"I Still Haven't Found What I'm Looking For" belted from the stereo, and all their voices rose along with it. Her grin burst forth. Another family memory. And contrary to the lyrics, she'd found exactly what she'd been looking for.

~

Claire continued to wave until Marina's car disappeared from sight. Man, she was going to miss them. What had, at first, seemed like an inconvenience had turned out to be a wonderful blessing. God sure seemed to be good at that—transforming less-than-stellar circumstances into unexpected gifts. Ashes into beauty. His specialty. Her hand caressed her stomach. Yet another example.

She turned to Bearett. "Let's celebrate. You up for brunch?"

"Celebrate what?" The corner of his mouth edged upward with his eyebrows. "Getting rid of the Stones?"

She swatted the air. "Oh, stop. You know that's not what I meant."

"I *do* know you hate to see them go, but I'm still confused about why we're celebrating?"

"The baby, you goof. Let's go out and celebrate this pregnancy."

His smile dropped as his forehead crinkled. "The pregnancy you were afraid to tell me about? The one you said you weren't happy with?"

"Yes. That one."

He stepped close and planted his hands on her waist. Heat from his touch traveled all the way to her toes. "What's gotten into you?"

She ran her hands up and down his arms. "This pregnancy terrified me at first, but it's growing on me." She tilted her head to the side. More like growing *in* her. "I didn't think I had what it takes to be a good mother, but I'm starting to realize that's okay. When I am weak, He is strong. And He will be with me every step of the way. He'll equip me with the grace I need to do this."

Bearett kissed her forehead. Her hands tightened on his biceps as she inhaled his earthy fragrance, a mix of bergamot and cedarwood with a whiff of something marine.

He cupped her chin, bringing her gaze up to his gorgeous green one. "You've never been more beautiful to me." Finger caressing her cheek, he captured her lips with his own. When he broke for air, his face remained close, his breath tingling her cheek. "I'm thrilled to begin this new adventure with you, sweetheart."

Her heart soared. That's what this pregnancy was, an adventure. One she would take with the love of her life. Grander than time-sailing. God had chosen her to be this child's mother. Whatever the future looked like, boring wouldn't describe it. "Is that a yes to a celebration brunch?"

"Absolutely."

As they sat across from each other at Six Chicks Scratch Kitchen over a huge cinnamon roll and yogurt parfaits, they spun sparkling webs of dreams. She'd teach classes on the *Duncan's Delight*—first pregnancy-friendly Pilates, then some motherhood-friendly ones. She could even do a baby-and-me class. A significant boost to their income. Since the classes wouldn't interfere with Bearett's cruise schedule, he could watch the baby while she taught.

"What about your dream to be a homeopathic doctor?" Bearett moved his empty plate to the side and took her hand across the table. "Do you want to go back to it? I'll support you in any way I can."

"Maybe." She wiggled her head back and forth. "I do think I'd love helping people address their health naturally. And I think I could do it. Pass the classes. Get my certification."

"Of course you could."

"But perhaps a new dream will replace that old one. I'm not sure how much of my desire to become a doctor had to do with a passion for it and how much had to do with proving myself to my parents, to anyone who thought I wasn't intelligent enough to pull it off." Had she really thought she could gain her parents' respect and approval by achieving such a status? It wouldn't work. They didn't consider homeopathy to be a valid practice. Impossible to please them. She'd become a dog chasing his tail.

"I don't know. From what you told me at the beginning, it seemed like you'd really enjoy it."

"I'm sure I would." She rubbed her belly with her free hand. "And maybe I could make it work while parenting. But we'll have to see. I don't want anything to compete with this." She looked down at her little bump. How amazing that the Lord was knitting a spunky little life within her right now. "Could be a timing thing."

"Could be." Bearett squeezed her hand. "No matter what, I'm in your corner."

"I know." And she did. She couldn't have asked for a more supportive husband. "What about your dream to continue to go on those mission trips each summer? You haven't given up on that, have you?"

"That's probably a timing thing too. There's no way I'm leaving my wife and baby to go overseas. My mission is right in front of me." He shrugged. "Maybe that will change with time. My capacity to travel, I mean. Not my dedication to you two."

Peace flooded her soul. "We're going to make it, aren't we?"

"No doubt about it. We have our faith to anchor us."

Yes, they did. And with His grace, they could weather any storm.

Epilogue

13 years later

Cheers erupted as Marina crossed the finish line with her little sister, Ava. She took Ava's hand and held it up in triumph. Brightly colored paint covered both of them from head to toe. Their first color run had been a resounding success.

As they moved toward the stands, Ava's parents and little brother rushed to congratulate them.

"That was so fun to watch." Ava's mom brushed a strand of purple hair from her daughter's cheek.

"It was fun to do too, wasn't it, Ava?"

"So fun." The girl bounced on her toes and looked toward the popsicle station. "Can I get a popsicle?"

Her parents nodded. "Absolutely."

"Grandma!" Hadley and Hayden ran up to Marina and hugged her legs.

"Uh oh. You're going to get paint all over you."

Aiden and Nevaeh strolled up to her.

"It's okay, Mom. It'll wash off."

"In that case …" She wrapped Aiden in her arms, smearing green and blue paint onto his white polo shirt and cheek.

"Mom!"

Nevaeh's laughter lilted in the air.

"I wanna run. Watch me run." Hayden took off, racing in the grass alongside the track for a few yards, then plowing back.

She ruffled his hair. "We'll have to do a color run together someday."

Brinley waddled up to her and kissed her cheek. "Good job, Mom."

"Where's Levi?" Marina looked around for Brinley's husband.

"He's getting me more water." She rubbed her lower back. Her pink tank top barely covered her bulging middle.

"Only three more weeks, honey. You can do it." She couldn't wait to be a grandma for the third time. Her cup certainly overflowed.

Ava returned with an already-dripping popsicle, purple juice running down her arm and merging with pink paint.

Ava's mom turned toward Marina. "We'd better get going. Thanks so much for doing this with her. It's all she's talked about for weeks."

"No problem. It was fun." She lowered herself to the nine-year-old's level. "Thanks for running with me. I'll see you in a couple of weeks for our zoo trip."

"Yay!" She hugged Marina's waist. "Thank you. See you later."

Marina waved as the family headed to the parking lot.

"You seem to really enjoy participating in Big Sisters," Aiden said.

"I do. It was hard when my first two little sisters graduated from the program, but we stay in touch. And Ava is precious."

Nevaeh twirled Hadley around in circles. "I'm still in touch with my big sister from over a decade ago."

How cool to think of these relationships lasting to adulthood and beyond. How could she have ever imagined her purpose in life would end when her children graduated and moved out? Though her role had metamorphosed, she would always be a mother. And a grandmother. Her role as a big sister was yet another layer of richness in her life. Another reason to thank God.

Brinley handed Marina's phone to her. "You missed a call from Claire. Hope you don't mind that I answered."

"Not at all. What'd she say?"

"She wants you to call her back." She rubbed her belly. "Levi has your purse. I didn't want to throw my back out from carrying it."

"Oh, stop." Marina chuckled. "It's not that heavy."

Both Brinley and Aiden scoffed.

"Hey, I didn't bring the kitchen sink today."

Brinley lifted a wry smile. "Only two umbrellas, a dozen snacks, and a battery-operated fan."

She shrugged. "See? Not bad." She pulled up Claire's number. "I'm going to call her back. Meet me at the house?" Saturday pizza nights had become a tradition.

"Yep." Aiden put an arm around Nevaeh's shoulder. "We'll pick up dinner and come on over."

On her way to the car, she dialed Claire's number.

"Hi! Brinley said you were doing some race with your little sister." Laughter rang in the background. Claire's daughter Zoey? She must be about twelve now.

"Yeah. It's over now. What's up?" She and Claire kept in touch, but mostly through texts and the quarterly video chats with Wendy and Stella.

"Something interesting arrived in the boat's mailbox." Her singsong tone teased.

"What? Did you have another time sailor?"

"No, this one is addressed to you."

"Me?" She stopped in her tracks. "How? Who?"

"It's from Miles. He was the time sailor you met in St. Louis, right?"

"Yeah." Miles's face emerged in her memory, the way he'd looked when he called her Mom. A good-looking teenager, like Aiden had been. Only, he'd no longer be a teen. It'd been … thirteen years since her adventure in 1849. She meandered forward, confusion clouding her brain. "I thought time sailors could only communicate with people on the boat they left from."

"So did we. His letter shocked us."

"What did it say?"

"Only one sentence. *I'm back on the water.*"

She gasped. "He did it. He got back on a boat. I wonder what changed to make him want to go home after all that time."

"No idea, but we're dying to find out."

As Claire explained her plan, Marina's excitement grew. It was time for another adventure.

The End

Miles's story continues in Braving Red Waters, *the third book in the Time Sailors series.*

Look for the next Time Sailors book *Braving Red Waters*.
Did you enjoy this book?

You might also enjoy these other books by Sarah Hanks:

Time Sailors Series
Braving Strange Waters
Braving New Waters (only available at sarah-hanks.com)

The Mercy Series
Mercy Will Follow Me
Mercy's Song
Mercy's Legacy

The Sister in Arms Collection
A Battle Worth Fighting
Fall Back and Find Me
Whatever It Takes

Stand Alone
Awakened to Life
New Creations
Every Voice Heard

Author's Note

I hope you enjoyed this second novel in the Time Sailors series. As a native of St. Louis, I was fascinated to learn more about my home city's history. I tried to stick as close as I could to the timeline of the cholera epidemic and the Great St. Louis Fire of 1849. However, to make the storyline work, I had to shift a few timelines here and there. The essence of what happened and how remains accurate. In reality, the term "forty-niners" wasn't used until 1852, but it was too much fun to mention the football team, so humor me there. Yes, they banned selling vegetables, assuming veggies were a cause of cholera. Other theories? Beer and sauerkraut. The hardest hit areas were the poorer districts where a lot of German and Irish immigrants lived, so you can see how they made the inaccurate connection.

The primary theory was that it was caused by "bad air." Fire, actually, was thought to clear or purify that bad air, so by that line of thinking, the Great Fire should have eradicated the epidemic. It did not. From 1849 through 1851, 5-10% of St. Louis's population died from cholera, over 4,500 people.

We now know that contaminated water caused cholera and that proper sanitation is paramount in avoiding many diseases. With no organized sewer or trash system in the city at that time, St. Louis was far from sanitary. Residents obtained drinking water from shallow wells near sewage-laden cesspools. Animal waste and trash littered the dirty/muddy streets. Lovely, huh?

Arsenal Island was renamed Quarantine Island. As mentioned, any boat that wished to dock in St. Louis had to stop there first for inspection. The sick were moved to hastily built quarantine wards. Some children were left orphans. The island graveyard filled quickly. If you come to St. Louis today looking for this historical island, you won't find it. It washed away, scattering graves all the way to the gulf, though some were moved to other graveyards.

Catherine Weber was a real woman who hung out on Quarantine Island. She was thought to be insane, made wreaths for graves, and seemed to know when someone was about to die. I had fun imagining Marina in her place.

As a mother of teenagers (in addition to littles), I enjoyed exploring the unique relationship teens can have with moms. My teens helped me with the lingo and made sure I wasn't too cringe. They are treasures and are some of my favorite people on the planet.

The next Time Sailors book will feature the USS Red Rover, a Civil War hospital ship I've been interested in for years. I can't wait to go on another adventure with you (and Miles).

Many blessings as you step forward and take risks, knowing Jesus is with you every step of the way.

Sarah

www.ingramcontent.com/pod-product-compliance
Lightning Source LLC
Chambersburg PA
CBHW071356300726
48976CB00006B/1899